THE SEASIDE GIRLS UNDER FIRE

TRACY BAINES

Boldwood

First published in Great Britain in 2024 by Boldwood Books Ltd.

Cover Design by Colin Thomas

Cover Photography: Colin Thomas and Alamy

A CIP catalogue record for this book is available from the British Library.

Paperback ISBN 978-1-80426-548-2

Large Print ISBN 978-1-80426-550-5

Hardback ISBN 978-1-80426-549-9

Ebook ISBN 978-1-80426-547-5

Kindle ISBN 978-1-80426-546-8

Audio CD ISBN 978-1-80426-555-0

MP3 CD ISBN 978-1-80426-554-3

Digital audio download ISBN 978-1-80426-552-9

Boldwood Books Ltd
23 Bowerdean Street
London SW6 3TN
www.boldwoodbooks.com

To family and friends — how would we ever get through life without them.

PROLOGUE

Frances had met Ruby halfway down the aisle, clasped hold of her hand and led her up onto the stage. It was the turning point she'd been hoping for. Every seat in the hall at the YMCA had been taken by lads in khaki uniforms, and those who had not been so lucky packed themselves into every available space around the rest of the room, craning their necks to see Ruby Randolph, star of the West End, and one half of the famous Randolph siblings, appear before them. It was a bittersweet concert, the last performance of the remaining Variety Girls for the foreseeable future. Ginny had already left to entertain the troops with ENSA, the Entertainments National Service Association, and in a few days Jessie would finally be on her way to perform in a London theatre.

Ruby leaned into the microphone. 'Hello, boys,' she said, her voice husky, and the place erupted with cheers and whistles. The three of them had gone into a medley of 'Pack Up Your Troubles' and 'It's a Long Way to Tipperary', calling on the rest of the cast to join them for a final rendition of 'Goodnight, Sweetheart'. The lads were on their feet with appreciation, the applause thunderous, and it took many curtain calls before the three of them could step down to join their audience, give them a little of their time, in a small exchange for all the boys were doing for them. It was only when the show ended that Frances truly appreciated that what they did was important. To see the smiling faces, witness the excitement, to listen to the boys say how much they enjoyed the show, how much it made them forget the boredom, their troubles. Could Ruby see how important it was too?

Frances was a married woman now, respectable, after years of having to keep her daughter, Imogen, a secret. She could let go of her own troubles, finding no sense in dragging them around with her; she hoped that Ruby could do the same.

'She's doing well, isn't she?' Jessie said to Frances as they came close, signing autographs and the small black and white publicity photographs they'd had printed. Ruby was surrounded by young men, and she looked across to them, gave them a smile. She appeared confident but Frances saw the hint of uncertainty in her eyes.

'I'm so proud of her. Johnny would be too,' Frances replied, understanding the immense courage it must have taken for her sister-in-law to go onstage again.

The Randolph siblings had risen to fame, darlings of the West End stage, before travelling to America, their career in the ascendant. They had been due to appear on Broadway when their mother, Alice, died, sending Ruby into a downward spiral of self-destruction. Her later discovery that she'd not only kept her brother and Frances apart, but that Frances had given birth to Johnny's child while they'd been in the States had all but destroyed her. It had culminated in a suicide attempt followed by a complete breakdown, and months in hospital receiving treatment for her nervous exhaustion. Her recovery had been slow, but she *was* recovering, thank God. A few weeks ago, Frances had been unable to get Ruby to leave the house, now here she was, taking her first tentative steps in the spotlight. Frances prayed that it would go some way to helping Ruby create a new life for herself, without Johnny.

Since her brother had been called up for army service, Ruby had lacked any kind of direction, seemingly not knowing how to function without him. They'd worked together since they were small children, their mother ruthlessly driving them to the top, pushing them forward, connecting them with the right people, their days taken up with endless rehearsals, then shows, important parties that involved much glad-handing, leaving little time for any kind of a private life. Johnny seemed to have taken it in his stride, but Ruby had borne the brunt of their mother's relentless ambition. It had been a terrible price to pay for fame.

'Do you think she enjoyed it?' Jessie mused. 'I mean, she's always been with Johnny, hasn't she?'

Frances shrugged. 'It must be incredibly strange for her. Uncomfortable even. But it's something she'll have to get used to. We have no idea how long this war will go on – or what we'll be called upon to do. But we all have to pull together and do something, no matter how small and insignificant it might seem. We'll all need to rebuild our futures, not just Ruby.'

1

CLEETHORPES, SATURDAY 24 AUGUST 1940

Grace Delaney snipped the red cotton thread with her small needlework scissors and scrutinised her handiwork. 'It's a good job you found the button, Jessie. It would have spoiled a lovely jacket.' She got up from her chair in the bay window and handed it over to her daughter. 'All packed for tomorrow?'

'I think so.' Jessie had taken everything out twice over. Yet still she was uncertain that she had all she needed. Tomorrow she would travel to London, leaving her mother and younger brother, Eddie, behind. It was thrilling to finally be taking such a huge step towards fulfilling her dream, but now the time of her departure was drawing close the doubts began to surface.

'Only think,' her mother teased. She slid around the high-back chair and began drawing together the heavy blackout curtains.

'Isn't it a bit early for that?' It was late August, the evenings still light and full of warmth, and people were intent on making the most of the daylight hours, dreading the coming winter when the darkness would press down on them all again. Jessie shook the thought away; this wasn't the time to think of dark things.

Her mother's room was on the ground floor of the terraced house in Barkhouse Lane, the best room as it was called. Jessie had lodged there with Frances when she'd arrived in Cleethorpes, a seaside resort on the Lincolnshire coast, the year before. Her mother and Eddie had remained in Norfolk, at the mercy of Grace's cousin Norman Cole and his insipid wife, Iris. For weeks Jessie had been unaware of her mother's rapid decline in health, of Aunt Iris's selfish neglect, until Eddie, in desperation, had turned to Jessie's fiancé, Harry, for help. Jessie had been compelled to bring them to join her, not knowing how they would manage but not caring either. Their landlady, Geraldine, had been wonderful, giving over the room to her mother, enabling her to recover from the walking pneumonia that had taken hold of her. Barkhouse Lane had been their sanctuary in a time of turmoil, Geraldine the steadying hand. With the support and guidance of the older woman, Jessie had been able to nurse her mother until her health improved *and* keep her job at the Empire Theatre to support them all. Once sufficiently recovered, her mother had found work as a seamstress and Eddie had been taken on as apprentice mechanic at the local bus station. None of them wanted to go back to the misery of their life in Norfolk – and Jessie was determined to make sure they never had to.

'Lil asked if we'd pop in to see her at the Fisherman's Arms,' her mother told her, coming to the centre of the room and checking her appearance in the mirror over the mantelpiece. 'You won't want to do it tomorrow. It's as well to do the blackout in preparation. You know how Lil loves to talk.'

'But it's Saturday. The pub will be busy. Lil won't have time.'

'She'll make time. She insisted.' Her mother took the jacket from her daughter and held it open for Jessie to slip in her arms. Jessie knew better than to argue.

'I thought Eddie would be back by now.'

'He had the opportunity to caddy and earn some extra cash.'

Jessie grinned. 'Hardly likely to pass up on that, is he.'

'No,' her mother said, proudly. 'He's been a good lad. He saves most of what he earns over what he pays for his keep.'

Jessie knew Eddie wouldn't cause their mother a moment of worry while she was away and that alone was a comfort, allowing her to concentrate on her singing career, a career that was going to make a huge difference to them all.

The Delaneys had been in dire straits when Jessie's father, Davey, died more than two years ago. He'd been ill for long periods that left him unable to work, and Jessie couldn't make enough money teaching music to her father's few remaining pupils to make a difference. When he died her mother had had no alternative but to throw herself on the goodwill of her cousin. The wretchedness of their life there was all the reason Jessie needed to drive her forward. One day she would earn enough to buy her mother her own home and, in doing so, keep the promise she'd made to her father to take care of the family.

It was a quarter after six o'clock when they left. Jessie linked arms with her mother as they walked up the incline of Barkhouse Lane, making their way to the Fisherman's Arms on Sea View Street via a series of alleyways and cut-throughs.

The pub was on the corner and Grace stood back while Jessie grabbed hold of the brass handle and opened the door. As she stepped inside, she heard her brother shout, 'She's here,' and a chap at the piano began to play 'Wish Me Luck as You Wave Me Goodbye'. Beside him, Frances and Ruby sang along, smiling broadly at her. Jessie stood, bewildered, until her mother pressed her gently on her back and moved her further into the pub, closing the door behind them. The place was crowded with friends, among them regular customers, happy to join in the celebration. Eddie was by the empty fireplace, grinning from ear to ear, Geraldine sitting on the banquette next to Frances's daughter, four-year-old Imogen, who was fussing over Lil's dog, Fudge. Bright coloured bunting was strung across the front of the bar, and an old white tablecloth had been painted with the words *GOOD LUCK JESSIE* and draped across the back wall. As the song ended, a great cheer went up and Frances stepped forward, taking hold of Jessie's hands.

'You didn't think we'd let you go without some sort of send-off, did you?'

Jessie couldn't find her voice, astonished that they'd gone to so much trouble on her behalf.

'Aren't you going to say anything?'

'Get the lass a drink.' Lil, the landlady, came from behind the counter. Her blonde hair was piled on her head, her best diamanté earrings glittering in the light, and she pressed Jessie against her well-endowed bosom as she hugged her. 'I can't run to champagne, ducky, much as I'd love to, but we've plenty of lemonade.' She released Jessie and pinched her cheek. 'Bubbles is bubbles in my book, and that foreign muck isn't all it's cracked up to be.'

'Jessie?' Her mother nudged her, and Jessie at last found her tongue.

'Lemonade will be perfect. Thank you so much, Lil.' She made a sweeping movement with her hand. 'For everything.' Her voice cracked with emotion and Lil squeezed her again, then returned to take charge behind the bar, queen of all she surveyed.

The chap at the piano carried on playing quietly in the background as Frances led her to the table where Eddie and Geraldine had saved Jessie and her mother a seat. She was still taking it all in, looking about her, finding friends who raised a hand and smiled in greeting. The stage doorman of the Empire, George, his wife, Olive, and their daughter, Dolly, lifted their glasses to her, smiled and nodded. She'd stayed with them when she'd first arrived in Cleethorpes all of a dither and found the theatre closed. They were good, kind people and she counted her blessings that she could call them friends. Jack Holland, owner of the Empire and a friend of her late father's, was standing at the bar with his snooty wife, Audrey – who was no doubt there under sufferance. Once she'd gathered her wits, she would thank them all, but as it was, she was truly overwhelmed. Frances pressed her gently down onto a stool, then went to the bar to get the drinks.

'I thought you might have guessed,' Eddie said. 'When I didn't come home for tea.'

'I did wonder,' Jessie replied. 'It's not like you to miss out on food.'

He grinned. 'Lil got me some chips when I'd finished hanging up the bunting. Looks good, doesn't it?' He nodded in the direction of the *Good Luck* tablecloth.

'It looks wonderful. Thanks, Ed.' He puffed out his chest. He would be sixteen in October. If Uncle Norman had had his way, Eddie would be back at school, studying, destined to take over the running of the family solicitors' practice. The Coles were childless and there were no other male heirs, Norman's brothers being lost in the Great War. As it was, Eddie spent his days tinkering with engines, doing the thing he loved. He'd considered it a lucky escape, but Jessie still felt a stab of guilt at spoiling his prospects. Frances handed Grace a port and lemon and placed the glass of lemonade on the table for Jessie.

'Lil says not to knock it back too quickly or the bubbles will go to your head.'

Jessie laughed and raised her glass to Lil behind the bar, who winked her acknowledgement. The dog slipped down onto the floor and trotted to join his mistress, and everyone shuffled up along the banquette as Ruby came to join them.

'Are you looking forward to London, Jessie? Frances said you had somewhere to stay.'

Jessie nodded. 'My mother has left nothing to chance. My room is booked with Mrs Croft in Albany Street.'

'Lovely.' Ruby smiled. 'You're not far from Regent's Park. A nice area. Safe.'

'As safe as anything is in war,' Eddie quipped. His mother frowned. 'Well, it's true, Mum.'

Jessie glared at him. It had taken an age to persuade their mother to allow her to go to London alone, Jessie insisting that she was perfectly capable of taking care of herself; hadn't she come to Cleethorpes on her own and made a success of it?

'That's hardly the same,' her mother had replied.

'I'm almost twenty.'

'Not until next April. And it's got nothing to do with your age, well, perhaps a little. But you'll be exposed to...' Her mother had chosen her words carefully. 'You're a young girl on your own. You'll be vulnerable. There'll be no one there to protect you.'

'Protect me. What from?'

Her mother had taken a breath. 'Things. Men.'

Jessie had smiled. 'Bernie has already said he'll keep an eye on me.'

Mention of her agent, Bernie Blackwood, had pacified her mother a little. He'd been her late father's agent and Grace trusted him implicitly. Little by little mother and daughter had compromised, Jessie allowing her mother to put things in place that would give her peace of mind. In an ideal world Jessie would have loved to take her mother with her, but she was loath to uproot them all again. Her mother loved it here, as did Eddie. They were settled, they had friends – and it was Jessie's dream to star in the West End, not theirs.

She had been beyond excited when she accepted Vernon

Leroy's offer to appear in his new production, *A Touch of Silver*, at the Adelphi on the Strand. The theatre impresario was putting on a variety show, similar to the one George Black, managing director of the Moss Empires theatres, had running at the Holborn Empire. *Applesauce* had opened last Thursday, Max Miller topping the bill. *A Touch of Silver* was a show in a similar vein, mostly variety but with a few ensemble pieces thrown in for good measure. Jessie found it hard to believe that she would be starring alongside such famous people in the West End. Pat Kirkwood was due to open in *Top of the World* at the Palladium after her success with *Black Velvet*. At nineteen, Miss Kirkwood was already being hailed as the new star of the war – a title Jessie coveted for herself. Her rise had been meteoric. Would Jessie's star rise as rapidly? She was determined to do everything she could to make it happen, and here, among her friends, their excitement reflecting her own, she felt that anything was possible.

She sipped a little of her lemonade and, once she had calmed herself, got up and went to thank those who had turned up to wish her well.

Jack Holland shook her hand. 'Your father would be so proud of you, Jessie.' His words moved her beyond measure. She dearly hoped he would, that, somewhere, he was watching over her, that she was making good on her promise to never give up, to keep reaching for her star. Jack and Davey Delaney had served together in the Great War. Her father's hearing had been impaired, which rapidly advanced his mental decline when he could no longer play the music he loved. Jack had not escaped without his own scars. He still walked with a pronounced limp, but it hadn't held him back him from doing his bit this time around, and he'd been quick to sign up with the Local Defence Volunteers – recently renamed the Home Guard. Finally, hoping she'd thanked everyone for coming along, Jessie went back to sit with her mother and Geraldine, who were deep in conversation. Frances appeared agitated, peering over Jessie's shoulder, smiling inanely when Jessie caught her. 'Anything wrong?'

'No. Not at...' Her face brightened, and she urged Jessie to turn around. Jessie did so, her mouth gaping in surprise when she saw who it was. She got up, her stool falling behind her, hurried towards the young pilot who had just walked in, and flung her arms about him.

'Harry!'

The chap at the piano whistled his appreciation and began to play 'If You Were the Only Girl in the World'. Harry laughed, good-naturedly, and removed his cap.

'I didn't think you could get leave?'

'I got an eight-hour pass. I couldn't let you go without saying goodbye.'

He slipped his hand in hers and she led him over to the table, Eddie vacating his seat. Jack Holland sent a pint over, and Harry nodded his thanks. 'I still have the car and, more importantly, enough petrol. It was worth it for a couple of hours with you.'

Suddenly, as much as she loved being with everyone, she longed to be alone with him, just for a few minutes, to kiss his lips, to tell him she loved him, increasingly aware of time slipping away from them. Two hours would fly by. He looked so smart in his RAF uniform, but so much older than he'd done when he worked in her uncle's office as junior partner. Back then he faced nothing more challenging than making sure conveyances went smoothly; now he faced the enemy head on – and it showed in every line of his handsome face.

Harry was with Fighter Command, his squadron part of Group 12 and based mostly in Lincolnshire. She knew his job involved providing cover for the industrial areas of the Midlands, and latterly the airfields of Group II as the attached squadrons went into battle over south-east England. The RAF aircraft were greatly outnumbered by the Luftwaffe, but they were more than holding their own as they battled for supremacy of the air. Yet even though our chaps were doing well there were the inevitable losses, and casualties. Harry had lost friends, not only in combat, but also in accidents, human error they called it, and Jessie could see each one was taking its toll. His face was thinner than it had been at the start of summer, his eyes less bright, but he was still her Harry, and always would be. She sat as close to him as she could, their hands clasped discreetly, trying to keep abreast of the conversation, but too distracted by the nearness of him, savouring his touch, the smell of his cologne. Harry squeezed her hand. 'Grace. Would you mind if Jessie and I went for a short walk. To get some air.'

Jessie could have kissed him there and then.

Her mother smiled. 'You didn't need to ask, Harry, But I'm glad you did.'

Jessie needed no encouragement and, not wanting to waste a second, she got up and allowed Harry to lead her outside.

'Excited?' he said as they walked away from the pub, the noise of chatter snuffed out as the door closed shut.

'Yes, and no.' She sighed, glad to be able to talk so freely with him. 'I wish I could take everyone with me.'

'It would be a tad crowded.'

She grinned at him, and he touched the strand of unruly chestnut-coloured hair that had fallen onto her forehead, kissed her cheek.

'You know what I mean.'

'I do. I wish the same. That I could take you with me wherever I go. That we might never be apart.' He slipped his hand about her waist, and they walked to the top of the street towards the seafront. Seagulls whirled high above them as they made their way through the ornamental gardens and up the winding slope to Ross Castle. The quirky stone folly had been built purely for tourists and not for defence, but from it you could get a view of the entire coastline. Alone at last, and away from prying eyes, they kissed, his lips full and warm on hers, and Jessie felt the rest of the world melt away.

After a while he pulled away from her and they put their hands on the rough wall, looking out over the River Humber. The evening was clear, and she could see the lighthouse at Spurn Point on the other side of the estuary, the city of Hull some way to the left of it. The tide was out, the promenade below all but deserted, save for a few people walking their dogs and others out for a stroll. How different it was from last summer, when war had been a whisper on the horizon, and not the reality it now was. She'd arrived here long before Hitler's army marched into Poland and Britain had no option but to take up arms. The town had been swarming with holidaymakers then, cheerful faced as they headed for their boarding houses and hotels. In no time at all best suits and summer frocks had been supplanted by uniforms of khaki and blue, men boarding the trains, kit bags on their shoulders, boots clattering along at a march. So much had changed – she had changed. She was stronger, of that she was certain, and more determined to make a success of her singing career than she had ever been. Yet still, there was that inner battle – should she go, or should she stay?

'Am I doing the right thing, Harry? Leaving all this behind.' She felt like she would never see it all again, that she needed to take one last long look in case she didn't. He drew her close, and she turned to face him. The breeze caught her hair, and he swept it away with his hand. She grabbed hold of it, held it by her cheek.

'Don't second guess yourself. It's fatal.' He freed his hand. 'You've made your decision, and you must see it through to the end, just as I do when I'm flying.' He held his index finger between his eyes and drew it forward. 'Set your target and go straight for it.'

She grinned, saluted. 'I will, Pilot Officer Newman. I will.'

Her heart was full as they headed back to the pub, conscious of all the people who had given up their evening to celebrate with her. When they'd refreshed their drinks, Lil rang the bell behind the bar and shouted to Jessie, 'Speech.'

She blushed, got to her feet and went to stand by the door where everyone could see her, and, more importantly, she could see them. She looked to her mother, her pride written on every line of her beautiful face, and Jessie felt her heart swell. 'I've never been one for words.'

'Yes, you have,' Eddie chimed, and the room was filled with laughter.

She shook her head at him, smiling. 'I want to thank you all for coming. To Lil, Frances, Ruby and Eddie for organising this wonderful send-off – which I appreciate more than I can ever say.' She felt her voice wobble. 'I suppose I should thank the RAF for giving Harry his pass.' Harry grinned and she knew she was the luckiest girl in the world to have him at her side. He wanted her to succeed, and as she took in all the other faces in the room, she knew that each and every one of them, family and friends alike, felt the same. It made her heart feel too full for her chest, but she took a deep breath and continued. 'Most of all, I want to thank my mum—' she paused, emotion making her throat thicken '—and my dad, for sharing their talents with me. I can't imagine a world without music and dance.'

'Nor can we,' Lil called from her position behind the bar. 'So let's have plenty of it before you leave us.' Lil nodded to the pianist, and he began to play 'Ain't She Sweet'. Frances nudged Ruby to her feet, guided Jessie over to the piano and the three of them led the singsong, Jessie wringing every last drop of happiness from the evening. It would carry her through when she left – and all the days afterwards. She was going to be a star and wouldn't stop singing until she was.

2

For as long as Jessie could remember, Sunday had been a day of trains: a day she looked forward to, and a day her mother had always dreaded. Sundays meant a new town and a new theatre, packing and unpacking. Starting over.

'I'll take this to the guard's van, Jessie,' Eddie told her, picking up her suitcase. It had seen better days, the tan leather battered at the corners, the labels that covered it the story of her father's wanderings during his time with the finest concert orchestras.

'Don't keep the guard talking, Eddie,' their mother chided. 'Time enough for that when Jessie's gone.' He winked at Jessie, and they shared a smile. Her mother took hold of her hand and Jessie felt the strength in her grip, reassured once more of her mother's good health. 'Another adventure begins, my lovely girl.' She put her free hand to Jessie's cheek. Jessie looked to Frances, who was standing beside her mother, Imogen at her side. If it hadn't been for their friendship this past year, she doubted she would have managed half as well. She only hoped that she would find such a friend in London. 'Have you got your ration book and your savings book? Do you know how to get to Albany Street from King's Cross station?'

Jessie nodded. 'Frances drew me a map. I know where I'm going, Mum. Don't worry.' As she said it, she knew her words were pointless. Her mother would worry whether she told her to or not and, if she was being honest, Jessie was a little unsure herself. The newspapers were guarded in what they reported but the actual city of London had suffered less from bombings than many other towns and cities, as far as she knew. The bombers were attacking the ports and industrial sites in an effort to bring the country to its knees. So far Grimsby had suffered little damage, Cleethorpes even less. She adjusted the strap of the box that contained her gas mask and gripped her handbag. 'If I get lost, I can ask...'

'A policeman,' Eddie finished for her as he stepped down onto the platform. The pair of them grinned at each other. How many times had their mother said that to them over the years? Grace smiled, gave a brief shake of her head.

'I'll be fine, Mum. Honestly.'

'I found you a seat in a compartment and left your flask and pack up on it.' He pointed to the window. 'The lady in tweed said she'll keep an eye on it for you.' That there was another woman in the compartment seemed to settle their mother and Grace gave her son a proud smile as he came to stand beside her.

Frances handed her an envelope. 'I jotted down the names and addresses of a few friends. Make sure you call on them. Tell them Johnny and I will be back before long.'

Jessie took it from her, glanced at her name written in Frances's elegant hand. 'I will.' Now the moment of parting was almost upon them she felt her courage waver. Coming to a small town in peacetime was one thing, but going down to London in a time of war was entirely different. The last time she'd visited the capital she'd not been much older than Imogen. She was not a child any more, but even so...

Frances gripped her hand and looked directly into Jessie's eyes. 'Make sure you do.'

'Will you send me a postcard, Auntie Jessie, when you get to London?'

Jessie squatted down on her haunches to speak to Imogen. Only a fortnight ago bombs had fallen in Grimsby, not far from where Frances lived in Park Drive. They had been unhurt, but a man had been killed, houses badly damaged. The war had come to their doorstep and brought with it an awareness that they were all under attack now. It had galvanised Jessie to action. If they weren't safe here, they weren't safe anywhere – and why hold back any more? The outbreak of war had curtailed her last opportunity to work in a London theatre – she was determined that it wouldn't happen again. She'd spent the last few weeks in a concert party, travelling about Lincolnshire in a bus, entertaining at army and air bases, which was rewarding and fun – but it wasn't enough. Time was ticking on – there couldn't be any more delays.

In May, Harry had suggested she take a year to actively pursue her dreams – a target to aim for. They'd become engaged last Christmas and she'd immediately wanted to plan their wedding, to make another of her beloved lists, tick things off as she achieved them. He knew her better than she knew herself, that she would never settle down unless she took a shot at making her dreams come true – to appear on the West End stage, to make records and sing on the wireless. One day she might make films as Gracie Fields had done. Anything was possible, she was sure of it.

She thought of him now, tried to imagine him safely on the ground and not in the air. He was brave; she could be brave too.

After all, she didn't have an enemy to fight. The thought gave her courage, and she beamed at her mother, hoping her nerves were well hidden, knowing it would be all too clear. A couple passed by. The train on the next platform pulled out and, when the smoke and steam cleared, revealed the promenade where she had walked arm in arm with Harry. She'd had the whole world then, right here, and the only obstacle to confront was whether she could settle down as the wife of a country solicitor. She hadn't wanted to admit it to herself, not then, but she knew she couldn't. War had curtailed many things, but it had also given her a freedom that might otherwise have been denied her. Eddie glanced at the clock atop the ornate station canopy and checked it against his wristwatch. 'Two minutes.'

Frances stepped forward and embraced her. 'Don't forget, you can always come back if you don't like it. It can be lonely in a big city. Don't be stubborn.'

'Me?' Jessie said, light-heartedly.

Imogen pushed between them and handed Jessie a hand-drawn card. 'Mummy said you can put it in your dressing room, and it will make you smile.' Jessie stared at her image as Imogen saw her, wearing a bright red dress, the widest of smiles, brown exaggerated curls, *Jessie the Star* written above, gummed stars about her like a halo.

'Oh, Imogen. It's wonderful. You're such a clever girl. It'll be the first thing I do when I get there.' A bunch of soldiers who had been hanging outside the guard's van pinched out their cigarettes and stowed them in their jacket pockets. There was little waste any more, what with rationing and shortages. Prices had shot up and were bound to keep rising as stocks fell short and supplies from overseas were thwarted. The station master began slamming doors and windows were pushed down; people leaned out.

Her mother drew her close, hugging her tightly, and it was

almost her undoing. She whispered in her ear. 'You did it before; you'll do it again.'

Jessie nodded, stayed in her mother's arms, breathing the scent of her skin, feeling the softness of her cheek pressed against her own before she pulled away. Tears pricked at her eyes, and she looked to Frances, who took her hands in hers.

'Make new friends, Jessie. But remember the old.' She gave her a quick hug. 'Now get on the train.'

Jessie stood aside to allow a middle-aged couple to board, the man placing a tender hand to his wife's back. Jessie was reminded of Harry doing the same, and a well of loneliness swelled. How long before she would see him again?

'You'd best get aboard, Jess,' Eddie warned her. 'The whistle's about to blow.'

'Look after Mum,' she whispered, knowing he would do his best. He'd promised to let her know if their mother's health deteriorated. She seemed better in the milder months, but autumn was nipping at their heels. Would she stay well if winter was as bitterly cold as it was last year? She stepped up into the carriage and he slammed the door shut, waited while she pushed the window down and leaned out. Her mum came forward and Jessie reached out for her hand, wanting to hold on to it for as long as she could.

'Your father would be so proud of you, darling.'

Would he? Knowing she was leaving them behind. Jessie's cheeks were wet with tears and her mother opened her bag and held out a handkerchief. Jessie took it from her and dabbed at her eyes, rubbed it under her nose. 'I was determined not to cry.' She held out the hankie to her mother, who dismissed it with a small movement of her hand.

'Keep it. I have another; I came prepared.' The simple remark cut home. How would she fare without her mother, without

Frances. 'No matter how many times we part, we know,' her mother half sang, 'we'll meet again.' It made Jessie smile. The song had become popular since Vera Lynn had recorded it last year. It seemed to speak for so many who could otherwise not find the words. The whistle blew, making Imogen jump then collapse into giggles. It was infectious and made them all laugh.

'That's better,' her mother said, stepping back from the train, the steam building up and billowing over them, a sigh as the brakes were released.

'Don't forget the postcard,' Imogen called to her.

'I won't. I won't.' Jessie waved, shouting over the noise of the engine as the train began to draw away and the figures on the station shrank as the distance between them widened. When she could no longer see them, she shut the window and waited for a moment or two before moving along the swaying corridor to find her compartment, squeezing between lads in uniform who winked and smiled appreciatively as she passed. Her lunch and flask were on the one empty seat, the other taken by the middle-aged couple she had seen earlier, and the lady Eddie had mentioned seated opposite. The other two seats were taken by two men, one reading the newspaper, another doing the cross-word. All very respectable. She could look after herself. Her mother would soon realise she had nothing to worry about. Nothing at all.

3

Eddie cycled in the direction of the golf course where he would caddy for his boss as he did every Sunday, while Grace and Frances made their way down the steps and onto the promenade. The weather was fine and warm; it was a shame not to enjoy it. It had been a quiet summer, many of the attractions closed, the boarding houses now billets and temporary home to the numerous servicemen and women who had descended on the town to defend the coast. The tide was out, the waterline only just visible in the distance, the horizon dotted with ships moving up and down the estuary. Eight miles west of Grimsby docks was the port of Immingham, which had become naval headquarters for the Humber. A submarine base and major refuelling depot were located there, along with a battery of anti-aircraft guns. Frances's awareness of the danger spots and possible targets had been heightened since the bombing in Welholme Road a couple of weeks ago; it was only a few streets away from their home in Park Drive. They'd hurried to the Anderson shelter in the garden for safety, trying not to frighten Imogen as the siren began to wail. The noise had been terrify-

ing, the explosion close enough to blow the front widows in. It
was far too close for comfort and brought home the reality of
how this war was beginning to reach each and every one of
them.

Imogen skipped a little ahead of them and Frances linked her
arm with Grace and said, as if to answer Grace's unasked question, 'She'll be fine. You know she will.' They crossed the road,
forsaking the canopy that covered the other side lined with gift
shops and a café, to walk in the bright morning sunshine.

'It doesn't stop me worrying.'

'No. But you had to let her go.' She watched Imogen, her dark
hair swaying as she skipped along. How on earth did those
parents cope whose children were still being evacuated, not
knowing where they were going, or when they would see them
again? 'I can't imagine how hard it is. It never crossed my mind
how my mother and father must have felt when I left Ireland. I
was too excited – and too selfish – to think of them.'

'You were young, Frances. Your future stretched before you.
As it does for all of us, make of it what we will.'

'I might not have left if I'd known how hard it would be.'
Things had started well enough, with a summer season in Blackpool. She'd been not quite sixteen, thrilled and frightened in
equal measure. Other summer shows and pantomimes had
followed, Frances filling the gaps in between by working in
touring variety shows. After that she'd joined a show that tried
out in Manchester before moving to the West End. Her big break
– or so she'd thought. She'd fallen in love with its star Johnny
Randolph, and he with her, much to the irritation of his mother,
who had better plans for her son than a lowly chorus girl – and
an Irish one at that. The show, *Lavender Lane*, had transferred to
America. Johnny had promised to send tickets for her to join him,
and he had, only for them to be intercepted by Ruby, who was

simply following their mother's wishes, terrified that Frances would take her place in their act. It was the worst of times.

'But it all worked out in the end,' Grace countered, well aware of Frances's struggle. 'It always does, if we just keep going, one step in front of the other.'

Frances glanced at the pier. As a defence against invasion it had been breached by the military earlier that year, half of it still accessible, the other marooned, the small tearooms on the end boarded up, cast adrift. It seemed to echo how she felt.

Johnny had returned from America at the outbreak of war, unaware that together they had a child. His mother and sister had kept it that way. She'd managed on her own, with the help of her friend Patsy Dawkins, who lived with her family in Waltham, a village a few miles inland. And now she was managing again, without Johnny. But at least marriage had made her respectable, and she no longer had to worry where the next penny was coming from. Her heart ached for him as it had done when they'd first met, but how could she complain when so many other women were in the same boat?

They climbed the commemorative steps and up onto the Kingsway. The Cliff Hotel had been taken over by Coastal Command, the high windows giving a clear view of the estuary. Out in the river, the two forts built during the Great War guarded the mouth of the Humber before it gave way to the North Sea and Frances wondered whether they would be enough to hold the enemy at bay. They crossed over to Sea View Street and parted at the rear entrance to the Fisherman's Arms. Not so long ago, she would have walked with Grace to the house they'd once shared on Barkhouse Lane. It made her wistful. In many ways life had been simpler then.

'I said we'd call in on Lil for an hour before she opens up,' said Frances.

'Give her my best wishes,' Grace replied, giving her a hug before walking purposefully in the direction of Cambridge Street. Her head was high, but Frances knew her heart was heavy. Jessie might be determined but she was also young and naïve.

Frances knocked and walked straight into the sitting room that was Lil's bolthole between opening hours. The *Sunday Express* was spread out over the table, Lil bent over it, glasses balancing perilously on the end of her nose. She was fully made up, not a blonde hair out of place, the top two buttons of her yellow blouse unfastened, offering a glimpse of her generous cleavage as she leaned over. She looked up when the pair of them walked in, her dog emerging from his place at Lil's feet and making straight for Imogen.

'Did she get off all right?' Lil asked, as she folded the paper and pushed it to one side.

'She did.' Frances removed her coat and hung it over the back of the chair opposite Lil. The room was a tad chilly owing to a high wall directly outside the long sash window, which blocked out most of the light. But it was cosy enough, with two comfy armchairs facing a gas fireplace, a gateleg table and two dining chairs pushed against one wall. To one side was a small partition behind which was a sink and small gas stove, a square of counter-top. More than enough for Lil, who spent most of her days and evenings behind the bar of the Fisherman's Arms.

'Old Fudge is pleased to see you, Imogen me darlin'.' Lil moved a pile of newspapers and envelopes to one side and pressed her hands on the table, made to get up. 'Have you time for a cuppa?'

'I'll do it,' Frances told her, peering into Lil's cup and regarding the tea leaves. 'Ready for another?'

'Aye, drop these in the pot again. Make 'em last a little longer. Tastes and looks like pittle, but I suppose it will have to do.' She reached for the biscuit barrel, removed the lid and tilted it towards Imogen. The child peered into it.

'May I take one for Fudge?'

'Imogen,' Frances reminded her. 'We have to be careful with food, remember.'

'She's all right,' Lil countered gently. 'Won't do Fudge no harm, nor me.' She patted her hip. 'I need to shift a few pounds.'

Imogen broke the biscuit and made the dog sit before handing over the treat and Frances went to put the kettle on the stove. When it had boiled, she took the teapot to the table, along with another cup. While she poured, Lil lifted the edge of the tablecloth and Imogen and Fudge crawled under it.

'How's things at home?' She raised her eyebrows, not mentioning Ruby by name for the sake of little ears. Frances would be able to talk freely here. Whatever she said, Lil would not think her unkind. She called a spade a spade, and although she was blunt, she had a big heart. When the theatres closed at the outbreak of war, Frances had found work behind the bar alongside her. The job had been a life saver when there was little work to be had, and too many people after it. Money was something she no longer had to worry about, thanks to Johnny's shrewd investments. He and Ruby had arrived back in England to headline a show at the London Coliseum. When war was declared, all the theatres had closed, albeit temporarily. Knowing that there was every chance he would be called to serve his country, Johnny had entered into a partnership with the Randolphs' agent, Bernie Blackwood, and Jack Holland. In the spring of 1939, Jack had purchased the Empire Theatre in Cleethorpes and reopened it with great success. Encouraged, he had enticed Bernie on board and bought the Palace Theatre in Grimsby and the Theatre Royal in Lincoln. Johnny had joined them in their endeavour just before Christmas. At the time he'd only been thinking of securing his sister's future, having no knowledge of Frances's whereabouts, or that they had a child, but it all had worked out to be very timely. Ruby had been too ill to be involved, and when Johnny left for the army Frances had assumed his place in the syndicate, overseeing the running of the Palace and booking in the shows.

'Better than it was but progress is slow. It's going to take a long time for her to mend. Mentally more than physically.'

'Well, bad enough all that business of—' Lil mouthed *Ruby being blackmailed* then spoke normally again '—by that nasty article Mickey Harper. But finding out about you and Imogen tipped her over the edge good and proper. And no wonder.' She tapped the table and they were both quiet, Lil no doubt remembering, as Frances was, the nude photographs that had been taken of her sister-in-law. Ruby had been in a pitiful state, drinking to blot out her misery, believing there was no way out of it until Johnny finally discovered the truth and they were able to get rid of Mickey Harper for good.

'Thank God for friends, eh, Lil?'

'Thank the good Lord indeed,' Lil said, smiling at her. 'She seems a nice lass, what I've seen of her.'

'She is, when she lets her guard down. Not that it happens very often. I think she's absolutely bewildered at the moment. It couldn't have come at a worse time, what with Johnny being in the army. It must feel to her that she's lost everything all at once.'

'Aye, but look what she's gained.' Lil arched her back then settled back in her chair.

'I don't think she sees it like that at the moment, Lil. She's too focused on the past, the damage that's been done.'

'It'll get easier as she gets stronger. She's still very thin. Looks like a gust of wind would blow her over the water.'

Frances grinned. 'Our housekeeper, Mrs Frame, is working on

it, but with butter and sugar rationed it could take a bit longer than it would have done before we were at war.' She sipped at her tea; it tasted sour. 'I'm only too glad we have girls from the WRNS billeted with us from time to time. It lightens the load and brings a distraction, not just for Ruby but for us all.' It was a delicate balance, keeping Ruby from falling back into the abyss of depression. 'It's not her fault; everything has always been done for her. She can just about make her bed.'

Imogen popped her head out. 'I can make my bed, Mummy. And I put my nightie under the pillow.'

'Good, lass.' Lil nodded towards her. 'That's what I do.'

'It's because I'm a big girl,' Imogen continued. 'That's why I'm going to school.'

'Aye, and I wonder what they'll make of you.' Lil laughed. The tablecloth was dropped again.

'And that's another reason.' Frances sipped at her tea. 'If it was just the two of us, me and Imogen, I'd let the house go. It's far too big and we could get something smaller out Waltham way, near Patsy.' She had been friends with Patsy since that first summer in Blackpool. Patsy had been the one she'd turned to when Johnny left her broken-hearted, the one who had taken care of her when she gave birth to Imogen and couldn't work. Patsy and her husband, Colin, were more than friends; they were family. 'I doubt it would help Ruby, though. I think she needs the familiarity of things for the time being. And Johnny wants us to stay where we are.' Ruby had still been in hospital when Frances and Imogen had moved into the house the Randolph siblings had rented last December. It hadn't helped matters when Ruby returned home from hospital. On the surface Frances had taken her place, onstage and off. It was taking time to adjust to living together, each of them wary of the other's feelings.

Lil nodded. 'I can understand that. I should think he can

picture the three of you there. There's a comfort to be found in that.' At present Johnny was based in Yorkshire, but she knew he could be posted anywhere, at any time. She tried not to think of the danger he might face, that they all might face in the coming months.

'Maybe I'm worrying over nothing.' Even as she said it, she didn't believe her own empty words. It wasn't a question of *if* more bombs would come, but when.

'You don't have to put on a brave face for me, lovey. I should think you've done enough of that these last few years, but you've the money now. Yer fella would want his family to be safe.'

Frances had hoped things would improve but they had not. Once France had been taken, Hitler turned his attention to Great Britain. Bombing had taken place across the south of England, the Midlands, and the north-east. It wasn't the end of it, merely the beginning; raids were expected again. It wasn't the only thing to be expected. Her monthlies had been late, and when she counted back to the last time she and Johnny were together it could only mean one thing. Another letter had been written to tell him of her pregnancy, just as she'd done when she found herself pregnant with Imogen. Only this time it had arrived safely. He had telephoned as soon as he could, absolutely thrilled at her news, and applied for leave. She was waiting to hear if it had been authorised.

'Well, you have to think of your little ones.' She tilted her head when she looked at Frances. There was no pulling the wool over Lil's eyes. 'You look a little different since I last saw you – around your face. Well, it doesn't take much to put two and two together.'

Frances gave the table a quick glance and mouthed *Imogen*.

Lil nodded, popped her head under the table and wiggled her hand. Imogen chuckled. Lil sat up again and reached across the table to take Frances's hand in hers. 'I'm delighted for you, lovely lass. We need good news in a time like this. The little one will be excited.'

Frances smiled. 'She will. Johnny's due leave. We want to tell her together.'

'And Ruby? Has she said anything?'

'She's too busy contemplating her own navel to notice any change in mine. But I worry how she'll take the news.' It was too early to get excited. If she'd got her dates right the baby would be due at the end of March and she wanted to break it to Ruby gently, knowing she could never have children of her own. 'I feel like it's rubbing salt in her wounds.'

'She'll be thrilled for you.'

'Outwardly she will, but I don't know, Lil. She's still very fragile. I don't want to set her back again.' She drained her cup and got to her feet. 'We ought to be getting back. It'll be time for you to be opening up.' She lifted the tablecloth. 'Time to go, Imogen.'

Lil came round and gave her a hug, rubbed her hand over her back.

'She's a lucky girl, having you to watch out for her. Doesn't seem like she's ever had that before. Not that her brother hasn't taken care of her, but I doubt she knew what good friends were until she met you and Jessie.'

'You'd do the same,' Frances said as Lil released her and Imogen scrambled out from under the table.

'I don't know that I would,' Lil told her. 'Not everyone would be so forgiving. I don't know that I've met a kinder lass in me life.'

4

There had been a long wait for the bus and Frances had felt a wave of nausea building as they stood in the sunshine. In an attempt to fight it, she had taken Imogen by the hand and walked the length of Alexandra Road to the bus stop on the High Street, the fresh air restoring her equilibrium. But it had been stuffy on the bus, and she'd been overwhelmed with tiredness as it slowly made its way down the long thoroughfare that linked the seaside of Cleethorpes to the industry of Grimsby, with its fish docks and warehouses in close proximity. She felt dead on her feet by the time they'd walked from the stop to their home in Park Drive. Thankfully it was a good distance from the docks, nestled in a leafy suburb on the edge of town. It was a fine house with large bay windows that looked out across the park on the other side of the road, People's Park, which was resplendent with all manner of trees and shrubs, a large lake in the centre. When Johnny was called up for service in January, Frances had been quite prepared to remain there. It was easy enough to get to the Palace, and war had not yet come so close, but last week's bombing had left her afraid of what might happen to them all, of what might happen to her unborn child.

She opened the wooden gate and Imogen ran up the path, reaching up to grab the handle and open the front door. A motorbike had been propped against the dividing wall, indicating that their latest guest had arrived, and the sight of it lifted her spirits. She had registered the spare bedroom with the billeting officer and a regular stream of young women from the Women's Royal Naval Service, popularly known as Wrens, and the occasional naval officer, came to stay for a night or two. It was someone else to talk to, young women with energy that Ruby sometimes ignored or embraced, dependent on her mood. Her sister-in-law had dithered that morning before they left for the station to see Jessie off, saying she would come, then changing her mind at the last minute, as was her habit. It was all very wearing as Frances battled with morning sickness that seemed to last all day. Still, Ruby was better than she'd been when she first returned from the hospital. Imogen had the ability to bring out the better parts of Ruby as no one else could, which only served to illuminate how much damage Ruby's mother had inflicted with her controlling and coercive behaviour. Frances instinctively pressed her hand to her stomach, thinking of the baby growing inside her. How could any mother be so cruel?

As the front door opened, the stray dog they had rescued ran out and dashed about her feet and back to Imogen. The child threw her arms around his scruffy neck as if they had been parted for weeks, not hours. 'Oh, Mr Brown, have you missed me like I missed you?' Wherever they went they would have to take the dog.

Inside the house, Frances removed her coat and gloves and placed them on the hall table, glanced down at the bag and thick jacket on top of it. Imogen was chattering to someone in the kitchen and Frances walked in to discover a blonde-haired girl with her back to her, opening cupboards, Imogen explaining where things were. The girl brought down a cup and saucer and, seeing Frances, lifted down another, placing them both on the table. She put out her hand.

'Hello, you must be Mrs Randolph. I'm Bridget.'

Frances shook her hand then let it drop.

'Can I get you something? Tea? I wasn't sure where anything was, but this young lady has been a grand help.' She beamed at Imogen, who swung her torso from side to side at hearing the praise.

Frances bit back her irritation. The Wren had been expected and Frances had left simple enough instruction for Ruby to take care of her. 'It's I who should be getting *you* something.' She recalled the bag in the hall. 'Has Ruby not shown you where things are? Your room?'

'Miss Randolph said she didn't feel well and went to lie down. She told me you'd be home shortly. I'm sorry if I—'

'Please don't apologise.' Frances stopped her. 'Here, let me get you something. You must be hungry?' She'd left cold pressed meat and bread in the pantry; Ruby only had to cut a couple of slices and put it on a plate for the girl when she arrived. It wasn't complicated. Frances indicated for the girl to sit down. 'Have you come far?'

'A hundred miles or so, not too bad.' The girls were deliberately vague, never giving more information than was necessary. Frances guessed she'd come from HMS *Europa* in Lowestoft, the headquarters of the Royal Naval Patrol Service. The links between the two towns were strong, both being home to large fishing fleets in peacetime. Many of the newer and larger trawlers had been converted to minesweepers, as they had been in the last war, fishermen young and old signing up for naval service. There could be few families in both towns that weren't connected to the sea in some vein. Bridget withdrew a chair and took a seat at the pine table while Frances busied herself in the pantry. Mrs Frame had Sundays off. It was a day Frances dreaded, not that she couldn't fend for herself, she'd been doing that for years, but Ruby was apt to drag herself about the house and there was no one else to lift the mood. It had begun to get on her nerves more than it should. She'd put it down to her hormones, hoping that things would settle down as the weeks passed and the sickness abated. Mr Brown sat by the back door and looked expectantly at Frances.

'Imogen, will you take Mr Brown out into the garden so he can have a run around, please.'

Her daughter nodded, standing on tiptoe to open the door, turning to her mother with a smile of great satisfaction that she'd managed it alone.

Frances put the bread and meat on the table, poured them both a cup of tea, leaving the teapot on the table, then sat down with Bridget. The girls they billeted were usually well brought up young women who had volunteered early. Many of the local Grimsby girls had also joined the WRNS, as after their training they were able to billet in their own homes. It was less pressure on the navy and the girls welcomed the fact that they could serve and still be with their families. The girls who had taken positions as dispatch riders had ridden motor-bikes before the war. Not only that, but they knew how to strip the engines down and repair them. Frances admired their spirit and capability. It wasn't something she would want to under-take, driving miles across country in daylight *and* in darkness. If only Ruby could embrace that same spirit and contribute in some small way. Frances was certain it would help her recovery but each thing she suggested was met with either apathy or an excuse.

Bridget pulled the plate towards her. She was a pleasant-looking girl with a round open face and a smattering of freckles across her nose. Frances offered her the bread, then the meat, and apologised for the lack of butter. Bridget helped herself. 'Of course, I recognised Miss Randolph as soon as she opened the door.'

Frances suppressed a sigh. No wonder Ruby had retreated; it would have ignited the weight of expectation she still felt, to be bright and gay, to be what other people expected her to be. Fame had not brought Ruby happiness and her thoughts flitted to Jessie, hoping fame, if she found it, would be kinder to her.

'I hope you didn't have to wait too long for her to answer it?'

'Oh, no. Well, perhaps a few minutes.' She shrugged, smiling amiably. 'I didn't mind at all. She was very apologetic. She'd been in the garden.' The girl glanced to the window. 'It looks very pretty out there.'

'Not as pretty as it used to be, before we added the Anderson shelter and extended the veg patch. But the trees and shrubs give it colour. And we have the park over the road. We're very lucky.'

Bridget took a bite from her sandwich. 'I saw the Randolphs in the West End a few years ago. *Lavender Lane*. It was a wonderful show.'

'It was.' It was the show that had brought her and Johnny together, but the memories were tainted, thanks to Ruby and her mother. All the same, it had been a magical time and far better to remember all the good things. Bridget hesitated before she spoke again.

'For some reason, I think it upset her.' The girl was apologetic. 'I got the feeling she didn't want to talk about it.'

Frances was cautious how she answered. She wouldn't want

Ruby to be subject to gossip. As far as the public was concerned, Ruby's brother and onstage partner had gone to war, like the majority of men of fighting age, and Ruby was taking time out.

'Ruby hasn't been too well. She wouldn't have meant to have been rude.'

The girl nodded but didn't ask any further questions and the conversation turned to the town and the things Bridget could do while she was staying with them. 'The Tivoli Theatre and the Palace offer variety shows. There are numerous picture houses and there's the Café Dansant if you wanted to go into Cleethorpes. The park is pleasant enough if you just want to walk.'

A short time later, Ruby came to join them. 'Feeling better?' Frances asked.

Ruby nodded, took a glass from the cupboard and went to the tap, sipped at the water then waved at Imogen out in the garden. When she turned, she was smiling. Frances knew it was fake, but the girl wouldn't.

'I'm sorry I had to leave you,' Ruby said, her voice overly bright. 'These headaches come on so suddenly.'

'It's quite all right,' Bridget told her. 'I was glad to be able to sit down and be quiet. It takes a while to settle the noise of the bike ringing in my ears.'

Ruby hovered by the sink and, sensing she was not going to be of help, Frances got to her feet. 'If you've finished, Bridget, I'll show you to your room.'

In the hall she bent to pick up Bridget's bag, but she swooped in front of her and picked it up herself. Frances stiffened. How could the girl possibly have guessed her condition? 'Not that there's anything in the bag, simply manners,' Bridget explained. Frances relaxed and led Bridget upstairs and into the back bedroom that overlooked the rear garden. The bed had already been made with fresh sheets and Mrs Frame had left towels on the chair by the window. Frances went to it and opened the casement a little to let in the air. The garden was still quite lovely, the Anderson shelter to the back of it. Mr Frame had dug it with a friend, and they had erected the corrugated iron shell, covering it with soil and turf so that it wouldn't be seen from the air.

'It's a lovely room.' Bridget came to stand with Frances at the window. 'Smashing garden. Have you lived here long?'

'Since last year.' Or at least Johnny and Ruby had. There was no need for Frances to tell every little detail. The garden was screened on all three sides with large shrubs and dense trees that were still in full leaf, though they were losing their green, a hint of yellow and gold here and there. Frances had found solace there, enjoying each season as it came and went. She had moved into the house in February when the garden was awakening. Then hellebores and daffodils were in bloom, and hot on their tails the tulips, and yet more colour as the roses blossomed and the shrubs gained their summer dresses. She doubted she'd find anything as lovely elsewhere.

'The bathroom is next door, the lavatory next to that. I should think you might want to freshen up? Rest?' She went to the door. 'I'll leave you to it. It's a cold supper I'm afraid.'

The girl flopped onto the bed and smiled. 'That's perfectly fine. You've been very kind.'

Frances went into her own room and switched on the light. The front windows had been blown out in last week's blast and were still boarded up. The glazier was due to come that week. She would be glad when things were back to normal – or as normal as they could ever be. At least they would be in place for when Johnny came home. He would call her at six, as he always did, and once again she appreciated the luxury of having a home telephone. The sound of his voice was all she had, but at least it was more than a lot of women could hope for. She sat on the end of the bed, longing to lie down on it to nap, but reluctant to give in to the fatigue. Instead, she changed her shoes for something less smart and went back downstairs. Ruby was still at the window, the table not cleared. Frances picked up the bread and returned it to the crock, put the things in the pantry. Ruby didn't even move aside when she took the dirty crockery to the sink, merely glanced at them.

'How's your headache, Ruby?'

Ruby looked at her from under her lashes. 'Much better, thank you.'

'That's good. Does that mean you'll come to the Empire later? It's the singalong evening. Grace was asking about you this morning. And I know the boys would appreciate it – as would Jack.'

Ruby began rubbing at her temple. 'Not this week. Perhaps next.'

Frances sat down at the table opposite her. 'But you were wonderful last week at the YMCA. And you coped so well in the pub last night. I thought you might—'

'That was different,' Ruby snapped.

'How?' Frances was exasperated.

'I don't know. It just was.' Ruby began to scratch at her wrist, her nails leaving deep red scores on her pale flesh; it was what she did when she was challenged, finding some physical means of hurting herself. Frances put a steadying hand on Ruby's arm to stop her. Ruby shrugged it away. Frances sighed, wishing she wasn't so tired, wishing that she had the answer to all Ruby's problems, knowing there was no easy solution – only time, and lots of it. Johnny felt that if his sister could get her confidence back their agent could get her work in films. Frances wasn't thinking of anything so grand.

'I'm sure you'd feel much better if you got—'

'How would you know?'

Frances briefly closed her eyes, not wanting to lose her temper. If she backed down each time Ruby snapped, they would never make progress. 'It's like riding a bike, Ruby. You keep falling off and you have to get back on.'

'It's nothing like it.' Ruby stopped talking as the back door opened and Mr Brown trotted in followed by Imogen.

'Oh, hello, Auntie Ruby. I thought you'd gone for a walk.'

'I was waiting for you.'

Imogen went to her side. 'You should have come with us. We went to see Auntie Jessie at the station. Then we went to see Auntie Lil at the pub.'

Ruby smiled and it transformed her face. 'You should have taken Mr Brown. He might like to have seen Fudge.'

'Oh no,' Imogen said, her little face suddenly serious. 'Mr Brown had to stay here and look after you. You saved his life.' She stood on her tiptoes, reaching for the lead that hung by the back door. Frances unhooked it and handed it down. The child had a knack for diffusing the bad feeling between her mother and aunt. Ruby was instantly disarmed.

'It wasn't quite like that—' Ruby started, but Frances interrupted.

'Yes, it was.' They had been in the shelter the night of the bombing and in his distress the dog had run out into the night. Knowing how much he meant to Imogen, Ruby had run after him. It was a stupid thing to do, but a brave one.

Imogen fastened the lead to Mr Brown. 'We'll wait while you get your cardigan,' she told her aunt. 'It can get a bit nippy in the park, can't it, Mummy?'

'It certainly can,' said Frances, trying to be serious. It was a phrase Mrs Frame used on a regular basis. 'Best to do as she says, Ruby. Don't keep Miss Bossyboots waiting.'

When they left, Frances went to the front room and watched

them from the window, the two of them walking hand in hand. Imogen took Ruby as she was, having no knowledge of all the hurt she'd inflicted upon mother and daughter. Nor did she have an understanding of all the pain that had been inflicted on her aunt. However much Ruby infuriated her sometimes, Frances would have to remember that. For Imogen's sake, if not for her own.

5

Jessie had been overwhelmed when she arrived at King's Cross. Everything appeared larger, faster, more intense. All humanity had swarmed from the train, soldiers and civilians, spilling out onto the wide platform and Jessie had been suddenly overcome with the enormity of her surroundings. The glass on the station had been reinforced with wire mesh and tarred to blacken it, and even though it was daylight outside, inside the station was grim and dimly lit. The dust had caught in her throat, and she stopped at the buffet to get a glass of water and use the lavatory. On a bench outside the buffet, she'd picked up a discarded newspaper and wished she hadn't. It reported fifty-five enemy losses in large print, our own in smaller type further down. She'd left it there and tried to forget. Knowing numbers wouldn't help. She queued at the telephone box and made a quick call to Lil, asking her to get a message to her mum, to let her know she'd arrived, then made her way out of the heavily sand-bagged exit, in the direction of Regent's Park, glad to have arrived in late summer while the evenings were still light. It would be difficult enough finding her way in daylight let alone during the blackout.

The weather was glorious but the air was heavy with smoke and fug from cars and buses, lorries and wagons. The streets were far longer than those she'd experienced elsewhere, the houses taller, and she walked slowly, each step she took a world away from the relative safety of Cleethorpes. Although there had been warnings there had been little damage, the Germans focused on hitting the ports and docks, concentrating on disrupting the supply chain and limiting goods coming into the country. She'd overheard talk on the train as passengers joined them from Peterborough – that Birmingham had been hit and the East End was still burning. Unable to bear it any more, she'd given up her seat and made her way to the guard's carriage, finding her father's case and sitting on it, taking what comfort she could, pushing away the doubts that had resurfaced: that she should have stayed where she was, been content with what she had.

* * *

Jessie stood before the house in Albany Street in north-west London and glanced again at the address her mother had written down. Surely there had been a mistake. It was far too grand to be theatrical digs. The four-storey house was part of a long terrace, each house having a wide stone step leading up to the front door, and a long cast-iron balcony above. There were two windows on each floor, each pane of Georgian glass taped with crosses to limit the damage if they should be caught in a blast. It looked like it would withstand anything. She checked the paper again. It was definitely the right place. Above her barrage balloons floated, silver whales tethered to the ground. It was nothing like she'd expected it to be, and the grandness of the property only added to the intimidation she'd felt as the train had come closer to London.

She stepped up to the front door and rang the bell, wondering if she should have gone down to the basement and used the servants' entrance. Before she could change her mind, the door opened to reveal a plain-faced girl, a little older than herself, wearing a black dress and starched white apron. 'I'm looking for Mrs Croft,' Jessie told her.

Without a word the girl came forward and relieved Jessie of her suitcase. Jessie rubbed the feeling back into her hands, her fingers sore from carrying it. She'd been bewildered as to which bus to take, choosing instead to follow the map Frances had drawn for her, cursing that the streets were so long. It had taken the best part of an hour to get there, stopping and starting as she put down her case to rest her aching arms and shoulders.

'Follow me, miss, if you please.'

Jessie did as she was asked, following the girl into a large hallway. The maid put the suitcase at the bottom of the stairs, directing Jessie to make her way to the first floor and take the door to the right. It opened into a grand sitting room at the front of the house, the two long windows overlooking the street. Jessie looked about her. The room reminded her of a theatre, the windows furnished with heavy red drapes that were edged with gold fringing. Two plump, generous sofas faced each other either side of a white marble fireplace and around them occasional tables were decorated with silver-framed photographs and china ornaments. Two armchairs nestled by the window, a small table between them, a copy of *The Stage* newspaper to one side of it. Mahoghany-framed playbills featuring Marie Lloyd and Vesta Tilley were displayed about the walls, and exotic bowls and vases sat atop every highly polished table and cabinet. Standing among the opulence, Jessie felt grubby and unwashed.

Presently she was joined by a buxom woman, her steel-grey hair set in a generous pompadour style about her cheery face. The manner in which she swept into the room left Jessie in no mystery as to Mrs Croft's background. No doubt her name was on many of the playbills that decorated the walls.

'Jessie, my dear girl. Take a seat, take a seat. No need to stand on ceremony here.'

Jessie hovered on the edge of a chair.

'Sit back, darling. Right back, that's it,' she encouraged as Jessie sank fully into the cushions. 'That's better. You must be tired. Long journey. It's a caper these days, isn't it?' The maid who had greeted Jessie earlier came in and set a tray of tea down on the table in front of Mrs Croft. 'I'll have Violet draw you a bath.' She looked at the girl. 'Half an hour, Violet. It'll give me time to show Miss Delaney her room.' The maid gave a small bob and left.

A bath. Jessie had been used to having a strip wash at Barkhouse Lane. Never in her life had she lived in a house with its own bathroom.

Mrs Croft poured the tea and got up and handed one to Jessie. 'I hear you're at the Adelphi.'

'I am, Mrs Croft.'

She smiled. 'No need to be so formal, Jessie. Call me Belle; everyone else does.' She took up her own cup. 'Not a bad place to start. Best to find your feet and get comfy before you venture a little further. It's a tough business and it will be as well to get a little experience under your belt, although...' The woman looked her up and down. 'I reckon you're one of those girls who won't take long to get in front of the right people. You've got the looks, and by all accounts you've got the voice.'

Jessie raised an eyebrow in question.

'Your mother wrote to me. And Madeleine of course. I

suppose you know that.' Madeleine Moore had topped the bill at the Empire when Jessie first arrived in Cleethorpes, forsaking her film career to go back where she started, appearing in small theatres, hoping to discover the joy in performing again. She had nurtured Jessie's talent, spotting her potential, introducing her to men of influence. That she was here at all was down to the woman's generosity.

Jessie nodded. 'They became great friends last summer. Miss Moore has been very kind to me.' As soon as Jessie had accepted Bernie's offer, Grace had written to Madeleine wanting to secure a safe place for Jessie to stay. But this house was nothing like the theatrical digs the Delaney family had lodged in when she was a child. By that time her father was already in his decline and the rooms they rented were shabby and dark. Jessie thought now that perhaps her mother and father had stayed in such lovely homes once upon a time.

Mrs Croft nodded. 'A lovely woman. Pity she hasn't found the right man. Not all of us are so lucky.'

'No,' Jessie agreed.

'Got yourself a young man, have you?' Mrs Croft said, glancing pointedly at Jessie's engagement ring. Jessie sipped at her tea, slightly taken aback by the woman's frankness. She'd hardly been in the house more than fifteen minutes.

'I do.' Jessie held out her hand for Belle to get a closer look and the older woman took it in hers, smiled admiringly.

'That's a beautiful ring. He must be a corker.'

'He is,' she said, warmed by the thought of him. 'He's a pilot in the RAF.'

'Brave boys.' Mrs Croft was quiet. 'There's been a lot of bother over the south coast these past weeks.' She was about to continue then thought better of it. 'Known him long?'

'A couple of years,' Jessie explained, glad to talk of Harry and not of what he was doing. Mostly she tried not to think of it at all, only prayed for his safety, remembering precious times when they were together – and would be again. 'He was working in my uncle's solicitor's office. As was I, for a time.' It all seemed so long ago now. She'd felt so trapped, the endless monotony of her life stretching before her.

'You didn't like it?'

Jessie shook her head. 'Oh, I know some people like a steady job, knowing where they are from one day to the next, but I felt...'

'Like you were suffocating?' Belle offered.

'Exactly like that.' It was good to be with someone who understood. Though she felt she had been suffocating on the train, the carriages packed to capacity, the corridors crammed with bodies, sweating, smoking, the heat stifling. Belle got up and placed her finger on the poster on the wall.

'That's me, Belle L'amour of the Three L'amours. And that one,' she said, moving to the next. 'I've been on the bill with the greats, as you can see. We were an adagio act, you know, telling a story through acrobatics, holding poses, like statues. Well, I've gone to seed a bit since then.' She smoothed her hands over generous hips. 'Can you believe I used to have a sixteen-inch waist?' Not waiting for Jessie to confirm or deny, she took down a silver filigree frame that contained a sepia photo of a dark-haired young man in doublet and hose, a girl either side of him, his arms about their tiny, corseted waists, the legs of their costumes cut high to accentuate the length of their limbs. 'My sister and my brother. Both gone now. God bless them.' She smiled fondly at the picture, remembering. 'What a life we had. I'll tell you some time.' She replaced the silver frame, took the cup and saucer from Jessie's hand and returned it to the tray. 'I talk too much. But it's always lovely to look back on the good times. Now, let me show you where everything is.'

Jessie followed her into the room next door.

'Dining room. Monday's an early start to account for rehearsals, otherwise breakfast is late, as is supper. You'll have something to take to the theatre if you choose, but there are plenty of cafés to be found.' She turned to Jessie. 'If you let me have your ration book, I'll make sure you get everything you need.'

Jessie opened her bag and handed it over, relieved that she wouldn't have to stand in line for hours. Another luxury granted to her.

Belle led the way down the corridor to a rear staircase. 'That's down to the kitchens and what have you. There's a cellar below, best to know in case you're about when the warning goes off. You'll probably be at the theatre, but better to be prepared. Just in case.' She moved her hand, signalling Jessie to go back the way they came.

Jessie followed her up two flights of stairs to a small room on the top floor at the front of the house. It was twice as large as any room she'd ever had, a large brass bed against the wall, her case already placed on the floor beside it. Beside the bed was a dressing table with a large triple mirror, a velvet cushioned stool placed in front of it. A full-length mirror made up one door of the double wardrobe.

'Bathroom's on the next floor down, the lavatory next to it.' She went to the door. 'Take as long as you want, my dear, then join us in the sitting room, if you so wish. Some of the others will have returned by then.' She checked her wristwatch, and smiled at Jessie. 'Is it all to your liking?'

'Oh, yes. Thank you, Mrs Croft. Belle.' Jessie couldn't hide her delight. She was glad her mother had insisted she come here. It was more money than she'd ever thought to pay. But she was in London – and opportunity had its price.

When Belle left, Jessie ran her hand over the highly polished wood, moving to each piece in turn, peering out of the window, looking down onto the street below, then back again to take in the room. It was such a luxury and one that was affordable on her wages of twelve pounds a week. Left to her own devices, she would have found something cheaper, allowing her to save *and* send something back home. But Grace had put her foot down when Jessie showed her the advertisements she'd ringed in the newspaper. 'Oh, no, that will never do. You *must* stay somewhere respectable or I'm coming with you.' Jessie had immediately acquiesced.

She sat down on the bed and smoothed her hands over the counterpane. One day she would be able to give her mother fine things, a brass bed, plump pillows with white cotton pillow shams, and a satin eiderdown. That was what she'd come here for; she hadn't expected it for herself, though she was glad to have it. She unpacked her case, hanging her few clothes in the cavernous wardrobe, and went to take a bath, still unable to believe that someone had run it for her – and that she had it all to herself.

Refreshed and feeling less soiled, she made her way back to the sitting room. A man of late middle age was lounging on the sofa, his cheeks flushed, eyes closed, his long fine fingers interlinked over his maroon waistcoat. He opened one eye when she came in.

'I spy with my little eye...'

Jessie froze.

'Victor,' a woman said firmly, holding him to heel. She got up from the high-back chair that had concealed her. 'Take no notice, darling. He's been at the pub.'

'Just a little snifter. Medicinal purposes,' he said, sitting more upright.

The woman sucked in her cheeks then gave Jessie a broad smile. 'You must be Jessie. Belle said you'd arrived. Velma, of Victor and Velma.' She moved to the empty sofa, patted the cushion next to her and Jessie sat down. Close up, the woman looked a little younger than what Jessie took to be the woman's husband. Older than her mother. Early Fifties, perhaps more. You could never really tell with theatre people. Her skin was smooth, though it creased about her brown button eyes. 'At the Adelphi. Belle told me. Funnily enough we've not long left there.'

'Pity,' Victor said, and his wife tutted, gave a little shake of her head.

'Who's your agent?'

'Bernie Blackwood,' Jessie replied.

Belle Croft came to join them, standing in front of the marble fireplace. The two women exchanged approving glances.

'She's got herself well set, hasn't she, Belle?'

The front door opened and the sound of heels and chatter and coats being hung interrupted their conversation. Two identical girls in their late twenties came in, dressed in suits, little hats perched on their heads. Victor sat up. The twins blew him a kiss. 'Evening, girls.'

'Jilly,' said the one on the left, shaking Jessie's hand.

'Jane.' Her sister offered her hand. 'Just arrived?'

Jessie nodded.

'Been here before?'

'My first time in London.'

'Ooh.' One turned to the other then back to Jessie. 'I meant at Belle's. But first time in London. Gosh, what a time to make its acquaintance.'

'I think I might have been once before.' Jessie was hesitant. 'I was very young, about four or five.' Her visit had been brief, if it had happened at all. 'I went with Dad to a concert. He used to play in the orchestra. But he was ill. It was after the Great War.' It was a vague memory, his hand in hers. Where had Mum and Eddie gone? She couldn't remember. It was only the two of them. Perhaps Eddie had been ill, her mother tired.

'The damage of the last war goes on and on. And here we are again.' Belle sighed, beginning to draw down the blackout blinds now that dusk was falling. 'Who'd have thought it.' She stopped, stared at the blackness, then jogged herself and began to switch on the lamps.

'Does your father still play?' Jilly asked, brightly.

Jessie shook her head. 'He passed away a couple of years ago.' It seemed so distant and yet so recent, and each mention of him brought back the familiar pang of pain and emptiness.

'Oh, I am sorry. That must have been very hard.'

'It was, especially so for my mother.' Her mother had not made any great drama of her grief, but it had been such a difficult time for them all, losing their home as well as her father, with little money to speak of to ease their way. There followed months of great distress and turbulence while their mother sought a safe haven for them all – not that living with the Coles had been any kind of haven, more akin to being caught in purgatory. But that was in the past and she wasn't going to look back anymore. She smiled at the twins. 'Thankfully, things are better than they were.'

'Well, you'll be safe enough here with Belle. Nothing for your dear mother to worry about.' They made Victor move up, and sat next to him; Jilly patted Victor's knee. 'I hear Max Miller is playing to good houses at the Holborn Empire.'

'And Pat Kirkwood's opening at the Palladium next month. That should be the one to catch. *Top of the World*,' Victor added. 'What with Tommy Trinder and Flanagan and Allen topping the bill, it'll take more than Hitler and his grotty gang to stop us.'

'Chase 'em orf with your umbrella, Victor,' Jilly urged. They all roared with laughter.

'I did my bit in the last lot,' Victor told them, 'though I'm more than happy to take them on again.'

'They'll call you if they need you, dear.' Velma smiled at him, her face full of love. They were a kindly bunch and as they chatted Jessie felt more at ease, glad that she'd found a home from home. And that was down to her mother. Grace Delaney might not have money, but she had friends who thought highly of her, and in her own quiet way she was drawing on everything she had to smooth Jessie's path. Jessie vowed to make her efforts worthwhile.

6

The siren had gone off in the early evening and the residents of Albany Street had made their way into the cellar, grumbling at the inconvenience. Velma told her that they'd had more than a few occasions to go down there just lately so it was all rather well organised. Small camp beds were set out around the walls, a pillow and folded blanket on each one, and a mixture of battered easy chairs, deckchairs and the odd dining chair filled a small area to the right of the stone steps. About the walls, wooden shelves were stacked with oil lamps, books, newspapers and numerous tins of food. A small pine table was pushed up against one wall and on it a Primus stove, tea and sugar caddies, a large brown teapot and numerous cups and saucers. Tucked at the rear was a half bottle of whisky and a couple of small glasses. No one seemed at all perturbed as they made themselves comfortable. It was almost as if they had been sitting in the dressing room after the curtain had come down. Talk soon turned to who had been a joy to work with, all very jolly and good natured, before they pounced on the horrors, sharing tales of the backstabbers and the jealousy, of getting gags and routines cut, the accidents and the mishaps where fault could never be proved. 'You'll put poor Jessie off before she's even started,' Velma said kindly, pressing Jessie's shoulder.

'Well, anyone in showbiz knows you have to take the rough with the smooth,' Victor warned. 'It's not all stardust and sequins. As we know only too well.'

Jessie knew of it but hadn't experienced anything too harsh. She had misguidedly thought Madeleine Moore had her song cut in the show, but that had been a misunderstanding on her part. That had been down to an ambitious comedian by the name of Billy Lane. And he hadn't wanted to hurt Jessie; she was just in the way – his target had been Madeleine, but it had backfired. She briefly wondered what had happened to him. He had abandoned the show, chasing after Bernie Blackwood for a spot on the wireless. She hadn't heard of him since. And good riddance to that. His treatment of her was nothing compared to the trail of misery he'd left behind. He'd been dating her best friend, Ginny, and got her pregnant. Thankfully, if you could call it that, she'd suffered a miscarriage, but it had been traumatic, and Jessie feared Ginny might never get over his abandonment. It had all been truly sobering, leaving Jessie determined that the same thing would never happen to her.

They heard engines in the distance and Jessie strained to hear, listening out for any explosions but there were none close by and eventually the conversation died as they either closed their eyes or picked up something to read. When the all-clear sounded they made their way back upstairs, Jessie having a bite of supper before going up to bed. She fell onto the marshmallow feather mattress, exhausted, Victor's words going round in her head.

* * *

Belle had made her eat breakfast even though she couldn't face it, nerves getting the better of her. 'You'll thank me for it later on,' she had insisted, giving Jessie directions to the theatre, informing her of which bus to catch if she didn't want to walk. She'd made a mental note of the numbers, but the weather was beautiful, and she'd got up in plenty of time to allow for the walk, hoping it would calm her nerves, wanting to get a sense of where she was in relation to the theatre, and all the places of note in between. At Trafalgar Square she marvelled at the height of Nelson's Column, the breadth of the National Gallery, stopped at the memorial to Edith Cavell and read the inscription.

EDITH CAVELL

BRUSSELS

DAWN

OCTOBER 12

1915

PATRIOTISM IS NOT ENOUGH.

I MUST HAVE NO HATRED OR

BITTERNESS FOR ANYONE.

She knew of the nurse and her heroism – that she'd tended to the injured, no matter what side they were on, and had been shot by a firing squad. Reading it Jessie felt strangely peaceful. Whatever she faced would never require so much bravery, and with a lighter step she carried on to the Strand and down towards the Adelphi.

She slowed her pace as she approached the theatre, and crossed the road, wanting to get a better view of the frontage, the canopy patterned with black and white diamond tiles. Above it a large hoarding advertised *A Touch of Silver starring Sid Silver* in enormous black letters, *OPENING THIS THURSDAY* printed on a paper banner and pasted across it. Below it sandbags were stacked either side of the entrance doors, the brass handles and finger plates gleaming. On the pillars in between glass cases contained details of the show and she waited for a gap in the traffic before crossing the road to get a better look. She searched the bill for her name and found it three lines from the bottom, the dancers and the orchestra below. She doubted she had ever seen anything more exciting in her whole life.

She doubled back to Bedford Street and found her way to the stage door on Maiden Lane and went inside. The stage doorman peered out of the office and checked her name off the list, then introduced himself. 'The name's Gus. Let me know if you need anything. Anything at all.' He reached behind him. 'Your keys, Miss Delaney,' he said, handing them over.

She clutched them and was about to turn away when he called her back.

'A postcard.'

On the front of it was a small posy of violets and she knew without turning it over that it was from Harry. The message on the reverse was brief.

Here's to new beginnings.

The man smiled at her. 'Someone special?'

She nodded. 'Very.' She almost floated up the stone stairs to her dressing room on the first floor. Singing came from the open door and she went in to find a girl in her mid-twenties, perhaps a little younger than Frances. Her coat had been hung over the back of her chair and her bag was on the dressing table, claiming her territory, leaving Jessie to take up the small place by the sink. She assessed Jessie through the mirror, thinly plucked eyebrows rising as she took in Jessie's ankle socks and flat shoes. Feeling that she had been found wanting, Jessie quietly removed her coat and put it on one of the empty hangers that hung from the metal rail at the back of the room.

'You must be Jessie Delaney,' the girl said as she smoothed her platinum blonde hair into place. 'Adele Blair. Soubrette.' Her eyes were startlingly blue, and carefully applied lipstick accentuated the cupids bow of her lips.

Jessie put out her hand. The woman took it in hers and gave it the briefest of shakes. She was no doubt well cast, the soubrette being coy and flirtatious in her performance. As such, her soprano would not clash with Jessie's crooning, and that alone helped her relax. There would be little cause for competition between them. Jessie had been booked 'act as known' which meant she was there to sing in her style. There would be production numbers that she would be a part of, as would other members of the cast. She could dance if it was required of her but Vernon had booked her because of her voice, nothing else.

'Crooner,' Jessie told her.

'Ah, hoping to steal Vera Lynn's crown, are we?'

'I'm not here to steal anyone's crown,' Jessie said pleasantly, putting her father's make-up bag on the dressing table. The familiarity of it steadied her, touching it, anchored her. Her talisman. The leather bag was falling apart, the hinges broken, the make-up ground into the ridges and corners but that didn't matter. It brought him close. Again, the raised eyebrow from Adele. It rankled but Jessie wasn't going to be intimidated. 'It was my father's,' Jessie said, her voice challenging. Adele looked at her blankly. 'I realise I must look like a country bumpkin to you.'

'I didn't mean to...' Adele took a breath. 'I'm sorry.' She lowered her chin. 'You weren't what I was expecting.'

'What were you expecting?'

Adele shrugged. 'I don't know. Someone who'd been around a bit I suppose.'

'Well, I have.' Jessie picked up her music. 'I've been working since I was eight. Granted, it was at my father's side, but I've had plenty of experience since.' She'd learned a lot during that first summer season when she'd first stepped off the train in Cleethorpes. More so these last few months, travelling with the concert party. She knew what songs worked and which ones stirred the emotions, when to sing the ballads, and when to uplift and delight.

Frances had warned her that not everyone would be welcoming. 'You have talent, Jessie, but that doesn't mean people will be supportive. Stand your ground from the off.' It had felt odd doing so, it wasn't in her nature, but Adele had judged her as soon as she'd walked into the room and it made her uncomfortable. She hadn't expected to have to defend herself before she'd even got on the stage. 'I did very well in Cleethorpes...'

'Cleethorpes!' Adele was incredulous and spun round in her chair to look directly at Jessie. 'You must have played some of the biggies – Manchester? Birmingham? Leeds?' She turned back to the mirror, picked up a powder puff and began dabbing at her cheeks, her chin, releasing pale clouds into the air.

Jessie shook her head, feeling the heat rise in her neck.

'Well, all I can say is you must be good.' She winked at Jessie through the mirror. 'Or did you do something else to get a spot in the show?'

'I'm sure I don't know what you mean,' Jessie spat, incensed by Adele's implication that she'd got here on anything other than her talent. The woman put down her powder puff and got up.

'Look.' Adele put out her hand. 'Let's start again. Adele Blair.'

Jessie took it firmly. 'Jessie Delaney.' The two exchanged smiles.

'That's better. I don't want us to set off on the wrong foot. Best to start as we mean to go on.'

'Agreed,' Jessie said. It would be unbearable otherwise. She tucked Harry's postcard behind the mirror in front of her place.

'Someone special?'

'My fiancé. Harry. He's a pilot in the RAF.'

'And he finds time to send a postcard? He must be some chap to do that.'

'He is.' His letters came frequently, sometimes more than one. They were safely in her drawer at Albany Street, tied with a red ribbon. She turned in her chair. 'And you? Is there someone special?'

Adele gave a small laugh. 'Why have one when you can have many. You'll soon see what I mean. Army, navy, air force, take your pick. A different one every night – or more if you're so inclined.' The girl picked up a neat handbag. 'Better go down into the auditorium and see who else is here. I'll wait while you get ready.' Jessie brushed her hair, picked up her music. 'That it?' Adele said, clearly unimpressed.

'It's all I need,' Jessie replied.

They made their way down the steps and through the pass door into the auditorium, Jessie placing her sheet music on the stage along with the others who had got there before her. By the looks of it she would be last to be called. It was strictly first come first served but today it didn't matter when she was called; she wasn't planning on going anywhere, wanting to take time to familiarise herself with her surroundings. It wouldn't do to be too pushy. She smiled at everyone as she walked down the aisle, suddenly conscious of how inexperienced she was. The dancers were scattered among the right-hand side of the first few rows and members of the orchestra were down in the pit, talking among themselves, and tuning instruments, limbering up. A few old pros were dotted about the other seats, some already in groups, and she worked out that they would have been the tumblers and the jugglers from their physiques. She was surprised to see that Sid Silver, the comedian who was topping the bill, had arrived on time and was talking in earnest to a man who Jessie assumed must be the director, and his assistant. They were older men, men too old to be called up, but men of experience and she wanted to learn all she could from them. Jessie slid into a seat next to Adele. The couple in the row behind them leaned forward and introduced themselves. Edgar was a magician, David a tenor. Among the other cast members were a troupe of comedy tumblers, an impressionist, and a trio of acrobats known as the Bernardis.

At precisely nine o'clock the director, Charles Lambert, went onstage and explained the running order for the days up to opening night. They were welcome to go out of the theatre when not called for, but they would start rehearsing the production numbers that afternoon – for which they all needed to be in attendance. Everyone who worked in the theatre would be required to take on fire-watching and other duties to help keep the theatre safe. There were to be no exceptions.

Adele groaned, but Jessie didn't care how hard she had to work. There would be time enough when the show was on to do all she wanted to do, to see the Palladium and all the other theatres she had heard so much about, as well as all the famous landmarks she had only seen in books and magazines: the Houses of Parliament, Buckingham Palace, Westminster Abbey. It was a thrill to be here, war or not.

They sat among the rows, watching and not watching, as each act got up to go through their music, or dots, as they were known in the business, some of them wanting a whole run-through, others just topping and tailing, making sure the orchestra was aware of the tempo, the comedy tumblers going through some of the routine to make sure the orchestra knew when to come in with their sound effects. Jessie was fascinated by the way the performers approached their work, the confidence and assurance of people who knew what they wanted and how to get it, taking ownership of their performance, not leaving anything to misinterpretation, and knew she must do the same. The music had to be the way she wanted it, and she was glad that she had a thorough understanding of it, thanks to her dad. She wished he could be there, sitting beside her, telling her to take her time, to remember who she was, and not to be afraid. Adele moved about the seats, chatting with the others with ease, flirting, throwing back her head when she laughed and Jessie envied her confidence, her assurance. Hopefully, in time, she would feel like that too, but today she only felt small.

The Adelphi was an unusual building, all sharp angles, with no hint of the curves and over the top flourishes of almost every other theatre she'd been in; but beautiful all the same. It had been rebuilt in the 1930s and decorated in orange, green and gold. The ceiling looked like the top of a jewelled casket, the centre light made of silver glass. Jessie drank it in – the carpet, the seats, the way the lights were hung and operated. In between she mostly listened as the other acts talked shop, of where they had been recently, mostly where they had been in the past – if it was something they thought might impress their colleagues. Jessie marvelled at their subtle one-upmanship. One or two had been at the Palladium, another had done a six-week stint with ENSA in France before being evacuated with the troops near Dunkirk. They talked of how dreadful it was and pitied the poor buggers who were killed and taken prisoner of war. Jessie couldn't bear to think of it, of the mothers and fathers who would not see their sons again.

At last, it was her turn to go through her music, and she took a deep breath as she got to her feet and walked down to the orchestra pit, hoping she appeared more confident than she felt. She'd chosen something lively to open with. 'I've Got a Pocketful of Dreams', which Bing Crosby had recorded, followed by 'The Sweetest Song in the World' and finishing with 'Till the Lights of London Shine Again'. It was a selection she hoped would sit well with Vernon Leroy's vision for the show. She'd taken an age over each choice, working with her mum and Frances to find something suitable for her voice. In time composers might bring songs to her as they did with all the big stars. But that was a long way off. These were early days and she had to choose well, prepared for them all to be unsuitable, and having to get something else together at short notice.

She went to the orchestra rail, talked with the musicians, confident in how she wanted to put the song over and what she was asking of them. There was no need to go through the entire song – they were professionals, and so was she, and she was delighted when they treated her as such. It gave her a wonderful boost and she merely asked them to play the opening to tempo and to close, and any parts that might be ambiguous. When she'd finished, she stepped down from the stage, and as she passed, the orchestra leader called to her. 'Miss Delaney, that was an absolute delight.' He winked at her, and it took her all her time not to skip down the aisle.

Adele left Edgar and took the seat next to her. 'Happy?'

'Oh, yes. It couldn't have gone better.' She couldn't wait to sing, but knew she had to hold herself in reserve. Frances had told her not to give everything away to begin with. She'd save it for opening night.

It was almost noon when the man in the camel coat opened the doors at the rear of the auditorium and came down the aisle, a slender, dark-haired woman at his side. He took a seat, and the woman went up to the front row, pressed her hand to Charles Lambert's shoulder. He motioned for the dancers to go on with their routine then followed her back up the aisle. The man in the beige coat got up again and the two men shook hands, then began to talk, their heads close. Jessie tried to work out who he was; he looked vaguely familiar, yet she just couldn't place him. She leaned into Adele. 'Who is that?'

'The chap who's paying our wages. Vernon Leroy.'

Jessie was shocked. 'It can't be.'

Adele laughed. 'Not what you were expecting?'

'No, I've met him before. He looks so different. Are you sure it's him?' She'd only met him once, when he'd come to the Empire to see Madeleine Moore. He'd seemed so much larger then, taller, wider, filling the space about him.

'When did *you* meet him?' It was clear from the tone of her voice that Adele didn't believe her.

'He came to Cleethorpes. The day before war was declared.'

Adele pulled a face and it annoyed her.

'Madeleine Moore was top of the bill. He came to see *her*.'

'Ah, that makes sense. Why else would he go?'

That belittling tone again. This time Jessie chose to ignore it. 'Madeleine was very kind to me. She made sure I got a spot in the show when Mr Leroy came to see her and gave me two of her own costumes so that I had something special to perform in. If it wasn't for her pushing me forward I might not be here at all.'

'You're making it up.' Adele glanced down at her red nails and sneered at Jessie. It irritated.

'Why would I make it up?'

Adele shrugged, her back straight, her head high, and turned her attention to the dancers as they stepped up onstage, leaving Jessie aggrieved.

After some time, the two men stopped their conversation and Charles made his way to front of the stalls, Vernon close behind. He called up to the dancing girls and all twelve of them quickly descended the steps at either side of the stage and took their seats in the first couple of rows. He was a thickset man with wide shoulders and a broad forehead, his black hair peppered with white. He was definitely the man she'd met that glorious night at the Empire, but he seemed shrunken, and Jessie could not for the life of her work out what it was. Perhaps it was a trick of the memory; he'd only appeared larger than life because the theatre was so small, as were the corridors backstage. It was only eight hundred people and this theatre held twice that. Now that she was in London perhaps everything would not be as large as it had once seemed, so far beyond her reach. The thought comforted her.

'Welcome, everyone. I'll be brief. We have a lot of work to do in a short amount of time.' There were murmurs of agreement. 'Normally, I'd have tried the show out in Brighton or Manchester, but as you're well aware, it's been far too dangerous these last few weeks, so we've had to change things about a bit. I know it puts a lot of pressure on some of you for the production numbers but it's nothing compared to what our lads are facing.' He paused for a moment, looked down at his hands. Everyone waited for him to speak again. He raised his head and smiled out at them. 'The costumes are ready. The scenery is ready. In an ideal world it's not what I would have wished, but we are far from living in the golden time of peace. We open on Thursday.' He paused again, looked out across the auditorium so that they knew he was talking to each and every one of them. 'When times are hard people want to forget their troubles and misery and find some escape. That's what we're here for.' There was a flutter of applause, which he

acknowledged with a small bow of his head. He thanked them
and wished them well, then he and the director took their seats
and the director got up and got the girls back onstage.

'Want to go for a drink somewhere? Stretch your legs?' asked
Bettina, one of the three Bernardis.

Jessie hesitated. 'We have our costume fittings.'

'Not until this afternoon,' Adele reminded her, getting up
from her seat. 'There's a café down the street.' She looked to
Jessie. It would be churlish not to join them, and much as she
would rather remain where she was, she needed to keep on the
right side of Adele, otherwise sharing such a small dressing room
for hours on end would be unbearable.

At the Lyons Corner House they found an empty table and
sat down.

'Have you worked for Leroy before?' Bettina asked Jessie.

'This is my first time.'

Bettina smiled. 'He's not in George Black's league, or Cockie's
for that.' She stretched out her hand and checked her nails,
rubbed at the thumb. 'But he's up there with them. He can put on
a good show.'

Jessie was impressed. George Black was in charge of the Moss
Empires circuit, the number one theatres that every act aspired
to, the flagship being the Palladium. And C. B. Cochran was a
legend of the theatre. Many of his Young Ladies at the Gaiety
Theatre had married millionaires and titled men. Not that Jessie
was interested in that, she had Harry, but working for such
powerful men almost guaranteed success. *Ever Green* had opened
in this very theatre, Jessie Matthews starring in the show and the
later film. Dare she dream that one day she might play the lead in
a musical, be feted by the likes of Ivor Novello and Noël Coward?
'Is he good to work for?'

'He's fair, I'll say that,' Bettina told her. 'And you can't say that about many men in his position.'

Adele laughed. 'Many? He might be the only one. They've all got their mistresses on the side.'

'We should be so lucky.' Bettina stretched out her arm. 'A new diamond bracelet would be simply divine.'

He didn't seem that sort of man to Jessie, not that she was an expert, but she wasn't so green as to not know that kind of thing went on. There had been a huge scandal when Jessie Matthews had been discovered to be having an affair with her co-star in *This Year of Grace*. At the time Sonnie Hale had been married to Evelyn Laye, another of Cochran's Young Ladies. Knowing it went on was one thing; thinking it was acceptable was another. She changed the subject.

'He seems very different to when I saw him last year.'

'We're all different to how we were last year,' Adele quipped. 'Didn't you know, his son was shot down over the Channel last week. I should think it's the show that's keeping him going.' The waitress placed their tea on the table and placed a cup in front of them in turn. Bettina pulled her cup towards her and when the girl had left, picked up the teapot and began to pour.

'I wouldn't want to be with a chap in the RAF; the odds are they won't last the war. That's why they're the ones living it up. Life is short. We don't know how long we've got.'

Jessie's blood chilled and she shivered. Bettina was concerned. 'Are you all right?'

'Her fella's in the RAF,' Adele said by way of explanation.

'He's all right, though?' Bettina stopped pouring.

'Yes. Yes, he is,' Jessie managed to reply. 'I was with him on Saturday. Just a few hours, that's all he could get. Hopefully he'll get an extended leave soon.'

'I doubt that, not at the moment. Our boys have been fighting over the south-east for weeks. The Battle of Britain, they're calling it,' Bettina said, adding a half spoon of sugar to her tea. 'The losses are less than the Germans, but they're still losses, aren't they? Each one of them is someone's son.'

Jessie tried to filter out her words, straining to listen to the background noise, not wanting to be any part of the conversation.

'Bettina!' Adele snapped.

'Sorry, darling. I didn't think.'

Adele reached for Jessie's hand and gave it a gentle squeeze. It was a small gesture, but one that made Jessie think more kindly of her. There was no more talk of war as they walked back to the theatre. Thereafter, the time was filled by sharing stories, much as she had done in the cellar last night with Belle and the other residents of Albany Street. Gradually, Jessie became more relaxed in their company, and when they broke for the evening she was sad to leave, eager to get back the following morning, but bone-tired all the same. She hoped for a good night's sleep, in her bed as opposed to the cellar.

7

After she'd performed her songs at Wednesday's dress rehearsal, Vernon Leroy called Jessie to one side. Charles Lambert had been thrilled with her choice and hadn't changed a thing. She'd thought it had gone well; Matthew, the orchestra leader, had smiled at her throughout, the delight clear on his face, and it had given her the reassurance she needed. But today, tiredness and overwhelm had caught up with her and she'd been filled with doubt as she walked to the theatre that morning. Over breakfast Victor had talked only of the bombers Churchill had sent to Berlin in retaliation for the attack on the East End on Saturday, the day before she'd arrived in London. The newspapers reported their success, but everyone knew Hitler wouldn't take that lying down, and they braced themselves for his reply. Surely it was only a matter of time before he responded in kind?

Now, she wondered what she had done wrong, but Vernon smiled at her, laid his hand on her shoulder. 'That was marvellous, young lady. I knew my instincts were right when I heard you last year. I'm only sorry it took me so long to get you here.' It was hardly his fault; Jessie hadn't been ready to leave. 'Settling in all right? Anything you're not happy with?'

'Oh no, Mr Leroy, everyone had been wonderful. So helpful.'

Close up he looked like he hadn't slept for weeks, the lines on his face deep, the skin beneath his eyes a bluish grey. She wanted to say something about his son, to acknowledge it, but who was she to console such a great man? He had a kindly face and she thought of George, who guarded the stage door at the Empire, and what she would say to him. He was a father too.

'I was sorry to hear about your son, Mr Leroy.'

He nodded. 'Thank you. It's kind of you to think of me.'

'And him,' Jessie added.

His smile became deeper. 'Yes, my dear. And him. Most people are afraid to mention it. I'm glad you were brave enough to do so.' He took her hand in his. 'Bravery is a wonderful quality. You're going to do well, Miss Delaney. I know it.'

That evening she'd hurried home, longing for her bed, hoping that the air raid warnings were short, if they came at all. Her mum and Eddie were travelling down tomorrow, and she prayed that their train journey would be smooth, that they would arrive in time before the curtain went up at 8.20. Harry had already sent a card and she knew flowers would follow, and though he couldn't be there with her she knew he'd be thinking of her.

Her mother had been worried by the headlines, calling the theatre each evening to check that she was all right. Still alive was what she really meant. Jessie had thought to put her mother off coming, but Grace had insisted. She wasn't going to miss her daughter's West End debut. Jessie was both thrilled and troubled. It was one thing putting herself in danger but not her mum or Eddie. That was the entire reason she'd left them behind in the first place. Belle had found room for them at Albany Street, reassuring Jessie that it was no trouble at all, preparing a bed for her mother, and fixing a put-me-up for Eddie.

Jessie hardly slept that night, going over her routines, over her steps for the three production numbers she was involved in – one to close the first half, the opening of the second, and a short number to close the show. That's if anyone remained – she wondered how many would choose to leave if the warning sounded.

Belle was in the dining room when she went downstairs, overseeing Violet as she set the breakfast table.

'Did you manage to get any sleep, darling?' she said, gently patting Jessie's cheek.

'A bit.' Jessie pulled out a chair and sat down, helped herself to a slice of bread. She wasn't hungry but knew she had to eat something. Belle moved a knife and fork, checked the other place settings, pointed to Violet to adjust a glass and dismissed her.

'I don't want you to worry about a thing,' she said, filling Jessie's glass with water. 'I'll bring your dear mother and brother to the theatre in plenty of time for you to see them before the curtain goes up. I'll get word back to Gus at the stage door. Alfred is going to meet them at the station.' She had met Belle's husband only once. By the time she returned from the theatre he'd already left for his position with the local ARP. 'All you have to do is concentrate on the show.' It would be easier said than done.

In the early evening, Jessie stood with her mother and Eddie in the black marble of the theatre lobby, grateful for her mother's insistence that she be there, nerves starting to get the better of her. Belle and Alfred had disappeared into the bar to allow them some privacy, and Jessie was appreciative of their kind consideration. Eddie had not been able to stop talking about the grandeur of Albany Street and his enthusiastic jabbering had been a welcome distraction.

'You'd better get back for the half hour call, darling. Don't mind us, we'll be fine.' Her mother squeezed her hand. 'Break a leg. You'll be marvellous.'

If only she had her mother's certainty. The nearer it got to curtain up the more the churning in her stomach increased.

'You've got your tickets?'

Eddie held them up.

'And you know where the shelter is if you want to leave. Only...'

Her mum gripped her wrist. 'Don't fuss so, darling. If there's a warning we'll stay in our seats, just as we would do back home.'

It did little to comfort her, only deepened the guilt, torn because she so appreciated their support, desperate for them to be safe.

'Now, go. Or you'll be late for the half. I don't want you to get a fine because of us.'

The thought of losing a few shillings was enough to galvanise her, and giving her mother and Eddie one last squeeze she went out of the doors and round to the back of the theatre. Even though the fines for lateness and bad form went to the Actors' Orphanage Fund she didn't want to part with her money if she could help it. Her reputation for being prompt and reliable meant too much to her. The same couldn't be said for Adele who didn't seem at all perturbed at handing over her cash for numerous small misdemeanours.

Despite her mother's worries, she was early for the half-hour call. Harry had sent flowers, as had the Randolphs, Lil and customers of the Fisherman's Arms. There was a huge bouquet from her agent, Bernie, who would be in the audience tonight, with his wife. Their thoughtfulness delighted her, and she struggled to dampen her natural excitement when the flowers and cards outnumbered those Adele had received.

The wardrobe lady, Tabby, was already in the dressing room when Jessie returned, hanging the freshly laundered clothing on the rail, checking the seams and hems, making sure all the buttons and other fastenings were in place. It was a luxury to have someone take care of it all and Jessie never wanted to take any of it for granted, least of all Tabby who had been so kind to her these last few days. As she slipped out of her jacket Tabby removed a hanger from the rail and took it from her.

'You've got them settled, have you, your ma and brother?'

'I have.' Eddie had told her that the train had been slow, as most of them were these days, allowing for goods trains to take precedence, stopping if the line had been damaged. They had got there safely – and that was all that mattered. Belle had been as good as her word and brought them to the theatre early, getting a message to Gus at the stage door. Because of it Jessie had been able to give them a quick tour backstage, proudly introducing them to Adele and other members of the cast, before taking them front of house.

'I'm glad they're here, but worried sick all the same.' Jessie sat down in front of her mirror and picked up her hairbrush. Tabby took it from her and began to draw it in long, gentle sweeps through Jessie's hair, one hand resting on the back of Jessie's head.

'Now, then, she's your mother. Where else would she want to be, you tell me? Mothers go through 'ell and high water for their babies. You'll be the same one day. Then you'll know why it was the only thing she could do.'

Jessie knew she was right, although she hoped it was a long time before she became a mother herself; as much as she loved

Harry, there was far too much she wanted to do before she settled down to have babies.

'You look tired, Tabby.' Jessie had always found her bright and cheery but today she seemed slower as she moved about the room.

'Got my sister staying with me. 'Er house is flat as a pancake. Got it bad down the East End at the weekend. Lost everything – what little she had.'

'Are the family all right?'

'Her and the kiddies are. Thank the good Lord. They're at my place. Sleepin' on the floor. That's why I come early. Give 'em the chance to get their heads down afore it all starts again. I reckon she'll send the kiddies away. They went last year but it seemed daft. We didn't have no bombing to start off with, did we? And she was sending money for 'em. They was miserable without her, and she was miserable without them. So she fetched 'em back.'

'And her husband?'

'Down the docks on watch with the auxiliary fire service since yesterday afternoon – an' she ain't heard anything to the contrary.'

'Oh, Tabby. How brave.'

Tabby shrugged. 'He's just doing what everyone else is doing, my lovely. Just as you are. You need to go out there and given 'em something to look at, something lovely to listen to. Make 'em forget what's waiting for 'em when the curtain comes down. Makes all the difference.'

Did it? Jessie wasn't sure that it could make *that* much difference.

'My father fought in France in the Great War. He said the men responded to the entertainment – whether laughter or song. For a brief interlude it took them somewhere other than where they actually were.'

'He was right,' Tabby affirmed. 'There's those who think entertainment is frivolous but it's essential.'

She was comfortable with Tabby, and their little chats settled her as she busied herself with the fittings and any costume repairs. She was sure she'd had the same effect on many a girl who'd sat in her place. Tabby had been with the theatre for more than thirty years, calming nerves, the steadying hand that curbed the jitters before curtain up.

'I sometimes feel he's with me.' Jessie reached up and touched her hair. 'Like a feather has passed over my head. A small disturbance – no more than that.'

Tabby put down the brush, rested her wrinkled hands on Jessie's shoulders, the gold band of her wedding ring almost covered by soft creamy flesh.

'I know exactly what you mean, my love.' She stopped as Adele came into the room and flopped down into her seat, surreptitiously taking in the flowers that had appeared throughout the day. Between her entrances during rehearsals she'd disappeared into other dressing rooms, exchanging gossip and catching up on the latest rumours. 'I feel my old mum with me,' Tabby continued as Adele wriggled into her seat, ''specially so when I'm troubled and more likely to need her help. I talk to her all the time.' She smiled at Jessie through the mirror. They saw Adele roll her eyes. 'Nice to have someone who'll listen without interrupting, ain't it?' She winked at Jessie. 'Miss Blair. What little titbits have you retrieved for our ears this evening?'

'I don't know what you mean.' Adele pretended to be offended then proceeded to tell them about the comedian's wife who had found the betting slip in her husband's suit when he'd staggered home drunk. *Forty pounds*, she mouthed. *Forty*. Almost as much as they earned in a month, possibly more than dear Tabby earned in a year.

'What a waste,' Jessie said.

'Imagine having that much money *to* waste.' Adele picked up a comb and pulled it through her hair. Tabby made no attempt to take it from her and Jessie got the impression that Tabby hadn't taken to her as she had to Jessie. Adele leaned forward into the mirror and ran her tongue over her teeth, rubbing at a tooth here and there where lipstick had adhered. 'I'll be glad when we've got tonight out of the way. Let's hope the gentlemen of the press are kind to us. If you can call some of them gentlemen.'

'And if they're not?'

'It'll be bye-bye, show.' She laughed when Jessie frowned. 'Hey, don't get so worried about it. There are ups and downs in this game. All. The. Time. You have to take the highs with the lows, or you'll go mad with it. Isn't that right, Tabby?'

Tabby didn't answer, only rested a hand on Jessie's shoulder in comfort. Jessie wanted to vomit.

'Don't you have any family in tonight, Adele?'

Adele glanced at the cards around Jessie's part of the mirror, her head tilted to one side. She opened her mouth to say something, obviously thought better of it and shook her head, became flippant. 'Nah. I'm a bit long in the tooth for all that. Besides, when you've been in as many West End shows as I have it all gets a bit flat.' Jessie found that hard to believe. She hoped she always felt the excitement that came with opening night, no matter where it was. There was a knock on the door and the fifteen minutes was called. Adele disappeared after the call boy.

'How can she be so relaxed?' Jessie said when they were alone.

'It doesn't matter so much to her as it does to you. In my experience the ones who care so much are the ones with the most talent. Doesn't matter how many West End shows they've been in. Come now,' she said kindly, but firmly. 'Let's get your costume on for the opening number.'

Jessie's skin tingled as if it was on fire when the orchestra struck up and the overture music crackled over the tannoy. The dancers opened the show, the Three Bernardis the first act. Jessie was to follow them. At least she didn't have to go out cold, before the audience had been warmed up, and she was grateful for that. When her call came she made her way into the wings, stood watching Bettina and the two brothers go through their moves, throwing Bettina around as if she was nothing more than a bag of feathers. The set had been kept simple, and all in all it was really a glorified variety show, with production numbers that involved most of the cast in various bright routines that lifted the spirits. After all, that's what they were there for. Tabby waited with her, and Jessie held on to her hand, wishing it were her mother's.

'I think I might be sick,' she whispered, wanting for all the world to run away.

'You won't. Your ma is out there. All you have to do is sing your songs for her.' She gave her hand a quick squeeze. 'And remember that your father is right beside you, wanting you to do well.' Jessie turned to her, the gentle words exactly the ones she needed to hear.

'Thanks, Tabby.'

When the opening notes of her intro music played, Jessie took a deep breath and smiled as widely as she could before breezing out onto the stage, almost at a little run, stopping in front of the microphone, then bursting into 'I've Got a Pocketful of Dreams'. The moment the spotlight caught her, any nerves and fears melted away and suddenly, she was home. Whole. All the pieces of her sliding perfectly into place. Nothing could stop her, not nerves, nor fear, nor Hitler's bombs. Nothing. She smiled out, for her mother, for Eddie, for herself, knowing she was where she was meant to be. It was the most thrilling feeling, to sing out into the darkness, to spread out her arms as she held the final note of her last number, hoping applause would follow, suddenly not caring if it did. But the moment she stopped the applause was terrific. She bowed to the front, to the left and the right, and glided off the stage, feeling she had wings, that she could float above the auditorium and look down on it all as the applause followed her. She stepped out again for an encore, stage left, bowed again and skipped off. The jugglers made their entrance stage right but the applause went on and on and they were unable to start their act.

'You'd best go back on,' the stage manager told her. 'Doesn't look like they'll stop until you do.'

Jessie did as she was told, and when she walked out the place erupted again. She couldn't stop smiling and laughing, so thrilled that her mother was there, and Eddie too, gazing out into the stalls, to the upper circle and the gods, dazzled by the light. The ovation rang on, and she glanced to the wings, wondering what she should do next. Mr Leroy appeared from the shadows, raising his hands in applause, a broad smile on his face. He mouthed to her, *Sing*. She nodded to the conductor and the band began to play the last verse again. The audience settled down, only to erupt again when she finished. She bowed, the audience calling for more, and she wished with all her heart that her mother was on the front row, that she could see her lovely face at such a special moment. She came off, shaking with the shock of it, the pure joy and bewilderment, as the show was allowed to continue. She had stopped the show, not the siren, nor anything else, but she, Jessie Delaney, had won the audience over. If she had ever doubted herself, this was the sign she needed, that coming to London was the best thing she could have done.

8

The air raid warning had gone off in the middle of Adele's song and dance number, the sound of Wailing Willie slicing through it. The orchestra had paused when the house lights came up, and the manager had walked on to make the announcement for those who wished to leave to do so. Adele waited for the few audience members to vacate their seats and make their way down the aisle. When the manager gave the signal and exited stage right, the lights were dimmed, and the orchestra took her music from the top. She had to win them over again, and although she succeeded, it wasn't easy, the interruption breaking the spell that had been created at the opening of the show. When she'd finished her act, the audience were generous with their applause, but nothing like they had been for Jessie. It had annoyed her more than it should, having the girl steal her thunder. It wouldn't last; she wouldn't let it.

After the curtain had come down for the last time, the cast had remained onstage and congratulated each other, Sid Silver making a beeline for Jessie. He was wearing a lounge suit, his thinning grey hair slicked back with oil, and Adele watched as he

put out his hand to Jessie. He should have come to her first. She
had a name, a reputation, and Jessie was only starting to build
hers. The kid had surprised them all, not just her, and Adele
smarted at being sidelined so swiftly.

'I've only seen a few acts stop the show over the years, but
that has to go down as one of the best, young lady,' Sid told Jessie.
'Take time to let it sink in and enjoy it. It doesn't happen very
often.' He congratulated Adele for carrying on like a trooper
before quickly moving on to speak with other members of the
cast, and when Vernon Leroy appeared onstage he commandeered him. Oh, how she longed to be the star of the show. Just
once.

By the time Adele got back to the dressing room, Jessie's
mother had arrived, sweeping her daughter into her arms, her
brother, Eddie, giving her shoulder a quick squeeze. Adele had
met them only briefly, when Jessie had brought them backstage
before the curtain went up. Grace Delaney reminded Adele of
one of the characters Greer Garson played in films, the gentle
type with impeccable manners, who suffered silently and always
came out on top. She was obviously thrilled for her daughter, but
Adele watched the way she gently brought her back down to
earth, her awareness of everyone in the room, the manner in
which she handled the fine balance of being enthusiastic without
gushing. Jessie had told her that her mother had been in the
business, a dancer with the corps de ballet. Adele might have
guessed her mother wouldn't have been a run-of-the-mill dancer
in the music hall. Still, she would be only too aware of how
swiftly the highs could turn to lows. Had she warned her daughter, and had Jessie chosen not to listen? She hardly knew her own
mother, who had dumped her with her sister a week after her
birth and boarded a liner to New York. Adele had a crumpled
photo, received the odd letter on her birthday – but not all of

them. Out of sight out of mind. Forgotten for the most part. Adele had been a mistake. Her aunt had reminded her of it often enough; the result of a failed affair with a married man. All her life she'd had to fight to be noticed, and once again she had been eclipsed.

As more people squeezed into the room, Grace came over to her. 'I thought you were marvellous, Miss Blair. It must be so difficult when you are interrupted like that, but you handled it so graciously and effortlessly. Jessie can learn a lot from you.'

It disarmed her. Had she known what it was like to be over-shadowed too? From everything Jessie had said, it had all been about her father and his career. How had Jessie's mother felt about that? At the end of the day, who cared about what the women felt? It was always about the men. The brother stood against the wall, not quite fading into the background, as Sid Silver and a couple of the other members of the cast buzzed around his sister.

Adele squeezed past them, reaching over Sid to get her dressing gown from the rail, wanting to get out of her clothes, wanting to be with the others whose stars had not shone so brightly that particular night. There would be other nights, though, and she knew how to deal with girls like Jessie. She was taking the pins from her hair when Vernon Leroy joined them, carrying two bottles of champagne – heaven only knew where he had got them from. Since the fall of France what would have been easily come by was now in short supply. Once again she felt the stab of pain that he had not brought it for her. He passed one to Sid Silver to open and he twisted it so that it opened with merely a puff of gas. The stage manager came in bearing glasses, followed by a man who introduced himself as Jessie's agent. Vernon went straight for Jessie and kissed her cheeks, handed her a glass of champagne.

'They loved you. I knew they would. You're fresh, you're exciting, and just what we need. Stay just as you are and the critics will adore you.'

Adele bit at the inside of her cheek. She'd been passed over for girls like Jessie Delaney since she was a kid; no matter how hard she tried, she could only get so far and then stall. At twenty-five she knew her moment had already passed; there was little hope of getting the accolades she deserved – and it certainly wasn't going to happen in this show. Not with the kid stealing the limelight. She caught Tabby's eye and fastened a smile to her face. Tabby returned it, but it possessed none of the warmth she had for Jessie. Some people were terrible liars. She dabbed powder on her nose and refreshed her lipstick, watching through the mirror as the men fussed around Jessie Delaney.

Grace interrupted her and handed her a glass, leaving her daughter to soak up the moment. Her generous action made Adele feel mean, but she couldn't be gracious; she wasn't that kind of girl, and she knew it. Perhaps Grace did too, and that was why she had come to stand beside her.

'Best to enjoy the moment,' Grace said. 'It won't last; it never does.'

'No,' Adele replied, feeling suddenly supported. 'Such a shame.' She found Grace Delaney oddly comforting.

When all the glasses were filled, Vernon raised his glass. 'I give you Miss Jessie Delaney, a star in the making. To Jessie.'

Adele raised her glass with the others and joined in the toast, catching Jessie's eye and forcing a smile.

'To Jessie.'

9

Jessie was delighted to discover that all the other residents had waited up for their return. The soft lamps were lit in the sitting room, and she walked into a sea of expectant faces. Belle clasped hold of Jessie's hand and raised it.

'Take a good look at this girl. A showstopper.'

Velma was first on her feet, drawing Jessie into an embrace, then kissed her cheeks, left and right, squeezing her hands, and looked at her, eyes shining.

'Good for you, girl. And to have your mother here to see it. Wonderful. Simply wonderful.' The twins were next, then Victor, all of them congratulating her while her mother quietly removed her coat and sat down on the sofa, Eddie sitting on the arm of it beside her, watching as Jessie answered a barrage of questions. Belle opened the drinks cabinet and brought out a cluster of crystal glasses and a bottle of sherry, poured one for everyone and handed them to Alfred to pass around.

They sat up until the early hours, Jessie next to her mum, not wanting to leave her side, knowing that in a few hours she would be catching the train back home. She wished they could have stayed longer but Eddie had already taken two days off work and her mother had her work with the WVS. On Sunday she would be at the Empire serving teas and sausage rolls, taking care of people as she always did, in her own quiet way. One day she wouldn't have to work at all, and Jessie sensed that might not be too far in the future, if things carried on as they were. Vernon Leroy had been delighted and although she was only a small part of the show, she knew she'd done well.

'Word will soon get around,' Velma said. 'It won't much matter what the press say, although they're bound to be complimentary,' she added, smiling at Jessie. 'You'll be the talk of the town.'

'I'll get Violet to go out for the early editions,' Alfred told her. 'Your mother can take them home with her.'

Her mother looked tired, but Jessie knew she wouldn't give in to sleep until Jessie was ready to retire. Belle noticed and began putting the empty glasses on the tray. 'Exciting as it is, it's about time we all went to our beds, especially if Jessie's to have a repeat performance tomorrow. You'll need to be on your toes now, my girl.'

Jessie didn't understand.

'Not everyone will be happy for you, darling. You're among friends here, but the further you get up the bill the tougher it will be.'

'Belle's right,' her mother added.

'Sadly,' Victor said, rubbing his hands on his thighs. 'But as long as you keep your feet on the ground and don't let success go to your pretty little head, you'll be just fine. Isn't that true, Grace?'

'It helps,' her mother replied before she began wishing them all a good night. They drifted out of the room and up the stairs, leaving Alfred to turn off the lights. Jessie stood at her mother's door. 'Tired?' her mother asked.

'Not really. My head is whirring with what happened. I'm so glad you were there, Mum, you and Eddie. It meant the world to me.'

'It meant the world to me too. I only wish your father had been there to see it.'

'I believe he was. Perhaps not in the flesh but he was with me all the same. I feel him around me all the time.'

Her mother nodded. 'He never really left us, did he.' She leaned forward and kissed her. 'Now off to bed and get some rest. You've got to do it all again—' she checked her watch '—tonight.'

* * *

Jessie had little sleep, reliving the evening's events, her brain wired, and was roused by a sharp rapping on her door. When she called out, 'Come in,' Eddie came in with their mum and flopped a pile of newspapers on her bed.

'You won't believe what they're saying about you, Jess.' Eddie pushed them under her nose, one by one, pointing out the column inches, reciting the words before she had a chance to read them. '"Sid Silver sparkled but Jessie Delaney was pure gold."' She read each one, and more than once, savouring every word.

'It's such a wonderful start, Jessie.' Her mother sat on the edge of the bed beside her and took hold of her hand. 'You should feel very proud. It was clear to everyone in the audience that you gave your performance everything you had.' Her mother would know that better than anyone else. 'But it's tiring, doing it night after night – and you must rest so that you have something in reserve, otherwise your inner light will dim and burn out. I wouldn't want that to happen.' She moved the newspapers to one side. 'I'm glad you're with good people, kind people. People who understand the pitfalls. It eases my mind to know Belle is watching out for you. You must write to Madeleine and thank her. Let her know how you appreciate her advice, her help.'

'Oh, I will. I wouldn't even be here without her. Vernon Leroy would never have noticed me.'

Her mother rubbed her hand. 'You'd have been noticed eventually, my girl. It's not just your voice; it's more than that. You possess that special something that can't be taught. Or bought. The audience knew it the moment you ran out to claim centre stage.'

'You knocked the spots off that other girl,' Eddie said cheerily.

'Now, now, Eddie. Don't be unkind.' She turned to Jessie. 'Belle was right when she said not everyone will be happy for you. Best to bear that in mind.'

Was it warning? Jessie wasn't sure. Everyone had been delighted. It wasn't just about Jessie, was it? The whole show had been a success. And she had been part of it. As first steps on the ladder went, it had to be a big one.

10

Jessie went with them to the station, Eddie carrying their small suitcase. Inside were the pages of newsprint carrying the notices of her West End debut. They would be carefully clipped and added to the pages of the scrapbook her mother had started when Jessie had first appeared at the Empire. Even Jessie had to admit it was quite the leap and understood why Adele had been sceptical when they first made each other's acquaintance. She hoped last night's performance had justified Vernon Leroy's faith in her, and that she'd proved she'd earned her place on the bill.

'Call me at the theatre when you get home. Or at Belle's.'

'I will,' her mother said, folding her into her arms. Jessie breathed in the scent of her, not wanting to let her mother go, knowing she must. She hated saying goodbye, and when the train had disappeared from sight she'd left the station feeling desolate. Sharing her triumph with her mum and Eddie had been wonderful, and no matter how kindly Belle was, from now on nothing would be the same.

At the stage door, Gus handed her a sheaf of envelopes, a wad of cards, a note from Bernie to ask her to call in his office next week. It lifted her spirits somewhat as she made her way up the stone steps to her dressing room, flicking through the envelopes. To her surprise Adele was already there, filing her nails, a copy of the *Mirror* and *Express* on the floor by her feet. As they passed, other members of the cast popped their heads around the door to congratulate her on the marvellous notices.

'They were very kind,' Jessie said as she removed her coat and sat down in her place in front of the mirror. 'I suppose they won't always be so. They know it's my first time. That's all it is.'

'Not everyone is so kind on your first time,' Adele said, leaning into Jessie and winking. Tabby tutted at the innuendo. Jessie ignored it, reading the handwriting on the envelopes and setting aside the ones she knew were from Harry, Frances and Ginny to one side; the others she would read later. Ginny was heading back home as her father was ill, and was dreading it. Jessie knew they'd never got on. It would be awful for her. She would be careful in her reply, not wanting Ginny to feel that while her dreams were on hold Jessie's were rapidly becoming reality. Frances wrote of life at Park Drive, that Johnny was due leave, Imogen starting school, that Ruby was slowly improving. And Harry wrote of his love, as he always did. She put the letter away and started to get ready, put her hand out for her make-up bag and stopped, her hand mid-air. It wasn't there. Her stomach lurched. 'Tabby, have you moved my make-up bag?' She looked under the table, moved her bags, her towels, magazines. She got up, frantic, scanned the room, began pushing the dresses aside on the rail. Tabby rested a hand on hers to stop her.

'Hey, hey, take a breath. It won't have gone far.'

'Tabby's right,' Adele said, tossing her emery board onto the dressing table and getting up. 'Where did you leave it?'

Jessie tapped the dressing table. 'Here. I always leave it here, to my right side. Someone must have taken it.'

Adele gave her a small smile. 'I don't think anyone else would want it. It wasn't expensive, was it, and it was very old. And tatty.'

Jessie felt sick to her stomach. 'It might not be worth anything to anyone else but it's beyond price to me. I've got to find it.'

'There were a lot of people in here last night...' Adele said, pulling her chair forward and moving her bags, kicking the papers aside. She looked at Jessie. 'Would your mum take it home with her?'

Jessie was incensed. 'Of course she wouldn't; she knows what it means to me.'

'Perhaps someone moved it for safekeeping?' Tabby offered, trying her best to calm her.

'Yes, when they brought in the champagne, they moved everything,' Adele said, suddenly sympathetic. 'Didn't you notice?'

Jessie shook her head, waves of panic swelling in her stomach. 'I didn't notice much at all; there were too many people.'

Tabby pressed Jessie into her chair. 'Stay calm, my darlin'.' She shifted the armchair, the shoes one by one, methodically moving about the room. Jessie ran her hands through her hair trying to work out where it could have gone. In her excitement had she mistakenly taken it back to Albany Street? Tabby pulled the rail out, picked up the large drawstring laundry bag that the girls dropped their soiled clothes into and put her hand into it. 'Here it is.'

'There you are,' Adele said, sitting back in her chair. 'All that fuss over nothing.'

But it wasn't nothing, not to Jessie. It was everything. It was the most precious thing she owned.

'I said it wouldn't have gone far,' Tabby said, handing it over. Jessie hugged her, then clutched the bag to her, opened it and checked the greasepaint sticks, glad to have them again. She wanted to cry with relief and would have done but for the thought that Adele would call her a drama queen. Frances would have understood, and Ginny, and she suddenly missed them and the camaraderie they'd shared. She'd hoped to build that same relationship with Adele but perhaps she was expecting too much too soon. The gap between them seemed too wide. Tabby spoke gently to her, her voice soothing, and began to brush Jessie's hair, the long strokes calming her, while Adele gave her opinion on who might have moved it.

'Probably the theatre ghost.'

'There isn't one,' Tabby countered.

'Every theatre has a ghost, Tabby.'

'Not this one. I've been here thirty years on and off and I've never heard of it. If you ask me, it's folks playing mischief.' Through the mirror, Jessie saw her look pointedly at Adele.

'Well, I don't believe in that sort of thing anyway. Ghosts and heavenly spirits,' Adele patted Jessie's leg and smiled encouragingly. 'Best get yourself ready, Jessie. You don't want to let the audience down, not when so many will have come to see you to find out what all the fuss is about.' She swung round on her chair and began to apply her own make-up. Jessie had to wait until she had a steady enough hand to do her own.

It had been nigh on five years since Ginny Thompson last walked down the once familiar Sheffield streets towards her childhood home. She'd hoped to never to walk them again, leaving a few months after her mother had died when Ginny was fifteen. She stopped outside Simpsons corner shop and put down her case, her arm aching from the long walk from the station. It would be easy enough to turn back, pretend she'd not received Aunt Maggie's letter, but there was no one else to take care of her father. As the only daughter it was expected of her, as her father's sister had been quick to remind her, and her brothers were already doing their bit. For the last six months she'd been part of Entertainments National Service Association, ENSA as it was more commonly known, travelling around the south-east with another half a dozen performers. Nightly bombings had not stopped their shows, rather they had given them in spite of it, travelling around in a rickety old bus for hours on end, appearing in garrison theatres, factories and warehouses. It was hardly what the boys were facing, but she was doing her bit too.

A trio of kids were playing marbles in the road and two

women were talking outside their front doors that opened out onto the narrow pavement at the far end of the street. They gave her a cursory glance and carried on talking, watching every step she took. Ginny ignored them. She'd been used to looks and whispers when she'd lived here and was well practised at walking by as if she hadn't a care in the world. As she approached the front door of the shabby terraced house, a wave of familiar shame simmered in her stomach and left a bitter taste in her mouth. It was doubtful whether the windows had seen a wash leather since she'd left, the glass filthy with grime, the sills black with smut. Inside, the nets hung, tattered and grey. Her poor mother would weep to see it.

She hesitated, wondering whether to knock, but decided against it, and went inside. The smell of damp and decay made her gasp when she opened the door to the narrow hallway. No matter what she'd imagined it was nothing as bad as this. The walls were black with damp, the paper peeling away, bits that had been torn off left where they fell. The one solitary armchair was dark with grease, her father not bothering to wash his hands when he came in from work. But then he never had when her mum was alive, taking pleasure in giving her more work to do.

She stopped at the bottom of the stairs and called out his name, and her shoulders dropped a little when there was no answer. She put down her case and went into the scullery. Fish and chip wrappers were in the grate, dirty crockery piled in the sink and open tin cans on every surface. Her feet stuck to the tiled floor as she walked across it. A board blocked the scullery window, and when she opened the back door a couple of large rats disappeared into the accumulated rubbish that was piled there: scrap metal, bits of wood, and anything else Les Thompson couldn't be bothered to dispose of. If a bomb fell on it, no one would know the difference. There was a narrow clearing that led to the outside lav and that was all, the door hanging off its hinges. She closed the door, looked around for something with which to wipe her hands and picked up an old newspaper. Gingerly, she made her way upstairs.

Her father's room at the front of the house was empty. It stank of urine and sweat, the bed sheets speckled with mould, as were the walls, and she wondered that anyone could bear to lie on the mattress. The door to her old cupboard of a room had a bolt fixed on it, and recently by the look of it. It was secured by a large padlock, and she gave it a tug, inwardly hoping it wouldn't give, dreading what might be in there. Nothing legal if she knew her dad. Warily, she checked the other room in which all four of her brothers had slept, topping and tailing in the double bed. It was much the same except parts of the floorboards had been pulled up and nailed across the windows, a permanent solution to the blackout. If she'd come up in the dark, she could easily have gone right through.

Downstairs again, she had made up her mind to leave when the front door opened and her father staggered in, coughing and spluttering. He cleared his throat, turned and spat on the pavement before closing the door behind him. He looked older than his fifty-three years, and had lost much of his bulk, his grey threadbare suit hanging off his wiry frame. He hadn't bothered to shave, and his greasy hair sat about his grimy collar. He blinked at her.

'Oh, well look what the wind blew in,' he sneered, staggering into the chair and dropping in it. 'I always knew you'd come grovelling back. Up the spout and nowhere else to go?' If he hadn't opened his ugly mouth, she might have felt pity for him.

'I'm not *up the spout*.' She wasn't going to let him goad her as he had done her mother until the day she died. Grinding her down with words. 'Aunt Maggie told me you were ill. Death's door she said. I turned down work to come back and look after you.'

'Shouldn't have bothered; you never have before.' He coughed again and fumbled in his pocket, brought out a filthy rag and spat into it. Ginny turned away in disgust.

'What's with the bolt on my bedroom door?'

'Hasn't been *your* room for years. Not that it's owt to do with you. I'm looking after a few things for someone.'

'Something that needs to be under lock and key? Something dodgy.'

'None of your business. And none of mine either. Keep your neb out.'

Ginny folded her arms. 'They don't trust you enough to give you a key. Huh, sounds about right.'

'I can't work. Me legs are too bad. And now me ruddy chest. Rent's got to be paid somehow.' He picked up the newspaper on his chair and tossed it to one side. 'Ruddy women, sticking yer oar in. Just like our Maggie. She'd be glad if I turned up me toes.' He shook his head. 'Just a ruddy inconvenience, that's all I am. A ruddy inconvenience.' He rubbed the rag under his nose and pushed it back into his pocket, looked her up and down. 'I bet you wish your poor old dad dead too.'

She didn't answer. She'd wished him dead many times, prayed for God to strike him down when he raised his fists to her mother and each blow and kick connected. Terry had been the one to stop him, her eldest brother knocking him off his feet with one almighty blow once he was strong enough to do so. Her father had never raised his fists in the house again and she'd learned a valuable lesson. Standing up to bullies was the only way to stop them.

'I'll put the kettle on, make you a drink.'

He smirked. 'Got money for the meter, have yer? Money for the gas? That suitcase full of coal?'

'Haven't you?'

'I'm at death's door, aren't I? I can't work. Haven't worked in weeks.'

'How have you managed, then? Other than *looking after things* upstairs.'

He glared at her. 'Our Maggie's fed me. She's got me ration book. Her Brenda brought me a meal now and again, but she's started working shifts at the steelworks.' More coughing. Something bit at her flesh. Fleas. She shuddered, resisted the urge to scratch, knowing once she started, she wouldn't stop. 'Maggie's at the canteen, doing extra shifts. Her three little 'uns are gone. Been 'vacuated somewhere or other. The lad's in the army.' He stared at her. 'Everyone being looked after 'cept me. But I don't matter no more, do I? You all buggered off and left.'

She wasn't going to argue with that. When their mother died this house was no longer a home, simply a roof and four walls.

'You've only got yourself to blame.'

'Blame?' He coughed again, spat into the grate. 'You're just like the rest of 'em. Bled me dry, you did. Bled me dry.'

Oh, how she longed to put him straight, but why waste her breath? She knew exactly where his money had gone – over the bar of the Rose and Crown and lining the bookies' pockets. Not that he'd have any of it. She picked up her handbag. 'I'll see if I can get some milk.'

'An' a bottle of beer.'

She closed the door, pretending she hadn't heard.

* * *

Twenty minutes later she returned with milk and a parcel of fish and chips. By some miracle she found an ounce of tea in the caddy and a small bag of sugar in the scullery and, clearing some space, relieved to find there was at least cold water, she made a hot drink and took it through. She placed it on the empty beer crate that served as a table and handed her father his share of the food still in the newspaper.

'What about me beer?'

'I don't have money for beer.' Things had been patchy since the outbreak of war, and she could no longer rely on a long summer season and a pantomime to tide her over. ENSA had been a godsend, a regular pay packet for as long as she needed it. She'd put a little by every week and wasn't going to waste any of her savings on alcohol.

He grumbled under his breath, picked up the mug and slurped the tea, then shovelled the chips into his mouth so fast it made him choke. He spluttered over his food and Ginny looked down at her own, her appetite for it suddenly diminished. The sooner he got back on his feet the better.

When they'd eaten, she found an old saucepan, threw the remnants of the meal in it and covered it with the lid. She would get the details of the local swill collection when she went to see her aunt. Her father's intermittent coughs and grumbles continued, and he called out to her as she worked so she made more noise than was necessary to drown him out. She found a sack and filled it with tin cans that would go to scrap. It barely made a dent on the mess, but she'd made a start, and that was as much as she could do for now.

When she went back into the room, her father had fallen asleep. He was a piteous sight and she wondered what her mother had ever seen in him – but there must have been something, one redeeming feature that she'd fallen in love with. What would she think if she saw him now? The thought of her mother's love softened her. There was an overcoat on the nail by the front door and she draped it over him. She guessed that was mostly where he slept. Picking up her torch, she shone the narrow beam in front of her and made her way upstairs, wary of where she put her feet, anticipating the missing floorboards, and went into the back bedroom. She spread her coat over the old iron bedstead that her brothers had slept in and lay on top of it, listening to the sounds of the neighbours either side. A wireless, an argument, a man whistling in the yard below. She wouldn't stay a moment longer than she needed to. A week, a fortnight at most. He didn't deserve any more than that.

12

Ginny had no idea what time it was when she made her way downstairs the following morning. She'd tied back her hair, pulled on her old slacks and a blouse, determined not to give in to the misery of her surroundings. She'd lain awake for a long time, miserable, defeated, hating that she was back under her father's roof. He was still in the chair where she'd left him and he opened one eye, closed it again and ignored her. She didn't speak as she went into the back room.

Her mother's pinny was still hanging from the hook on the scullery wall, as if she'd just popped out to the corner shop. Ginny took it down. She squeezed the blue floral fabric, wishing it were the squeeze of a hand, then slipped her arms through the sleeves and tied the strings at the side of her waist to secure it. She fed coins into the meter and filled the largest pan she could find with water and placed it on the gas ring, then set about clearing the rubbish and taking it out to the dustbin. She was walking back when her father staggered out to the lavvy, dishevelled and unkempt. When she'd cleaned the kitchen, she would make him wash and shave. Not for any notion of making him feel better, only to lessen the shame that had settled about her shoulders the minute she stepped down from the train.

'Yer still here, then?' he rasped as she stepped to one side.

'I am. Unfortunately.' She hated herself for being so sharp, but he brought out the worst in her. This wasn't who she wanted to be, but it was who she was when she was with him. She made her way back to the house muttering at him under her breath.

'Is that thee, young Ginny?'

'It is, Mrs Smith. How have you been keeping?'

'Not so bad mesen. Eeh, it's grand to see thi, lass. I suppose thi's come back to help thi fatha. That's good of thi.' Mrs Smith's eyes were rheumy and she squinted at Ginny as she leaned over the red brick wall. 'I can't see much, but I can see thi glorious red hair. Just like thi mother's, God rest her soul.' Her father came out and the neighbour called out to him. 'Morning, Les.'

'Ethel,' he mumbled without looking up.

'Well, I'll let thi get on,' she said kindly. 'Looks like thi's got thi hands full.'

Back in the house, her dad had returned to the chair. Ginny had little to say to him and got down on her hands and knees to scrub the kitchen floor, the water not remaining clean for long, black when she emptied it down the drain. After an hour or more she took a break and made them both tea, using the leaves from the previous day.

'There's nowt to eat,' he grumbled.

'I haven't been out. I wanted to get the scullery clean before I brought any food into it.' She placed a bowl of hot water on the floor and handed him a scrap of towel and some soap. 'Clean yourself up. I'll get your razor sharpened.'

'To cut me throat with.'

'Oh, how I wish...' She stopped herself from saying any more. 'When you stop feeling sorry for yourself, perhaps you'll think on the lads who are out on the front line. Including yours.' She prayed they were safe but how long was it since she'd last seen any of them? All four wrote from time to time, but only a line or two. None had done well at school, and all had enlisted at the first call for recruits. When she had a little spare cash she sent them cigarettes, and she'd knitted scarves and socks to keep them warm when she was lodging with George and Olive in Cleethorpes – though she could hardly have called it lodging. They had taken her in as one of the family, and their simple generosity had been of great comfort when she was most in need of it. It made her wistful of their kindness for she'd not get any of it here.

'I did me bit in the last lot.'

'So you said.' He'd never enlarged on what his 'bit' was and she wondered if he had ever enlisted at all.

By mid-morning she had made the scullery reasonable. Tomorrow she would wash the sheets. The rooms needed airing, but she couldn't open the windows for the wood nailed across them. She would order some coal. At least she could get things dry if the weather was bad, and it might make a difference to the damp. She picked up her handbag.

'Buggering off already.' He coughed, great hacking coughs, thumping his fist to his chest.

'I'll get something from Simpsons on the corner. Then I'm off to Aunt Maggie's.'

* * *

Mrs Simpson was serving another customer and came out from behind the counter. 'Well, if it isn't our own little Rita Hayworth.' She gripped Ginny by her forearms in greeting. 'I suppose you've come back to take care of your father.'

Ginny nodded.

'I thought so. Nothing else to come back for is there, love? Not that he deserves it, but blood is thicker than water, so they say.'

Ginny didn't want any of his blood; she didn't want to think any part of her was anything to do with him. She made polite conversation with neighbours and was introduced to newcomers. They wanted to talk about what she'd been up to these past five years, the shows she'd been in, the stars she'd worked with, and although she answered as best she could she didn't have the time or the inclination to talk about it this morning. She excused herself, promising to come back when she'd caught up with her chores.

She bought her rations and some extra cans of beans. Mrs Simpson overweighed the biscuits, and winked at Ginny. The woman had been an angel to her mother when she'd walked into the shop battered and bruised, more often than not sporting a black eye, or swollen lips. Nothing was ever said, and no one would have encouraged her to leave – for where would she go? And five children to care for? Her mother had lived her life through Ginny, accepting her lot in life but determined that Ginny would have better. To that end she took in washing and mending, anything she could to bring in the pennies needed for Ginny's dance classes. Ginny was not going to let her sacrifice go to waste.

* * *

Aunt Maggie lived on Millmount Road on the other side of town, closer to the steel works where Uncle Derek was foreman. He'd never liked her dad; he had good taste, and he had morals. He was the union man and sought fairness. She opened the front door and called out, 'Auntie Maggie?'

Her aunt answered. 'Come through. I'm in the back way.'

Ginny closed the door, walking through the narrow hall and into the scullery. Her aunt was sitting at the Formica table peeling spuds, a scarf knotted about her head in a turban, a cigarette hanging from her mouth. She removed it, flicked the ash onto the newspaper, and nodded her head for Ginny to take a seat. 'How is he?'

'Cantankerous.'

'No change there, then.' She plopped a potato into a pan. 'Sorry I had to bring you back, duck, but I've got me hands full – and I can't look after him when he won't look after himself. I had our Brenda take him meals round, not that he ate much. He'd rather fill himself with booze.' She put down her knife. 'Brenda got herself a job working shifts down at Brown Bayley's steelworks and I'm out most of the day at the canteen. We just don't have the time and he does need looking after or that cough will turn to pneumonia.' She smiled sympathetically. 'I know he can be a nasty old sod, but I can't let him rot. He's family after all.'

Ginny didn't know why she bothered. Les Thompson had never bothered about anyone but himself. Her aunt got up and put the pan on the stove, checked the clock over the table. 'Now, then. Tell me what you've been up to since we saw you last. What about them Variety Girls you were with? Still see them?'

'Not since February. Jessie has gone out on her own and Frances married Johnny Randolph.'

'*The* Johnny Randolph?' Her aunt was impressed.

'The very same.' Ginny laughed, as if there was only one man in the entire world called by that name. 'She lives in a big house these days, with a housekeeper.'

'That'll be you one day, love. In a fine house with an inside lavvy and running hot water. You'll be too good for us, then.' She pulled the cigarette from her mouth and balanced it on the edge of the table. 'Still going with that chap you met last summer? Billy. Billy Street?'

'Lane.'

Her aunt chuckled. 'I knew it were something like "road". Street. Or the like. Didn't it work out?' Her aunt and uncle had spent the week in Cleethorpes, staying in a boarding house on the seafront, so they knew she was walking out with the comedian from the show. It had been nothing but a summer fling to Billy, but she'd wanted it to be much more. She'd felt special walking out with him, Billy the second top of the bill. It made her feel like she was someone instead of no one. He'd left before the end of the show without a thought to say goodbye and she'd been devastated. More so when she discovered she was pregnant. What happened was bad enough, but it could have been so much worse, and she chose to think of it as a dangerous lesson learned. It would never happen to her again.

'No. It didn't.' She didn't want to talk about Billy. It was a dark part of her life that she didn't want to think about, and one she would never share. Only Jessie, Frances and the women of Barkhouse Lane knew of her subsequent miscarriage, and she wanted to keep it that way.

'Plenty more fish in the sea, Ginny love. Especially at the seaside.' She laughed at her joke.

Ginny smiled. 'There was a chap. In the panto. Joe. We write. But I can't see it going anywhere.'

'Married, is he?'

'No! Nothing of the sort.' She scratched at a mark on the

table. 'He's just... oh, I don't know.' Something had never felt quite right, but she never knew what it was. 'He played the wicked uncle in the panto.'

'Oh dear, the baddie. That's unfortunate.'

'No, he was the opposite. Kind and thoughtful.' He was everything Billy was not. 'He's sweet on me.'

'Are you sweet on him?'

Ginny shrugged. She had no idea whether she loved Joe or whether she was simply looking to be loved. All the same, he was kind, and that counted for a lot.

'I thought you'd be fighting them off.'

Ginny laughed. 'I don't get asked that often. You'd be surprised.'

'They probably think you're out of their league, lovely-looking girl like you.' She picked up her cigarette again, took a quick drag on it. 'Well, you'll be around awhile, and you might meet someone just around the corner.'

Ginny hoped not. If she met the love of her life she wouldn't live here. Once her dad was better, she'd be off again.

'How's dad been managing for money if he's been out of work?' She didn't mention the locked bedroom, curious to see if her aunt knew anything about it.

'We helped a bit. I wrote and asked your brothers. They've sent the odd postal order. I keep what money there is and dole him out a bit of beer money now and again.' She lit the gas under the potatoes then bent down and opened the oven door. Ginny peered in. 'Rabbit pie. Lord, how Derek'll grumble when he comes in.' She folded her arms. 'Sick of it, he is. But I'm not a ruddy magician. I tell him, "Don't you know there's a war on?"' She wafted the tea towel. 'Ooh, you should hear him. Turns the air blue.'

Ginny laughed.

'That's better, love. You know you're such a bonny lass when you smile.' She wrapped the peelings in the newspaper and went out into the yard to dispose of them. When she returned, she washed her hands at the sink, gave them a quick rub with a tea towel and turned to Ginny, giving her an encouraging smile. 'Let's hope it's not too long before your dad's back on his feet. Then you can get back to living your dream.'

Ginny nodded. It wasn't really her dream, it was her mother's and Ginny had gone along with it, knowing it was an escape, a way out.

'Something like that.'

13

In spite of the upset over her missing bag, Jessie had managed to calm herself and hoped she'd given a good performance. No one could doubt that the audience had loved her by the extent of the applause, but she hadn't enjoyed it, not as she had the previous evening, unable to fully appreciate it. 'You're tired,' Tabby reassured her. 'You've had to say goodbye to your ma and brother. It's been a big week for you.'

'It's been a wonderful week for her, Tabby. She's the talk of the town. We should go out tonight, celebrate.' Adele put her legs up on the dressing table. Jessie was reminded of Frances doing the same thing, but the two women were nothing like each other. Frances was calm and level-headed whereas Adele was overconfident and brash. Yet hadn't her mother said she could learn a lot from Adele? 'Come out with me after the show. I'll show you a good time.'

'Not tonight. Tabby's right. It's been a big week.' It had been overwhelming, and she wanted time to be quiet, to reflect on all that had happened just as Sid Silver had urged her to.

After the show on Saturday night, she went straight home,

ignoring Adele's attempts to persuade her to do otherwise. She continued with her invitations the following week, Adele insisting a night out would do her good. During the Wednesday performance, Adele was insistent.

'Tonight's the night you're going to say yes, Jessie Delaney,' Adele said. 'It's been a full week since opening night. That's worthy of celebration, is it not?'

Tabby glared at her through the mirror and Adele flashed a smile in response. 'It will do her good to get out.' She turned to Jessie. 'You must be the only girl I've ever met who goes straight home after the show. You'll get yourself a reputation.'

'It's the better reputation to have.' Tabby was snippy. Adele tossed her head.

'Each to their own, darling. Life's a feast and I want to take a nibble of it wherever I can.' She made biting movements at Tabby, then laughed. 'How about it, Jessie darling?'

Jessie didn't feel she was missing out too much, though she'd been entranced by tales of the bands Adele listened to as she danced the night away. Supper was ready when she got in and she enjoyed sitting around the dining table with the others at Albany Street. The night was full of talk of other shows, the backstage gossip and the tales of the old days, the highs and lows, money and reputations made and lost. Belle was kindly and protective, and Jessie didn't want to give her mother any reason to worry for her safety – from bombs or otherwise. There would be time enough for partying when Harry came to stay.

'That's cos she's got a good head on her shoulders,' Tabby retorted. 'You'd be as well to do the same now and again. An early night wouldn't do you any harm.'

Adele pouted. 'But how boring would that be! We're young, Tabby. We should be out enjoying ourselves.' She put down her legs and leaned towards Jessie. 'There's plenty going on – and it won't cost you a penny. The lads haven't anything else to spend it on.' She tilted her head from side to side. 'Unless they walk along Piccadilly in the dark.'

Tabby tutted at her. Jessie had seen the young women who loitered around waiting for men and gave the area a wide berth, fearing she might be propositioned. Adele would no doubt laugh at that too, if she mentioned it. She hadn't been fully aware of all the things she'd have to navigate in a city, things she'd had no knowledge of back home.

'I promised my mother. And unless it's a quiet dinner I'm not interested.'

'Well, that can be arranged.'

Jessie laughed. 'Not your style, though?'

Adele reached across and tapped Jessie's knee. 'Tell you what. I'll meet you halfway. We'll go down to Sam's Caff in the morning. That's where the pros go to find news of anything rumbling under the surface. Looks like we're going to be here a long time. The box office is doing good business and Vernon Leroy's happy. You really do need to make a few friends your own age. It's not good for you, living in a house full of oldies. No offence, Tabby. I'll even get up early for you. Say ten? Outside the stage door.'

Jessie could hardly refuse, not when Adele was being so accommodating. It had been an awkward seven days since the show opened, Jessie quite obviously the sweetheart of the show as far as the audience was concerned. She knew she was blossoming with every performance, but it was how she had to handle herself offstage that gave her problems, and she still had occasions where she felt totally out of her depth. Adele thought her an oddity and she was beginning to feel she was. How many of the others thought the same? Somehow she knew she had to strike the delicate balance of fitting in *and* doing as her mother advised. Perhaps this would be the answer. 'Okay,' she said, hoping she sounded enthusiastic. 'That will be lovely, thanks, Adele.'

Adele appeared delighted. 'Don't mention it. It's about time you met a few people. It can get claustrophobic in the theatre, seeing the same people day in, day out.' She picked up a few coppers and got up. 'I need to make a call.'

Tabby closed the door behind her. 'Don't let her lead you astray, Jessie.'

'I'll be all right, Tabby. She's being kind.' Adele might be devil-may-care but that didn't mean she would be bad company during the day. And truth be told, Jessie was lonely. She didn't have the companionship of the dancers now that she had her name on the bill, and she was slowly beginning to realise that the climb to the top would be lonelier still. She thought of Madeleine Moore, of her broken marriages and broken heart.

'I'm just marking your card. Girls like Adele can get you into trouble, but they'll be the ones coming up smelling of roses.' She pressed her hands on Jessie's shoulders and looked at her through the mirror. 'I've seen it all over the years, my darlin'. Just an old lady looking out for you.'

Jessie took hold of her hand. 'Thanks, Tabby. I'll bear that in mind. But not much can happen in broad daylight.'

Tabby shook her head. 'You'd be surprised, my lovely. Bad things can happen anywhere and at anytime.'

* * *

Jessie was at the stage door for ten minutes to ten. By the time 10.30 came around, she was ready to leave when Adele came breezing down the street towards her. 'Bang on time,' Adele said, checking her wristwatch.

'You said ten.'

'I don't think I did.' Adele gave Jessie a puzzled look. 'Don't tell me you've been waiting outside for half an hour?'

Jessie nodded.

'You are daft.' She kissed her cheek. 'Let's be off then.'

Jessie was certain she'd said ten, but it wasn't worth getting upset about. What was half an hour when people were getting bombed out of their homes and being left with little more than what they stood up in? 'Doesn't matter.' She smiled. 'My mistake. Which way are we going?'

Adele linked her arm through Jessie's. 'Today, Miss Delaney, I'm going to introduce you to the delights of Soho.'

Adele led the way, over Trafalgar Square and towards Piccadilly, then on to Brewer Street, down towards the seedier end of Soho. Doors were open and men came and went; a woman hollered from a window and threw a tin can, which the man ducked as he hurried away. Adele called up to the woman. 'Forgot his wallet, did he?'

'Forgot he had to pay, more like,' the woman called, pushing down the sash. Jessie felt her cheeks burn. She would never have come here on her own and would have turned back if doing so hadn't given credence to Adele's opinion of her. She stuck close to Adele and leaned towards her.

'What if we get mistaken for, you know...'

Adele frowned, then realising what Jessie meant, roared with laughter. 'Well, I might, but no one's going to proposition you.' She laughed again. 'Gawd, I've never met anyone like you, Jessie. Have you been living in a convent?'

'No, but I've never been to a place like this.'

Adele smiled. 'Don't worry. I'll look after you.'

It did nothing to reassure her and soon after they stopped outside a café in the middle of a terrace of shops. The window was taped in criss-cross fashion even though it was a single pane, and a net covered the lower half, revealing the vague shapes of customers inside. Adele stopped at it and stood on her tiptoes, peered in, then turned to Jessie. 'There's a few in there already. Good timing.' She opened the door and led the way, a few of the men giving her appreciating glances. At the rear of the café, near the counter, two tables had been pushed together and half a dozen people sat around it, getting in the way of the girl who was going backwards and forwards with food and empty crockery.

A tall blonde got to her feet when she saw Adele. 'Room for another two. Move your chairs, lads.' One of the men had his back to the door and he got up to expand the circle and pull forward another chair. As he turned, he stopped and stared at her. Jessie couldn't move. The last person she'd expected to see was Billy Lane.

14

Billy moved towards Jessie. 'Great to see you. Just great. I had no idea you were in town until Adele said you were on the same bill.' He hugged her and she didn't respond. He frowned as he released her, holding on to her shoulders, but he was still smiling. 'You're looking terrific.'

She made for the other vacant chair, only Adele beat her to it and quickly sat down. 'You two should sit together. You'll have so much to talk about.'

Jessie's face was rigid, but she tried to appear pleased as some of the other girls moved their chairs and allowed space for Jessie to sit next to Billy, the last place she wanted to sit.

'Let me get you a drink. Tea? Coffee? Well, I say coffee. It's some dandelion muck but it's the best we're going to get.' He kept looking at her, his smile wide, shaking his head in disbelief. He turned to the others. 'I was with Jessie last summer. Madeleine Moore was topping the bill. It was a cracking season. Me and Jessie did a duet that nicked the show, well, Jessie here did. I was just there to look good for the ladies.'

The girls laughed. Jessie sat down, feeling like a schoolgirl in a party of grown-ups.

'Why aren't we surprised, Billy.'

Jessie didn't say anything, conscious of Adele scrutinising her every move. She fought to stay calm, inwardly furious with Billy. How could he make light of everything, after all the trouble he'd caused? But hadn't that always been his way?

'Let's ask Jessie, shall we. She looks the truthful sort,' one of the girls said. Her dark hair was set in large metal curlers, and she had a headscarf over them, which was knotted at the back of her neck. She held her hand out across to Jessie. 'Eve.' She introduced the others. 'Stan's a comedian, as is Billy – but you know that.'

'The audience don't,' Stan quipped, and the girls laughed. Billy gave him a good-humoured nudge.

'We're all Windmill girls. Billy included,' she teased. Jessie knew of the revue at the Windmill, where the girls were semi naked and posed in tableaus to get around the Lord Chamberlain's restrictions, but the girls didn't look cheap, far from it. Still, she wouldn't want her mother to know she'd been here, or Tabby, feeling certain neither would approve. 'So, Jessie, dish the dirt. How badly behaved was he?'

'Where would you like me to start?' Jessie said sourly.

The others laughed. 'Now you're for it, Billy.' He shrugged, lifted his hands, palms upwards and there was another burst of laughter.

'He left the show in rather a hurry,' Jessie said. There was no need to tell them anything else. It was none of their business, and Billy would only make a joke of it.

'Jealous husband, was it, Billy?' Eve joked.

Billy grinned. 'Not this time, girls. I got a better offer.'

'Oh, do tell.' Adele held out her cigarette and leaned across for a light from Stan, clasping her hand over his as he sparked his lighter, inhaling. She tipped back her head as she exhaled the smoke, wafting it away with her hand. 'We're all ears.'

'Sorry to disappoint you, Delly. Nothing exciting. I fancied my chances down here. Got wind of a radio opportunity and left the show a wee bit early. Bad form, but as we know, opportunity waits for no man.'

'Or woman,' Adele reminded him.

'What happened?' Eve probed.

'The bloody war happened, didn't it. The theatres shut and I enlisted.'

'Don't tell me you did the right thing?'

'Only cos he didn't have no choice,' Stan quipped.

Billy smiled. 'None of us had a ruddy choice.'

'Some less than others,' Jessie said quietly. She wondered why he wasn't in uniform now.

He turned to her, but she purposely avoided looking at him. 'Everything all right, Jessie? Nothing happened to your chap, Henry, wasn't it?'

'Harry,' she corrected. 'He's fine.' She was curt. She wanted to say he was brave, he was putting his life on the line for people like Billy. It crossed her mind that he could be a deserter – there had been many of them after Dunkirk, disappearing into the milieu of Soho – but she dismissed it. Being onstage wasn't the best place to hide.

'Still your fella?'

'Why wouldn't he be?' Her voice was sharp.

He held up his hands. 'Hey, what did I say?'

Jessie was aware that all eyes were on her. 'Nothing.' She looked to Adele, who drew on her cigarette. A cup was placed in front of her, and Jessie took a sip. The coffee was too hot, and she burned her mouth and cursed herself.

Eve turned to her. 'Your first time in town?'

'It is,' Jessie said, grateful for the chance to talk about something else. 'I'm still getting my bearings.' The woman seemed nice enough.

'She goes back to her digs straight after the show,' Adele said, rolling her eyes.

'Are you sharing a flat with Adele?' Billy asked. She turned to look at him and tried not to stare. His left eye was clouded over and there was a smattering of pitted scars about his cheek. So, he wasn't hiding after all. It made her feel a little less hostile.

'Not with me,' Adele answered for her. 'She's got digs in Albany Street. Pro digs.'

Jessie glanced at Adele. She didn't need to tell Billy all her business.

'Bit of a walk from the theatre,' Billy said. 'Especially with what's been going on the last few days.'

There had been warnings most days and each night Jessie had braced herself for the bombardment Victor had warned of, but nothing had happened and the residents of Albany Street had trudged up and down the stairs into the basement, grateful that they didn't have to be up as early as so many others did before doing a day's work.

'Well, if you get stuck you know where we are,' Eve told her. 'Plenty of room in the basement at the Windmill.' She got to her feet. 'Come on, girls. We need to get back for the half-hour call. You too, Billy.' She smiled at Jessie. 'Nice meeting you. See you around, Delly.'

Billy got up, put out his hand, which she reluctantly took hold of. 'Good to see you, Jessie. I hope we see you here again.' He leaned forward to kiss her cheek and she instinctively leaned away. 'Hey, don't hold it against me.' He grinned. 'I was the fool. Lost chances, and all that.'

Anger was eating away at her, for Ginny and what she went through when Billy left but, conscious that Adele was watching her, she managed a curt goodbye. There was the usual commotion while they got up and paid their bill, leaving Jessie and Adele at the table. When the last one of them had left and the door had closed behind them, Adele leaned across the table.

'What did he do?'

Jessie looked blankly at her. 'Who?'

'Come off it. Billy.'

'He told you. He left the show.'

Adele shook her head. 'It was much more than that. You could hardly look at him.'

Jessie shrugged her remark away, trying to appear as if she didn't care. 'Did you know he would be here?' She didn't know why she bothered to ask. It was obvious to a blind man that Adele had set her up.

Adele looked hurt. 'He saw the handbill, recognised your name. I said I'd bring you over. I thought you'd be happy. I was trying to do something nice.'

Her answer caught her unawares and Jessie apologised. 'It was a thoughtful thing to do, thank you.'

Forgiven, Adele brightened. 'So, what did he do?' She called over to the counter and ordered two more coffees. Jessie had been ready to leave and now she would have to stay – but she didn't have to tell Adele anything. It wasn't her story to tell. Billy had done plenty of other things to upset her. And Harry.

'He got my brother drunk – on more than one occasion.'

'There are worse things,' Adele replied. She added a little milk to her coffee, then passed Jessie the jug.

'Harry doesn't like him.'

Adele looked up. 'But you do.'

'Did. That was before...' She had already said too much.

Adele leaned forward and whispered, 'Before what?'

'He hurt a friend of mine.'

'Hit her?'

Jessie looked away. She would never forget the night Ginny miscarried and recalling it sent a fresh shiver down her spine. The pain that man had caused was endless. Adele sat for a while, sipping at her drink. 'And your friend – is she all right now?'

'She is.'

Adele screwed out her cigarette in the tin ashtray that was full of ash and spent matches. 'I thought Billy looked the love 'em and leave 'em type. Except...'

'What?'

Adele smiled like a cat. 'Couldn't you see it?'

Jessie had no idea what Adele was getting at.

'How his face lit up, when he saw you. He changed completely. Didn't take his eyes off you.' She turned her hand, studied her nails then looked to Jessie. 'I'd put money on it that Billy Lane's in love with you.'

Jessie felt her blood run cold.

'Huh,' she spat. 'I wouldn't give Billy Lane a second glance if he was the last man on earth.'

15

Life in London had not turned out as Jessie had expected and on Friday she'd been swamped by a wave of melancholy. The cast were friendly enough, and she loved being with Belle and the others, but she missed being with people her own age, her mum and Eddie, the friendship of Frances and Ginny. The three of them had been through so much together during their time as Variety Girls, and she felt lost not having them to turn to. Billy's presence aside, she'd quite enjoyed it at the café; the girls had been welcoming and she'd been comfortable enough in their company, especially Eve's. She didn't take any nonsense from Adele and Jessie got the sense that Eve had suggested that all of them leave the other day, aware of Jessie's feelings towards Billy, knowing it was none of their business – unlike Adele, who had pestered her for more information. It was a shame she wouldn't see them again, not while Billy was around. She intended to stay well clear of the café in future.

On Friday night, between houses, Jessie took out her Basildon Bond notepad and settled down to reply to her letters. There was a freedom in writing to Frances, not having to lie about how well the show was going, but Ginny was having a rough time, and Jessie had to stop and think before she wrote each line.

'Writing to your mum?' Adele asked. She'd been cutting out a picture of Carole Lombard from a magazine and was fixing it to the mirror in front of her.

'No, my friend. Ginny.'

'The one Billy upset?'

Jessie didn't answer directly. 'I did an act with her and another girl, Frances. Song and dance. A bit like the Andrews Sisters.'

'Nice. What are they doing now?'

'Frances is married.' She didn't tell Adele who to. Mentioning Johnny Randolph would lead to endless questioning. Adele would talk, and the Randolphs needed to keep a low profile about what had happened. The newspapers would have a field day, depending on what slant they took. *Johnny Randolph abandons lover and child. Randolph marries unwed mother.* The truth was more complicated than could be explained by a simple headline. 'Ginny went with ENSA for a time. She's had to go back home to Sheffield to look after her dad for a while.'

'The ties that bind.'

'Hmm.' Jessie went back to her letter, not wanting to be drawn into giving away any more detail.

Adele picked up her scissors and began flicking through the magazine on her lap. 'Billy was asking after you this morning. Wondered if you'd be going to the café again.'

'Maybe.' She was deliberately vague. She picked up her pencil and settled down to reply to Ginny, thoughts of Billy floating in her head, the night of Ginny's miscarriage flaring once more. She couldn't think of one without the other. Although Frances's situation had a happy ending it hadn't turned out that way for Ginny. She decided not to mention meeting Billy in her letter; there was no point stirring up old hurts. Tabby came in and began pairing the shoes that Adele had tossed carelessly aside. Jessie looked up, smiled, and carried on with her letter. When she'd finished, she wrote Ginny's address on the envelope, folded the pages and slipped them inside. She linked her fingers and extended her arms in front of her, got up and stretched her legs, moving her hips from side to side to loosen them off.

'Are you all right, Miss Delaney?' Tabby asked.

Jessie nodded. 'Just feeling a little out of sorts, that's all. But as my mother would say, "There's no sense giving in to it." I find if I get up and move it helps shift my mood.'

Adele was sympathetic. 'Why don't you come out tonight? I'm sure your mother wouldn't mind. She wouldn't want you to be lonely. I certainly don't. It's all a bit overwhelming at first, isn't it, being in the West End? And doing so enormously well at it too. There's no wonder you feel "out of sorts", as you put it.'

Jessie caught Tabby's expression in the mirror. She shook her head. 'No, I'd rather get back home.'

'Well, I think you're missing out on a big part of what it is to be in the West End, darling. You really are. All the fun to be had. There are plenty of thrilling places you haven't even seen yet. The Café de Paris, and Hungaria and Oddenino's at Piccadilly Circus. They're all bomb-proof.'

'I doubt anywhere is bomb-proof,' Tabby said flatly. 'They can say what they like. You should come with me and have a look down the East End. There are ruddy great craters where houses used to be.'

'I've seen it for myself, Tabby. But we can't stop living, can we? We have to carry on as best we can.'

Tabby turned away.

'Just this once?' Adele pleaded. 'I want to show you what you're missing.'

Jessie smiled. 'I'm not missing anything I'm bothered about. But thanks for thinking of me, Adele. It's really kind of you.' She found it hard to get the measure of the older girl, never quite sure if it was truly down to kindness, or an attempt to get the better of Jessie offstage when she couldn't manage to do it during the show.

'Suit yourself.' She became rather snippy. 'I'd put money on it that once Harry puts the phone down, he's down to the NAAFI with the WAAFs.'

'He's not like that.' Jessie was shocked by how quickly Adele had turned when she didn't get her own way.

'All men are like that. All the ones I've ever met. Out for what they can get. It's the quiet ones you have to watch, the ones you think are real gents, and all they want is to get you in a dark alley and have a feel.' Adele began to touch up her make-up. 'When you've been around like I have, you'll know I'm telling the truth. You can't trust anyone in this game.'

* * *

Tabby came in and out more than she usually would during the show and hovered about in the background, reassuring Jessie with her quiet presence. When the curtain came down, Adele slipped into a dress with a low neckline and nipped in waist, dabbed scent behind her ears, on her pulse points and her cleavage. She checked her reflection one last time in the mirror and picked up her bag. 'Are you sure you don't want to come?'

Jessie managed to smile. 'No, thanks.'

Jessie listened to her clattering down the stairs, the bang of the door that led out into the corridor and down to the stage door. Tabby pressed her hand to her shoulder. 'You're not like her, Jessie, and neither is your young man.'

'But you haven't met him.'

'I don't have to,' Tabby said, picking up the rags that Adele had left piled on her chair and putting them into the laundry bag, pulling the cord tight. 'A lovely girl like you deserves a lovely chap. Don't let Adele's words worm their way into your head.'

Jessie nodded. If only Tabby had known how close she'd been to saying yes before Adele had mentioned Harry.

16

Jessie was already at the theatre on Saturday when the siren sounded at around a quarter to five in the afternoon. She'd been sitting in the green room with Edgar and Bettina and they had strained to hear themselves above the monotonous wail that set their teeth on edge, wondering if it would affect the five thirty performance.

'The warnings don't seem to keep people away,' Edgar said, getting up from the battered armchair, one of many that were dotted about the room they used between shows to give them a chance to mingle and break the tediousness of endless hours in the dressing room. 'A lot of them think the theatre's as safe as anywhere else during a raid.'

'I suppose it is,' Bettina mused. 'Though I'd rather sit in the front of the stalls. I wouldn't want to be in the dress circle.'

'Or below it,' Jessie added, imagining the ceiling falling in on those below.

It was the end of the first complete week of performances and Jessie had become accustomed to the routine when the warning sounded. Only a small number of the audience ever got up to leave, and if the all-clear hadn't sounded before the end of the performance, the cast would carry on and entertain, ad-libbing, leading singalongs, or simply chatting until it did. Jessie had learned to adjust to the brief interruptions if the siren sounded during her spot. It didn't throw her as it once would have done – she simply waited for the orchestra to pick up at the start of a verse or chorus and carried on. They heard the first distant blasts while in the dressing room before curtain up. Jessie glanced to Adele, who didn't even look up from her magazine.

An hour later it was obvious this was no ordinary raid. 'The sky's full of the bleeders,' one of the stage crew said as she came downstairs ready to go on. 'Hundreds of 'em. Looks like the East End is taking a right battering. I reckon there'll be nowt left of Tilbury Docks, or Poplar at this rate. You can see the smoke for miles.'

'Are they close?' Jessie asked, trying to stay calm before she went on. She had looked through the spyhole in the wings and seen that it was a good house, with only a smattering of spare seats dotted about the auditorium.

'Close enough,' the chap said. 'Best keep down here. Just in case. Lower down you are the better.'

At the interval, Adele picked up her tin hat. 'I'm going on the roof. We'll have to take our turn up there on watch at some point. Might as well get a look at what we'll be facing.'

They had all taken part in the fire drill and a rota had been put in place. No one was exempt and no one wanted to be, but still Jessie was afraid at what she might see. For the last hour she'd tried to ignore the chatter as people moved up and down the corridors and stairs, talking about what was happening, that it looked like Goering had sent every bomber in the Luftwaffe to London that evening. Jessie wrapped her coat over her dressing gown and picked up her own tin hat, following Adele and some of the other theatre staff up the stone steps and through the door that opened up onto the roof.

Jessie smelled and heard the devastation before she saw anything, the noise of engines and explosions, the faint sound of fire engine bells and ambulances racing through the streets. She made her way to the wall that looked over to the east. The buildings opposite were too high for them to see directly across but a few of the crew had scaled the ladders that connected them to the roofs of the buildings next door. Jessie climbed with them and was astounded by what confronted her. The sky to the east was aglow with red light. It looked like a beautiful sunset, only it was far too early in the day for that, and in totally the wrong direction, the planes above it having the appearance of blackbirds, the German fighters circling above them, keeping our lads at bay. The sound throbbed in her ears but she couldn't move her hands to block out the noise, paralysed by the horrifying spectacle that was playing out before them. Huge fires had broken out and the air was thick with smoke and heavy with the smell of burning wood and oil, the drone of engines dulled by the thunderous explosions as the bombs hit their targets.

'They're giving 'em the whole damned lot, this time.' Edgar pushed his trilby back on his forehead and rubbed at it in disbelief. 'A ruddy stirrup pump and a bucket o' water ain't gonna be much cop against that.' He shook his head. 'The poor buggers on the ground won't have much chance to get away from that. We all knew it would happen. We just didn't know when.'

Jessie watched, disbelieving what was in front of her eyes. Where were all the people? An Anderson shelter would not protect anyone from such onslaught. She thought of the shelter back home, how small it was. How vulnerable they were. She didn't want to watch any more and turned away, went back inside. Adele followed her and they ignored their dressing room and went into the green room, dropped into the chairs. Bettina was at the sink drying some teacups and setting them out on the counter beside the hot water urn. Edgar came into the room. 'Gerry's changed tactics. We won't be going home tonight. Got any grub in, Bettina?'

'I'll just call the Ritz and see if they can send over some caviar. Will that do you?'

'That'll do nicely. Off you pop.'

Bettina threw a dishtowel at him. They were light-hearted but it didn't hide the unease they felt. Jessie couldn't bear to think of the people who lived along the docks and the river where the houses were packed tightly and cheaply built. It was beyond comprehension. 'How will the show go on when this is happening. How?' She could hear the tremor in her voice. What on earth was she doing here with a group of strangers? The pounding was relentless. They couldn't stay here; they had to go lower, lower, down to the stage area – it would be safer there. She made to get up.

'It will. It has to,' Edgar said flatly. 'What would you do? Take your chances and stay put or make your way out into the streets? Cos the shelters ain't up to much and they're refusing to let people into the Underground.'

'I think things might change after this,' Bettina said quietly.

* * *

The all-clear sounded just after six and the show carried on but it wasn't long before the warning siren sounded again and, during the break between the first house and the second, the dressing rooms on the higher floors were abandoned and they went down to the stage area, everyone finding some small space where they could put their belongings, the stars who had rooms on that level opening their doors to the rest of their colleagues.

She watched as people came and went, most of them outwardly calm, but Jessie wondered if they felt as she did, like it was all slightly unreal. She'd always felt the war was some distance away, that somehow it wouldn't touch her. How wrong she had been.

At the end of the second house, the curtain had come down after they had taken their calls, and then risen again and stayed there. The lights had gone up in the auditorium and members of the cast began taking it in turns to sing, to tell stories and entertain, Sid Silver taking the lead, keeping the audience laughing. When it was her turn, she went out onstage, free to sing whatever the musicians could play for her. It was all very relaxed and enormously special, able to fully see the faces of the people in the rows facing her, all of them joining in the refrain of well-known songs such as 'Tea for Two' and 'Side by Side' and, ironically, 'Isn't This a Lovely Day?'. It was an odd thing, to carry on like this, cheerfully singing along, ignoring the fact that the world as they knew it might very well be at an end. That days from now, they might well become an occupied country as France and Belgium and the Netherlands had become. The orchestra took over for a while and Jessie went to sit backstage. Chairs had been brought from elsewhere and cast and crew sat about, talking in low voices.

'Well, I've died onstage a few times, but I never thought I'd end me days like this,' Edgar quipped.

'That'll be a first,' Sid Silver cracked. He got up and stretched his arms. 'This don't look like it's going be over anytime soon. We might as well make ourselves comfortable.'

They gathered coats and old curtains and whatever items of comfort they could and took it in turns to rest on them, wondering when it would come to an end. Jessie thought of the devastation she had witnessed. It had been her dream to appear in the West End. Never for one minute had she imagined it would be like this.

* * *

When the all-clear sounded, Edgar looked at his watch. 'Nine hours. Nine ruddy awful hours.'

A few of them went up onto the roof again. Fires raged, smoke drifting in huge clouds as far as the eye could see. The sky was still except for the ghostly shapes of barrage balloons that strained on their cables, the planes gone, only the evidence of their visit visible. A series of alarm bells rang out across the city as rescue vehicles drove to where they were most needed. Below them people poured out of buildings and onto the streets even though it was the middle of the night.

When she returned to the green room, Bettina looked all in. Edgar picked up his trilby. 'We must be grateful for small mercies,' he said, tugging it into place. He had lost his light-heartedness, they were all too tired for that, and they silently gathered their belongings before making their way home. Jessie and Adele parted at the stage door.

'Will you be all right, walking back on your own? Only you can come back with me if you'd rather,' said Adele. It was kind of her to offer and Jessie was touched by her concern.

'I'd better let Belle know I'm safe. I can call my mum once I'm there, and let her know I'm all right. I should think news of it will be in the Sunday newspapers.'

Adele scribbled her address on the end of a cigarette packet. 'That's where I am if you need me.'

Jessie watched her walk away and disappear into the black of the night, hesitating whether to call after her but decided against it. Something made her hold back. Self-protection? She wasn't sure, but she knew she'd be better off being with Belle and the others. She switched on her rubber torch, a strip of tape to the bottom and the top of the glass narrowing the beam, as per regulations. There were too many traps for the unwary. Stories of people falling down manhole covers and pub cellars were rife. The last thing she needed was a broken ankle, or worse. She only needed to see one or two steps ahead of her. It didn't matter how long it took, as long as she got there in the end.

17

Jessie returned to Albany Street and crawled into bed, set her alarm for noon, grateful it was Sunday and she didn't have to go to the theatre. Her clothing and hair were full of dirt, but she was too tired to wash, and fell onto the bed, covering herself with the eiderdown.

When the alarm clock rang, she sprang out of bed, thinking it was a raid, then remembering it was only a wake-up call. She ran her hand through her hair, coarse with dust. Her mouth was dry, and she found the small flagon of water Violet had set by her bed and poured a glass. For a time, she hadn't been able to sleep, the night's events going round in her head. Images of what she'd seen from the roof, the huge fires, the clouds of black smoke were intermingled between her view of the audience as she sang, their smiles, the way everything going on outside the theatre faded away, so that only what existed between the four solid walls of the theatre was real: how safe it had felt, and how comfortable she'd been among them.

After she'd washed and dressed, she went downstairs and found Belle in the sitting room with Victor and Velma. The curtains were drawn back and if it wasn't for the acrid smell of smoke and cordite that seeped through the gaps in the window it could have been any other September day. Light flooded into the room, leaving crisscross patterns on the furnishings. Victor was in the chair by the window, a copy of the *Sunday Telegraph* on his lap, his hand flat against it. He lifted his head when she entered, a grim look on his face. Velma and Belle stopped mid-conversation and Belle got up and gave her a warm hug.

'I'm so glad you were safe. I can't tell you how relieved I was when I checked your room this morning.'

'I spent the night at the theatre. I didn't want to chance it.'

'Quite right too. If it happens again, darling, go across to The Savoy. Their basement shelter will be safe enough. I'll have a word with the doorman. He's a good friend of Alfred's.' She pulled the cord at the side of the fireplace. 'I'll get Violet to get you some breakfast. Have you had anything since last night?'

Jessie shook her head. 'No, not really. We had biscuits. And tea.'

'There's always tea.' Velma smiled. 'That's what we British survive on.'

'It's going to take more than tea.' Victor was sombre. 'They'll be back again. No doubt about it. I wouldn't count on the theatre opening Monday.' Jessie turned to him. He patted the newspaper. 'There's a rumour that George Black's going to close all his. If he does the others will soon follow. I bet half the warehouses of the East End have gone up. Trying to cut us off, aren't they? Stopping the supplies and burning what we have in store. This is our Guernica.'

Belle snapped at him. The mention of the Spanish town that was the scene of such carnage had raised her ire. 'That's not the attitude, Victor. We'll not be beaten. We weren't the last time, and we won't be this.'

'Last time was different, Belle. The war was mostly fought on land and sea – and not our land neither. I was in France. There wasn't a tree or blade of grass to be seen in some places. We didn't see much more here than a few zeppelins. But this.' He pointed to the ceiling. 'The lads have seen the Germans off in the Spitfires so far, and if they can't beat us in the air they'll try and bomb us into submission.'

'They wouldn't have enough bombs,' Velma insisted.

He was beginning to frighten Jessie.

'Victor, you're upsetting the girl,' Belle warned.

But he wouldn't be stopped.

'She has to know what she has to face. We all do.' He put the newspaper on the small table to the left of his chair. 'They've been well ahead of us, the Germans. They signed the treaty of Versailles. Well, it's not worth the paper it's written on. Lavatory paper. They weren't meant to build armaments, but they have – and submarines, and planes. And ships. And we've let them. All the allies talked about was appeasement. Pah! None of us wanted another war. Not after the last one. Good God, they called it the war to end all wars to make us feel better.' He shook his head. 'But ruddy Adolf. Well, you can't argue with a bully. They don't listen. Oh, they'll smile and tell you exactly what you want to hear because that's how they get what they want. Peace for our time! Chamberlain was a fool to believe his empty promises.'

Jessie felt her legs go weak and sank down into her chair.

'We don't need to hear this, Victor, not now,' Velma said quietly.

'We do,' he insisted. 'Then we'll be prepared.'

18

Saturday evening was not for the faint-hearted as the Luftwaffe once more rained bombs on Grimsby. It was nothing to the extent of what they'd suffered in London but frightening all the same, especially as an incendiary had landed on a house only a few doors away from the Randolphs' home. It had set the house alight but the fire service had been quick to respond. Frances had been relieved to learn that though the house was damaged there had been no casualties.

They were all in the kitchen when Mrs Frame called on Sunday morning, Imogen curled up in the dog basket with Mr Brown. The stray dog had turned up just when they needed him most. As, it seemed, had Mrs Frame, even though it was her day off.

'I couldn't rest until I knew you were all all right.' She pressed her hand to her chest. 'When I heard a house on Park Drive had been hit... I was beside myself. Ted told me. Hare Street and Welholme Road got it as well, but thank the good Lord there's been no...' A quick check to see if Imogen was still asleep. '... casualties and such like.'

'We've been very lucky,' Frances agreed. They had spent most of the night in the Anderson shelter at the bottom of the garden, wincing at the sound of the incendiaries falling, the crackle of the ack-ack guns as they blasted in retaliation, Mr Brown growling at the invisible raiders. Amazingly Imogen had slept right through, but Frances and Ruby had sat it out, waiting for the all-clear. They had taken a flask but neither of them had touched it, shaking too much to hold a cup let alone drink as the air filled with wails and thuds. Thankfully there had been no one billeted with them, and they had been able to sit along the benches, their legs stretched out, a blanket over them, a cushion behind. They'd been safe enough, though it hadn't felt like it at the time, and Frances dreaded the thought of ending her days buried under the tin can that was the shelter.

She pulled out a chair and gestured for the housekeeper to sit down. Her husband, Ted, had volunteered for the ARP and spent his evenings checking that homes were observing the blackout, and making sure everyone in his immediate vicinity was safe. Last night would have been much more of a challenge for the wardens who, when everyone else was taking cover, were out and about. Mrs Frame sank down into the chair. Frances doubted she'd had a wink of sleep herself with the additional worry of Ted out on the streets.

'Is he still on duty?'

'He's in the Land of Nod. Black as the Ace of Spades when he came in. I had to boil some water up so he could get a wash.'

'God bless him,' Frances said, appreciating the luxury she had of hot and cold running water, an inside bathroom. How her life had changed. No more rushing out to use the backyard privy. It was a far cry from her home in Ireland and all she'd had since. She would never take it for granted.

'All night they've been at it, assisting the auxiliary fire service.

As far as I know there's only damage to buildings, thank the good Lord – and that can be put right.'

Frances pressed her hand on Mrs Frame's shoulder. 'It can indeed. Thank heavens people like Ted are doing their bit on the home front.'

'We all need to do what we can,' Mrs Frame said. She practised what she preached, involving herself in any small duty that would contribute to the war effort. With such close proximity to the docks of Grimsby and Hull, and with Immingham only a short distance away, she and Frances had been knitting comforts for the minesweeping crews, inviting other neighbours to join them. Each Thursday afternoon they gathered in the sitting room to knit sweaters and regulation socks from the patterns supplied by the ministry. Ruby never joined in. When the other women arrived, she would disappear into the kitchen, or if the weather was fine, into the garden with Ted. Frances tried to include her, but it was an uphill battle, and she had battles enough. The combination of interrupted sleep and morning sickness was taking its toll.

'Will you be going to the singalong at the NAAFI this evening?' Mrs Frame whispered. 'Only I was wondering whether you'll be wanting me to have Imogen. Unless of course she'll be staying with you, Miss Ruby?'

Ruby looked to Frances. 'I thought you'd stay here tonight. In case...'

Frances waited. 'In case?'

'There's another raid?'

'No. I'll carry on as normal. Just as everyone else is doing.' She smiled at Mrs Frame. 'Thanks for the offer, Mrs Frame. I'll be taking Imogen with me.' If anything happened, she wanted her child with her. They would not be separated again. There'd been too much of that these past four years.

'You can't leave me alone.' Ruby became agitated. The bombing had set her back again, which was such a pity, when she'd been doing so well. It had exacerbated her anxiety, which, when it took hold, left her afraid to go out, and afraid to stay home alone. Frances didn't want to be unkind, but to give in to Ruby's whims would make them all miserable in the end.

'Ruby, I can't, and I won't let the lads down, or Jack.' She reached for Ruby's hand, wishing she wasn't so tired. 'People are depending on us too. Isn't it good that we do whatever we can to help?'

* * *

The bus dropped them across the road from the Empire at half past five, and even though there was still half an hour before the canteen opened, there was a queue. An assortment of lads in uniform leaned against the walls and sat on the windowsills of the shops either side of the front doors. A few of them gave Frances and Ruby admiring looks as they approached the entrance. Having Imogen with them neutered any saucy comments the lads might make, and Ruby was glad alone for that. One of them held open the door.

'Thank you, Clarkie,' Frances said, guiding Imogen forward. He saluted and Imogen giggled and returned it. One of the young lads who couldn't have been more than eighteen winked at Ruby and she offered her best smile. She'd spent almost her entire life pretending; she could manage it for the next couple of hours if she forced herself.

The box office was closed, the foyer carpet removed, but the brass handrails leading to the circle and the rooms above it still gleamed. The Ministry of Works had requisitioned the building in the early part of the year and turned it into a canteen. It was staffed entirely by women from the Women's Voluntary Service and opened three times a day. On Thursdays, the lads were entertained by visiting concert parties and on Sundays there was a community singalong.

This was where her brother had found Frances last year. While they were in America, Ruby had not given Frances O'Leary another thought. Yet, for a time, she'd thought of nothing else, thanks to her mother's carefully sown seeds of doubt, leaving her afraid that Frances would take her place onstage, as well as in Johnny's affections. Alice Randolph had instructed her daughter to intercept any letters between Johnny and Frances and she'd done so, willingly. Her mother had made her keep them. Unopened. Insurance, she had told her. She'd never explained why, and Ruby had never dared to question it until it was too late. Alice Randolph had returned to England to die without telling her children and Ruby had been angry, then afraid. Johnny had thrown himself into his work, and she had thrown herself at men. There had been lovers, most of them unsuitable, along with secret visits to clinics, drink, and drugs – whatever helped to blank out her rage and despair. Her grief, turned inwards, almost destroyed her – would have done if not for Johnny. Some days she wondered why he still cared for her at all. He had turned down a show on Broadway to bring them back home, trying to distance her from the intrusive press and a string of disastrous dalliances. And for what? They had nothing here – or so she thought. Until he found Frances. Worse still was the fact that he had a child. The knowledge that she'd deprived Imogen of her father was unbearable. It brought back all the feelings of her own loss, and no matter how hard she tried to push them down they kept coming back up to haunt her.

The three of them made their way into the theatre bar where the only drink on offer was tea and coffee. Grace and three of her colleagues were behind the counter setting out white mugs, ready to be filled from the big teapot. Behind them were piles of sausage rolls and buns, which would soon disappear once the main doors were opened.

Imogen ran forward and reached up to the counter. One of the women gave Grace a nudge and she turned around.

'Well, hello, Imogen. Would you like your usual glass of squash?'

Imogen nodded.

'Do you want to come round and get it?'

The child didn't need to be asked twice.

'Good to see you both,' Grace told Frances and Ruby. 'Especially you, Ruby. You've been missed.'

Ruby smiled at Grace's kindness. Grace might be slight, but she was strong, deceptively so. She was lithe and fine-boned, the small traces of her career as a ballerina evident in the way she stood, the way she moved. She was the kindest person Ruby had ever met. Grace had visited her in the psychiatric ward of the hospital when Ruby had been too ashamed to see anyone else. When all her misdemeanours had come to light, she'd not been cast out as she'd imagined but had been treated with love and forgiveness. She didn't deserve it and being here was a constant reminder. But there was nowhere else to go.

'Jack in his office?' Frances asked, as Imogen settled herself on a chair next to Ruby.

'I believe so.'

She turned to Ruby. 'Can I leave Imogen with you? I need to have a chat with Jack about the Palace. Unless you want to come with me?'

What was the point? Frances was more than capable of looking after both their interests. When the Randolphs had returned from America, Johnny had gone into business with Jack

and their agent, Bernie Blackwood. It was a long-term invest-
ment. He knew he would get called up at some point and, left to
her own devices, Ruby would have wasted her own share of their
savings. It provided a tidy income to keep the house going and
gave them money to spare. Not that she'd had cause to spend any
of it. She didn't go anywhere, and her wardrobe was full of
clothes she didn't wear. There were no more parties – and if there
were she wouldn't go. A wave of self-pity washed through her.
There was nothing she could contribute to the meeting that
Frances wouldn't have thought of first.

'You're more than capable.' She hadn't meant it to sound so
sarcastic, so biting, but she saw the glint of annoyance flash in
Frances's eyes before she turned away. She looked to Grace,
whose expression betrayed nothing, but she felt miserable all the
same.

Imogen tugged at her hand. 'Are you going to sing tonight,
Auntie Ruby? I do love it so when everyone joins in together. It
sounds beautiful.'

'It does, Imogen. But I'll leave it to Mummy tonight.'

'But you can sing with her,' the child insisted. 'She won't
mind.'

Ruby didn't know how to reply. Imogen was a curious child
and Ruby loved her as she had loved no one else in her entire life.
And she knew it wasn't driven by the guilt of what she had done.
Imogen knew nothing, only that her father had been away
working for a long time. She had accepted it, just as she had
accepted Ruby. But if her niece knew what she'd done, how
would she feel then? The thought made her heart splinter.

Imogen looked up when a girl of about fourteen bounced in,
a five foot nothing bundle of enthusiasm.

'You're late, Peggy,' Bea Armitage quipped good-naturedly.
'You're usually here before we are.'

'I missed the bus and had to walk.' She was in a coat that was too short for her, and when she removed it, so was her dress. Always the same dress. Red and white gingham that reminded Ruby of a tablecloth. Her shoes were worn at the toes, but her hair was tidy and clean and tied in a matching gingham ribbon. She waved at Imogen and bobbed a little curtsey at Ruby.

'Miss Randolph,' she gushed. 'It's so lovely to see you.'

Ruby had to smile. How could she not? Peggy told all and sundry she was going to be a star. In her eyes, Ruby had everything she coveted. The girl didn't understand the reality of fame; she had never tasted it, and if she did, would she find it as bitter and empty as Ruby had? The Randolphs had played in the best theatres, both here and in America, had been wined and dined, courted by the rich and the powerful – but it was always a means to an end. And in the end, it was all about money. Or sex.

The bar filled quickly once the main doors were opened, and Ruby took Imogen up to the dress circle. Frances and Jack came out of the office and joined them. He was a good man to go into partnership with. Johnny had chosen well. But then he always had. Frances was the right choice too, steady and solid, with none of the gushing enthusiasm that a lot of theatricals were prone to, herself included. And she wasn't hard, which she could have been given her circumstances. That she'd kept Imogen when so many girls would have chosen adoption only increased Ruby's respect for her.

'Ruby.' Jack embraced her, holding on to her shoulders and kissing her cheek. 'Good of you to come. I know the lads will appreciate your coming to perform. We've had some mediocre concert parties just lately, so to have a star in their midst will be a thrill. Something to remember.'

'I wasn't—'

He looked at her, his dark eyes so intent. He was a lovely man;

that she was surrounded by the kindest of people only made her feel less deserving of it. He'd taken the Empire on and reopened it, putting on variety until the very last, holding out until the Ministry of Works would wait no longer to requisition it. He kept the Palace in Grimsby going, and the Theatre Royal in Lincoln, and in between he served with the Home Guard, doing his turn on the roof during the night hours. How he ended up with his harridan of a wife she would never understand. He deserved so much more. Kind people did. He'd been Johnny's best man when he married Frances. Ruby had been in hospital and had not known of it until she saw a photograph it the *Daily Express*. She swallowed away the bitter taste in her mouth. Frances might have forgiven Ruby, but she hadn't forgotten. Perhaps neither of them ever would.

All four of them walked to the front of the circle and looked down at the lads below. The seats had been removed and replaced with tables and chairs where the boys could play cards and board games, read and write letters home. There were so many of them, and yet it was years since she'd played to an audience so small. Some of them looked up and Jack held up a hand to acknowledge them. 'I'll go and give the lads in the band the heads-up. Give me five minutes,' he said before rushing off. Imogen began to walk between the rows of seats, tapping each one of them in turn, pushing down some of the cushions to take in a different view of the stage until she found one to her satisfaction.

'Jack's thinking of turning the Palace over to cinema,' Frances told her. 'We don't have the staff backstage, and it's hit and miss with the musicians.'

Ruby had thought it would go that way. It was more manageable, and more profitable. And everything was about the profit. 'He's right.'

'Do you think so?'

Ruby stared ahead, taking in the curve of the proscenium arch. 'It will be less work. I'm not interested. And you...'

'I what?' Frances prompted. Ruby turned to face her. Frances might have been able to keep some secrets, but she couldn't hide from someone who'd had a whole lifetime of practice.

'I what?' Frances repeated.

'You'll have your hands full.' It was hard to say the words. Frances already had all that she would never have, and she fought the desire to be envious of her but couldn't stop herself. 'When the baby comes.'

Frances twisted sharply but didn't deny it.

'I heard you in the bathroom. Too many mornings. I know your reason for being sick would never be the same as mine.' It had been hard, listening to someone else and not want to get in there and do the same. A competition she could never win.

'Ruby, I didn't want to say anything. Not yet. It's early days.' She lowered her voice. 'Please don't say anything to Imogen.'

Ruby was affronted. 'I would never hurt that child. Never.' There were already too many regrets.

Frances pressed a hand to her arm. 'I know that, Ruby.'

Did she? Ruby hoped with all her heart she did. She wanted to bridge the cavernous gap between them but didn't know how, or why, Frances would ever want to. Ruby suspected she was there to be tolerated, nothing more.

Jack signalled to them from the stage.

'Looks like I need to start things off.' Frances went downstairs and a few minutes later appeared by Jack's side, the pianist playing 'Ain't She Sweet' as she came up on the stage. Frances welcomed them all, inviting the audience to sing along with her and opened with 'Run, Rabbit, Run', encouraging them to join in.

Imogen went to the front row and peered over the rail and

Ruby went to stand at her side. The accompaniment was a small band of mostly retired musicians, window cleaners and decorators, plumbers and office workers, men too old or too ill to fight. The singing was patchy at first, a few holding back, but as they gained in confidence more joined in, the lads' voices hearty and strong. When they were nicely warmed up, Peggy bounced onto the stage and belted out 'Sing As We Go', the song made famous by Gracie Fields, dropping easily into her ever-expanding repertoire of impressions to make them laugh. Ruby had to smile. It was impossible not to. Alice Randolph would have been appalled by someone like Peggy, but Ruby admired her. She was rough at the edges but what she lacked in style she made up for in enthusiasm. If anyone could make a career of it, Peggy was the girl to do it. Ruby watched for a while then took Imogen down into the auditorium. Grace was on a break from her duties, and she and the other women were standing at the back of the stalls, singing along with the boys. She envied the women their companionship, sensing she would always be on the outside of things, never really knowing how to join in. Imogen tugged at her hand. 'Auntie Ruby, please sing with Mummy, like you did last time.'

Ruby was about to say no, but Imogen put her head to one side, and, unable to resist, said, 'For you I will, but only for you.'

She made her way up onto the stage and Frances moved so they could share the microphone. There was another whoop of applause and appreciative whistles. Ruby smiled out to them and waved, blew kisses. Below she could see young faces. Men younger than her brother, boys most of them. Boys who had no choice whether to fight or not. Ruby smiled out again and from somewhere deep inside, found her voice and began to sing. Frances left her to it for a while and when the band stopped for a break, Ruby held the stage and chatted with the lads who called out to her. 'What was it like in America?' 'How's Johnny?' 'Will you be in films, Miss Randolph?'

She answered them all as truthfully as she could. 'Perhaps.' 'Who knows.' Simple answers that seemed to satisfy. She sang again, alone this time, then asked Peggy to join her. The girl looked behind her, then placed a pointed finger to her own chest.

'Me?'

Ruby nodded and Peggy came beside her. She could see the look of disbelief in Peggy's eyes. That the girl should hold her in such high esteem, that they all could, filled her with shame. They thought she was someone special. If only they knew what she had done, how cruel she'd been, would they think the same? Standing onstage made her feel naked and exposed and she was filled with a sudden panic for it to end.

Frances must have noticed for she quickly returned to the stage for the last medley and when it was over they were greeted with rapturous applause, the lads stomping their feet and calling for more. In the end Ruby was glad she'd been able to contribute something to the success of the evening, but it had only served to expand the hollowness she felt inside. The joy of performing, if it had ever existed within her, had gone. And she wasn't sure it would ever return.

19

On Sunday, Londoners suffered another night of bombing, and it was almost light when the all-clear sounded at 5.40 a.m. the following morning. Jessie tried to sleep as much as she could before going early to the theatre, knowing that things were in the balance as to whether the show would go on – or any show for that matter. At the Adelphi, cast and crew gathered in the stalls, waiting for Vernon Leroy to join them.

'I'm all for carrying on,' Edgar said as they waited, his arms folded across his chest, his trilby having a seat of its own beside him. Others voiced their agreement. 'We can't just shut up shop and go home, not when so many others are getting on with vital work. We're in no more danger here than we would be anywhere else. If a bomb's got your name on it, it'll get you no matter where you are.'

Jessie didn't want to be so fatalistic, but all the same she hoped the bomb with her name on it would never find her.

At half past three, Vernon Leroy strode onstage with a vigour he hadn't possessed the last time she'd seen him, and the conversation petered out as he came to the front of the stage, beckoning with his arms for those sitting further back to come closer. When things were settled, he thanked them all for coming.

'I've just finished a meeting with the theatre board. George Black is closing his London theatres.' People looked at each other, shrugged. He was only confirming what they'd all expected. 'The Palladium will go dark tonight, as will the Holborn and Finsbury Park Empires – and others in the Moss theatre circuit. I don't have any definitive news of other establishments, but I expect them to follow suit.'

Edgar shook his head, and leaned towards Jessie. 'Now for the bad news.'

She tensed, watching Vernon closely. He didn't look defeated – but then what was a show closing compared to losing your only son? He paced to the left.

'There's no official news that we have to close and, as far as I can gather, Black's insisting this is a temporary suspension of performances.' He smiled out to them. 'I'm not willing to shut up shop yet, if you're willing to carry on – on a day-to-day basis?'

Jessie could see people nodding their heads in the rows in front of her.

Sid was the first to speak up. 'Do you reckon any punters will come out to see it?'

Jessie knew that was the bottom line. The box office receipts dictated the run of the show. If they fell below a certain income they would have to close, bombs or not.

Vernon flipped his right hand. 'Who knows, Sid. But if you're willing to back me, I'm prepared to give it a go. Unless the government tells us otherwise.'

'Or a ruddy great bomb,' Sid replied.

'Well, that could happen anywhere,' Vernon replied pragmatically.

The vote was unanimous. Things would be assessed on a daily basis.

'In the meantime,' Vernon told them, 'I will be working on alternative ways to keep the show going. We are in calls with theatres all over the country. If we find we can no longer carry on as we are, the show will tour in the provinces. I'll give you more details as I have them.' He spread his hands. 'Until then, the show will go on – for the time being anyway.'

He stepped down from the stage and stood in the aisle, answering questions from anyone who wanted to ask them. Jessie didn't linger, there was nothing Vernon could add to what he'd already told them, and she went out onto the street and walked down the Strand towards Waterloo Bridge, wanting to clear her head. A suspension, Vernon had said, temporary. But how long was temporary? She found a phone box and called her mother, who she knew would be at the Empire with the WVS.

* * *

That evening the house was light, only a quarter of seats filled in the stalls and no one in the dress or upper circle, but the cast gave everything they had to those who had made the effort. The *Evening Standard* that evening announced the closure of the Palladium and Hippodrome. The Strand and Wyndham's were to close, as was the Aldwych and the transfer of *Thunder Rock* from the Globe to the Haymarket had been postponed, as had the production of Daphne Du Maurier's *Rebecca* at the Queen's.

On Wednesday evening they had huddled around the wireless set in the green room and listened as the prime minster gave his broadcast, warning them of the grave situation they were in. That an invasion could happen at any time. Hundreds of barges and merchant ships were massed in French, Dutch, Belgian and Norwegian harbours. The troops were waiting. He had given the good and the bad, asking that every person do their duty, whatever that might be. He had reminded them that the Germans had not gained mastery of the air and that our air, naval and military strength were greater than ever.

'Well, tonight the show might go on,' Adele said after it had ended. 'But I can't see it lasting much longer. There's only a handful of theatres left open. The Coliseum, the Criterion. Oh, and the Windmill. Let's hope Vernon's got something lined up so we're not out of work for long.'

Jessie's mother had urged her to come home but Jessie couldn't give in. Not because of a few nights of bombing. Other people were carrying on and so would she. The show went on as normal, pausing when the siren sounded and going on after the all-clear. There was talk of changing the performance times to 2.30 and 5.30, in an effort to avoid the worst of the nightly onslaught, of dropping the show to matinees only. Everything was up in the air and she found the only way to cope was to take each day as it came, just as Vernon had advised.

At the end of the evening, she gathered her things and left the theatre by the stage door. The sky was heavy with cloud and it had begun to drizzle, the rain spattering the dusty pavements. She had not gone more than a couple of yards when someone came running up behind her and her heart began to pound. She stopped, turned and shone her torch, finding the serviceman's face. He didn't look much older than Eddie.

'Miss Delaney. I wanted to say how much I enjoyed the show.'

'I'm so glad.' He looked harmless enough. Not the sort of boy Adele would be seen around town with. 'Are you in town for long?'

'A few weeks. Working on the battery. Got the night off.' He hesitated. 'A few of the lads. We're going on to the Hungaria at Piccadilly Circus. Some of your girls are coming along. I wonder if you wanted to...'

'That's very kind but I'm meeting my fiancé in a minute,' she lied.

'Lucky chap,' he said cheerfully. He wished her good night and turned away, disappearing into the darkness.

She hesitated. It wouldn't be too much, would it, to join them all, just once? She thought of the bases she'd toured with the concert party, the concerts with Ginny and Frances. Most of the chaps only wanted to talk, to be with a girl, missing their own. Adele's words came back to her. Was Harry being true? She carried on, hearing steps behind her. She stopped, hoping whoever it was would pass when someone caught at her elbow and she screamed.

'It's me. Billy.'

She struggled to free herself, bumped into an elderly man, and apologised. 'What the hell are you playing at, Billy?'

He pulled her back and they stopped.

'Jess, we were friends. Can't we be friends again?' He walked beside her. 'I know I did some stupid things but believe me if I could go back and put them right I would.' The siren began to wail. It was not unlike the noise Ginny made that dreadful night. The searchlights swept across the sky.

'Let me go, Billy.'

He released her and she began hurrying down the street. He came after her.

'You shouldn't walk the streets alone at night – regardless of the bombs. Women are getting accosted all the time.'

'I've been fine.'

'Then you've been lucky.'

She'd thought the same thing. The walk home was getting more fraught with danger and though she tried to tell herself she wasn't afraid, she was. She stepped out into the road and was yanked backwards when he pulled at her bag, narrowly avoiding a car that raced down the street. She wanted to vomit. Her heart was beating, the siren wailing, and she could hear the alarm bells ringing on the fire wagons. He pushed her into a doorway. She couldn't make out his face, only feel his breath on hers. She wasn't frightened of him, not one bit, but she didn't push him away. More of Adele's words came into her head. 'Couldn't she see it in his eyes?' She hadn't really looked in his eyes. She lifted her torch and shone the thin beam on his face, seeing the scar tissue about his right eye, the cloudiness of the pupil. For a split second she thought he might make a move to kiss her, and she pushed him away. His left hand caught her right arm and he held on to her.

'Be mad at me by all means, but don't put yourself in danger because of it. The shelter's a couple of yards from here. We need to be in it.' The words were scarcely out of his mouth when the first explosion shook the pavement. As they ran she didn't try to free herself, glad to be with someone – even if it was Billy.

He hurried them down the staircase and onto the platform. People had settled themselves anywhere they could and the two of them stepped between them, looking for a place to stand. It was hot and airless, and the smell was appalling, but it was better than being on the street. Billy clasped her hand and dragged her towards a small gap. People shuffled up to give them a little of the precious space and she sat down on the platform and tried to make herself comfortable. He took off his jacket then rolled up his sleeves, his right hand awkward, his skin puckered and shiny on his right forearm, the result of a burn. She tried not to stare but whatever happened must have been painful. He made a pillow of his jacket and pushed it behind her. She thanked him for it, all the time fighting her discomfort. It was a kind gesture but being with him was betraying Ginny, and heaven only knew what Harry would make of it.

Outside there was the familiar drone of engines followed by the whistle of bombs, the thud of explosions, one after another, and the relentless rattle of the anti-aircraft guns as they valiantly fought back. She hunched her shoulders at each one, trying to judge how close they were. Billy sat with his hands dangling in front of his knees.

'How is Eddie? Your mother?'

'Both well. Thank you for asking.'

He gave a small smile. 'How very formal.'

'What do you expect?'

'Well, more than this.'

He chatted to the old lady beside him, wiggled his ears and thumbed his nose at a little boy nestled at his mother's lap and made him laugh. It was the better side to Billy, and she softened towards him. After all, he had no idea what had happened to Ginny. Around them other people had come well prepared, with blankets and cushions, books and flasks. She'd seen the queues from the roof of the theatre, hundreds waiting in line at the end of the day, the elderly, women with babies and small children. How tiresome it must be for them, night after night. The hours passed and she put her head forward, resting it on her knees, trying not to breathe in the bodily smells, blocking out the snoring and other sounds. Somewhere to the left of her a child was crying, a mother singing a lullaby. She closed her eyes, and opened them when someone broke wind.

'Pity I ain't got a kite,' Billy quipped and the folk around them laughed. Jessie lifted her head and laughed with them. 'Ah, got you in the end,' he said cheerfully. He was different to when they'd first met. He was still overly confident and quick-witted but some of his sharp edges had become rounded. It intrigued her. He leaned back against the tiled wall.

'What do you do at the Windmill?' she asked him.

'Keep me clothes on.'

She sighed with disappointment. 'Oh, Billy, can't you ever give a straight answer?'

He shrugged. 'My act. Jokes, bit of the old soft shoe, bit of patter, a song. I do whatever they want me to do.'

'The perfect place. You and a load of naked girls.'

'Have you been to see the show?'

She shook her head.

'They don't all strip off. And those that do can't move.'

'Does that make it all right?'

'In the eyes of the law.' He sat forward. 'There are worse things a girl could do. They're lovely. Quiet, studious some of them...'

Jessie raised an eyebrow.

'They are. They can be quite motherly. They knit and paint and read. You've met some of them. They're just like any dancers.'

'Except they take their clothes off.'

He shrugged. 'The lads like it. Most of them have never seen a naked girl before, might never get that chance to – you know.'

She knew exactly what he meant. She thought of the serviceman who had stopped her earlier.

'What happened?' She moved her finger to the side of her own face where his was disfigured.

'Got stuck in France with the lads.' He moved his legs to allow a woman to pass by, dragging a small boy by the arm, snot running from his nose, which he wiped on his sleeve.

'Your eye?'

'Shrapnel. Didn't move quick enough.'

'Don't joke, Billy.' It was what he always did, making light of something so serious. It had infuriated her then and it infuriated her now.

'I don't know how to cope otherwise.'

She didn't press him, feeling she had already been too forthright, and for a time both of them were quiet.

She woke with a start when the all-clear sounded, embarrassed to discover that she'd fallen asleep on Billy's shoulder. All about her people began gathering their belongings and beginning to move. Billy got up and held out his hands for hers. For a moment she hesitated, before taking them and allowing him to pull her to her feet. They waited for the crowds to disperse a little before queueing to get out and up into the street. Over to the east, the sky glowed a vibrant orange, dense smoke billowing into the air and the sound of bells clanging as the fire service raced to where it was needed echoed all around. A WVS van was serving the wardens and those who had not sought shelter but had braved the onslaught. Women like her mother who would not weaken. Dawn was breaking and already the clean-up operation was underway, men clearing the pavement of glass, a cart following close behind. Billy rolled down his sleeves and put on his jacket, lit a cigarette, took a draw on it and blew out the smoke. The two of them stood to one side and watched as hundreds of people poured out of the Underground station and made their way home. Jessie began to walk in the direction of Albany Street and Billy fell into step beside her. She stopped. Underground it had been different, but out in the open she knew she had let her guard down, let him get too close.

'Good night, Billy.' She turned and walked away, feeling his eyes bore into her. This time he didn't follow her and for a brief moment she was disappointed, then she quickened her step and made her way home.

20

Frances didn't have to keep her secret from Imogen for long, as Johnny arrived in the early hours. Ruby had heard the doorbell ring, Frances hurry down the stairs to open the door, their voices soft and echoey in the quiet of the night. She resisted the urge to go down and join them. It wasn't her place to welcome him home, not any more.

In the morning, she stayed in bed as long as she could, delighting in listening to Imogen's excited squeals as she woke up to find her daddy had come home. She joined them in the dining room while they were having breakfast. They looked such a happy family, all three of them seated at the table, Mr Brown beneath it, hopeful for scraps.

Johnny got up, embraced her, took hold of her hands in his. His hands were not as soft as they once were, his hair shorter, and he looked more muscular than before he had left for training. 'You're looking well, Ruby. So much better than when I saw you a few weeks ago. It must be all the sunshine we've been having.'

Imogen was wriggling on her chair, trying desperately to

empty her mouth of food so she could speak. She slipped from her chair and ran to Ruby, took hold of her hand.

'We're going to have a baby, Auntie Ruby. The stork's going to bring him.'

'Oh, how exciting,' Ruby said, squatting down beside her and putting her hands to her tiny waist. Imogen turned to her mother.

'Is it going to be a brother or a sister?' Imogen asked her mother. Frances got up and gave Ruby a warm smile.

'We don't know yet, Imogen.' She put out her hand for her child to take. 'Let's ask Mrs Frame for more toast for Auntie Ruby. She'll be hungry.'

Ruby hadn't the slightest hunger, she never did, but she appreciated Frances's consideration in giving her a few moments with Johnny. He led her to a chair and took his seat only after she had taken hers. He couldn't hide his joy; it shone from his eyes, from every pore of his skin.

'It's wonderful news, isn't it? About the baby.'

'It is. The best, the very best.' She was so happy for him, for both of them.

'Frances said you were all at the Empire last night. That you sang a few songs.'

She nodded. 'Just a few.'

'How did it feel?' No one but Johnny would ask that question. He knew her as no one else did and she was pierced with sorrow for all she had lost and would never have again.

'Strange.'

He nodded. 'It is strange. It's the same for me too.' They had never worked apart. Did he feel as she did onstage, that there was always something missing?

'You're doing shows at the camp?'

He nodded. 'All sorts. Quite a few chaps are musicians,

amateur and professional. A few fancy themselves as comics. It keeps me busy. Breaks the monotony.'

She poured herself a glass of water.

'I might go into producing. I quite like it.'

She felt her stomach tighten. There would be no going back to being the Randolphs, no chance of picking up where they had left off when all this was over, and the thought of it made her panic again. She grasped for the back of a dining chair, holding on while the world rocked around her. Frances came back into the room.

'Sorry to interrupt.' She looked to Johnny. 'But if you want to walk Imogen to school, we need to leave in a few minutes.'

He got up. Imogen was already in her hat and coat, and she hugged Ruby, kissed her goodbye and leaned under the table to Mr Brown. 'Look after Auntie Ruby,' she said to the dog then took her father's hand.

Johnny kissed Ruby's cheek. 'We'll talk later, Ruby.'

After they'd gone, Ruby remained at the table. She couldn't stay here forever, the cuckoo in the nest, but what could she do without Johnny at her side?

* * *

'So, what do you really think?' Frances asked Johnny once they'd seen Imogen into school and turned for home. It was a fresh morning, the sun already high in the sky. They had already told Imogen they would take her to the park after school.

'Still a long way to go. Ruby's better than she was, but she's not there yet.'

Frances agreed. It was so much easier to talk about things face to face instead of by letter, or on the telephone.

'I'm so sorry she's such a worry to you, especially now.' He pressed his hand to her stomach. 'Oh, God, Frances. Let's hope this damn war is over soon.'

'We know it won't be.' There was no sense in thinking it would. 'In a way it's a good job that Ruby didn't go to Aunt Hetty. There wouldn't have been the opportunity to build bridges.' For the last few weeks she hadn't felt there'd been much progress at all, but then she hadn't been expecting miracles. Ruby would have to recover at her own pace, there wasn't much Frances could do to hurry it along, much as she wanted to – for her own sake as well as Ruby's.

'I suppose every cloud has a silver lining.' He pulled her close as they walked. The leaves were beginning to change colour, the intense green giving way to golds and reds. It was a wonderful place to be, opposite the park.

'I was talking to Jack about putting on a panto for two or three weeks,' she said, getting him up to speed with business before they got home. 'Opening Boxing Day. I know it's a lot of work for a short amount of time, but I'm sure local families will appreciate it.'

'I'm sure they would,' he agreed. 'I think it's a great idea.'

She clasped his hand, glad that she could be so close, wanting to cherish every moment at his side. 'It would be the perfect opportunity for Ruby to get involved.'

'It would.' He lifted her hand to his mouth and kissed it. 'And it wouldn't be too much pressure.' He gave her a sideways glance. 'You and Jack are quite a formidable team. Ruby doesn't stand a chance.'

'She's lost without you.'

He grinned at her. 'And you're not?'

'Not lost, no.' She'd spent too many years alone to not be able to cope. 'I miss you, yearn for you. But Ruby has no direction and that's a terrible feeling to have. I think we have to wean her into going solo bit by bit.'

'Do you think it will work?'

'Who knows, but she needs something to aim for. To keep her going forward.'

He opened the garden gate and stood back to let her pass, stopped her on the porch before she opened the door and kissed her. 'You go and rest for a little while. Leave me to talk to Ruby.'

* * *

Ruby was in the garden, a pair of secateurs in her hand, a trug at her feet, deadheading the last of the roses.

'Well, I never thought you'd become so domesticated, Miss Randolph.' She turned and smiled. He looked so smart in his uniform, the buttons glinting in the sun.

'I'm not very good but I'm learning. Thanks to Ted. He's been very patient, teaching me the names of flowers and shrubs.' She pointed them out to him. 'Hebe, hydrangea, cosmos, delphiniums, agapanthus.'

'I'm impressed,' he said, walking beside her. 'How have you been, Ruby?' He put a gentle hand to her arm, made her stop and look at him. His eyes were full of warmth and love, and she shrank a little, knowing she didn't deserve it.

'I've been...' She took a breath. 'Much better.'

'Ready to get back into the swing of things again?'

She shook her head. 'Oh no, not yet. I don't feel I could—'

He caught hold of her hand. 'Jack's thinking of putting a panto on at the Palace. Just a couple of weeks over Christmas.'

She could feel her pulse starting to race. 'That's a lovely idea. The children would enjoy it. I loved going to the pantomime with Mummy and Daddy.' It was one of the few happy memories she had, all four of them together, looking up at the stage as opposed to being on it. How fleeting happiness had been. Life was never the same after Daddy died.

'I was thinking...'

She knew what was coming next and, feeling unsteady, she walked away from him and sat down on the bench.

He took a seat beside her and continued. 'We've never done a panto. It would be such fun—'

'For who?'

'For you, Ruby.' He was looking at her, but she looked away, staring at the pile of leaves under the cherry tree.

'I don't think so. I'm not well enough.'

'But you're getting stronger all the time.' He reached for her hand again and she felt his strength run through her, knowing it would leave when he let go. Tears pricked in her eyes and she pushed her finger into the corner of each one to stop them from falling.

'Just because I got up and sang a few songs at the Empire doesn't mean I can carry a show. People will expect too much.'

'But you are more than capable of carrying a show, Ruby. Any show. You've been doing it for years.'

She looked at him. 'With you I have, but never alone.'

He spent some time trying to persuade her, the two of them side by side as they had always been, but no matter what he said, she couldn't face it. The mere thought of headlining, even in the provinces, was unbearable. She pressed her hand to her chest, closed her eyes, concentrated on slowing her breathing to calm herself. He stopped talking as she had hoped he would.

'Okay, okay, Ruby. I understand. We'll forget that idea.' He sat with her until her breath slowed and she opened her eyes again, watching the light dapple the leaves. He gave her a moment or two to consider then spoke quietly.

'I really think it will help if you can get involved in some way though. I'm keeping my hand in producing shows for the lads. It could be something we do in the future, as Randolphs.' He stretched his legs out before him, leaned back into the bench and stared ahead. 'Would you consider the choreography? I can't think of anyone better qualified.'

She thought about it, nodded. It felt terrifying to accept but she had to keep facing her fears. He took her hand in his. 'Small steps, Ruby. Small steps.'

21

Ginny had been looking after her father for over a month and in that time his health had not improved. It was almost as if he was willing himself to stay ill because it suited him to have her there. She was determined not to be reduced to an unpaid skivvy with nothing better to do than pick up after him, but he was becoming increasingly less mobile. It was rare that he got up out of the chair, grumbling at her as she cleaned the fire and set it. He ate his meals there but thankfully struggled out to the outhouse to do his business. That she couldn't bear.

She'd bought some sheets from the pawnshop down Leopold Street, and had tried to fix things up at the house as best she could, though she did so filled with resentment. The walls were less damp, and the wallpaper had dried out. It wasn't worth patching up the pieces that had lain on the floor when she'd first arrived, but she had pasted back the panels where it could be saved. Each morning she opened her father's bedroom window and let whatever breeze there was blow through the upstairs. She stood in his room and looked out onto the street below. Four washing lines were stretched from one side of the street to the other and sheets were billowing in the breeze like sails. Oh, to be by the sea right now, anywhere but here. She thought wistfully of her time in Cleethorpes. In spite of all the tawdry business attached to Billy Lane, she'd been happy there. For the first time in her life she'd felt she actually belonged. One of the women called out to her from the street below, waved, then went into her own house. Ginny went downstairs.

'I need to go out.' Les Thompson struggled to his feet and sat down again, yelping with agony, which sent him into a fit of coughing, gasping for breath in between coughs.

'I'll fetch whatever you need. What is it you're wanting?'

He griped at her. 'Keeping me prisoner in me own home.'

'I'm doing nothing of the sort. You're too unsteady on your feet to go out.'

He grumbled again.

'Well?' She picked up the ash bucket and began to clean the grate.

'A man could die o' thirst. They'll be missing me at the Rose and Crown.'

'I doubt they'll be missing you, but they'll certainly miss the money you've thrown over the counter for the last twenty-odd years.'

'By, you've become a hard lass. You've nothing of your mother in you.'

That hurt, as he knew it would. He'd goaded her mother until she bit back, all he needed to excuse his first blow. She gritted her teeth as she swept the warm ash into the metal bucket and set it to one side then began twisting old newspaper into kindling, adding offcuts of wood she'd found around the backyard and a few lumps of coal, trying to make things last as best she could. There was no money coming in above what her brothers sent, and what she'd saved was gradually being eaten away. She'd seen no sign of the man, or men, who were storing black-market goods in her old room – that's if there was anything there – nor of any money they might be paying her father. If they had he wouldn't admit to it. There was no alternative but to get a job to keep things going. The thought of being there any longer made her miserable, and she got up and went through the scullery and out into the yard with the coal bucket.

'Is that thee, lass?' Mrs Smith called over the wall. 'Weather's on turn. Thi can smell it in t'air. How's thi fatha doin'. Any better?'

'Neither in health nor temper, Mrs Smith.' She tried to be cheerful, but her dad's lack of progress was getting her down. She made another mark on the back wall with a piece of brick, a calendar of misery marking the days since she'd first arrived.

'Don't get trapped with t'owd bugger, lass. Thi mam would be turning in her grave if she thought thi'd got lumbered with him like she did. I remember how hard she worked to see thi got away. Don't thi leave it too long afore thi go off again.'

Ginny heard the bin men come clattering down the alley, gates opening and closing, the day already half over for some men. She wondered how her father had got away with doing so little in his life. He'd been known as a hard man, back in the day, and younger men knew better than to cross him. They wouldn't be so afraid of him now, and she wasn't afraid of him either. She was here not for love but for duty – and when her duty was done, she'd leave him to it.

When she went back in the house, he'd fallen asleep again. There was no point waking him, so she quietly put on her coat and hat. As she walked down the street, the postman handed her a letter. She recognised Joe's handwriting and read it on the bus on her way to Aunt Maggie's. He had two days' leave and was visiting his mother in Preston. Would she be able to meet him for a few hours? She folded it and put it in her handbag, staring out of the window, unsure of how to answer, uncertain of her feelings towards him. She didn't want to lead him on.

Her aunt was in the yard, the hall rug over the line, thrashing the hell out of it with the wicker beater, dust flying out of it as it swung back and forth with every wallop. She stopped when she saw her niece and took a breather, resting on the dustbin while she listened to Ginny's woes.

'I can't make things stretch, not for two of us.' She put her shoulder against the back of the house. 'I swear he's not getting well on purpose, just to keep me there. He enjoys seeing me suffer.'

'I'm not going to argue with you, love, but I don't know what I can do. I'm stretched as it is.'

Ginny let out a long sigh.

'Have you tried the Empire or the Lyceum? They still have shows each week, as far as I know. Most of the others have gone to picture houses.'

'It's the same everywhere. It makes finding steady work that much harder.' Each time she checked *The Stage*, the columns for calls had shrunk. 'What shows they have will be booked in complete with the acts. It'll be a tour, going from theatre to theatre, same people each time.' Ginny fiddled with the strap of her handbag. 'I suppose I could ask, let them know I'm about. You never know, someone might fall ill and I could step in at short notice.'

'That's the ticket,' her aunt said, pressing her hands to her knees and getting back on her feet. 'You can make it work; I know you can. It's only for the short term, to tide you over, then you can get back to doing what you love.'

It wasn't so much that she loved it, more that she didn't know how to do anything else, not that her aunt would ever understand. As far as she was concerned, Ginny had escaped the drudgery that was her mother's lot and had a bright future ahead of her. Her aunt chattered on about her boys, about how Brenda was earning good money down the factory and was walking out with a lad from Woodseats. 'You heard from that chap? Abanazar, wasn't it?'

Ginny smiled. 'Joe. I got a letter this morning. He wants to meet.'

'Ah, that's nice. Something to look forward to.'

It was perhaps the only thing.

Sandbags were piled high around the entrance to City Hall and stacked against the windows of the co-operative and Banner's department store. It was the same as every other town Ginny had visited while she was touring with the ENSA concert party. Queues stretched down the street outside butchers' and greengrocers', women resigned to waiting in line, with bags, with prams, with toddlers. She called at the Empire and the Lyceum, and every cinema in the city, writing her name and address on slips of paper so that they could contact her should an opportunity present itself.

She was tired when she got back, her feet sore with walking so far, and she hoped her father had at least managed to put a match to the fire. When she opened the door, he wasn't in his chair, the fire unlit. She heard him calling out, his voice muffled, and hurried through to the scullery, thinking he had fallen there. A pile of crumpled plaster was scattered about her clean floor and, looking up, she saw an old boot sticking out from the ceiling – and in it was her father's leg. She raced upstairs and into the back bedroom to find him groaning in agony. The top of his leg was visible, ulcerated and weeping, the rest of it having gone through the floorboard. She knew exactly why he was there – and had not an ounce of sympathy.

'Find what you were looking for?'

His face was distorted with agony. 'For Christ's sake, help me. Help me.'

For two pins, she'd have stamped on his fingers.

'I stopped hiding money under the floorboards a long time ago. All that effort for nothing.' He had taken what they had before, money her mother squirrelled away to pay the rent, the bills. He was trying to do the same to her, but she'd learned how to protect herself the hard way. Anything of any value she kept on her, in a small money bag strapped about her waist under her skirts. In it was her savings book and any cash she possessed. She watched him struggle to free himself.

'Get me up, damn you, lass! Get me up!'

She didn't rush to link her arms under his armpits and try to free him, but it wasn't easy when she did. She pulled, shouting at him to push himself free with his hands. It took time and effort, and little by little they managed to release him. His leg was in a bad state, swollen and purple, the accident aggravating what was already a large weeping sore that he'd kept to himself. It would necessitate a visit from the nurse – and more dwindling of what little money she had left. She wanted to weep with frustration. He wasn't the only one who was trapped. So was she.

22

In October, Sunday once more became a day of trains and Jessie waited at Victoria with Adele for the 11.48 to Brighton. Their bags were stacked on the porter's trolley, along with those for the rest of the cast. The show had closed a week after the Blitz had begun and in the days that followed Bernie had advised her to fill the empty hours by taking acting lessons. She began frequenting the Buddy Bradley School of Stage Dancing in Soho, used by stars such as Jack Buchanan, as they worked to keep themselves in shape. It would be all too easy to idle away the days. She called into Bernie's office three times a week, hoping for work to keep her going but there were few opportunities and what there were had been quickly snapped up by those who were better connected. Jessie felt she had fallen through the gaps, not wanting to commit to anything other than the odd night here and there singing with a band in one of the many restaurants that remained open. When *A Touch of Silver* was ready to tour, she wanted to be ready too. Her mother had asked her to come home, to wait for news in safety, but Jessie didn't want to. When things changed, and they could change at any moment, she wanted to be there.

When Bernie told her that *A Touch of Silver* had bookings from October to mid-December, she'd been delighted. She'd bid a tearful goodbye to all at Albany Street. Belle had almost squeezed the breath from her as she readied herself to leave.

'It won't be long before you're back with us again, darling. Stay safe until then.'

'You too, Belle.' They'd gathered on the step at the front of the house to wave her off and when she looked back before turning the corner they were still there, Belle and Velma waving their handkerchiefs in the air, Victor and Alfred standing guard behind them.

Now, as she sat with Adele on the bench outside the ticket office, she couldn't wait to get to Brighton. Adele ground her cigarette out under her heel.

'I thought I'd left all this behind me, traipsing from station to station, staying in digs with dubious landladies,' Adele said, looking up to the boards. Their train had already been delayed by two hours. Any later and they would arrive in the blackout, which was never a good thing. Not when they weren't familiar with the streets.

'At least we're still working,' Jessie replied. 'It might not be for long.'

Adele huffed. 'You're a little too much of the glass is half full for me, girl. We don't know what we'll be coming back to. Nope, this is it for the foreseeable so we might as well get used to it.' Adele went to get herself a packet of mints and no sooner had she left than the guard came to stand at the gate. Adele ran back and the two of them tore down the platform after the other passengers, Adele pushing her way through while Jessie uttered, 'Excuse me, please.'

Adele shouted over her shoulder, 'We ain't got time for manners if you want a seat.'

Adele smiled sweetly at the guard who pulled her into the carriage, and she grabbed hold of Jessie and dragged her along. Two soldiers, one dark, one fair, were spread out over a bench and sprang to their feet, brushing the dust from the slats. 'After you.'

'What gentlemen,' Adele said, wriggling her hips as she sat down. Jessie sat beside her. 'Where are you headed, boys? All the way down to the coast?'

The fair-haired one patted the side of his nose. 'Now that would be telling but we've got our buckets and spades with us.'

Adele flashed her eyes. 'I do love a trip to the seaside,' she flirted. 'We're at the Hippodrome for the next few weeks. You should come and see us. Shouldn't they, Jessie?' Adele took out a cigarette. The dark-haired soldier took a lighter from his top pocket, put his boot up on the bench and leaned over her to light it. Adele took a drag then exhaled the smoke.

'We'll take you up on that,' he told her, returning his lighter to his pocket. A few of their mates came along and they moved further down the train.

Jessie felt uncomfortable. 'What did you say that for?'

'They were harmless enough. We can handle them. Well, I can. I can always give you lessons.'

Jessie felt the heat rise on her neck. 'I don't need lessons.'

Adele didn't answer but her smile let Jessie know what she was thinking. A few of the other girls came to join them and Jessie stared out of the window as the train began to journey out of London, seeing the devastation from a different perspective. Halves of houses, curtains still at the windows, a bathtub, an armchair, remnants of people's lives laid bare for all to gawp at. It was hard to comprehend, and she was reminded of Victor's warning. It was only going to get worse.

* * *

They found their way to the theatre and got directions to the digs. Most of the hotels and boarding houses had been taken over for military use or for billets, and they were left to lodge with a sour-faced woman who looked them up and down when she opened the door.

'We're the girls from the theatre,' Adele said cheerily.

She blocked the doorway, her arms folded across her chest. 'I'll let you know right from the start, I'll have no funny business. I lock my doors at ten.'

'Oh, we're not the comedians,' Adele trilled. 'You'll get no funny business from us.'

The woman's face didn't crack, and Adele continued to smile until the woman relented and let them in. Jessie bit at her lip to suppress her laughter. Touring with Adele might be fun after all.

23

Ginny had commandeered a neighbour to help bring her father downstairs then paid for a nurse to minister to his leg. Once the blood had been cleaned up, Ginny could see the ulcerated weeping sores on his shins and calves.

'In a way it's a good job you went through the floor, Mr Thompson, or you'd never have got it seen to. You might have had to have your leg off.' The nurse left Ginny with instructions on how to care for his wounds and a feeling of utter desolation.

She would remember it as one of the most miserable times of her life. How long she would stay there was anyone's guess. Her father didn't help himself and seemed to revel in the fact that she was there at his beck and call. She feared she was turning into her mother. She'd warned him that if he raised his hand to her, she would walk out and never look back.

'My, yer a hard-hearted lass and no mistake. You've not an ounce of compassion for a poor old man.'

'You're not old. There are men older than you walking the streets at night keeping us safe, contributing to the war effort.

Any suffering you've brought on yourself. I've not an ounce of pity for you. You have more than enough for both of us.'

Two days later she'd found work as an usherette at the Central Picture House on the Moor, one of the main shopping thoroughfares. It would keep the roof over their heads and give her a break from her father's continual jibes. She was determined the old sod would get better and religiously dressed his wounds and kept them clean, wanting them to heal more than he did himself.

* * *

Ginny had arranged to meet Joe at the railway station. She had two hours before she needed to be at work, the doors of the picture house opening at 1.00 p.m. His train was due at 10.30 and she'd arrived in good time, taking a corner table in the station buffet, watching people come and go, fighting the urge to leave herself. She'd never been sure how she felt about Joe – or how he felt about her – but when he walked in, her heart fluttered like a butterfly. He looked nervously about the room and she raised her hand to attract his attention. His face brightened when he saw her, and he immediately removed his cap and pushed it into his pocket as he walked over to her. She got up and he hesitated, unsure of how to greet her, so she stepped forward and put her hands to his shoulders, kissed his cheek. 'Good to see you, Joe.'

'And you, Ginny.' He glanced at her empty cup on the table. 'Can I get you another drink?'

'That would be lovely.' He waited his turn at the counter, briefly looking back at her, smiling awkwardly when he caught her eye. His hair was cropped shorter than it had been when they'd appeared in the pantomime together last Christmas. She'd seen him only a couple of times since then, but his letters came regularly. In them he seemed to write all that he was unable to say when face to face. He returned with two teas and placed them on the table, then pushed one gently in front of her.

'You look lovely.'

She didn't feel it, but it was kind of him to say so.

'You look very smart,' she countered, taking a sip from her cup.

'Do I?' He looked embarrassed. 'My mother was surprised when she saw me.'

'Is she well?' His mother had been widowed when Joe was young and had gone to live with her sister in Preston when the war broke out.

'Yes, my aunt too. They've seen relatively little bombing where they are in the countryside, so they're quite safe.' He looked about the buffet. 'It's all a bit different to when we last met.'

'It is,' Ginny agreed. 'Do you get a chance to do any of your magic for your mates?' Joe had been an amateur magician before war broke out. He had resigned from his job at the bank to enlist – only to be turned down. Twice. He took the opportunity to follow his ambition to appear onstage, only to get called up.

'Yes, it's very popular. The lads like it. It keeps us entertained when there's nothing else to look forward to.'

'Don't you get concert parties? Don't ENSA send anyone?'

'They do but it's not all worth watching. Some of it is dire.'

Ginny nodded. 'Well, you know what they're calling it, don't you. Every Night Something Awful.'

He smiled. 'But your show wouldn't have been like that.'

'It wasn't, thank heavens.' She laughed. He sipped at his tea.

'Will you go back, when your father is well?'

'Yes, I'm counting the days.' She didn't enlarge on it, not wanting to bring her father into the conversation. There was an awkward silence and he picked up a spoon, made it disappear, then produced it from his top pocket. She smiled.

'Did you bring a photo?'

She opened her bag and handed it over. He'd asked for a small picture, one he could keep in his battledress pocket. He gazed at it appreciatively, then looked up at her, rubbed his hands together and when he opened them it had disappeared. He rubbed his hands again and produced a silk rose and presented it to her with a flourish. It was the sweetest thing anyone had ever done for her.

They spoke of nothing in particular, mostly going over what they had already said in letters. She told him of the films she had seen in her brief time as an usherette. Talk of it reminded her to check her watch. 'I need to leave, or I'll be late for work.'

'I'll walk with you. If that's all right with you?'

'Course it is. As long as you don't miss your train.'

'It would be worth missing,' he said quietly. 'If it meant extra time in your company.'

She smiled at him, linking her arm in his as they walked along. She felt safe with Joe. He wasn't a man for words, not the spoken ones anyway, and he was never going to be a man who swept her off her feet, but he was strong and reliable, and most of all, he was kind. And in a world with such cruelty that meant a lot. Out in the street, he talked more easily, and she wished they'd not bothered with the tea and had just walked. Joe was more relaxed with no one to hear him and she was sorry when they arrived at the entrance to the picture house and had to part. Reluctantly she released her arm from his.

'It's been good to see you, Ginny.'

'Only good?' she teased, feeling a little more confident.

'More than good. I...'

She didn't want to wait for words that wouldn't come so she

kissed him, knowing he would never make the first move. She wasn't surprised when he kissed her back, out on the street, and in broad daylight. They had wasted too much time already. It seemed to give him courage.

'Can I ask you to wait for me, Ginny? Would you?'

She laughed and kissed his cheek. 'I was already waiting, Joe. I just didn't know it.'

When she went into the building, her friend Mavis grinned at her. 'Kissing in the street, Miss Thompson. Tut, tut. What would your mother think?'

'She'd be delighted,' Ginny replied, knowing that a man like Joe would be all she had dreamed of for her only daughter.

24

A Touch of Silver had opened in Brighton to good notices. It was a pared-down show, with only half the dancers they'd had at the Adelphi and minus a couple of principles who had found work elsewhere. Jessie had been given an extended spot and to her delight had moved further up the bill. When she'd first seen the posters outside the theatre it had been hard to contain her excitement, her name side by side with Adele's. Sid Silver had found her that first morning as they rehearsed the new format.

'You've got the opportunity to do well here, young lady, but you need to work on your patter between songs. Give them a little more of your personality.' He winked at her. 'I'll give you a few pointers if you like. Help you along.' He'd been as good as his word, providing her with a few lines that would get the audience on her side. Jessie had thought it generous of him.

'Well, you're no competition,' Adele told her. 'He's the only comedian in the show so you're hardly a threat. Wait until you steal his laughs, then you'll see a different side of him. Comedians can be nasty bleeders if you cross them.'

Jessie ignored her, deciding to make up her own mind about

people she met. Sid Silver had been good to her, and that was all that mattered.

The weather had been lousy during the second week, and although they'd had gusting winds and heavy rain to contend with, it hadn't kept the audience from coming out in it to see the show. For the first week Jessie had slept long hours, catching up from all she had missed from the nightly bombings in London. And it was still going on, there being no let-up, the Luftwaffe turning out in numbers. Since the first nightly London bombings in early September, they'd been sleep-deprived, going about their business in a daze yet determined not to give in to the relentless attacks. Slowly they had adjusted their routine, and life went on as normal, or as much as it could in the circumstances. Tonight, she didn't care if she slept at all. Harry was on his way to Brighton from his base in Lincolnshire and she wanted to make the most of every precious minute.

In their dressing room at the Hippodrome, she leaned into the mirror and poked at her chin. 'Of all the times to get a spot,' she wailed.

'Leave it be. You'll make it worse.' Adele handed over a small bottle. 'Dab a bit of witch hazel on it. I'll guarantee he won't even notice.' Jessie took it from her and picked up a piece of cotton wool. The two of them seemed to get on better without Tabby coming between them, Adele less forceful, more charming. 'Is he bringing a friend?'

'You don't need him to bring a friend, Adele. You have them queueing at the stage door every night.'

'True, but it would be nice to go out as a foursome.'

Jessie put her hands down from her face. 'I was hoping for time alone.'

'Of course you were.' Adele poured herself a glass of water, and handed one to Jessie. 'Forget I ever said anything.'

* * *

It had been one hell of a journey, but Harry would have made it twice over if he got to see his girl. Of his three days' leave almost half would be spent travelling but he chose not to think of it, only of the reward of being with her. He had hitched a lift on one of the trucks leaving the airfield and had walked the rest of the way to the station. Thereafter he had spent the best part of eight hours squashed into a carriage with forty other men of various services. Everyone was on the move again. They were always on the move. He hurried away from the station and down towards the seafront. The sky was heavy with cloud, and he hoped they'd be in for a quiet night, not that it had prevented the bombers from indiscriminately dropping their load over London. He was glad Jessie was well out of it, though it was a shame not to have caught her on the West End stage. Even so, at least Grace had been there and that would have meant everything to Jessie.

He found the theatre easy enough and waited with the stage doorman while one of the stagehands went up to let Jessie know of his arrival. It was a step up from the Empire in Cleethorpes, but he was always surprised by the drabness of the backstage areas, most of them with chipped paint and scuffed walls, the plain and serviceable seating. The money was spent front of house for customers who revelled in the red plush, the gold paint and brass rails that made going to a theatre such an occasion. It had been an eye-opener, seeing it as it really was, without the glare of the spotlights, which made everything look much brighter than it was in reality. Artificial and exaggerated. He would never understand what made it so enticing.

He was waiting on the stairs when she raced down towards him and threw her arms about him. The pressure of her lips on his was all he had longed for as he'd travelled south. He wrapped his arms about her waist and when she drew back her eyes were shining.

'Oh, Harry darling, it's so good to see you.' She linked her arms about his neck, standing on tiptoes. Her face was thick with make-up, her eyes exaggerated, her lashes too black, looking not half as pretty as she did without it. But she was beautiful, and she was his girl.

She grinned at him, planting small kisses on his cheeks, his lips. 'I was so worried you wouldn't make it. Was it an awful journey?'

'I've had better.'

'I can't believe you're here.' She stopped on the turn of the stair and kissed him fully, holding his face in her hands then wrapping her arms about his neck and pulling him closer. Someone passed by them, but he didn't open his eyes, savouring the feel of her lips on his, the smell of her skin, the softness of her hair. There was another set of footsteps and someone squeezed past, and muttered, 'Don't eat him, Jessie.' He felt the smile on her lips, and she pulled away.

'Come up to the dressing room. Meet Adele.' She kissed him again, and the delight on her face made him forget the journey. He'd been tired enough at the start of it, but knowing he would be with Jessie gave him all the energy he needed to keep going. Taking hold of his hand, she led him up the stairs and into a dressing room that was crowded with costumes. A girl, older than Jessie, was sitting in front of her mirror wearing only a silk under slip and white stockings, painting her lips dark red with a stick of make-up, her lashes spidery with black mascara. She turned round when she saw him and looked him up and down.

'Well, I had no idea. What a lucky girl our Jessie is.' She held out her hand. 'Adele Blair. You must be Harry.'

He took her hand and she held on to it. It made him feel

slightly uncomfortable. She was nothing like Frances and Ginny. There was a hardness to her face that no smile could disguise. He knew what Frances had endured over the years, but it had made her guarded, not hard and he worried about Jessie being too long in her company.

Adele made conversation through the mirror and he replied to her reflection, all the time watching Jessie out of the corner of his eye as she applied her own lipstick. He longed to kiss her again. As if she could read his thoughts, she grinned at him and carried on, pressing her lips together and pouting.

'Do you want to go out front?' she asked him. 'See the show.'

'Of course he doesn't,' Adele interrupted. 'He's come all this way to see you. I can keep him entertained while you're onstage.'

Jessie frowned at her. Was she jealous? He hoped so. He smiled and she got up and took hold of his hand. 'I thought you might like to see it. It's a marvellous show.'

'I'm sure it is,' he said. 'But I'd rather stay with you.'

When she got her call, Jessie led him downstairs and into the darkness of the wings. She stepped in front of him and when he wrapped his arms about her waist she put her hands over his while she waited to go on. When it was almost her time, she released his hands, kissed them, stepped forward a little, ready for her cue, and when it came he watched her stride confidently out, almost a little run to centre stage, the audience greeting her with applause. He stepped forward as far as he dared, to watch. It was odd how she suddenly became something other than who she was, transforming in front of his eyes, as if she was made of air. She turned his way and beamed a smile that warmed him before turning her back and giving herself to the audience. He watched, enchanted, and wished she would give herself over to him so completely. She did a little patter with the audience before she went into the next song. It was new; she was more confident in the way she spoke to them and walked about the stage. She was becoming more sophisticated and somehow it took the edge off the freshness she'd had when he'd first seen her perform at the Empire.

At the end of the show he waited in the dressing room while the two women changed, turning away as Adele removed her clothes without a care, glad Jessie had more modesty. 'Come and join us at the pub, Harry,' Adele said, adjusting her skirt. 'Just a quick one. You must be dying of thirst.'

He could murder a beer. He looked to Jessie.

'We could go for a quick one?' she said.

'That's settled, then. We'll be at the Duke of York's.'

* * *

They stayed for half an hour, then Harry whispered into Jessie's hair, 'Is it selfish of me to want you all to myself?'

'No, not selfish at all.' She felt exactly the same.

They said their goodbyes and headed down towards the seafront, crossing the road to walk along the promenade, peering into the ornate shelters, looking for one that was not already occupied by courting couples. It might have been cold and miserable, but they weren't the only ones looking for a quiet spot of their own, and the beaches were out of bounds. Large concrete blocks prevented access and rolls of barbed wire curled along the railings of the esplanade. Lookout posts were spaced at intervals, platforms surrounded by sandbags, sappers keeping watch throughout the night. Eventually they found a spot where they could stand and watch the churning of the distant sea. 'Did you manage to get somewhere to stay?' She huddled close to him, and he lifted his arm to put it about her shoulders.

'One of the lads has an aunt who lives off The Lanes. She's put me up for the night. Very kind of her.'

'People are kind, aren't they, on the whole. Of course one has to make an exception for our landlady, Mrs Barrett.'

He laughed. 'Is she still as bad?' She had written of her in her letters. It had made him laugh when she told him of all the excuses the woman had made about the lack of hot water and skimping on the rations.

'She's worse. Can you believe it? I've never met such a mean and miserable woman in my life. She's worse than Aunt Iris, and that's saying something.'

He laughed at her, babbling away. It was so good to be in her company, to smile, to forget. He looked out across the dark sea, the grey clouds sweeping over the sky, glad that for a couple of days he didn't have to be up in the air. The headlines were focused on London, but the lads were still battling elsewhere, trying to protect the industries in the Midlands, the Rolls-Royce factory, the steel manufacturing in Sheffield, the railway works in Derby. He briefly wondered when the Germans would move away from London and bomb the major cities. At least Jessie would be well out of it. The show would leave Brighton and move to Eastbourne. He hoped she'd be safer there.

She shivered and they began walking again to keep warm. A couple came out of the shadows of a shelter and Harry quickly pulled Jessie into it, the two of them glad to be sitting down on the bench. She stopped talking and he switched off his torch, laid it behind him. He drew her close put his hands to her face, kissed her, then kissed her again, each time longer and harder. He could taste the salt on her lips and on her skin. She smelled fresh and clean, and he wondered if she wanted him as badly as he wanted her. He removed one hand from her face, unbuttoned her coat, her blouse, and placed it inside, felt the warmth of her breast, the beat of her heart. She didn't object, kissing him more fiercely, unbuttoning his jacket and shirt. He felt the cold air on his skin, and she placed her hands on his chest. He wanted to go further, wanted to be a part of her and she a part of him. They kissed until he knew he had to draw away, before he went too far, frightened her away.

He released her and the two of them buttoned themselves up in the darkness, and he slipped his arm about her shoulder again. She leaned her head on his chest and for a time they didn't say anything, the two of them listening to the crash of the waves on the shore, the suck of water on the shingle as it receded. He kissed the top of her head. 'Is being onstage all that you dreamed of, Jessie?'

She hesitated. 'It is. But not quite.'

'Because of?'

She sat up. 'The war of course. It's been all stop and start. I don't feel I've made any progress.' She reached for his hand, linked her fingers with his. 'I feel such a child sometimes, moaning about not following a dream. But I want Mum to have her own house, one that belongs to her, with her own key and her own gate...'

'And roses around the door,' he said, finishing the picture for her.

She put her head on his chest again. 'Something like that. Is it stupid to still have a dream, Harry?'

'We all have to have our dreams, Jess. Of what the future might look like. Something to keep us going through the bad times. Dreams are good. I don't want to imagine a future under German occupation, do you? That's what keeps me focused.'

'Gosh, that's a bit morbid.'

'It's not, darling. We both want the same – something better.' The wind picked up and he felt around for his torch, shone it on his watch. 'Better get a shift on to get you back in time for Mrs Barrett's curfew.'

'But you didn't tell me what your dream was?'

He took hold of her hand, kissed her fingers and they started walking.

'That's easy.'

She stopped. His eyes had adjusted to the darkness, and he could see her hair flapping wildly about her face. He would fight every enemy that existed to keep her safe.

'What is it?'

'That I won't have to leave you on the doorstep when I kiss you goodnight.' It was all he thought of. Being with her made the world worth fighting for. 'Now come on, droopy drawers, or I'll have to fight Mrs Barrett the Battleaxe to let you get your beauty sleep.' They ran along the promenade, laughing at the very thought of it. One day they'd be going home together. Until then, like all of his pals, he had a war to fight.

25

Mrs Frame had not been allowed to remove her coat. 'You look awful,' Frances told her. 'You should have sent Ted with a message instead of dragging yourself out here.'

'I didn't want to let you down. I know Bridget was expected. Did she get here before midnight?'

Bridget had become a regular visitor as she delivered her messages to the Admiralty along the length of the east coast. She got on well with Ruby, the two of them often going off to play tennis at Barretts Recreation Ground if the weather was favourable. Not that there'd be any opportunity for it now. They were already a week into November.

'She did. I've had plenty of sleep. Don't you worry.' She pressed her hand to the woman's shoulder. Mrs Frame was a stout woman and strong as a horse, but she was suffering with a dreadful cold. 'I don't want you struggling on and then going down with something much worse. There's very little to do that I can't do myself for a few days. Imogen's at school and Ruby's on hand.'

Ruby was useless regarding anything domestic, but lately Mrs

Frame had managed to rope her in to doing small chores, such as helping her peg the clothes on the line and bringing them in when they were dried. Mrs Frame pursed her lips. 'She's better than she was.' They exchanged a smile and Mrs Frame ran a handkerchief under her nose. They both agreed it was important to get Ruby to do something, although Mrs Frame was reluctant to let her have too much run of the kitchen. 'How I laughed when she had to hang up her own underwear. Good job she didn't have to hang my Ted's long johns.'

Frances grinned. 'We'll save that for another day. Now, will you get yourself home and back to bed.'

The housekeeper reluctantly agreed and when she had gone, Frances went into the pantry to sort out what they would have for dinner. She had lied to Mrs Frame. Bridget had arrived in the dead of night. She had lain there listening for the sound of her bike along the road. The last few nights had been relatively undisturbed by visits from the Luftwaffe, but she would often lie awake, worrying about Johnny, the baby, the theatre, everything a jumble, tossing and turning, wondering whether she was doing the right thing by everyone. It had been wise for Jack to suggest they turn the Palace to film, for that was where the profit was, and it was much less of a worry than seeing shows in and out each week – but the panto would require lot more effort on her part. She only hoped Ruby would honour her commitment to take care of the choreography or that would fall on her shoulders too. She pressed her hand to her bump. Please God it would be an easy pregnancy.

When she came out of the pantry, Ruby was sitting at the kitchen table. 'I thought I heard Mrs Frame.'

'You did. I sent her home.'

Ruby looked worried. 'Have you given her notice?'

'Dear Lord, of course not. She's ill. Too ill to run around

looking after women who are perfectly capable of looking after themselves. We can manage for a couple of days, can't we?' She tried to sound encouraging. Mr Brown was laid in the middle of the kitchen floor, basking in the warm sunlight that streamed through the window and Frances stepped around him as she made her way to the table with a bag of flour.

'It's very quiet without Imogen,' Ruby said as Frances placed the weighing scales on the table.

'It is.' Frances picked up a weight and placed it on the plate.

'It must be awful for the parents who've had to send their children away from the cities again.'

Frances nodded, got up to fetch some cold water, skirting around the dog, thinking how lovely it must be to stretch out and snooze all day. 'If they bombard as they are doing elsewhere, I'll have to consider going away myself.'

Ruby paled. 'What would I do?'

'Stay here? You wouldn't be able to come with me, Ruby, unless I was able to rent something privately. It's always an option.'

Ruby started wringing her hands together and Frances pressed her own gently on Ruby's to stop her. 'We'll sort something out. Don't let's worry about these things unless we have to.' Ruby nodded and Frances's heart went out to her, but she had to think of her children first. 'Why don't you take Mr Brown out for his walk. Unless you'd like to make the dinner?' Frances had learned that the easiest way to calm Ruby's anxiety was to distract her. As she had expected, Ruby got up and went to get Mr Brown's lead. The dog quickly found his feet and sat in front of her.

'I'll walk the dog.'

'You could do both?'

'Maybe tomorrow.' She picked up the lead and fastened it to his collar, and slipped out of the house.

* * *

When Ruby returned, Frances was on the telephone in the hall. She turned her back to her as she entered so Ruby took Mr Brown into the kitchen and closed the door. When Frances joined her a few minutes later, she was obviously distressed, fastening her coat buttons and looking about the room for her handbag. 'I have to go. Patsy needs me. You'll have to take care of everything.'

Ruby lifted the handbag and passed it to Frances.

'Is everything all right?' It was rare to see her sister-in-law so flustered.

'What?' She opened her bag, checked inside it, snapped it shut. 'No. No, it isn't.' She sank down into a chair. 'Colin's ship has been torpedoed. I must go to her and the boys.' She put her hand to her mouth. 'Oh, dear God, those poor little boys.'

Ruby had met them only a handful of times and both Patsy and her husband had been kindly enough to her, considering they knew all about the problems she'd caused in the past. Frances and Patsy were as close as sisters and she was distraught. Ruby wished she could do something to help. 'Shall I call for a taxi?'

Frances shook her head, got up. 'No, I'll take a bus. By the time I walk to the stop there'll be one due.' Frances seemed all of a dither, unable to think, and it jolted Ruby into action.

'I'll take care of Bridget. Don't worry.'

'Thanks, Ruby. That will be...' She paused, pressing her lips together. Ruby wanted to comfort her but didn't know how.

'Would you like me to collect Imogen from school?'

Frances put her hand to her forehead and stared down at the floor. She looked close to tears but didn't give in to them. 'Yes, yes please. If you will.' She fixed her beret into place. 'I don't know when I'll be back...'

'It's all right, Frances,' she said, hoping to reassure her. 'I'll manage.' She followed her out to the front door. And as Frances stepped out, Ruby grabbed hold of her arm. 'Tell Patsy I'm sorry for her loss.'

Frances gave her a small smile, tears pricking at her eyes. 'I will.'

* * *

When Bridget got up, Ruby was doing her best to peel potatoes. She had spread a sheet of newspaper over the kitchen table, as she'd seen Mrs Frame do so many times, a large pan to one side of her and a colander full of King Edwards covered in soil to the other. Mrs Frame would despair of the thickness of the peel on the first few, but she was slowly getting the hang of it. 'Is it the army, Ruby, or the navy?'

Ruby frowned.

'The potatoes. How many are you expecting to dinner?'

Ruby dropped her hands to the colander. 'I wasn't sure how many to do so I just kept peeling.'

Bridget pulled out a chair and sat opposite her. 'Where's Mrs Frame? Frances?' Ruby told her. 'Oh, Lord, how very sad. It's damn awful. How I wish we could put an end to it. Like a tennis game. Love all. That would be enough.'

'If only,' Ruby replied, wishing things could be settled so easily. She sat for a while, deep in thought until Bridget spoke and snapped her back into the present.

'Want any help?'

Ruby hesitated. 'I think Frances was going to make a pie. I've never made pastry before.'

Bridget laughed. 'You've not done much at all by the look of those potatoes. Finish that one and we'll see what's what in the pantry.'

'I'm supposed to be looking after you.'

Bridget corrected her. 'We're all looking out for each other, don't forget that.' She lifted cans and moved jars of preserves. 'You're not alone, Ruby,' she said over her shoulder. 'We're all doing things we've never done before.'

Her words struck home. 'I thought I was the only one making a hash of things.'

'You're not, believe me. But the more you do something the easier it becomes. I can't sing or dance.'

'You could if you wanted to.'

'Exactly. You could ride a motorbike if you wanted to.'

Ruby put down the knife and took the pan to the sink, filled it with water then put it on the stove. 'I doubt it.'

'Of course you could. We've never been allowed to try most things, have we, us girls. But we can do anything if we put our mind to it. Let's get this out of the way then you can have your first lesson.'

Ruby laughed. 'You're not serious?'

'I am.' Bridget found an apron and tied it about her waist. 'Chop, chop, Ruby. We haven't got all day.'

Ruby found some apples in the pantry and they stewed some down with a little honey then left them to cool. She enjoyed working alongside Bridget, less afraid of getting things wrong. Frances intimidated her. She was never unkind, but Ruby knew that her incompetence annoyed her.

'You never talk much of your time on the stage,' Bridget said as she wiped down the table after the pie had been made and put in the oven.

'That's because I want to forget it.'

'It can't have been all bad.'

Ruby considered her answer. 'It wasn't, but I've had enough of it. My brother and I have been working since we were small children, six or seven. We were either rehearsing or performing. It's not as glamorous as it looks.'

'I didn't think for a minute that it was. Some people think my job sounds thrilling. But it's not all riding along with the breeze. There are bumps and potholes on the road. Nothing is ever as it seems, is it?' She rinsed the cloth and hung it over the tap, then leaned against the kitchen cupboard. 'It must have been wonderful to travel, especially around America.'

Ruby couldn't argue. 'It was. We met some really wonderful people.'

'A man?'

Ruby changed the subject. She'd already revealed too much. She took off her apron and hung it on the back of the pantry door. 'Ready for my first lesson when you are.'

They went outside to the front of the house and Bridget pushed the bike off the prop stand, talked Ruby through the throttle, brakes and gears, and gave her a general lesson of how the bike worked and started it up by kicking down on the kick start lever. Bridget put on her cap and pulled down her goggles and shouted, 'Get on the back.' Ruby hitched up her skirt and put her leg astride the bike, positioned herself behind Bridget who called over her shoulder, 'Put your arms about my waist and hold on.'

Ruby did as she was told and Bridget twisted the throttle and roared off down the street, leaving a trail of dust and petrol fumes in their wake. Ruby gasped then burst into laughter, loving the freedom, the speed, as Bridget rode around the block. She stopped the bike at the entrance of the park and shouted for Ruby to sit up front. 'Get your balance. Feel the floor either side. Now, tell me how you're going to start and more importantly how you're going to stop.'

Ruby recited back the things Bridget had told her. Bridget nodded her approval. 'Take it slowly and only to the house. I'll run along beside you.' She handed over her hat and googles and Ruby put them on. She was terrified but Bridget had such confidence in her that she was sure she could do it. If she fell, then so what. A little bit of damage to herself, maybe some to the bike. At least she would have tried. Following Bridget's instructions she engaged the gear, twisted the throttle and released the clutch. The bike moved with a sudden jerk and she giggled nervously. She wobbled, stalled, started again, and in that manner, stopping and starting, she made it back to the house, Bridget trotting along by her side. When Ruby came to a stop Bridget took hold of the handlebars. 'That's enough for today. I might get into trouble for wasting fuel, but we'll make a messenger of you yet.'

They walked together to collect Imogen from school and Ruby told Bridget that she would be choreographing the pantomime. 'Oh, I do hope I'll be here to see it. I love a pantomime. Nothing quite like it, is there? And the best of it is that the baddy always gets caught in the end.'

Bridget linked her arm in hers and Ruby was taken aback. She'd never been close enough to anyone but her brother to link arms, not offstage, but as they walked along in the autumn sunshine, she became more comfortable with it. 'I hope you're here too, Bridget.' For the first time in weeks Ruby began to think she might enjoy it after all.

26

Frances had had plenty of time to think on the bus, working out what she could possibly do or say to be of comfort to Patsy. They'd been friends for years, Patsy taking her under her wing when she first came over from Ireland. Frances was meant to be living with her mother's sister in Blackpool but her aunt had not been interested in babysitting her young niece, and had left her to her own devices. Patsy had stepped in and made sure she was safe, taught her how to manage her money and numerous other things that Frances had no knowledge of back then. Patsy had been the first person she turned to when she found she was pregnant with Johnny's child, and Colin had been like a father to her in many ways, his calm and steady presence reassuring when she was most in need. Oh, dear Lord, how would Patsy manage without him?

The bus turned into Cheapside and stopped opposite the forge. She could hear the children in the playground of the school a little way down the road. The airfield of RAF Grimsby was rapidly expanding and a gaggle of girls in WAAF uniform sauntered along towards their camp, located in the fields close to the windmill. It was hard to think back to a time when they weren't at war. It had seeped into every corner of their lives, and with Colin's death the true cost of it was brought closer to home.

She got off and walked up to the small turn in the road, to the white cottage set a short way back from the footpath, and stopped at the gate before opening it. A few brave roses still bloomed and the bold hydrangeas either side of the front door were hanging on to the last bit of colour. So many times she had walked down this path to her child, taking comfort in knowing Imogen was cared for, was loved. It was her turn to give comfort now. This was the house she had come to when Imogen was born, and where Imogen had stayed when Frances got work and couldn't take her with her. The Dawkins family were her family, and Imogen loved the boys as brothers. Frances ran her hand over her swollen belly. Would it be a boy or girl this time? Would Johnny live to see his child born? She pushed the thought away. Colin's death had made everything more fragile and, right now, she needed to be strong.

Patsy was in the kitchen, watching her sons through the window. She turned when Frances walked in, and gave her a weak smile. Frances dropped her bag to the floor and hurried to hold her friend in her arms. Patsy was limp, her life force drained away and she held her as long as she could, hoping to somehow imbue her with strength. Frances kissed her forehead and released her. 'Oh, darling. When did you find out?'

'This morning.' She dragged a small telegram from her apron pocket and handed it over. 'I got the boys out of school. I didn't want to be on my own.'

Frances read the simple statement, that the minesweeper he'd been on had been mined and that Colin was missing presumed dead. Patsy bit down on her lip and tried not to cry and Frances embraced her once more, holding on to her as the tears silently fell. 'Do the boys know?'

'I didn't want to tell them, not yet. How can I steal their joy?' They stood shoulder to shoulder watching them play in the garden. Bobby, the eldest was only eight, his brother Colly six. The two of them had been raking leaves into a pile but the rake was quickly tossed aside, and they both fell into it, wafting their arms like wings, scattering leaves, undoing all the work they had just done. But they were having fun, and that was all that mattered.

'It doesn't seem real,' Patsy told her. 'I read the telegram over and over again. Do you think it's a mistake?'

Frances wanted to tell her that it was, that there was every chance that Colin would be found, but when she looked at her friend she couldn't lie. This woman had made her face up to her own painful situation and make plans. She would never have been able to keep Imogen otherwise.

'I don't think they'd send it unless they were certain.'

Patsy held it again, staring blankly at it, then pushed it back in her apron pocket, holding on to it as if she were holding on to Colin's hand.

Frances felt her throat thicken. She swallowed hard and removed her coat and hat, then guided Patsy into a chair. 'I bet you've had nothing to eat all morning. Let me get the kettle on and we'll share something.' She opened the cupboards and took out some bread and jam, conscious of using their rations. She would make it up somehow; what did it matter at a time like this? She made the boys sandwiches and lemonade and took it out to them.

They sat up in the pile of leaves when they saw her, cheerful at their unexpected release from school. 'Is Imogen with you, Auntie Frances?'

'Not today, Bobby.' She placed the plates and tumblers on the garden bench. 'Picnic today, boys.'

'Yippee.' They snatched up the sandwiches and ate greedily. She tousled Colly's hair and went back inside.

'Have you been able to contact your mother? Your sister?'

'I phoned a neighbour to get word. It's times like this I regret not living nearer to my family.'

Her words hit home. Frances had not been back to Ireland since before Imogen was born and had only told her parents by letter once she and Johnny had been reunited. As an unmarried mother there would've been no question of keeping her unborn child if she'd gone home, and she couldn't countenance the thought of giving her child away. That things had all worked out, she could only describe as a miracle. But happy endings didn't mean they were easy.

'Your mother will perhaps already be on her way.'

Patsy nodded. 'I'd better make a bed up for her.'

'I can do that.'

'We can do it together.'

Frances didn't stop her. Patsy's way of coping was keeping busy, but it didn't follow that she had to do it alone. Frances took sheets from the airing cupboard, and they went into the small box room that had once been Imogen's. It had been painted the colour of calamine lotion and small framed pictures of pixies adorned the walls.

'Do you know what you're going to say to the boys?'

Patsy tucked in the top corner of the sheet and looked out into the garden. 'Only that Dad won't be coming home.' She threw back her shoulders. 'I can't let them see me being weak. It will frighten them even more.'

'They'll want to take care of you.'

Patsy gave a small smile. 'No, it's me who's here to look after them.'

* * *

After making the bed, they went into the sitting room. Colin's ashtray was still on the arm of his chair, waiting for his return. Patsy picked it up and held it for a while before placing it gently onto the mantelpiece. 'His minesweeper, HMT *Reed*, was hit by a mine. I phoned the Royal Naval Patrol Service headquarters in Lowestoft to find out what information I could, but they couldn't tell me much more than I already knew.' Frances made her sit down. Patsy stared at the windowsill where the framed wedding photo took pride of place. 'I always lived with the fear that his ship wouldn't come back. A lot of women are in my position these days.'

'It doesn't make it any easier to bear.'

'No. No, I suppose it doesn't.' She fumbled in her pocket again and Frances knew she was reaching for the telegram.

'Have you enough to manage on?' she asked, then offered, embarrassed, 'Do you need any money?' It was such a reversal of fortune. Those very words had been said to her more times than she cared to remember by both Colin and Patsy over the years.

Patsy shook her head. 'Colin is... was a good earner. We put money by. It'll keep me going while I work out what to do.' She got up and turned the knob of the wireless until she found some music and let it play in the background. She smiled at Frances. 'You're much bigger than when I last saw you. Felt the baby kick yet?'

'All the time.' Frances smiled. 'I think this one is definitely a tap dancer.'

Al Jolson came on the radio singing 'You Made Me Love You'.

'That was playing when I met Colin on Cleethorpes Pier.' Patsy paused, remembering. 'What a wet and windy summer that was.'

'He always said he caught a mermaid,' Frances reminded her.

She gave a teary smile before her face crumpled and she reached for her handkerchief. Frances got up and went to her and held her in her arms as the tears came, then the sobs. 'That's it, lovely girl. You have a good old cry.' She wanted to cry herself; Colin had been such a kind and steady sort. How she longed for him to be here now, with his words of comfort and wisdom. In time she settled Patsy on the sofa and eventually she fell asleep. Frances covered her with a blanket and left the room, gently closing the door behind her.

The boys came in, hungry, and Frances made them something to eat and when the phone rang, she answered it, keeping her voice low. It was Patsy's mother telling her she was on her way but wouldn't be there tonight. The train had been cancelled and she would get the early bus in the morning. Frances promised to stay with Patsy until she arrived. When she hung up the receiver, she called Ruby.

'Did you remember to get Imogen?'

'Of course I did.' Ruby asked about Patsy.

'It's the shock.' She could feel her own voice breaking. The boys were in the kitchen playing Ludo. Chattering away. It didn't matter if their grandmother came today, tomorrow or next week; telling them would be the hardest thing Patsy would ever have to do. 'I won't be back tonight. I'm waiting for the boys' grandma to arrive.'

'Don't worry about anything here, Frances,' Ruby told her. 'Believe it or not, I've got everything in hand.'

Frances quietly replaced the receiver, grateful that after so long Ruby sounded confident.

It was the one bright glimmer in the saddest of days.

27

Jessie had waved Harry off at Brighton station not knowing when she would see him again. That had been more than a month ago and, in that time, there had been no let-up on the bombing of London. Each day the newspapers carried the same reports, of how the Londoners were carrying on, the Underground platforms full each night, thousands of people homeless, the unbearable loss of loved ones. She wondered how they could bear it – but what else could they do but endure. She read a report of a cinema that had been bombed, the usherettes tearing their blouses to make bandages, and thought of Ginny. Her letters came in a steady stream, mostly Ginny venting her frustration at being lumbered with her father, but also of the friends she'd made while working at the cinema. She wrote of Mavis, a young mum who worked with her most nights, trying to make ends meet while her husband was away in the army, her mother looking after the kiddies. Things were dreadfully hard, but it was bringing out the best in people – and sometimes the worst, if Ginny's father was anything to go by. Ginny had replied that her father was like that long before the war came along.

It was mid-November and the shops were already decorated for Christmas and Jessie had taken every opportunity to visit the department stores, choosing small gifts to take home to her mum and Eddie, for Geraldine and her friends. The selection was far less than last year and the quality poorer, but she wanted to get something. She bought her mother a knitting bag and Eddie a toolbox, imagining their delight when they opened them. By far the best part of earning good money was being able to treat those she loved.

They'd left Brighton and travelled to Eastbourne for a week, then west to Torquay and had recently arrived in Bournemouth. The show would end mid-December when the theatre closed for panto rehearsals. She hadn't expected to be appearing in one herself, but to her delight Frances had written to ask her if she was available to star in the one they were producing at the Palace. The subject was Dick Whittington; would she consider playing the title role as principal boy? It had been an easy yes on her part, if she could work things out with Bernie. She tempered her excitement, waiting for his response, which when it came was positive. Vernon Leroy couldn't confirm a date when *A Touch of Silver* would return to the West End so she was free to accept the part. She'd been absolutely thrilled, knowing she could spend Christmas with her mum and Eddie. Topping the bill at the Palace was a huge step forward and she was truly grateful that Frances had thought of her. It was such a kind gesture, but she expected nothing less from her friend. Frances had been looking out for her from the first day they'd met and it appeared would continue to do so. The script had arrived two days later, giving her plenty of time to learn her lines in the dressing room of Bournemouth Pavilion.

'You're not concentrating,' Adele snapped. 'I need the line when you go on board the ship.'

Jessie put her hand to her brow and tried to remember the words, but her head was all over the place. 'I can't think, Adele. I just can't.'

Adele had put down the script. 'Hey, don't get so upset. I thought it might take your mind off things, a distraction. It's not working, is it?'

Jessie shook her head. They were between performances, the first house having gone well. Jessie had arrived in the theatre at four and waited for Harry's call at the stage door but it hadn't come. She'd lifted the receiver numerous times, checking that there was a dial tone until the stage doorman had told her she was interrupting the line, and it would prevent the calls from coming through. She'd still been by the telephone when the show went up, and in the end, Adele had come to find her. That morning the *Daily Telegraph* had carried a photo of Coventry Cathedral – or what remained of it, and details of the raid. It was unthinkable that so much destruction could be wrought in one night.

'He'll be fine, I'm sure,' she'd said, trying to be of comfort. 'The phone lines might be down. He might be sleeping it off. There might be any number of reasons he hasn't called.' She'd taken Jessie by the elbow and led her back to the dressing room. 'Come on,' she said, taking charge. 'You've got a show to do.'

Jessie had no recollection of her performance that night, but she'd done the best she could, and by the sound of the applause the audience hadn't been aware of anything untoward. Adele had remained in the wings, watching her the entire time and it had helped her concentrate. Jessie had never been quite sure how to take Adele from one day to the next, but tonight she had been grateful for her solid presence. When the curtain came down at the end of the show Jessie raced offstage and to the stage door for news – but there was none.

Back in the dressing room, she went through the motions of taking off her costume, her make-up. She rested her hand on her father's make-up bag, closed her eyes and whispered a silent prayer for him to keep Harry safe and as she did so, the tears she'd been holding back all evening fell onto her cheeks. Adele put her arm on her shoulder.

'You're making it more than it is. It's a missed phone call.'

Jessie rubbed the tears away with the back of her hand. 'Something's wrong. Harry always does what he says he will.'

'Well, he's not like all the men I've ever met.'

Jessie wiped her nose on a rag. She'd seen some of the men Adele went out with. There seemed to be no discrimination on her part. 'He's special.'

'He is. He's probably down the pub right now – which is where we should be.'

'Oh, no, I couldn't, Adele. Not tonight. I just want to go back to the digs.'

'Same as you do every night.' She took Jessie's hand and pulled her to her feet. 'This is exactly the night you need to come out. Have a drink. Forget everything. That's what we're all doing, trying to forget. You might as well come and join us.'

So far she'd resisted going out after the show with Adele. She didn't mind going in the pub in the daytime; that was different. Most of the cast seem to adopt a local close to the theatre and when she became melancholy and longed for home, she would join them for an hour or two. Adele picked up Jessie's bag and pushed it into her hand. 'Come on. One little drink won't hurt.'

Jessie hesitated.

'You know that the girls are saying you think you're a cut above. That you're too good for the likes of us.'

Jessie was appalled. 'That's not true. How could they even think it?'

'I know that, but you know what people are like.' Adele refreshed her lipstick, picked up her own handbag. 'You do know that when you get back to London you'll have to change or you won't last five minutes when things start taking off? People will expect it. Best to get used to it slowly while we're here, wean yourself in. You don't want to make enemies of people you have to work with, do you?'

There was sense in what she was saying. Bernie was taking her to The Ivy when the show returned to London. He'd told her she needed to be seen in all the right places, meet the right people. That was the way to make those all-important connections. It would all happen when they got back. But what if they didn't get back? What if Harry...? Tears threatened again. She wanted to stop the thoughts exploding in her head. She wanted to be sick. She didn't know what she wanted, only for it all to stop.

'Just this once,' she told Adele. 'But only one drink.'

* * *

Adele linked her arm in Jessie's and led her away from the theatre, weaving down the side streets until they came to a door at the side of a shop, a small blue light glowing over it. Adele knocked on the door three times. It was opened by a thickset man who ushered them in, closing the door quickly behind them. They went down a flight of stairs and into a large room beneath the shop. It was packed with bodies and a thick fug of cigarette smoke hung above their heads. She glimpsed Bettina standing in the corner with three of the dancers and a couple of lads in naval uniform. Adele weaved them through the crowd to join them. Bettina couldn't hide her surprise and Jessie saw her glance to Adele, eyebrows raised. 'Jessie, glad you could make it.'

'I tried hard enough.' Adele laughed. Bettina introduced her to the lads in their company as Bruce and Stan. The dancers smiled but Jessie could sense their animosity, that she was an intruder. Adele had been right, she should have come sooner. They must think her an awful snob.

'I'll get you a drink,' Adele said.

'No, you won't,' Bruce said. 'I'll get these. What would you like?'

'Lemonade,' Jessie said. The girls sniggered and Jessie felt the heat rise in her neck. She didn't want to be here anyway; she should have gone home.

'I'll come with you,' Adele said. 'Help you carry them.'

When they came back, Adele handed her a drink. Jessie sipped, spluttered. 'That's not lemonade.'

'It is.' Adele smiled. 'I told them to put a gin in it.'

'Adele,' Bettina admonished. 'That's a nasty trick.'

'It's not a trick,' Adele said quietly. 'She needs it. Her chap's missing.'

'He's not missing,' Jessie cried. 'He didn't call. That's all.'

'There you are,' Adele said, lighting up a cigarette and blowing out the smoke, wafting it up into the air with her hand. 'I told you it was only a missed phone call. Nothing to worry about.'

Jessie sipped at the gin and lemonade. It tasted nice, refreshing, and she slowly began to relax and get to know the girls. With the noise and the chatter there wasn't really room to think, and she had a sudden understanding of why her father drank; to forget all he'd been through in the Great War, and to wash away the fear. Someone handed her another drink, and she took it, then another, the smoke stinging her eyes, her head beginning to swim. After a while it was hard to stand, and she began to sway. 'I think she's had enough,' Bettina said to Adele. Jessie felt she was going to vomit. Adele grabbed hold of her elbow.

'Come on, little star. Better get you home.' No sooner were they out on the street than Jessie retched and was sick in the gutter. She wiped her mouth with her hand. Her head felt as if it was filled with concrete, her legs as if they were made of rubber, and she stood up a little, staggered and was sick again. What would her mother think if she could see her now?

Adele put her arm under Jessie's to support her and walked her home, led her up to her bedroom. Thankfully they were in a small hotel and there was no Mrs Barrett, no curfew. Jessie fell on the bed and Adele removed Jessie's shoes and let them drop on the floor. Through blurry eyes Jessie watched her moving about the room. Adele pressed a towel into her hands. 'Use that if you want to be sick again.' Jessie managed to nod her thanks and mercifully, fell asleep.

* * *

Adele lit a cigarette and sat down on the stool in front of the dressing table. Through it she could see Jessie spark out on the bed and thought she'd better hang around, just in case the girl was sick again. She'd never met anyone like her, green as a Brussels sprout and just as tempting, but she had star quality written all over her. On the dressing table was a half-written letter and a pile of envelopes. Adele figured she envied Jessie's friendships more than her talent. It seemed unfair she had both when Adele had neither – well, not to the same extent. She'd receive the odd postcard now and again, a letter from her mother if she ever gave her a thought, but her friends came and went with whatever show she was in at the time. She'd learned to let go and move on whereas it appeared Jessie held on to things and took them with her.

She picked up a couple and skimmed them, more for filling

time than an expectation of finding anything to gossip about. Reading reaffirmed her suspicions; there was nothing riveting, just stuff about a load of people Jessie talked about, the lady from the pub, the couple who lived by the theatre. She saw one with a Sheffield postmark and began to read. In it, her friend Ginny had written about it being the anniversary of something terrible.

At least it freed me from forever being connected to Billy Lane. What kind of life would it have been for me otherwise?

It had to be a miscarriage, or an abortion. The girl hadn't written in it so many words but reading between the lines it was blindingly obvious. She checked Jessie through the mirror. No wonder little Miss Perfect had been so upset with bad boy Billy. God, the girl hadn't lived at all. He wasn't the first bloke to get a girl in trouble. She'd had a narrow escape herself more than once. But if you knew the right people... Jessie moaned, leaned over the side of the bed and was sick into the towel. Adele quickly replaced the letter in the envelope and went over to her.

'Oh, darling. Do you want a glass of water?'

Jessie managed to nod. Adele poured her a glass and took it over to her, helped her sit up a little. 'Sip, don't gulp,' she urged Jessie, pressing her hand to Jessie's forehead.

Jessie did as she was told. 'Thank you so much, I'm sorry to keep you awake.'

'Shh, don't be daft. Anyone would do the same. It was my fault. I didn't realise you couldn't take your drink.' She took the glass from Jessie and placed it on the bedside table, then tucked the sheet around her. 'Try to get some sleep. Hopefully you'll feel better in the morning.'

* * *

When Jessie woke it was almost noon and she struggled to sit up, her head thick and her throat like sandpaper. She reached for the glass at the side of her bed and saw a note, picked it up and read it.

Harry called at 10. Airfield communication down.
Told you not to worry! Delly

She put the glass down and sobbed uncontrollably. She had never felt so wretched in her life.

28

December brought much colder weather, mornings of either crisp frosts or thick fogs. Ginny eked out the coal and other supplies as best she could, wanting to keep her father warm and nourished if only for the selfish reason that it would allow her to finally leave. The thought of spending Christmas with him brought back bitter memories, of how he'd spoiled so many with his drunken and loutish behaviour. He wouldn't have the opportunity this time. Ginny had kept him well clear of the booze. Aunt Maggie had invited them to join her family for Christmas and Ginny had been quick to accept. At least she wouldn't have the strain of being cheerful for his benefit, and if he gave her the runaround his sister would soon put him in his place. As would Uncle Derek. But that was almost two weeks away, and there was a lot she could do before then.

She made her father something to eat and, checking the blackout was in place all over the house, she picked up her gas mask and put the strap over her shoulder.

'I've asked Betty next door but one to check in on you at five. I won't be back until ten,' she told him, pulling on her woollen hat and wrapping her scarf about her neck.

'I don't need no bugger checking on me. It's like being in prison.'

'If the coppers find out what's in the room above your head you might very well be.' At least if he was locked up at His Majesty's pleasure she'd be free of him.

'Pah, what do you ruddy know. Piss off to work. I'm sick o' the sight of yer.'

She needed no encouragement and left the house without saying goodbye.

A few kids were running down the street with an old bicycle wheel and whooping as they went along, their cheeks and noses red with effort and cold. Their joy was infectious, and she smiled as she made her way towards the Central Picture House. Wednesday was half-day closing and as the shops pulled down their blinds and turned the open signs to closed, people spilled out onto the street.

At the Central there was already a line of people waiting for the doors to open, not just for the cinema but for the billiard hall in the basement. Ginny went into the office, placed her bag and gas mask in her locker and took out her overall and cap, securing it with grips, then smoothing her hair in place with her hands. Two of the girls came in, chattering ten to the dozen.

'All ready for Christmas?' one asked the other.

'Trying to make the best of it. Got my mum some slippers from Banner's and my dad a nice bit of tobacco. It's the kiddies I want to make it special for.'

Ginny's mother would always do her best to make things special before her father rolled in drunk and spoiled things, shouting at her for wasting money they didn't have. On Christmas Day her mother was usually wearing a paper crown made from an old newspaper and sporting a black eye. Ginny was very young then, the boys too, and none of them dared say anything. Once her brother stood up to him and they saw the result, none of them were scared any more. They loathed Les Thompson, and it would have been hell but for their mother, trying to keep the peace. But at what price?

She waited for Mavis to arrive and the two of them went into the auditorium to take tickets and show people to their seats. When the lights dimmed, she took her place on the back row next to her friend. The curtains drew back and the Pathé newsreel started up. There was a reel showing bombed-out London, people sleeping on the Underground and in basements. It had looked jolly cheery, but she knew it wasn't. There was nothing cheery about smiling through at all. But what else could you do when things were so bad? This week's offering was a double feature with *The Blue Bird* with Shirley Temple, and *That's the Ticket* starring the comedian Sid Field, the latter being the most popular. People wanted to laugh. She supposed it was the release they all needed from the constant grind of getting through each day.

The first feature started and Shirley Temple sprang to life in front of them. 'It's not been a bad week, has it,' Mavis whispered, 'but we'll be packed out next week. The Lyceum and the Empire will be closed. Rehearsing the panto. Jack Buchanan in *Cinderella*.' She couldn't disguise her glee. 'One thing about the war, it's brought all the big stars up north now they can't work in London. I'm taking the kiddies on Boxing Day.'

It sent pangs of envy through Ginny. If she'd have known she was coming back to Sheffield she could have auditioned for a part. She might not have got one, but she could have tried all the same.

She showed latecomers to their seats, walking backwards,

shining her torch so they could see their way, the constant up and down of silhouettes on the screen as people went along the rows. The film wasn't her cup of tea. She preferred the musicals with Fred Astaire and Ginger Rogers. She'd hoped one day she'd be up there on the silver screen too. It only took one or two lucky breaks – and surely she was due one.

It was around seven when the film paused to the accompaniment of groans from the audience, and the familiar warning flashed up on screen that a raid was imminent. They had grown accustomed to them. The manager came on the stage and asked all who wished to leave to do so quietly and calmly. Ginny moved quickly down to the exit doors and drew back the heavy plush curtains, waited to let a few people pass before she pulled them over the doors again. The lights went down once more, and the film resumed where it had left off. Ginny went back to sit with Mavis. The hum of planes could be heard over the film, drowning out some of the dialogue. 'It sounds bad out there,' Mavis whispered. 'I hope the kiddies are all right and Mum got them down the shelter.' She didn't wait for Ginny to respond, telling herself, 'Yes, yes, of course she will. They'll be safe.'

Ginny reached across and held her hand and they sat together, quietly watching the film they had already watched many times before, the ground shaking beneath their feet.

At nine the film ended, and the manager asked people to leave and go home, or to the shelters. They were invited to stay in the billiard room on the lower floor if they wished. He opened the doors to let people out and Ginny hardly dared look at what was going on outside, hearing it was enough and the smell of smoke made her gulp for air.

'Looks like we're going to get the lot tonight,' the manager said to Ginny, and he pulled the doors to. 'They must be giving London a night off.'

She followed him down into the billiard room where hundreds of people had decided to take shelter. It was stuffy and airless and when it seemed there was a lull in the bombing, the manager came to them. 'It would be best if we made our way to the shelters, ladies. I think we'll all be safer there.' He made an announcement and they formed groups of ten, making sure there were enough men to accompany each group of women as they went out into the street.

Mavis was agitated. 'You go,' Ginny told her. 'I can manage.'

'I want to get back to my girls.' Mavis was tearful and Ginny hugged her. 'I'd rather be with 'em. Good or bad. I'll be all right; it's not far.'

Ginny watched her as she hurried in the direction of Rockingham Street. All around buildings were alight, flames leaping up into the sky. It was a clear cloudless night, a bomber's moon, allowing the Luftwaffe good vision of their intended targets. She watched people dash off into the night, the dark shapes becoming smaller, indistinct. For the first time that night she thought of her dad, and wondered whether he was thinking of her.

When the last of the groups were ready to leave, she ran with them. Every street seemed to be on fire, the night air filled with screeching and thundering as buildings crumbled and collapsed. Her heart hammered in her chest and felt like it would burst up and out of her mouth. She held her handkerchief over her mouth and nose, having no idea what to do, or where to go as she ran away from the devastation all around her. Someone said the Marples Hotel was gone. It stopped her in her tracks. The whole of the city was alight, or so it seemed to her. The blackout served no purpose; the city was laid bare: department stores, hotels, shops, churches, entire streets. It all felt like a bad dream, a waking nightmare. She stumbled along in a state of utter disbelief as people hurried past, pushing her forward with them as they made for a place of safety. At one point, she pressed herself against a wall to catch her breath and stared at a mangled bus, at cars blackened and warped. Searchlights traced through the sky and she heard the crackle of the anti-aircraft guns as they fought to bring the bombers down. It looked like hell. It looked like the end of the world.

* * *

Someone had given her a tin hat and Ginny spent the night helping where she could, escorting the lost and bewildered to the safety of the library, until someone pushed her into a chair, handed her a cup of sweet and milky tea. Her mouth was parched and her eyes stung. To the right of her people with blackened faces and burns were being tended to by women wearing Red Cross and WVS armbands. She felt totally useless as more wounded came forward. There were so many of them, and still they kept coming. She hoped her aunt was safe and her cousin, and Uncle Derek at the steel works. It was bitterly cold and away from the fires frost sparkled on the pavement in the morning light, and among the broken glass that littered the pavement.

It was after four when the all-clear sounded. She stayed there, doing what little she could, directing people towards further help, comforting crying children, praying that Mavis had got home safely to her children, until she couldn't carry on and one of the WVS ladies made her go home. She walked down the streets in a daze, her teeth beginning to chatter, not only from cold but from the shock of it all. Somewhere ahead of her 'Silent Night' was playing on a gramophone and she stared at windows, Christmas trees in the centre of them bright with tinsel, and wondered how many Christmases had already been ruined. Would there be any place for celebration after this?

The sight of Simpsons corner shop shook her as she came closer to home. It looked like it had been sliced with a knife, the roof and entire frontage gone, and as she turned onto her street her legs felt they would go from under her. The right-hand side was intact, the other like a mouth with teeth missing. Though she felt ready to collapse, she willed herself to get to where her front door should be. A team of wardens milled around, and she recognised Mrs Smith's son-in-law, Mick, standing among the rubble. A handful of her neighbours were climbing over brick and blackened wood, searching for what they could salvage. Mick came towards her. She opened her mouth, but no sound came out. Mick's face said it all, but she had to ask.

'Did he get out?'

He shook his head. 'We tried to get him to go to the shelter, but he wouldn't budge. I had to think of the wife and the mother-in-law.' He was most apologetic. 'There was nothing we could do, love. I'm sorry.'

Ginny nodded dumbly, picking her way over the rubble. There were no happy memories attached to this house. Perhaps this was the best thing that could have happened to it. She stood where the scullery had been, the yard where her mother scrubbed other people's mucky clothes to pay for Ginny's classes, and saw a scrap of blue fabric. She hobbled over to it, carefully lifting the brick and mortar, brushing away the dust from her mother's apron, and held it to her face. A huge wave of anger swept up from her toes, flooding over her entire body, and she filled her lungs and let out a huge roar. No tears, nor sorrow, but sheer anger at the misery of their lives in this house, and her sorry excuse for a father.

Mick rushed over, wrapping his arms about her, but she

couldn't find it in her to cry. When he released her, he walked her over the rubble and back onto the pavement. Ginny put her hand to her hair, knew she was a mess. She brushed at her clothing, torn and covered in soot, trying to smarten herself, to have a bit of pride, and it registered that she was still wearing her overall from the cinema. She put her hand in her pocket, and touched the silk rose Joe had given her when they'd last met. It was the only time she'd ever wished he was at her house, now that there was nothing left of it. She crumpled the apron in her hands, not knowing what to do, or where to go. Ginny wanted the comfort of her mother but knew she could never have it again. That was when the tears came, and Ginny cried for all the misery that was at last at an end.

29

The week before Christmas, Jessie boarded the train, glad to be going home. She'd bought a second-hand suitcase, which carried her Christmas presents but also the other items of clothing she'd purchased, encouraged by Adele. 'It'll all be rationed before long; everything will be bloody rationed – and you need to think ahead. You'll be wined and dined when we get back to London and you need something suitable.'

She'd told her of Bernie's promise to take her to The Ivy.

'There you are, then. You can't go in your ankle socks and flat shoes, can you?'

They had gone to Beale's department store, and she'd bought a navy two-piece and matching court shoes and bag. Adele had said it made her look old. Jessie thought it made her look sophisticated. She remembered how elegant Madeleine Moore had appeared wearing something similar. Her mother could have made her one for half the price, but it had been so exciting to go into the shop and have the assistants mill around her as she made her purchase.

Dusk was falling when she arrived at the station and she left her cases at the office, asking for them to be delivered the following morning. She walked briskly up the steep slope towards Alexandra Road, wanting to walk past the Empire for old times' sake, remembering how daunting her arrival had seemed to her back then. She'd come a long way since that first summer in 1939.

As she reached the top of Barkhouse Lane, she quickened her step and gave a gentle tap on the front window to alert her mother before opening the front door. Inside the house she took a moment to pause, full of gratitude to be home, the place where she didn't have to be anything other than herself.

Her mother was at her door by the time Jessie stirred herself, her arms open, and Jessie walked into her embrace. When her mother released her, she held on to her arms and looked her up and down. 'You look well, darling,' she told her quietly, then raising her voice said, 'I have a visitor.'

Jessie followed her mother into her room.

'Ginny! Thank God.' Her friend was sitting in one of the two armchairs that were set in the bay window and she got up to greet her. She'd lost weight, and her hair, though still the glorious red, had lost its shine. Ginny smiled, but her eyes were devoid of any warmth, and when Jessie threw her arms about her, she felt limp and lifeless. 'I read about the bombings on the train and prayed you were safe.'

'I am. I'll tell you about it, but not now. I didn't realise you were coming home today.' She smiled at Grace and picked up her battered leather bag. 'I'll leave you to it.'

'There's no need,' Grace insisted.

Ginny waved away her comment and smiled at the two of them. 'We'll have plenty of time to catch up. You must be tired.'

No matter how tired she felt, Jessie knew she was in much better shape than Ginny. But the girl couldn't be persuaded and after saying goodbye to Grace, Jessie went to the door with her, and her mother went into the kitchen.

'Where are you staying?'

'With Dolly. George and Olive invited me to stay with them over Christmas and New Year. They've been kindness itself to me.'

Jessie didn't dare ask but felt she had to. 'Your dad?'

Ginny shook her head. 'Everything's gone. My auntie Maggie and her family were bombed out. Thankfully, they were at the shelter but there's nothing left, nowhere else to go.' She hugged Jessie. 'You spend time with your lovely mum. We can see each other tomorrow.'

Jessie closed the door behind her, drew the blackout curtain over and removed her hat and coat, hanging it on the row of hooks in the hall. Back in her mother's room, she sank into the chair that Ginny had vacated. A length of twine had been hung over the mirror above the mantel and Christmas cards slipped over it. Beneath it, the gas fire burned low, the ceramic plates glowing red along the bottom row of squares. Her mum came in and handed Jessie a mug of hot milk.

'Tough journey?'

'Not too bad. How long has Ginny been here?'

'This house? A half hour. She arrived a couple of days ago. Dolly let me know she was coming.'

'She looks terrible.'

Grace nodded. 'She's been through the mill. She was caught up in the Blitz. I gather her colleague didn't make it home to her children, which was upsetting enough for her without everything else that happened.' Her mum checked her watch then tugged at the curtains in the bay window and sat down. 'When Ginny got home, her house had suffered a direct hit. Her father was killed outright.'

'Oh, how awful. For all of them.' The girl had had more than her fair share of bad things. 'Poor Ginny. I know she and her dad didn't get on, but it must have been dreadful to go back and find nothing there.'

'It must have been very traumatic for her,' her mother said, 'though she tries hard to hide it.'

Jessie thought of that first night of bombing at the Adelphi when the planes had been overhead, the sound of the explosions, the wail of bells.

'I was frightened when I was in London. It was horrendous when the planes came like a great swarm. The sound was deafening, a great throbbing of engines, the bombs whistling as they fell, the crunch and thunder when they landed. I kept hearing it long after they'd gone. And the fires. The smell. She'll be in shock, won't she?'

Grace nodded. 'And no one to turn to. That's the worst thing.'

Jessie couldn't bear to think of life without her mother. 'Makes me think how lucky I am.'

'How lucky we all are, darling.' She kissed Jessie's head. 'It's as well you're here together. It might help her get through these darkest of days.'

Eddie arrived soon after six and Jessie boiled a pan of water for him to wash the oil and grease from his hands and handed him a bar of carbolic soap. 'Glad to be back, Jess?' he said as he rubbed at the dark marks. His hands were strong and broad, nothing like their father's. Eddie's were practical, like the boy himself.

'What a daft question,' Jessie said as their mum handed him a piece of old towel to dry his hands.

'No, it's not. You must be disappointed that things didn't work out in London.' How typical of Eddie to get right to the point. He grinned at her. 'Of course, I know you came back because you missed me.' She laughed, and her mother did too. Eddie leaned against the sink. 'You must have been miffed when it all shut down. For the second time.'

'Can't be helped,' Grace said. 'There are people going through far worse.' Eddie was suitably reprimanded. Their mother moved him aside with a gentle push of her hip and went to pick up the bowl of dirty water, but he wouldn't release it to her. He went outside to empty it down the drain, Jessie swiftly pulling the curtain over the back door as he came in and out.

'Did Mum tell you she's learning to drive?'

'I haven't had time,' their mother said, removing a tablecloth from the drawer of the dresser. Jessie took it from her, opened the two ends and with a deft flick of her hands shook it over the table. When it settled, Grace smoothed out the creases with broad sweeps of her hand. 'It's so I can take my turn in the WVS van.'

'Golly, that's wonderful, Mum. You're full of surprises.'

'Life is, if you don't give in. We never know what's around the corner for us, do we?'

Jessie thought of Ginny. She couldn't have imagined what had been lying in wait for her.

They waited for their landlady, Geraldine, to come home from her work at the dock offices before they ate. She was delighted to see Jessie and even though she knew Geraldine would be uncomfortable, Jessie couldn't resist giving her a hug. Though she looked stern and indomitable, Jessie knew she had a soft centre. She washed her hands and took her place at the table.

'How was Brighton, Jessie? The last time I was there was at the end of the Great War.'

'There's been a lot of damage in the past few months. The

piers are out of bounds, as are the beaches. It's the same most places, I suppose. It'll be a long time before the seaside towns get back to how they were.'

'I hear the west coast is not so affected,' Grace chimed. 'A lot of the Christmas cards are from the girls and boys who were here. The people need rallying as much as the troops do.'

'They do indeed, Grace.' Geraldine scraped the thinnest sliver of margarine on her bread. 'It's going to be another long winter.' It did nothing to cheer them.

* * *

Afterwards, they gathered in Grace's room and listened to the wireless, Eddie sprawled on the bed with a comic, her mother and Geraldine taking the armchairs and Jessie sitting in a chair she'd brought in from the other room.

'I'd like to think we'll hear you on the wireless one of these days, Jessie,' Geraldine said.

'It's on my list,' she replied. 'As soon as the shows start up in London I'll be back.'

'That's the spirit,' Geraldine said. The room was warm and for the first time in weeks she felt able to totally relax. She was awfully tired and made Eddie move up, settling herself on the bed next to him, putting one of her mother's pillows behind her back, and closed her eyes, listening to the wireless, the dull hiss of the fire in the background, the steady flick as Eddie turned the pages.

She startled when her mother gently shook her shoulder. 'Up to bed, my girl.'

'Did I miss the end of the programme?'

'You did.' Eddie helped her to her feet.

Wishing Geraldine a good night, she went upstairs, closely

followed by her mother, who kissed her, the child she was, and whispered, 'Sweet dreams.' Her nightie had been placed under her pillow and she quickly undressed and got into it, pulling back the sheets to reveal the hot water bottle her mother had put in earlier. She put her feet on it and warmed her toes, luxuriating in what it was to be so loved.

30

Jessie was up early the next morning. She needed to be at the Palace Theatre for rehearsal at ten but first she had to make a call. It was before eight when she quickly dressed and braved the cold to run to the telephone box on the promenade to call Frances. A few minutes later she returned to the warmth of the kitchen. Eddie and Geraldine had already left for work and her mother was putting some water on to boil.

'Where did you go in such a hurry?'

'I called Frances. I wondered if she might have a part for Ginny in the panto.'

'Oh, Jessie. They've been in rehearsal for a week already. They won't have anything for her unless someone falls ill.'

'They have,' Jessie said, skirting around her mother as she popped an egg into the roiling water.

'Who?' Her mother was puzzled. 'Everyone was quite well when I saw them on Friday evening.' Grace had been employed as wardrobe mistress for the panto and was happy to do it, adapting costumes the girls already had, making others from bits of fabric and old curtains she had hunted down.

'Frances.'

'Oh, Lord,' her mother said, sinking to a chair. 'It's not the baby, is it?'

'Frances is fine, Mum. I know she was going to play Fairy Bow Bells but when I told her about Ginny she was more than grateful to relinquish her part. She'd only taken it on in case she could coax Ruby to do it.'

'Jessie Delaney, you're an interfering little minx,' her mother said, getting up to see to the egg. 'But one with a good heart.' She spooned the egg from the water and put it in front of Jessie along with a slice of bread with a scraping of margarine. Jessie picked up her spoon and bashed the shell, taking her time to savour the egg. They were only allowed one each week, so she wanted to enjoy the experience.

'I was shocked when I saw her, Mum. She looks so awful. So... defeated.'

Grace took a seat next to her. 'She'll bounce back. In time.'

'I hope so. She's had rotten luck, hasn't she? It seems to be one horrid thing after another.'

'We all get our share of ups and downs. That's why friends are so important.'

'And family,' Jessie said, finishing the last of her egg.

* * *

Although the windows were taped and sandbags were stacked across the frontages of the town hall and the shops, the streets looked much the same as when Jessie had left. Unlike London and the cities that had been blitzed, there was little obvious damage. Geraldine had told her that Grimsby had borne the brunt of most of the raids, the area of docks and industry their target. She was glad her mother was here, for it seemed safer than anywhere else she'd visited in the last few months.

It was a grim day, with little light, and the wind sliced though her coat and pinched at her cheeks, making her eyes water, and she hurried down Dolphin Street to give Ginny the good news. Dolly answered the door, greeting her friend with a hug, before leading her down the hallway, and into the back sitting room. Olive was sitting in her armchair by the fire and she got up, smiling broadly when she saw Jessie. 'Here's another of our lovely Variety Girls, Dad,' she called over her shoulder. George came in from the yard, carrying a bucket of coal, and quickly set it down. He hurriedly washed and dried his hands to embrace her. Ginny got up to give him her seat, but he shook his hand, pulled out a chair from the table that nestled in the bay window for Jessie, and another for himself.

'How long are you home for, young Jessie?'

'Until the theatre reopens – or I'll have to think again.' She hadn't even considered that the London theatres might be closed for the duration of the war.

'Can I get you anything, Jessie? Tea, a spot of something to eat?' The couple had always been generous, but she didn't want to take any of their precious food supplies.

'No, thank you. I'm in a bit of a rush. It's Ginny I came to see.'

Ginny furrowed her brow. 'Aren't you meant to be at rehearsals?'

'I am, but I need you to come with me. They need a fairy and Frances asked me to ask if you'd step in.'

'But how—?'

'I called her last night, from the station,' Jessie interrupted her, not wanting to give her too much time to think. 'She asked me to let her know that I'd arrived in case they needed to rearrange things this morning.'

Ginny looked confused.

'Please say you'll do it, Ginny. It will help Frances out of a hole. And it will be so good to work together again. I've missed you.'

'Oh, isn't that wonderful, lovey,' Olive enthused. 'It'll do you the power of good to get back to work.'

Jessie beamed at Olive, glad to have her support.

Ginny seemed flustered. 'I don't have anything. No make-up, no shoes. I have what I've got on – and what Dolly lent me. Everything...' Her voice wobbled and Jessie took hold of her hand.

'You don't need anything. You can share my things. Frances is the same size shoe; Mum can easily adapt anything; you know she can.'

Ginny was unsure but Jessie wasn't taking no for an answer. When she agreed, Jessie helped her get ready and the two of them walked to the bus stop.

'It's going to be wonderful, Ginny. We can share a dressing room again. It will be just like old times.'

* * *

When they went into the auditorium, Frances was standing at the bottom of the aisle facing the stage, watching Ruby put the dancers through their paces. The two of them walked down to her and Jessie tapped her on the shoulder. When she turned, Jessie smiled at the neat bump in front of her. 'I was going to put my arms about you but I'm not sure they'd fit.'

'We can give it a try,' Frances said, grinning, and the two friends hugged. Frances took hold of Ginny's hands. 'Thank heavens you're here, Ginny. I just couldn't cope with anything else. Are you sure you don't mind stepping in? I mean, I know it's all last minute but if you could—' Ginny looked close to tears and Frances stopped. 'Oh, darling. I am so sorry. So, so sorry. I can't imagine what you've been through.'

Ginny stiffened. 'I'm all right. Nothing has happened to me that hasn't happened to a thousand other people.'

'But even so,' Jessie told her.

'Please. Don't,' Ginny said. 'I've come to work. The same as you.' She looked embarrassed.

Frances immediately changed her tack. 'Of course you have. Let me get you a script.' She reached into her bag and handed it over to Ginny. 'It's not a huge amount to learn. Most of it's rhyming couplets. I've starred them in pencil. Grace will be in later. I'll get her to take the costume in. At least the magic wand fits all sizes.'

Ginny smiled at her joke. 'I'll go somewhere quiet and read through them.'

'Sure. You can use the office. Or dressing room number one. That's where I've put you and Jessie.'

Ginny nodded and headed backstage.

'Poor Ginny,' Frances said when she'd gone. 'She's obviously still in shock.'

'I thought it best if she had something to keep her busy,' Jessie offered. 'I hope you didn't mind me asking. I didn't expect you to stand aside. I thought you might be able to fit her in as a villager or something small.'

'You did me a favour. I've been hoping Ruby would take over. I wanted to get her onstage, but she wasn't having any of it – and I know better than to push.'

Jessie watched Ruby as she demonstrated to the girls, and they followed her steps. There were ten in all, girls aged from fourteen to sixteen who attended one of the local dance schools. The schools had broken up for the holidays, so they had a week to rehearse the routines before it opened on Boxing Day, which was a week on Thursday. Frances indicated for Jessie to take a seat and when she did, Frances sat down next to her.

'Ruby looks much more relaxed than when I last saw her.'

'She is. It's given her something to focus on. It's what she needed. It's perhaps what Ginny needs too. To keep busy, not giving either of them too much time to think. Johnny thought Ruby could play Alice Fitzwarren but Ruby wasn't having any of it. She's happy to appear in the programme as the choreographer, but not as a headliner.' She nudged Jessie. 'That glory goes to you, my girl.'

'Oh, heavens,' Jessie said. 'I hadn't given a thought to the pressure, only to the fun.'

'Keep it that way,' Frances advised. 'It should always be fun.'

31

It had been a blow when Johnny called to say that he couldn't be with them for Christmas but would be there for the New Year instead. Frances had been hoping they could spend their first Christmas together as a family, but it was not to be. There would be others, she hoped, in years to come. Her thoughts went to Patsy's boys, who would never know another Christmas with their father. She worried for Johnny, and for the coming baby – who seemed to enjoy wriggling for hours once she lay down to sleep.

She'd spent long days at the theatre during rehearsals, and on the Sunday morning before Christmas she lay in bed as long as she could, grateful for a few quiet moments to gather her thoughts and rest a while. Imogen had gone downstairs, and Ruby had put her head around the door, telling her that she would take care of her.

'Have a lie-in. You deserve it.'

Frances had not argued. She was exhausted and there was still so much to do. Thankfully, Mrs Frame had taken care of the shopping for Christmas week. She'd invited Patsy and the boys for Christmas dinner. Mrs Frame had managed to scrabble together the ingredients for a Christmas pudding, and they'd been fortunate enough to get a capon, which the butcher would deliver on Christmas Eve. Vegetables were plentiful, thanks to Mr Frame turning the majority of the lawn over to growing produce. She'd bought a few presents and made a few others, finding time to knit while Imogen had been at school. But there was still the house to decorate, and it would have to be done today.

* * *

While Frances rested, Ruby went up into the attic and brought down every box of decorations she could find, taking them into the sitting room and setting them about the tree that had been bought on Freeman Street Market the day before. Mr Frame had secured it in a bucket of soil and placed it at the centre of the bay window. Last year Mrs Frame had decorated the house; Ruby had had no interest in it, angry with Johnny for bringing them to such a drab and smelly part of the country. Worse still was the crushing discovery of Imogen. The child looked at her now, her eyes wide with excitement as she stood amid the boxes. 'Which one shall we open first?'

'Whichever one you want.'

The child leaped upon them, pulling open the flaps that had been tucked inside each other. Together they carefully unwrapped the tissue paper protecting the glass baubles, unravelled the tinsel, and fastened together the paper concertina stars and globes in red and green and white. Another box contained a wooden reindeer, nativity figures and stable, a lantern and a string of electric lights. Ruby set the lantern on the hearth and placed the two red wooden candle holders on either side of the mantelpiece. Together she and Imogen fastened the stars and globes into shape and hung them from the crepe paper streamers they had draped across the sitting room, then the two of them went into the garden to gather some greenery. Ruby took a trug and secateurs from the shed and cut branches of holly and strings of ivy, some rosemary and bay for scent. Mr Frame had pointed them all out to her in the days when she'd first arrived home from hospital. Home. The thought made her smile. It had been so long since she'd called anywhere home. She was putting the final piece of ivy over a picture frame when Frances joined them.

'Oh, Ruby,' Frances said from the doorway.

Ruby froze. 'You don't like it?'

'It looks marvellous.' Frances walked into the room, taking in the greenery Ruby had arranged on the mantelpiece.

'I thought it would save you. You've looked so tired lately.' She frowned. 'Should I have waited?'

'No.' Frances shook her head. 'No, not at all. I was lying in bed trying to summon up the energy to do it.'

Imogen ran up to her, taking hold of her hand.

'I helped, Mummy,' she said, her eyes shining. 'I wanted to put the angel on the top of the tree, but Auntie Ruby said we had to wait for you.'

'Well, that's very kind of her.'

Ruby had never thought of herself as kind and it made her uncomfortable that Frances, of all people, should think it of her. 'I'll go and get the stepladder,' she said, suddenly overcome, and went into the garage to fetch it. When she returned, she set it in front of the tree and Imogen made her way up the steps, her mother standing protectively behind her. Frances handed the angel to her daughter, who reached out, her tongue poking from the corner of her mouth in concentration, balancing it on the top branch. When she succeeded, she clapped her hands in delight and Frances put out her arm to steady her. Ruby moved the steps, Frances switched on the lights, and they all stood back to admire it. The room sparkled with light and warmth. She only wished her brother was there to enjoy it.

* * *

On Christmas morning, Imogen had woken at the first glimmer of light, delighted to find the stocking she had left at the bottom of the bed filled with small treats: a handful of nuts, a notebook and tiny pencil, a yo-yo, and sweets that Frances had saved from the ration. While Imogen wrote a message to daddy in her notebook, Frances treasured the quiet moment, wishing with all her heart that Johnny was beside her. As Imogen snuggled close, she whispered a silent prayer that God would keep him safe and bring him home.

After a while Frances pulled on her dressing gown and went downstairs, Imogen racing ahead. She flung open the door to the sitting room. 'Oh, he's been, Mummy. Father Christmas found our new house.'

'Of course he did. Father Christmas knows where all the children live.'

Imogen dropped down on her knees in front of the small pile of presents that had appeared beneath the tree. Although she heard Ruby moving about upstairs, she did not come to join them, and in the end, Frances went with Imogen to fetch her. Imogen was about to rush in, but Frances cautioned her to knock. 'It's only polite, Imogen.'

'Even though it's Christmas?'

'Yes. Manners are important every day.'

The child rapped quickly, not waiting for Ruby to answer, and climbed onto the bed beside her.

'Father Christmas has been, Auntie Ruby. There are presents under the tree.'

'Have you opened them?'

'No, we were waiting for you.'

Ruby was about to make an excuse, but Frances interrupted her. 'We can't start without you.'

Mr Brown came to join them in the sitting room and Frances gave Imogen his present to unwrap first. Imogen unwrapped a bone and gave it to him. He chewed noisily in the background and Frances put the wireless on, the sound of Christmas carols almost drowning him out as he slobbered over it.

Together they helped Imogen carefully unwrap her gifts, setting the paper to one side. It would be stored away with the decorations and used next year. They had to be careful with so many things and Ruby thought of the extravagant Christmases in the past when she had torn off the paper with abandon and tossed it aside. There was a doll and small items of clothing that Frances had knitted for it. Ruby had bought her a book and she watched Imogen intently as she opened it. The picture of the fairy on the front had charmed her when she'd seen it in the shop and she'd thought Imogen would like it, resisting the urge to buy several more. It was one of the many things she'd learned from Frances. That spending more money didn't equate with bringing more pleasure. The delight on Imogen's face was its own reward.

Ruby had bought Frances some leather gloves. 'I thought it was the only part of you that wasn't expanding.'

Frances smiled. 'Thank you, Ruby. They're quite beautiful.' She handed Ruby her own gift. Frances had knitted her a beautiful navy-blue jumper, with cable knit on the front and on the sleeves. She recognised the wool as being one of Johnny's old jumpers. Emotion gathered in her throat and struck her dumb.

'I hope it's not too big,' Frances said quietly. 'I think I might have been a little too generous with the size.'

Ruby stared down at the sweater, tears dropping onto the wool.

Imogen immediately got up and put her arms about her, squeezed her tightly, and Ruby's tears came in a flood.

'Are they sad tears or happy tears, Auntie Ruby?' she asked, concerned.

Ruby laughed, wiping them away. 'Happy tears, Imogen. I've never been given a more wonderful gift in all my life.' She smiled at Frances. 'Thank you.' Frances leaned forward and kissed her cheek.

'Merry Christmas, Ruby. Let's hope we have many more.'

* * *

Patsy arrived before noon and, after removing their outdoor clothing, the boys went into the sitting room and played in front of the fire, sharing their presents with Imogen, demonstrating the planes and boats, a cap gun and a cowboy hat they had each received. The two friends went into the kitchen, leaving Ruby to watch over the children.

'How are things, my love?' Frances asked.

'Some days are better than others.'

'The boys?'

'Coping better than I thought they would.' She shrugged. 'They're used to their dad being away for long periods. Colly sometimes asks when Dad is coming home. Then he remembers, and...'

Frances rubbed her friend's shoulder. 'Oh, Patsy.'

Patsy drew her handkerchief from her sleeve. 'I'm not the only one, am I? In a strange way that helps.'

Frances nodded. There was an odd comfort to be had in knowing you weren't alone, that others felt as you did. She filled the kettle and put it on the range, got three cups and saucers from the glass-fronted cupboard and set them down on the table. Patsy pulled one towards her. 'Ruby seems better. I do believe she's put on weight.'

'We both have.'

Patsy laughed.

'I feel like an elephant. I was never this big with Imogen.'

'It's a good job you weren't. You worked until you almost dropped.'

'I had to.' There had been no alternative. She'd thought ahead, knowing she couldn't rely on anyone else to support her. This time around things were different.

There were squeals of delight from the sitting room and then a record being played. 'Sounds like they're having fun.'

Patsy picked up the tray and the two of them joined Ruby and the children in the sitting room. She handed Ruby a drink then settled down on the sofa and looked admiringly about the room.

'You've made a lovely job of the decorations, Ruby. You have marvellous style.'

Ruby looked at the lights twinkling on the tree, the angel atop it, looking down on them. 'I enjoyed doing it.' It had been wonderful to go out in the garden and forage to add to all the decorations that belonged to the house. 'I wanted to make it lovely for... everyone.'

'To make amends?'

Ruby looked at her. There was nothing Patsy didn't know about Frances and her struggles. She would know all about Ruby too. 'I've spoiled so many Christmases for her and Imogen in the past.'

'They'll be forgotten. One day you'll look back and only remember the good ones.'

Would she? Ruby got up and placed a log on the fire, watched the flames lick around it. She smiled at Patsy. 'Here I am feeling sorry for myself, when you have...' She stopped. 'I'm sorry about your husband. It must be very difficult.'

'It is,' Patsy said, 'although I've spent many a Christmas without him. Men at sea don't come home just because it's Christmas. We have a small Christmas, just me and the boys, then again when Colin comes...' She corrected herself, '...came home.' She looked down at her hand as she brushed it over her skirt, her wedding ring glinting in the soft glow of the flames. 'Things are as they are. I can't change the fact that Colin will never come home, but I can try to make sure the boys have a good life without him. We can all do that, Ruby. Make the future better than we had hoped for.'

* * *

After dinner, Jessie arrived with Harry, Grace and Eddie. Geraldine had gone to sit with a friend who was on her own. While they were wishing each other merry Christmas, Ginny arrived with Dolly and her parents. Ruby took their coats and other belongings and went upstairs to lay them on her bed.

Frances embraced Harry. 'Good to see you. When did you get here?'

'Last night. I kicked young Eddie here out of his bed.'

'Ah, but he's had to pay dearly for it.' Jessie laughed. 'Eddie has been bending his ear about Hurricanes and the new bomber that's taken to the skies.'

'Come into the sitting room and get yourselves warm,'

Frances said, ushering them into the house. 'We've got a good fire going in there although it's a little parky elsewhere.'

In the dining room, Ruby had moved the table against the wall and Frances and Patsy put together some of the cold cuts and trimmings left over from their Christmas dinner and set them out on it. To one side was a bowl of tinned fruit and a small glass jug filled with a can of Carnation evaporated milk, a dozen crystal glasses and a bottle of sherry. Harry filled the glasses while Eddie and Dolly rolled back the carpet and Jessie sat down at the piano and began to play, Ruby dancing with the children like the Pied Piper.

As the light faded, they drew the blackout curtains and went back into the sitting room to play charades while Frances and Patsy put the children to bed. When they returned, Frances lit the lantern on the hearth and the two candlesticks on the mantel, the flames reflecting in the mirror behind them. The room was warm and cosy and full of friends and Ruby thought she'd never had such a wonderful Christmas in all her life. If Johnny had been home, it would have been perfect.

32

On Boxing Day, just after noon, they got themselves ready to go to the Palace for the opening performance of *Dick Whittington*. Ruby assisted the children with boots and coats, and as all seven of them had stepped out onto the pavement, Imogen took hold of her hand. She walked with the children, leaving Patsy and Frances to talk together, two friends who had supported each other through such difficult and lonely times. Patsy was a lovely woman. Ruby had watched her with her boys, and with Frances, and saw how kind she was, how caring. Despite her circumstances she showed not a trace of self-pity and it strengthened Ruby's resolve. She could do nothing about the past, but she could try to make a better future.

Patsy remained with the children in the front row of the dress circle while Ruby and Frances went backstage to rally the troops – not that there was any need, for the dressing rooms rippled with excitement and electricity as the two of them visited each one, wishing the occupants to 'break a leg' and telling them to enjoy every minute. They called in on Jessie and Ginny last. Jessie was up and down like a jack-in-the-box while Ginny sat quietly in the corner, her back to the wall, reading over her lines one last time.

'Anything you need, ladies?'

'A large glass of something alcoholic might do the trick,' Jessie said.

Ruby wasn't sure whether she was joking. It was far too early in her career for Jessie to start using alcohol as Ruby had done.

'You don't need it.' Ruby smiled. 'Not ever. Hearing the audience enjoy themselves is the only tonic you'll need.' She watched as Frances talked quietly to Ginny, taking her hands in hers, the girl smiling back at her, nodding in response to whatever pep talk Frances was giving her. Ruby was worried that they'd perhaps, even in kindness, inadvertently put her into the limelight too soon. When they walked back to join Patsy and the children, she voiced her concern. 'Do you think Ginny will make it through the performance? She was very subdued.'

'I believe she'll be all right. And I can easily step in if she falters. But she won't,' Frances said confidently. 'She's much stronger than she looks; perhaps not on the outside, but inside she's made of Sheffield steel.'

When they returned to their seats, Grace had arrived with Eddie and Geraldine. In the row behind them were many faces she recognised: Dolly and her parents, Lil from the pub and Joyce from the café. Jack and Audrey Holland took their seats just before curtain up, Audrey making her grand entrance, not that anyone noticed, and she sat down in a grump. Ruby suppressed her amusement.

There was a sudden ripple of excitement as the house lights went down and the orchestra played the overture. She leaned forward to catch the look of absolute pleasure on the children's faces, the three of them already sitting forward on their seats to get a better view. By the time it came to the interval, they had already abandoned them, leaning on the rail of the circle, wanting to be as close as possible to the magic unravelling onstage. Things had gone well so far. There had been plenty of laughter and in all the right places, and King Rat had been greeted by thunderous boos each time he walked out onstage. Jessie had been a revelation, owning the performance and, to her relief and admiration, Ginny had not faltered. No one in the audience would have any idea what the poor girl had gone through, and Ruby took a moment to think of her own performances in the past. That was the art and the artifice, the willingness to deceive not only the audience, but oneself.

When the show came to an end, the applause was terrific, and the cast took plenty of calls before they brought in the final curtain. The dance routines had looked good, the girls had been faultless, and Ruby felt a small flutter of pride at what she'd achieved with them. Frances leaned forward and mouthed *well done* and they all got to their feet, wanting to go backstage and congratulate the cast for their marvellous efforts. As they moved up the aisle towards the exit, Jack came over and shook their hands. 'That was wonderful, ladies. I think we can call that a huge success, do you agree?'

'The first of many, Jack. Looks like the Randolph women are taking over the theatre.'

She caught Ruby's eye, held her gaze and smiled. Ruby returned it. She hadn't thought of anything beyond the pantomime; perhaps it was about time she did.

* * *

Ruby and Frances took it in turns to attend each performance, Frances taking the matinees so that she could be home to put Imogen to bed. Two days before New Year's Eve, she stood in the wings, watching Jessie give King Rat a hard time. She was delighted to see her friend blossom, knowing that Jessie was extracting every drop from each performance, making small changes to discover what the audience responded to and taking it to the edge of what excited them most. Frances didn't move when someone came behind her, knowing she was not blocking anyone's entrance when whoever it was kissed her gently on the neck. She twisted quickly, only just remembering that she couldn't make a sound. 'Johnny. Oh, Johnny.' She reached up and caressed his face, and he took her hand and led her away to a dark corner and kissed her. Some of the dancers walked past, giggling quietly, and Frances smiled into Johnny's lips. She would've done the same at their age. He stood back, releasing her and she held on to his hand. 'Just arrived?'

He nodded. 'I came straight from the station. I guessed it was where you'd be. Mother hen, keeping watch.' He placed his hand on her tummy. 'My, my, Mrs Randolph. How you've grown. Too much Christmas pudding?'

She punched him playfully on the arm.

'How's it all going?'

'Better than I could have hoped. Every performance is sold out. We could have gone on another couple of weeks at least.'

He placed a thumb on her chin. 'We'll know for next year.' She didn't want to think that far ahead, wanting to savour only the moment they had right now. She took him by the hand, and they stood back in the wings watching the performance from the shadows, intermittently whispering updates to get him up to speed with all that had been going on. 'And Ruby hasn't caused you any problems?'

She shook her head. 'You'll hardly recognise her.'

* * *

That night, Imogen shared a bed with her aunt, allowing Frances and Johnny precious time alone. He put his warm hand on her naked belly, and she moved it slowly until he could feel the baby kick. He had laughed in delight, and showered her with kisses, and she thought of all that he had missed, and the times she'd had no one to share the miracle of new life with. 'It's definitely a boy,' he said, propping himself up on his elbow.

'Do you hope for a son?'

'I want a happy, healthy child – and a happy wife.'

'You have one; perhaps you'll soon have the other.' She turned to him, and they kissed, and all the longing of the past few weeks finally found a release.

* * *

The following morning, they were woken by Imogen, who came in excitedly, wishing them both merry Christmas and wriggling in between them. In her hand was her Christmas stocking once again filled with small treats. Ruby had rewrapped the yoyo, the notebook and tiny pencil and added nuts and sweets she'd kept to one side.

'What's this?' Johnny asked, laughing.

'It's our other Christmas,' Imogen explained. 'It's just like Auntie Patsy does with Bobby and Colly.' Her mouth turned down at the edges when she looked at him. 'Only poor Uncle Colin won't come home this time. They don't have a daddy, any more.'

It was too much for Frances and she caught a sob in her throat. Johnny reached for her hand and clasped it fiercely.

'Auntie Patsy has Mummy,' Johnny told Imogen. 'And Bobby and Colly can share me with you. Just like you shared Uncle Colin on those other Christmases. Does that sound right to you?'

Imogen nodded and snuggled into the crook of his arm, showed him the little notebook and Frances had to turn away, blinking back her tears.

* * *

After the second performance on New Year's Eve, the cast and some of the crew squeezed in with the customers of the Palace Buffet next door to the theatre. It was crowded and smoky and Frances didn't want to stay too long but knew it was important that they all stick together. It was difficult to comprehend that it was exactly a year since Johnny had learned of his child, and that Ruby had tried to take her own life. The knots of their troubled relationship had gradually worked themselves out, but she was afraid of what the new year might bring. The war showed no sign of ending and women between the ages of eighteen and forty were being asked to sign on at the labour exchange. It was an odd celebration, saying goodbye to a year that had been dreadful for so many, not knowing what was to come. As the clock struck twelve, she got to her feet and joined in with Johnny, Ruby and the others to link arms as they sang 'Auld Lang Syne', then followed them into the street where crowds of people stood listening to the ships out in the Humber as they blasted their horns to herald the new year. Johnny took her in his arms and kissed her, and she closed her eyes, wanting to hold the memory of it forever.

* * *

They had taken Imogen to the panto on New Year's Day, sitting together as a family to watch the performance, Imogen between them. But although Johnny had enjoyed it, he had been distracted and continued to be so as they walked through the park on the way home. He was leaving tomorrow and if he was troubled about something, she wanted to know. While he was upstairs, putting Imogen to bed and reading her a bedtime story, Frances tended to the fire and lit the candles on the mantel. When he came down, she saw no sense in pretending there was nothing wrong and as he joined her on the sofa she asked him outright.

'Is there something you need to tell me?'

He shifted uncomfortably. 'What makes you ask?'

'Please don't hide things from me. I'll only frighten myself with what it could be. I'd rather know what it was.'

He slipped an arm about her shoulder and pulled her close and she listened to the strong beat of his heart.

'I didn't want to spoil things. It's been such a wonderful few days.'

'But?'

He let out a long sigh. 'It's nothing definite but they put a few chaps forward to coordinate the entertainment overseas.' She sat up and he traced a finger down her cheek. 'It won't be for some time yet. It might come to nothing. I may not be the best man for the job.'

She knew he would. He was solid and reliable, and she couldn't think of anyone more qualified.

'Will you let me know?'

He nodded.

'Promise.'

'The minute I find out. But let's not think too far ahead.' He placed a protective hand on her tummy. 'A lot could happen before then.'

She stared into the flames, watching the shapes twist and sink as they licked around the logs. She'd so wanted him to be there for the birth of their child but there was nothing any of them could do about it. It was in the lap of the gods.

* * *

Johnny left on the second of January, the house feeling empty without him. Soon it was Twelfth Night and during the afternoon, while Frances was at the theatre, Ruby took down the decorations with Mrs Frame. The holly and ivy had withered and dried, and she took it outside to add to the bonfire Mr Frame had lit an hour ago. It was smouldering nicely, and he was disturbing it with a hoe. 'That's the end of the gaiety,' she said as she emptied the final bits from the basket.

'For the time being,' Mr Frame said. 'Mind, the crocuses will be popping up, soon enough, shaking their little white bonnets in the wind. Then the daffs and their sunny heads. Plenty to look forward to.' He leaned on the hoe, smoke curling up from the bonfire and into the air. 'To everything there is a season.'

'And a time to every purpose under the heaven,' added Ruby.

He smiled at her, the deep wrinkles of his weathered face creasing as he did so. It was a familiar biblical verse, one she'd heard Aunt Hetty utter many times. Ecclesiastes, she seemed to recall. It had given her comfort when things hadn't worked out as she had wanted them to, hoping that things would get better.

'Hope is good, Ruby,' Aunt Hetty had agreed, 'but that doesn't mean you can stop working at things.'

She was desperate to make things better, but now that the panto was coming to an end, she had no idea where to start. She was wearing the jumper Frances had knitted for her and she wrapped her arms about herself, rubbed at the sleeves, watching the smoke spiral up then dissipate in the cold air, feeling it bite at her cheeks and redden her nose, deep in thought.

'All right, Miss Ruby?' Ted asked after a while.

'Fine, thank you, Ted.' Clearing the house had helped clear her head, leaving space for new ideas to form. She recalled Johnny's words to her, about taking baby steps. It wasn't the grand gestures that mattered, it was the small everyday things that made the difference to how people felt, like Patsy's kindness, and Ginny's hope. Mr Brown sniffed about her feet and she bent down and rubbed at his fur. Mr Frame was right. There was plenty to look forward to; she only had to wait for the right time for it to grow, herself included.

33

While the panto was playing to packed houses, Jessie had not been idle. In her free time she'd been making enquiries about getting back with the concert party she'd been with before she left for London. She still had to pay her way until *A Touch of Silver* opened again and was loath to tap into her savings. Her bank account was showing a healthy balance, in spite of her extravagances in Brighton and elsewhere. Here there was less to distract her, especially away from Adele's influence, and every pound she saved was a step closer to a down payment on her mother's house. In the meantime, she had the best of both worlds, spending more time with her mum and Eddie, able to see more of Harry. In the process she'd wanted to help a friend. It had been obvious to Jessie while they were in the panto that Ginny was still far too frail to try for work on her own, and it seemed sensible for them to team up together. Grace had cautioned her to be careful when she suggested the idea.

'Ginny might see it as pity, and she won't want that.'

'I want to help, Mum, and I can.'

'Even so, darling. Be careful of her feelings.'

Jessie had decided to propose it as being fun, that she would find it miserable on her own, and it would be a little revival of the Variety Girls, albeit as a duo. 'It will give us such an advantage, Ginny. I can do a song spot, you can dance, and we can sing and dance together. We already have the music, and we know the routines. They're getting three acts for the price of two.'

Ginny hadn't put up much of a resistance, still subdued from her ordeal during the Sheffield Blitz, and they had joined a small concert party that comprised a magician, a ventriloquist and a pianist. Their diary was full for the remainder of January until the middle of the following month. Jessie was disinclined to book any more than two weeks in advance, certain that a call from Vernon Leroy's office was imminent.

'But what if you don't get a call?' Ginny had asked.

Jessie was adamant. 'I will. It's the only thing I'm certain of.' The thought of it kept her going when the days were miserable, and they rattled around the countryside in the dark after already doing a lunchtime and afternoon shows. There was plenty of work, people crying out for entertainment, wanting to be uplifted and escape the slough that came after the New Year festivities had ended. Even in peacetime, January was a drag, miserable and cold, spring always seeming so far away. Last year they hadn't experienced bombing, and rationing had only just begun. Now they were all feeling the effects of war, resigning themselves to a long fight. Those who had lived through the Great War had prepared for it.

Earlier that day they had played two shows at the NAAFI on Grimsby Docks and in a warehouse down by the water where they performed their routine on a makeshift platform made of fish boxes, trying to ignore the smell emanating under their feet. That evening they had travelled to a village hall on the outskirts of Lincoln, one glorified hut seeming much the same as any other. There had been a narrow stage at one end, with little in the way of heating other than the number of bodies crammed into the building. Satisfyingly, they were greeted with tremendous applause when the show finished, and whoops and appreciative whistles when the audience finally let them go. It revived them enough to carry on for another hour or two.

Jessie and Ginny changed in the ladies' toilet and went out to chat with the boys in the audience. It meant a long evening, but it was part and parcel of what they did, under the watchful eye of the pianist, Arthur Cleverly, their unofficial chaperone. A retired accountant, he'd played in the orchestra at the Palace Theatre after putting in a full working day – as had many of the other musicians who were too old to fight. He'd seen many weird and wonderful acts over the years, and often regaled them with stories of the goings on, both backstage and front of house. It made the long journeys to and from the isolated venues more fun than they might otherwise have been.

It was after midnight when the five of them got on the bus to head for home. While Jimmy and Fred took seats close to the driver, the girls moved further down the aisle, away from the doors where a draught whistled through and bit at their bare legs. They had learned to travel with numerous cushions and blankets, for the seats were hard and the nights desperately cold once they left a show, travelling through the countryside in the early hours.

Jessie slid into the left of the back seat, Ginny taking the right and they stretched their legs out, the soles of their shoes almost touching. They made a nest of their bags, leaning on them instead of the wooden slats that played havoc with their thighs. The engine thrummed to life and crawled slowly out of the compound.

There was little snow in Cleethorpes but out in the countryside it spread across the fields like cotton wool, casting light up to the sky and outlining the spiky limbs of trees and hedgerows. It was sleeting heavily and there was still a long way to go, the roads increasingly more difficult to navigate, now that there were few vehicles on the road to keep them clear.

Ginny huddled in a coat that was too big for her; everything she possessed had belonged to someone else first. She'd arrived in Cleethorpes with what she stood up in. Jessie's mother had taken her to the WVS store and found her items to wear. Jessie had given her a jumper and a skirt, Dolly a blouse, and some underwear. Frances had lent her a couple of her Variety Girls costumes, telling Ginny that she would have no need for hers for a long time. Jessie took it as a sign that Frances was stepping back from her onstage career, perhaps for good.

Jessie leaned her head back on the window. It was cold and she pulled on her woolly hat and sat back again. 'That Charlie bloke was an absolute pain,' she said as she settled herself. 'He couldn't keep his hands to himself.' She'd slapped them away, smiling as she did so, trying to be gracious, but he had gone too far and she'd told him so. 'Some men don't know to behave.' She should have handled it better, but it had been a long day and it was difficult to keep smiling when the high of performing began to leak away.

'He wanted my address.' Ginny pulled a scarf about her neck and tucked it into her coat. 'He wouldn't take no for an answer, so I scribbled down Lil's. She told me to, if I was ever stuck.'

Jessie laughed. 'I can imagine him turning up at the Fisherman's Arms and getting a mouthful.'

Ginny tucked her chin down into her scarf. 'I'll bet he already has a sweetheart.'

It reminded Jessie of what Adele had said, about Harry going off with other girls. 'Perhaps that's what Harry does.'

Ginny was shocked. 'What on earth are you talking about?'

'Well, I wouldn't know anything about it, would I? What if it's out of sight, out of mind?' She rubbed at the window with her fist and peered out into the darkness.

'You don't know how lucky you are,' Ginny snapped, and Jessie was immediately ashamed.

'Ignore me. I'm just tired.' She smiled and was relieved when Ginny returned it.

'What about Joe? It's such a shame he couldn't get down to the panto. We could have had a little reunion.'

The two of them hadn't really talked in the dressing room when the panto was in progress. There was too much going on and Jessie was onstage for most of the show. Ginny had been reluctant to talk about anything for a long time, still processing all that had happened when she was in Sheffield, the fire and the loss of her home, and her father. Whether she had got on with him or not, it must have been a terrible shock. Jessie had gently teased it out of her, bit by tortuous bit. She would unburden herself a little then clam up and Jessie would quickly turn the conversation to local gossip that she'd heard from the dancers and the usherettes, avoiding any talk of London, of Adele, or Billy.

'It was a relief in a way. I'm glad. I ought to write and tell him I've found someone else. Let him down gently.'

Jessie sat up. 'Why?'

Ginny lowered her voice so that Jessie had to lean forward to hear her above the noise of the engine as the driver changed gears and the bus laboured up a small incline. 'He asked me to wait for him and I said I would. But I'm thinking now that I shouldn't have.'

'Why on earth not?'

Ginny's voice was barely a whisper. 'He'll expect me to be a virgin.'

Jessie blushed. 'You don't have to tell him.' She knew she'd have to tell Harry, she couldn't keep a secret as big as that from him, but Ginny was still so fragile and she wanted to give her hope. And comfort. 'What good would it do? He might have, you know, already.'

Ginny gave her a sad smile. 'I doubt it. Joe isn't very forthright, is he? Not like a lot of men. And all men want to marry a virgin – even if...' She leaned her head against the back of the seat. 'I might never have to tell him.'

'Oh, Ginny, please don't talk like that.' Jessie didn't want the thought to enter her head. It was all too easy to think the worst. The newspapers were full of reports of young men who had died before they had learned to live.

'But what if he doesn't come back? Geraldine's fiancé was killed in the Great War and she never found anyone else.' She was one of the million 'surplus women', as they were called. A whole generation of young men had been lost and there was not nearly enough of those who survived for the young women to marry. 'I could tell him, and it will all be for nothing. Best to let him think I'm not that kind of girl than to tell him I am.'

'Oh, Ginny. You're the best girl ever. He knows that.'

'He doesn't know me at all.' She tilted her head back and slowly moved it from side to side, staring up at the ceiling. 'I wonder what Mr Bigshot Lane is doing now?' she said bitterly. 'I've never heard him on the wireless. Have you?'

Jessie thought it best to lie. There was no use adding to Ginny's misery and nothing to be gained in telling her that she'd met him in London, not that she'd sought him out. She shifted on the bench, uncomfortable at betraying her friend. It was a dilemma, but not as uncomfortable as the one Ginny faced. 'No, I haven't.'

'Serves him right,' Ginny said forcefully. 'He thought he was going to hit the big time.' She thumped the cushion behind her. 'I'm glad it didn't work out for him.'

Jessie knew different but what could she say? 'He might have been called up.'

Ginny put her head down, stared at Jessie and raised her eyebrows. 'Do you think so? I reckon he'll have made some outlandish excuse to get out of it. Billy never cared about anyone but Billy.'

Jessie wanted to tell her that he wasn't all bad, that she'd seen a different side to him. He'd fought for his country after all – he might even have fought for Ginny had he known. But Ginny wouldn't want to hear that, not tonight. Maybe not ever.

Arthur walked down towards them, holding on to the back of the seats as the bus swayed along the country road.

'All right, girls? Another successful show. You're doing a grand job.'

'We all are,' Jessie said. The days were long and tiring, and he was much older than them. She noticed that his energy flagged as the evening wore on, but his enthusiasm never faltered. Jessie guessed that each performance revived him whereas, at the moment, each show appeared to drain Ginny of what little interest she had, that it was simply something to do to fill her empty days. Jessie couldn't begin to imagine how that felt.

'Do you think it makes a difference, Arthur?' Ginny sounded dreadfully miserable and Jessie began to doubt that it had been a good idea to get her involved. It was too arduous and, physically, she wasn't up to it. Without her make-up she was deathly pale and the circles under her eyes grew darker by the day. 'I wonder that after this I shouldn't sign up for one of the services. Song and dance isn't going to win the war.'

Arthur gripped the back of the seat. 'You'd be surprised what wins a war, girls. Courage, bravery, fearlessness. *Morale*,' he said with emphasis. 'Believing that you will win even when the odds are against you. Them young lads in there don't need reminding what they're fighting for, but they certainly need to forget about it for an hour or two. I think we managed to help them do that.'

They couldn't disagree, Charlie's wandering hands aside. Wherever they went, the audiences were always glad to see them, none more so than the boys in uniform. Having said his two penn'orth, the old man pushed his hands in his pockets, sank back in the seat and tucked his chin down into his chest, closed his eyes. A few minutes later he let out a rasping snore. The girls grinned at each other then settled down, hoping to get some sleep. It would be another early start tomorrow.

34

On Valentine's Day, Jessie received what she'd been hoping for –
a telegram from Bernie Blackwood telling her that *A Touch of
Silver* would reopen at the Adelphi the first week in March. She
called his office in high excitement. 'Not only that,' he told her,
his satisfaction evident, even down the crackly phone line. 'Sid
Silver has been working on a new sketch, a two hander. You and
him.' She was thrilled, barely able to get the words out when she
told her mother. Grace was delighted then worried.

'Your star is rising a little too fast. Perhaps I should come with
you.'

'No. You have to stay here.' London had been bombed for
months without respite and there was no sign of it ending. There
had been relatively little action in Cleethorpes, other than a few
air raid warnings while Jessie had been home. 'Eddie has his
apprenticeship, and he needs you.'

'And you don't?' her mother teased.

'I'll always need you. But I've already been away on my own
and I'll know my way around things much better this time.'

Two days later, she received a letter from Adele, who had

secured a flat off Shaftesbury Avenue. Did Jessie want to share? Jessie was elated. It seemed things were finally slotting into place.

'I'd rather you go back with Belle in Albany Street,' Grace said when she told her. Jessie knew her mum didn't think much of Adele, but she was being practical.

'It's nearer the theatre. Adele said flats are hard to find. So many have been damaged by the bombing.' It would be much cheaper and she could save a lot more. Soon she'd be able to give her mum a stability that no one could take away from them. She had seen the beautiful houses owned by the stars; there was no reason she couldn't rise to the top and have one for herself. Then her mother would never have to worry. The theatres might close again at short notice but if she could make the right contacts and secure a recording contract, or get on the radio as Billy had intended, she would have other means of bringing in a good income. It made her wonder why it hadn't worked out for him, especially when things had looked so promising. Bernie might have the answer and she made a mental note to ask him when she next saw him. 'I'll be quite safe, Mum. I know my way around better than I did when I first went. And I get on with Adele. I know she's a bit...' She sought the right words.

'Flighty?' Grace suggested.

'Flirtatious. But she's a good sort. She's put me right on so many things. She has experience.'

'That's what worries me.'

She kissed her mother's cheek. 'I don't want to get sidetracked by Adele. I felt like a fish out of water when I went there last year but I've done so much since then. I've played principal boy for the first time and headlined a show. I'm not the girl I was a few months ago.' Jessie caught a brief look of regret pass over her mother's face.

'No, you're not. But it's important to stay true to who you are.

That's what makes you so special, Jessie. Make sure you hold on to it at all costs.'

Jessie promised she would, though she wasn't sure what her mother meant. How could she stop growing and developing as an artiste? Wasn't that the point of it all? To learn and improve.

'Ginny is going to miss you.'

'And I'll miss her. But she always knew that I would go back to London as soon as I got word. That I was only filling in time until then.'

Grace turned the skirt she was working on and began unpicking the hem with a hook. 'You've been very generous to her, Jessie. I'm sure she appreciates it.'

Jessie looked at her mother.

'I think she knew that you could have kept all that work for yourself.'

'She'd have done the same for me.'

'Perhaps. But I'm proud that you did it without any prompting from me.'

Jessie pulled the net away from the window. Women from the little laundry at the top of the street were leaning on the wall and smoking cigarettes. Ginny had worked there for a few months when the theatres closed and had hated it.

'I feel bad leaving. She seems so alone.'

'George and Olive will see her right. They've been very kind.'

Jessie sat down beside her mother. 'Makes me think I must be mad to leave you and Eddie behind.'

'But leave you must, darling.'

She was glad her mother understood. 'I think I'll go and see her.'

Grace put down her sewing. 'If you wait, I'll walk with you. I'm on the tea urn at the Empire at noon.'

Her mother changed into her WVS uniform and donned her

green overcoat and smart hat. They linked arms as they strode up towards Humber Street and onto the Kingsway. Jessie adjusted her scarf, wrapping it about her face, trying to cover as much as possible to stave off the bitter cold. Her coat was little shield against the wind that blasted from the estuary. Trawlers lined the horizon, going off to war or coming home, many of them minesweepers going out to keep the east coast safe from Scotland down to Lowestoft, protecting the fishermen who still went out to make a catch even though the seas were thick with mines and they were under attack from the air. She thought of Colin and men like him. So many had already been lost, and still no sign of peace.

She left her mother at the entrance to the Empire and turned the corner into Dolphin Street.

Dolly answered the door and led her through to the back sitting room, where Olive was in her chair. Dolly walked through to the kitchen and began filling a hot water bottle.

'Where's Ginny?'

'Bed,' Olive said, indicating for Jessie to take a seat. 'Terrible she was when she came down this morning. I sent her back up again. Dolly's doing that bottle for her now. Poor little lass. I think everything that happened to her before Christmas has finally hit her.'

Jessie waited while Dolly filled the bottle, then followed her up the steep staircase and into Ginny's room. There being no heating to speak of, the room was decidedly chilly, but Ginny was wrapped warmly, numerous blankets and eiderdowns covering her, so that all that was visible was her head. Her skin was so pale it was almost alabaster; her nose was red with the cold. Jessie was glad she'd kept her coat on.

'What's wrong?'

'I felt dreadful,' Ginny managed to utter. 'I knew I was

hankering for a cold but then my bones just ached so much. I made it downstairs then collapsed. Dolly helped me back to bed.'

'Oh, Ginny. You are—' She stopped herself.

Ginny managed to smile. 'In the wars?'

Jessie nodded. 'Sounds daft to say it now, doesn't it? When we are actually at war.'

Dolly perched on the end of the bed and Jessie gingerly sat at Ginny's side. Her friend shuffled over a little to make room. 'I'm sorry to let you down. I don't think I'll be able to work this last week, and I was so looking forward to it.'

'I was looking forward to it too. It won't be the same without you.'

'You didn't need me.'

'I did. I wasn't—'

Ginny brought her hand from under the blankets and took hold of Jessie's wrist. There was no strength in her grip, and Jessie shivered, not because of the cold but because it reminded her of her mum, how ill she had been when Jessie left her with Aunt Iris. She smiled away the dark memory. Her mother was long recovered, and it wouldn't happen to Ginny because she was being loved and cared for.

'You were being kind. I knew that from the beginning. I want you to know I'm grateful for it.'

Dolly went downstairs, came back with a mug of tea for Jessie and Ginny. Someone hammered on the front door and Dolly ran down to answer it. Ginny managed to lever herself up on her elbows and Jessie held the mug for her to sip from.

'When you're well you'll have to come to London and stay with me and Adele. We're going to be sharing a flat.'

'I will. I'd already decided that I was going back with ENSA. There's nothing for me in Sheffield.'

'What about your auntie Maggie?'

'She's got her own life. And I want to have mine. I'm lucky really. I can go anywhere, do anything. There's no one to hold me back.'

Jessie knew she was trying to be brave. Her mum had never held her back, only cautioned her as she went forward. She knew how lucky she was.

'I'll tell Arthur. He'll be glad to know you'll be winning the war with...'

'...song and dance,' they said in unison. Ginny smiled, then groaned, and lay back on her pillow.

Dolly stuck her head around the door.

'You've got a visitor.' She stepped back and Joe walked into the room. Ginny dipped her head, brushed at her hair with the flat of her hand.

'Oh, Joe. You never said you were coming. I look such a mess.'

He twisted his cap in his hands. 'You look beautiful, Ginny. You always look beautiful.'

Jessie patted her hand and went to stand with Dolly. 'We'll be downstairs. I won't go without saying goodbye. Good to see you, Joe.'

Jessie waited until Joe came downstairs to say goodbye.

'Where are you staying?' Jessie asked him.

'I'm not. I delivered a lorry to Doncaster. I had a few hours and I managed to hitch hike most of the way. I just wanted to see her while I could.'

'Well, I reckon you're the medicine she needs,' Olive told him. 'How long before you have to get back?'

'An hour. I've got a lift lined up.'

'Sit yourself down, then, lad. We can have a brew together and you can get yourself warm before you have to be off again.'

Jessie left, promising to call and see them before she went to London, and walked round to the Empire to tell her mum about

Ginny and Joe. He'd turned up just when Ginny needed him most, and somehow Jessie knew that he would be there for her through thick and thin. He loved her and that was all that mattered – and if Ginny could believe that too, they had every chance of finding happiness together.

35

Jessie arrived in London at the beginning of March and was shocked to see the damage that had been wrought on the city since she'd last been there. So many buildings had been reduced to rubble – homes as well as businesses. Windows might have been missing glass but where they had been boarded up there had been painted signs declaring they were open as usual. Undefeated. Adele had given her instructions on how to find the flat and they had been easy enough to follow. Juggling her handbag, her suitcase and her gas mask, she got off the bus on the main road and walked the rest of the way, searching for number 156 Greek Street.

It was a real step down from Albany Street, the red-brick buildings three stories high with a small shop frontage below. The front door opened into a dark hallway displaying a raft of notices with rules about noise, and keys, lights and mail. On one wall hung a set of shallow pigeonholes and she checked the one for flat 4D, just in case Harry had sent something in advance of her arrival. It was empty.

He hadn't been too happy when she told him her plans. Not

that he'd tried to put her off; he knew her well enough to know that nothing he could say would hold her back once she'd made up her mind. It was just the impression she got, that he didn't approve of Adele. Truth be told, she didn't exactly approve of Adele herself. As she took hold of the rail and looked up at the flight of stairs she was filled with doubt; this was not what she'd been expecting. The staircase wound its way up over three floors and she took a deep breath, taking one flight at a time, resting a few seconds on the half landings, hearing the wireless, light seeping out from under the doors, someone playing a gramophone. A couple of kids squabbled and their mother bawled at them to pipe down. She was glad to reach the top floor, relieved to put down her case. Her shoulders ached and small blisters had erupted on the pads of her palms under her middle fingers. Taking her handkerchief from her pocket, she wiped the sweat from her brow and her hands. She would have taken off her coat, but it would have been something else to carry. She knocked on the door. After a few seconds she rapped again, louder this time, pressed her ear to the door, hoping to hear footsteps. When no one came she tried the handle. It was locked. Too tired to go elsewhere, she sat on her case, hoping Adele hadn't gone far. After a while she went down to the lower floor and pushed open the door bearing a chipped sign with the letters WC. The door next to it was the bathroom and she peered inside. The sink was marked by a dark brown stain, the bath with similar, a boiler with a coin meter beside it for the hot water and another sign: instructions on how to use the boiler, for residents to clean the bath after use – which by the looks of it had been ignored. The sight of the meter brought childhood memories flooding back, her mother not having the change to operate them. The lack of privacy, traipsing from town to town, her mother trying to make a small room home, the decline as her father's health failed. She had forgotten the misery of it.

She made her way back to her suitcase and heard the front door open and close, something fall on the floor – a key? – a female voice curse, then light steps tripping up the stairs. Jessie leaned over the handrail and saw Adele's blonde head. She looked up and smiled, held up a bottle of milk. Jessie brushed her hands over her skirt as she joined her on the landing. 'No need to stand to attention, Miss Delaney.' Adele opened the door and went inside.

'I thought you might want a cuppa when you arrived, and the milk was sour.' She flung her bag on the chair and set the milk down on the small countertop that housed a compact stove. The flat was of a reasonable size with two doors on the right-hand wall. In the centre of the room was a sofa, behind it a fold-down table pushed against the wall, a dining chair either side. On the table was an ashtray full of cigarette ends, and half a dozen stockings were draped over the chair backs. Adele rinsed a mug in a small sink, taking down a packet of tea and adding a spoonful to a small metal teapot with *Property of the GWR* stamped on it. 'Stick your bag in there.' She indicated to a door on the right, as she filled the kettle and put it on the small gas ring.

Jessie opened the door. The room was a glorified cupboard, with a single bed and just enough space to stand and undress. A third of the way around the wall was a picture rail from which she might be able to hang her clothes. She put her case on the bed and went back to join Adele.

'I know it's on the small side, but it'll do, won't it?' She looked worried and Jessie smiled to reassure her. 'Mine's a bit bigger but I figured you wouldn't mind, being as I got the flat. I adjusted your share of the rent accordingly.'

'Of course it is. It'll save me a packet and I won't be in it much. Thanks for thinking of me.'

'You're welcome.' She pushed a mug of tea into Jessie's hands. 'Glad to be back?'

'I am. I didn't think it would be so long.'

'What have you been up to? Get plenty of work?'

Jessie filled her in. 'Did you?'

'Bits and bobs.' She was vague, more interested in what Jessie had been doing. Jessie didn't press her. Who knew what people were going through in times like this – and she knew Adele had no family to speak of. But she had a lot of friends and Jessie knew Adele knew how to survive whereas that was a skill Jessie had to hone. 'How did you come across the flat?'

'One of the girls at the Windmill. Remember Eve?'

Jessie nodded.

'She told me it about it. I thought it was perfect. Close enough to the theatre and all the places we'll want to go to after the show. Piccadilly is only a short walk away.' She paused, looked at Jessie. 'It's hardly Mayfair but it's all right for now, isn't it? Just to begin with. We can find something a little more your style once the show's up and running.'

Jessie didn't want her to think her a snob, even though her mother would be horrified to think she was living in Soho when she could be safely ensconced with Belle. 'It's a great find,' she reassured her. 'So much closer. It will be far easier to get to work from here.'

Adele stood by the window, looking down onto the street then suddenly disappeared into her room and came out with a towel in her hands. 'Now you're here I can have a bath. Got any sixpences for the meter?'

Jessie went to her bag, opened her purse. 'Two. Will that be enough?'

Adele took the money. 'What a doll. There'll be plenty of hot water left for you. I bet you'd love a wash after being stuck on the train for hours.'

When she'd gone, Jessie looked around, checked inside the cupboards, found a place to hang her coat and store her case. She opened the door to Adele's room. It was more than twice the size of Jessie's, with a double bed and room for a bedside table and a small wardrobe. She was a bit miffed by the disparity but Adele had found the flat and Jessie would rather pay less rent. Someone knocked on the door and Jessie went to open it.

'Hope I'm not too early?' Billy Lane grinned at her. When she didn't move he prompted her. 'Aren't you going to let me in?'

She took a step back, allowing him to enter, and closed the door behind him.

He sat down on the sofa. 'Delly not about?'

'She's in the bath.'

He stretched his arm across the sofa, made himself comfortable, and she suddenly realised why Adele had been so intent on looking out of the window. She sat down on one of the dining chairs and Billy twisted to look at her. 'Glad to be back?'

'I was.' The smell of the cigarette ends made her feel nauseous and she picked up the ashtray, searched for a waste bin, and when she couldn't find one stuck it on the counter and went back to the chair. She fidgeted. 'Are you walking out with Adele?'

Billy laughed. 'Hell, no, she's not my kind of girl.'

'Not like Ginny?' She thought of her friend, how the last few months had beaten her down. She was a shadow of the bright girl she'd been before she'd got involved with Billy. That had been the start of it. The thought inflamed her.

'Ginny was a nice girl.'

'Too nice for you.'

'Everyone's too nice for me.' He got up. He was obviously

puzzled by her attitude, but she couldn't help herself. He seemed to be breezing through life while poor Ginny's went from bad to worse. It didn't seem fair. He spoke softly. 'Would you prefer it if I left?'

She shrugged. 'It's rude of Adele to go in the bath when she knew you were coming.'

Billy was about to reply when Adele came in wearing nothing more than a towel and a big smile.

'Forgot my soap and flannel.' She went into her room, came out with a small drawstring bag and disappeared. Jessie wanted to throttle her.

Billy started to explain. 'Adele said—'

'Forget it.' She got up and went to the sink. It wasn't his fault, was it? He'd come here on Adele's invitation, but Jessie wasn't going to pushed into anything. Whether Adele was right that Billy thought more of her was irrelevant. She would never have any feelings for him. 'Do you want a drink? There's tea – or tea.'

'In that case tea would be perfect.' He got up, leaned against the window watching her. She rinsed Adele's mug and refreshed the pot using the same tea leaves, showed him the milk bottle and he nodded; she added a splash. 'I don't think there's any sugar.'

'I'm sweet enough.'

She gave a small laugh. 'That's debatable.'

He made his way to one of the easy chairs and this time she sat opposite him.

'Have you been in London the whole time?'

He blew over the tea to cool it, sipped. 'For my sins. The Windmill's one of the few places that stayed open. We never closed – although a wag said, "We never clothed".'

She gave him a wry smile. Much as she wanted to ignore him Billy was good company. When they'd first met she'd felt him predatory; now she could see it as confidence – or overconfidence, to be more precise. She imagined he would be having a hard time at the Windmill. No one went there to see the comedians.

'What happened with being on the wireless, Billy? I thought Bernie had contacts?'

She was curious as to why nothing had come from it. Maybe Bernie didn't have the connections he said he had. He put his mug on the floor by his feet. 'I upset someone. Someone with a lot of clout. I'll not get anything on that front. Not until the bloke's gone somewhere else.'

'What on earth did you do?'

'Not much. You don't have to do much. These men hold all the cards. Blokes like me, we're ten a penny.'

'I was hoping to get on the wireless. Like Vera Lynn and Anne Shelton.'

He smiled at her. 'You will. You've definitely got the talent. All I'll say is watch your back.' He huffed. 'And your front.'

'Don't be coarse, Billy.'

He put his hand up, smiled at her. Beneath the cockiness he was a nice person. She could see that.

'Sorry.' He shrugged. 'I forget myself sometimes. I'm not used to being in polite company.' Now he was mocking her and she was annoyed with the way he flipped from being one person to another, much like Adele did, leaving her unsure of how to take them. He got up, handed her his empty mug and made for the door. He turned before he opened it.

'Don't fall out with Adele over this. Best to have girls like her as friends, not enemies. Tell her I said cheers.'

She watched him walk down the stairs, whistling as he went, and closed the door. Moments later Adele came in, her hair damp, rubbing at it with a small towel.

'Billy gone?' She was trying her best not to look surprised.

'Yes, you missed him. He said to say cheers.' Jessie was all smiles. 'Enjoy your bath?'

'Lovely. Ta for the sixpence. Remind me I owe you.' And with that she went into her room and shut the door. Jessie went to the window, looked along the street. In the distance she could just make out Billy crossing the road, hands in his pockets, no doubt still whistling, mulling over what he had said. Sometimes it was hard to tell who were friends, and who were enemies. Sometimes they might be one and the same.

36

Three days before the show reopened, Jessie had a meeting with Bernie. She'd left the flat early and queued outside the National Gallery for the daily recitals. They'd been started by Myra Hess and had become most popular, people seeking beauty when faced with the ugliness of war. For a brief time the audience were transported away from the devastation that lay outside the doors. The walls of the gallery were bare of paintings, most having already been removed to a place of safety and Jessie wondered where it could possibly be. People had huddled in basements and been buried alive, and sixty-six people had been killed when a bomb exploded on Balham Station Underground in October. While she listened to Chopin's 'Nocturne No. 9', she was reminded of Edgar saying about bombs having a name on them and wondered if there was any truth in it. Was it all down to fate in the end, and if so, what was the point in running away?

Afterwards, she stopped in a café and bought herself a coffee, sat by the window, watching the people pass by in the street, filling in time until her three o'clock appointment.

She arrived at Bernie's first-floor offices in a building off

Piccadilly ten minutes early, waiting around the corner until Big Ben chimed the hour, feeling slightly nauseous as she ascended the stairs. His secretary informed him of her arrival. He came out of his room, beaming, and fussed over her, giving Shirley a potted history of Jessie's father. 'What a marvellous talent he was. And now I have his little girl under my wing. We must take good care of her, Shirley.' His kindness immediately put her at her ease. 'Can I get you a drink?' he asked, holding out his arm as an indication for her to go through to his office.

'No, I'm fine. Thank you, Bernie.'

He showed her to her seat and closed the door behind him. She took in the dark furniture and oak-panelled walls, the framed playbills and signed photographs that adorned them.

Bernie sat down at his desk. 'Looking forward to getting back to work?'

'I've been counting the days.'

He smiled indulgently.

'I felt like I was wasting my time.'

He leaned back in his chair. 'You're young; you're impatient. That's to be expected.' He steepled his hands. 'My only consolation to you is that everyone is in the same predicament. It will all be back to normal before long.' He told her which of the theatres were already bringing back shows. 'Be patient a little longer. These are early days. We have no idea if we'll get the audience back, but the raids are getting less.' He pushed a piece of paper in front of her. It was an offer for Jessie to advertise Alka-Seltzer for the princely sum of £50.

Jessie looked at him.

'I turned it down.'

She sat back, disappointed.

'It's not right for you. You'd be the "effervescent Jessie Delaney" for all the wrong reasons. Now, a shampoo advert, or perfume, clothing and the like, that's different. It has the essence of glamour, of the reader aspiring to live like a star.' He smiled at her. 'Don't worry, there'll be plenty more opportunities coming your way. But we have to hold back for the right ones, or the next thing we know you'll appearing at the Windmill. Your mother would never forgive me.' He picked up a cigar, rolled it between his fingers. 'My dear, you must remember that plenty is going on behind the scenes, even when it doesn't look that way.'

It was the perfect opportunity to ask about Billy. 'Billy Lane's in the show at the Windmill. I thought he came to London to be on the wireless.'

'Ah, Billy.' He opened a drawer, took out a pair of silver cutters and snipped the end from his cigar. 'That's exactly what I meant about the right opportunity. Not all of them are a good fit.'

'What did he do?'

'Interfered in a...' He paused, searching for the right word. 'Relationship.' Jessie waited for more. Bernie was being polite. 'He upset someone important. Not the best of strategies if you want to get on in life. Got a little too friendly with the chap's lady friend. The chap was a married man, so Billy, quite reasonably I suppose, thought he was safe. I'm afraid he got his fingers burned.' Bernie picked up a lighter, warmed the end of his cigar and puffed on it. 'Why do you ask?'

'I've met him once or twice while I've been here.'

'Then my advice to you is to learn by his mistakes. He upset a man of power, who could make or break his advance up the ladder to fame. Whichever way he turns at the moment he'll be faced with metaphorical brick walls. Doors can close as quickly as they can open.' Bernie got up from his desk, and Jessie did likewise, knowing she'd already taken up enough of his time. 'It will be a good while before Billy can put his head above the parapet again.' He placed his cigar in a crystal ashtray and came round to stand with her, putting a fatherly arm on her shoulder. 'Unless he wants to tour the Outer Hebrides for the rest of his life,' he chuckled, escorting her to the door. 'I want better for you, Miss Delaney.' She smiled at his being so formal. 'Better to wait for the right thing to come along. Will you trust an old man on this?'

She shook his hand. 'Of course.'

He took hold of the brass doorknob. 'You concentrate on the show and let me concentrate on your pathway to stardom. That's what you pay me for.' He walked her out to the reception desk. 'I'll get Shirley to check my diary and we'll go for that lunch I promised you at The Ivy.'

Jessie strolled along the Strand with a spring in her step, gratified to have someone like Bernie looking out for her. She stopped at the Adelphi and read her name on the revised posters, her name in larger letters alongside Adele's. Bernie might have turned down the advert, but things were beginning to happen; she was in the right place and the day was hers. She cut through Covent Garden, walked past The Ivy, and stood on the opposite side of the road watching people enter and leave, no one she recognised, but she imagined they were important. All the stars went there or to the Savoy Grill. Soon she might be one of them. She cut through to Shaftesbury Avenue, back onto Wardour Street and finally onto Argyll Street and stopped outside the entrance to the Palladium. Two men were fixing a hoarding above the entrance, Max Miller's name spelled out in huge red letters. One day they'd be putting her name up above the canopy and she wouldn't give up until they did. The doors were open, and she went up the steps. Inside the lobby, cleaners were buffing the brass rails and door plates and it filled her with excitement that they'd be doing the same at theatres all over the city. As she passed them, the woman in the box office looked up. Jessie smiled and walked confidently towards the doors to the auditorium. If she could just see inside...

A door opened to her left and a man in an expensive suit came towards her. 'Can I help you?' He seemed kindly enough – but she cautioned herself. It was all about confidence; that what's her dad always said. Walk in as if you own the place and people will think you do.

'I wondered if I could look in the auditorium. I'm appearing at the Adelphi – or will be by the end of the week.'

He smiled. 'Of course – and you are?'

'Jessie, Jessie Delaney.'

Her answer seemed to satisfy him. 'If you'd like to follow me.' He led the way, opened the door for her to step through and gave a flourish with his arm that made her grin. He walked briskly along the back of the stalls and invited her to stand in the aisle. The safety curtain was up and men were working on the scenery, the light bar lowered, and a man was sliding gels into the frames, slotting them into place. 'Pretty little place, isn't it?'

It was delightful. She imagined the King and Queen and the two princesses sitting in the royal box as she had seen in a photo in *Picture Post*. How wonderful it would be to appear in front of Their Majesties. She closed her eyes, seeing herself onstage, the audience, royalty looking down on her, a curtsey, a bouquet, the applause... 'One day I'm going to be on that stage. Topping the bill.'

'Would you like to go up there now? See what it's like to look out on your audience?'

She opened her eyes, blushed, unaware she had been speaking aloud her thoughts. 'Oh, I... oh, yes please. Would that be all right?'

'Be my guest.' He slipped into a row, his hands on the back of the seat and she hesitated, wanting to savour the moment before walking up the steps to the stage. The lighting man gave her a nod of acknowledgement and continued with his work, leaving her to stand stage centre looking out. She gazed up at the dress circle, to the spotlight box, imagined the light of it on her face, turned to look at the royal box. Gracie Fields had stood on this very stage, as had Jessie Matthews and Evelyn Laye. One day it would be her turn. One day...

'How about testing the acoustics? What about a little song. Just for me?'

She came towards the front and leaned down to him. 'Are you sure it will be all right? I don't want to get you into any trouble.' She could tell he was trying not to laugh.

'I promise you won't get me into trouble.'

She thought for a moment, looked up to the royal box and a tingle ran the length of her spine. 'I'll sing you one of my father's favourites.' She smiled, knowing he was there with her and began to sing 'When I Leave the World Behind'. She smiled out to the invisible audience, to the kindly man who had given her the joy of this moment and sensed the men behind her stopping their work. When she came to the last note they gave her such warm applause that she turned and curtseyed to them. She was deliriously happy as she skipped down the steps and shook the man's hand. 'Oh, thank you so much. That was one of the best moments of my life.'

'It was my absolute pleasure.' He walked back up the aisle with her and once again held open the door. 'And you're at the Adelphi, you said, Jessie?'

'Yes, opening on Thursday. Do come.'

'I will,' he said, holding out his hand. 'Nice to have met you.'

37

When Ruby returned the Christmas decorations to the attic, she'd seen the trunks that contained the Randolph costumes along with many of her old clothes that she'd worn in America. Over the last couple of weeks, she'd gone through them, taking out the beautiful dresses she'd worn onstage and off. They seemed to belong to another lifetime, and she'd been happy to leave them there, under lock and key. Afterwards she'd gone through her wardrobe, putting to one side the clothes she knew she would never wear again, sick at the thought of how much it had all cost, knowing the most precious item she owned was the sweater Frances had given her for Christmas. It was time for it all to be put to better use. She thought of all the kindnesses she had been shown this past year and she wanted to give something back.

* * *

On Thursday afternoon the rain had been relentless, and she'd folded the garments into a pile and taken them into the kitchen where she was going to wrap them in the brown paper that Mrs Frame always kept to one side. The housekeeper was busying herself with preparation for the Park Drive Comfort Fund, as it was now called, adding cups and saucers to the lower level of the tea trolley, the milk, sugar and a plate of biscuits on the top, before wheeling it through to the sitting room. The dining chairs had already been arranged there, in readiness for the half a dozen or so women to arrive.

Ruby was searching the odds and ends drawer for a length of string when Frances came in and saw the pile of clothing. 'Having a clear-out?'

Ruby closed the drawer and went back to the table. 'I thought Ginny might find them useful for when she goes back to ENSA.' When the panto ended they had been able to give her work at the Palace, as an usherette and in the box office. It had not been too arduous for her, once she'd recovered her health, and slowly she was becoming the stunning-looking girl Ruby remembered.

'I should think she'll be thrilled.' Frances picked up a dark brown cardigan. 'Is this cashmere?'

'It is.'

Frances raised her eyebrows. 'Are you sure you don't want to hold on to them?'

She shook her head. 'I'm not the person I was before.'

'That's a shame,' Frances teased, folding the cardigan and replacing it. 'I shall miss her.'

'I won't,' Ruby said, slipping the string under the brown paper. 'She wasn't very nice.'

'Yes, she was. Is.' Frances watched her fold the paper and start tying the string.

'I was a mess.'

Frances put her finger on the piece where the string crossed and Ruby tied the knot. 'You were bright, and bubbly, and fascinating.'

'I was wild and over the top,' Ruby corrected. 'Too busy being who I thought people wanted me to be.'

Frances nodded her understanding and when Ruby looked at her, she smiled. 'Then it's about time you became who *you* want to be.'

They were interrupted when the doorbell rang, and Mrs Frame called out, 'I'll get it.'

Ruby heard the women coming into the house. Frances glanced at the window, rain running down the glass. 'Why don't you come in and join us? You can't hide in the garden in this weather.'

'I wasn't hiding,' Ruby said, feeling the heat prickle at her neck. She knew Frances didn't believe her but she was running out of excuses. In the end she blurted out the truth. 'I can't knit.'

'Oh, Ruby. Why didn't you say? And all this time I've been thinking that you didn't want to sit with us in case the ladies asked too many questions.'

Ruby fiddled with the string on the parcel. 'I felt stupid. Every woman knows how to knit.'

'Did anyone ever teach you?'

'No.' Her mother hadn't wanted her to knit, telling her that she could buy anything she wanted.

'Then how could you know what to do?'

Frances took her hand and led her through to the sitting room, introducing her to the ladies who had been coming to the house for months. 'Norah, Ada, June, Louise, we have a new recruit. This my sister-in-law, Ruby.'

They welcomed her with smiles and kind words. Mrs Frame patted the chair next to her and Ruby sat down. Frances went to a large bag stuffed with needles and another packed with wool then took the chair the other side of her. The women resumed their knitting and carried on with their conversations and Ruby was enthralled that they could talk and knit at the same time.

'I'll cast on and start you off,' Frances told her, 'then we'll see how you go.' There had been no fuss, no dramas, and Ruby had watched intently as Frances took her time to add stitches to the first row, demonstrating the process. She handed the needles to Ruby, showing her how to hold them, talking her carefully through each step until she felt confident enough to do a row on her own.

She wasn't competent enough to talk while she worked, that would take time, but she listened as the women spoke of their families and exchanged snippets of gossip, discussed what they thought Mr Churchill should do next. Ruby was deep in concentration when the telephone rang, and she looked up only briefly as Frances went to answer it. When she didn't return after some time, Ruby went to check on her. She found her sitting at the kitchen table, dabbing at her eyes with a damp handkerchief and felt her stomach tighten with fear. 'What's wrong?'

Frances turned away, not wanting her to see she'd been crying. 'It was Johnny.' It was a while before she spoke again and Ruby braced herself for the bad news. 'He got the posting. He's got embarkation leave.' She turned to Ruby, her eyes red and swollen and pressed her hand to her enormous bump. 'I so wanted him to see his child before he left but it looks like he'll be gone long before the baby makes an appearance.'

She had never seen Frances so vulnerable, and Ruby went to her, lifted her arms, hesitated then embraced her, hoping to bring a little comfort to the woman whose unwavering kindness had changed her life.

38

There was little fanfare when the show reopened at the Adelphi, more of a relief that things were getting back to some sort of normal. Jessie's expenses were less, thanks to Adele, which was just as well as they had taken a cut in pay until the show was established and audiences hopefully returned. They need not have worried; there were plenty of uniforms taking up the seats and the civilian population were desperate to laugh again – but the houses weren't as full as they would have been in peacetime, and it was still early days to know whether the shows could make enough to keep them running. Performance times had been brought forward to 2.30 and 5.30 in an attempt to avoid any raids they might still be subject to in the coming weeks.

Jessie's costumes were pressed and hanging on the rail, a cloth spread out on the dressing table in front of her mirror. She put her father's make-up bag down and tapped it three times. They were both back where they belonged, and it felt wonderful. Tabby came into the room and Jessie hugged her.

'Oh, Tabby. I missed you so much.' She told her of Brighton, of the landladies. 'Adele was marvellous. I wouldn't have had a clue. I might well have starved.'

'I doubt that,' Tabby said, not wanting to give Adele too much credit. 'I'm sure you'd have survived well enough.'

Jessie wasn't so sure. 'Sometimes it was dire, really bad, Tabby. But we had such a laugh as well.' Adele had made it much more fun; she would have been miserable without her.

The first performance was well received and during the gap between shows Jessie received a message from Bernie.

'What's that?' Adele asked, seeing her excitement.

'It's my agent. He's taking me to The Ivy for lunch next week.'

'Sounds promising. Something else to celebrate tonight. I'll get a message to Eve and the girls at the Windmill.'

'Oh, I don't think so.'

'Tut, tut,' Adele told her. 'We'll have none of that, remember. You need to get a taste of London nightlife – or what are you doing here?'

Jessie briefly thought of what her mother would say to that, but she was young, and she wanted to experience all the exciting things that were literally on their doorstep. It was just so wonderful to finally be back in town and this time she really did want to make the most of all that was at her feet. 'You're right,' she agreed. She could leave whenever she wanted to now that they were in such close proximity to everything. 'But just a taste. I don't want to stay out all night.'

They rolled home at three in the morning, Jessie giggling as they staggered up the stairs to bed.

'Had a good time?' Adele asked, flopping into an easy chair.

'The very best,' Jessie said, dropping into the other. Her feet stung like the devil with dancing all night, but they'd had such a wonderful time. There had been a fabulous dance band at Hatchetts and when they'd had enough they carried on to Oddenino's in Piccadilly. They could have danced until dawn if they'd wanted to, safe in the reinforced basement of each venue.

'That's just the start,' Adele replied. 'There'll be more to see tomorrow night. If you want to, that is?'

* * *

Jessie wore her new navy suit for her lunch with Bernie, wanting to look like she belonged in such exclusive environments. She stood in front of the full-length mirror on the back of the wardrobe door in Adele's room. 'What do you think?'

Adele sighed. 'Like I said when you bought it. I think it makes you look older.'

Jessie smiled. 'Sophisticated?'

Adele was lying on the bed and she tilted her head to one side. 'Hmm, I suppose so. It's not what I'd wear.' Which was exactly what Jessie wanted to hear.

At The Ivy, Bernie was already waiting for her and the maître d' took her name and led her over to his table. He stood up while the waiter pulled out her chair and sat down only after she did. She wanted to look about her, at the other diners, to see if she recognised anyone but she didn't dare, not yet.

'You look lovely, my dear. Very much like your mother.'

The waiter handed Bernie a menu and one to Jessie. 'Would you like wine with your meal, Jessie?' She nodded, afraid to speak lest her voice came out as a squeak. 'Would you like me to choose?'

'Yes, please. That would be lovely.' They ordered food and as Bernie talked, Jessie slowly relaxed, looking about at the people on the tables in front of her. At a table to their left she was amazed to see the gentleman from the Palladium. He caught her eye and gave a slight movement of his head to acknowledge their acquaintance. She smiled. The waiter came with their meal, and when he left Bernie told her that an advert had come in for shampoo. It would appear in the magazines. He thought she should take it. He was speaking to someone at Decca about Jessie making a recording. Before she could ask any questions, a man stopped by the table and said hello to Bernie. Bernie got up and shook his hand. He looked to Jessie.

'Jessie, this is Dexter Parker. He's in radio—'

'And pictures, Bernie, moving into motion pictures. Might have a few opportunities for some of your people.'

Bernie smiled at Jessie. 'Jessie here is playing the Adelphi with Sid Silver. Quite the sensation.'

'So I've heard.'

She smiled, words not readily coming to her. That people knew of her, important people, was too much to take in. She listened while the two men exchanged pleasantries before he got ready to take his leave. 'My apologies for interrupting your meal.' He smiled at Jessie. 'Lovely to make your acquaintance, Miss Delaney.'

When he'd left Bernie leaned forward. 'All those acting lessons might be about to pay off, Jessie. You could be just the girl he's looking for.' The man from the Palladium got up and left with his two colleagues, resting a hand on Bernie's shoulder as he passed.

'Bernie. Long time no see. We must have a drink sometime.' Bernie made to get up but the man put up a hand. 'No, don't get up for me. I'll be in touch.' He gave Jessie a polite nod. 'Miss Delaney.' And left.

'Who was that?'

'Don't you know? He knew *your* name.'

'I met him at the Palladium, after I came to your office. Should I know him?' She took a sip from her glass.

'It's George Black. He is the Palladium.'

Jessie nearly choked on her wine. She told Bernie what had happened, and Bernie roared with laughter.

'Oh, Jessie. What an innocent you are.'

For a second she was disappointed that her attempt at sophistication had failed, then she began to laugh too.

39

The nightly raids continued and by the end of March, the people of London had endured seven months of almost nightly bombing. Although Harry would rather Jessie was elsewhere, he admired her spirit. She was not a quitter.

The stage doorman gave him directions to Jessie's dressing room on the first floor and when he rapped on the door a middle-aged woman opened it. He guessed it to be dresser Jessie had spoken of her in her letters; she looked the motherly sort. 'Tabby?'

Hearing his voice, Jessie suddenly appeared over her shoulder. 'Harry!' The door opened wider, and Tabby stood back, allowing her to pass, and she took his hand, drawing him into the room. Adele was sitting in front of her mirror, filing her nails. He offered his hand to Tabby, who gave it a warm shake.

'Pleased to meet you, young man.'

The room was not so cramped as it had been in Brighton but was still on the small side, more suitable for one person than two. There was a sink and a rail of dresses, shoes paired beneath them in a neat row. Tabby pulled forward a comfortable chair and asked him to sit down, went to her bag in the corner and drew out a bottle of beer. 'I know it's early, but all the rules have gone out the window these past couple of years.'

'Tabby!' Jessie said in delight. 'You absolute darling.' He took it gratefully, bemused by Jessie calling everyone darling.

'Now you're settled that your young man is here safely, you'd best get on with getting ready. And stop all that jittering.'

Jessie looked at him through the mirror, a stick of red make-up in her hand that she traced over her lips. He longed to kiss them, but it would have to wait.

He remained in the dressing room while the show went ahead, fascinated by the comings and goings, chatting to Tabby and getting to know her. She was a kindly sort, and he was glad that Jessie was under her watchful gaze – at least while she was in the theatre. Adele didn't have the steadying presence of Frances and, in a way, he hoped Jessie would soon move on to another show. He patted his jacket pocket, checking he had his smokes on him. 'I'm popping outside from some fresh air,' he told Tabby.

Outside the stage door he lit up a cigarette and walked around to the front of the theatre. There was already a queue forming: a fair number of lads from the army, the navy and a few chaps of the air force. He knew many of them would be in line at the Windmill, hoping to get an eyeful of a naked girl. He was glad Jessie had nothing to do with shows like that.

Backstage the air was prickling with excitement when he returned, the stage crew relaxing when they saw it was him. It was obvious they were expecting someone else. In the dressing room, Jessie was frantically trying to wriggle out of her costume and into her dress, Tabby doing her best to calm her. 'Oh, Harry.' She looked disappointed. 'I thought it was him.'

Tabby shook her head.

'Him?' Harry was bemused.

Adele licked her finger, ran it over her eyebrows, moved her head from left to right, checking her make-up was perfect. 'Dexter Parker.'

Harry shrugged.

'Surely you've heard of him.'

He had no idea who these people were. He'd heard of Noël Coward and Ivor Novello, hadn't everyone, but this was not his world, and he hadn't the slightest idea who Dexter Parker was.

'He's a big shot in this business. Recording, films.'

Jessie fidgeted with her necklace, moving the clasp to the back of her neck. 'How do I look?' Before he could tell her, there was another knock on the door and Tabby stepped forward to open it, chivvying Jessie to take a deep breath before she did so. A tall man in a dress suit was at the threshold, his fair hair slicked back with pomade, his eyes piercingly blue.

'Are we decent, ladies?' he asked, his voice like melted butter. The entourage behind him hovered in the open doorway.

'Wonderful show, ladies, wonderful. Jessie, you were a delight.'

She beamed at his praise, her eyes shining.

'We met at The Ivy?' His intention had been to charm Jessie and Harry could see it had worked.

'Yes, I was with my agent.'

'Bernie. I'll have a word with him. We must do lunch?'

Jessie looked like an excited puppy; if she'd had a tail, it would be wagging furiously. Harry wanted to laugh, but he also felt a sliver of fear. Dexter Parker acknowledged him with a nod of his head and went on his way, his lackeys close behind. No sooner had Tabby closed the door than Jessie squealed in delight. 'It's happened. I knew it would. I could feel it.' She threw her arms about him. 'You're my lucky charm, darling.' She turned to Adele. 'Isn't it wonderful, Adele?'

Adele wasn't too impressed. 'If anything comes of it. I've heard it all before.' She smiled at Harry. 'A few of us are going to the Havana tonight. It would be lovely if you two lovebirds could join us.'

Harry had planned to take her to dinner, just the two of them but Jessie was radiant with excitement.

'You choose.' She chewed on her lip, looking at him under her lashes, and he knew what her answer would be. 'It would be fun. Just for an hour?'

Harry nodded. How could he disappoint her?

* * *

The girls were checking in their hats and coats and Harry waited while Jessie went into the powder room. He held her hand as they went down the stairs to the lower floor. It was more high class than Harry had expected, and waiters extended their arms to carry trays above the heads of the crowd as they weaved through. He saw more than one bottle of champagne disappear into the dark corners. The band was in full swing, the brass section on their feet, the dance floor busy with couples. Adele quickly introduced him to other people in their circle, and when she was done Harry leaned close to Jessie and almost had to shout. 'What do you want to drink?'

'Gin and lemonade,' she said brightly. 'If they've got it.'

He was surprised and she noticed. 'Adele got me onto it.' He went to get the drinks, wondering what else Adele had got her into. He leaned with his back against the bar while the barman served him, watching her as she laughed and joked with the others in their group. She was relaxed and happy, comfortable in their company. In her letters she'd written of the bands she'd heard play when they'd gone dancing after the show, and it was clear she was at ease in this environment. He looked about him. It was a fancy place, but it wasn't for him. A few weeks ago he would have thought it wasn't for Jessie. She hadn't come down off her cloud since her brief meeting with Dexter Parker and he worried for her. She was hungry for success, and that left her, in his eyes, quite vulnerable. How could he warn her without bursting that lovely bubble she was floating in? She looked over his way and beamed and he lifted his hand to her then turned back to the bar. This was her world, not his, and if she was intent on staying in the West End, he wondered how they could ever make their relationship work.

The barman passed him the drinks and he went back to the group and handed Jessie her gin and lemonade. She was gushing at her good fortune. Adele was listening, smiling, encouraging, but there was a bitter undertone to her reply. Adele caught him watching her and flashed him a generous smile. He'd thought it was for him, but realised when she raised her hand to beckon someone over that he'd been mistaken. He turned to see who it was and was stunned to see the double of a chap Jessie had worked with in Cleethorpes coming towards them. He frowned, doubting it could be him, but as he came closer, he knew that it was Billy Lane. He spun round to Jessie but she was deep in conversation with a dark-haired girl Adele had introduced as Eve.

Billy joined them, putting out his hand to Harry. 'Harry, old chap. Good to see you.' At least the man had called him by his correct name. He'd delighted in getting it wrong that summer in Cleethorpes when Jessie first returned to the theatre. Back then Harry had wanted to knock his smug head off his shoulders. 'Spending time with Jessie?'

At the mention of her name, she turned, and her cheeks

reddened. She looked guiltily at Harry, and a million thoughts swam into his head. He wanted to ask her what was going on, but if they left now it would look like they were leaving because of Billy.

'Dexter Parker came backstage after the show.' Adele was speaking to Billy, but she never took her eyes off Harry and Jessie, and he knew she was loving every minute of it, aware of Jessie's discomfort. He tried to hide his own.

'What did he want?' Billy took out a cigarette, offered one to Harry, who declined.

'Jessie of course. Everyone wants Jessie.' She winked to Harry and Jessie blushed a deep crimson.

'Don't be ridiculous,' Jessie stammered.

Billy got a light from one of the girls and lit his cigarette, blowing the smoke out over their heads. 'I'd give him a wide berth if I were you. Wait for something better.'

'You're jealous,' Jessie snapped.

He shook his head. 'Marking your card, that's all. He's a powerful man but not a nice one.'

Harry had had enough. He leaned towards Jessie and spoke close to her ear. 'Time we left.'

The band struck up and, no doubt sensing a reprieve, she said, 'But we haven't danced.' She was stalling on him, he knew that, but only delaying the inevitable. All the same he led her to the dance floor and took her in his arms.

'You didn't tell me Billy Lane was in town.'

'You didn't ask.' She wouldn't look at him.

'Don't be obtuse, Jessie. You know what I mean.'

'I knew you'd be annoyed that he was here. It's nothing to do with me. I can't tell him where to work.'

'And where is he working?'

'The Windmill.'

Harry shook his head. 'Would a man like Billy work anywhere else?'

'Work is work.' Jessie became defensive. 'He was injured at Dunkirk. You can see the scars.'

Harry released her. 'Oh, so it's more than a casual bumping into him, then? You obviously had time to chat.' He walked from the dance floor and went to collect his cap from the table. Billy had disappeared, but the damage had already been done. He couldn't stop wondering what else Jessie was keeping from him. He said a curt goodbye to Adele and the others and made his way through the crowd.

Jessie hurried after him. 'Harry, wait.'

'Why? So you can make a fool of me in front of your friends?' He stopped on the stairs. 'I don't know who you are any more, Jessie. You've changed.'

'We've all changed, Harry. We've had to.'

It wasn't what he meant. 'You're spoiling who you are, trying to fit in with people who can't hold a candle to you. You're better than that.'

She hung her head and when she looked up her eyes sparkled with unshed tears. He wanted to sweep her into his arms and take her away, far away from the shallowness of these temporary friends but he couldn't make her, and he wouldn't. She had to see through them for herself.

'I wanted to fit in; I didn't want them to think I was a snob. Or a country bumpkin.'

'Want who to think? Adele?' He took hold of her hand. 'You didn't come here to fit in, Jessie. You came here to stand out. God knows what your mother would make of it all.'

She pulled her hand away. 'Leave my mother out of it.'

'Oh, Jessie. Can't you see? This is what she was afraid of, that your head would be turned.'

She leaned against the wall. A couple walked past them, and the doormen opened the doors onto the street, letting in a burst of cold air.

'I'm going outside for a smoke. You go back to your friends. I'll be back later.'

* * *

Jessie watched him go, unsure of what to do. Should she go with him or should she go to Adele and the others? Harry would be gone tomorrow, and she'd be on her own. She didn't want to make things awkward again. People pushed past on their way down the stairs and she remained there, dazed, not knowing what to do. How could he do this when everything was going so well? When she was on the brink of something so exciting? Her chest felt heavy, her legs too weak to bear the weight of her, but she couldn't move. Being onstage was uncomplicated: she knew exactly how to behave, how to move, how to speak; she hardly had to think about it. It was when the curtains closed, and the lights went off that her life became difficult. She longed for her father's arms to be about her, for her mother's wise words.

Billy came up to her. 'Where's Harry?'

'Outside.' The tears fell then. From misery and from anger.

'Hey, hey.' Billy pulled a handkerchief from his pocket and handed it to her. She dabbed at her eyes. 'What happened?'

'We had a row. He's outside.'

'Is he coming back?'

She didn't answer. She wasn't sure that he would.

'Jessie?' Billy grabbed hold of her arm and she looked at him, his face blurred by her tears. Billy would understand how she felt. He had that need in him too, to perform, to stand in the limelight and hope for applause, feel like you were flying when you got it. She didn't have the words to explain, and Harry would never understand if she did. She'd never been this close to Billy before and when she looked into his eyes, he smiled.

'Go to him. Decent chaps like Harry are few and far between. You'd be a fool to let him go.'

His response surprised her and she suddenly knew beyond doubt what she wanted. She gave him back his handkerchief and dashed up the stairs and outside. Harry was standing in the doorway, the ruby of his lit cigarette glowing in the darkness and she went to him. 'Will you wait while I get my hat and coat?'

He nodded. 'I'm not going anywhere. I was waiting for you to make up your mind.'

* * *

At the station the next day, they were both subdued. Jessie hadn't slept, hearing Adele return as dawn was breaking. She waited with him as long as she could, watching passengers pour down the platform and board the carriages. She walked down with him, standing at an open door, ignoring men and women who were saying their goodbyes. There had already been too many of them.

'We need to think about *our* future, Jessie. What it's going to look like when this damn war is over.' He took her face in his hands and kissed her, and she closed her eyes, wanting the world to stop spinning relentlessly on. Everything was happening too fast, and it was making her dizzy.

He released her and got up onto the train, pulled the door shut and leaned out. She reached up for his hand. 'I love you, Jessie. I hope that's enough.'

'More than enough.' A lump rose in her throat. There was so much she wanted to say and never enough time to say it. The whistle blew and the train began to draw away. 'I'll write,' she shouted over the noise of the engine. He nodded and she waited until he was out of sight before walking away. She didn't want to go back to face a stream of intrusive questions from Adele, finally admitting to herself that she'd made a mistake taking the flat. Her mother was right. She should have paid more attention.

40

Frances had tried everything to bring the baby on, downing spoonfuls of cod liver oil at regular intervals and walking endless circles around the lake in the park across the road, all of it fruitless, for the baby was not ready to make an appearance. Olive had sent a tin of pineapple and Frances had guiltily eaten the lot. Still there was no movement.

It was the last day of March and Mrs Frame had gone to Victoria Street to pay some bills, Mr Brown was settled in his basket and Imogen was at school. There was nothing much for either of them to do but Frances had insisted on cleaning the silver, attacking each spoon with such vigour that Ruby feared they'd be worn right through. 'Isn't it better to leave that for Mrs Frame?' Ruby offered, disturbed by this sudden burst of activity. Frances had already cleaned the windows that morning, even though Mrs Frame had done them only the day before.

'I have to do something to take my mind off things, Ruby. I'll go mad otherwise.' Johnny was due home in three days and Frances had become more distressed as his return drew closer, not having experienced a twinge, let alone a contraction.

Ruby had not known what to do, feeling a sense of helplessness as she watched Frances work herself into a frazzle. When her sister-in-law had polished the last spoon, Ruby gathered them up to take back to the dining room. 'Why don't we go for another walk around the park instead. It's drizzling but that won't hurt if we take an umbrella. Perhaps the fresh air will help.'

Frances got up, pressing her hands to the table to stabilise herself. She winced, putting her hand below her belly and there was a sudden splatter of water on the tiles and Ruby turned back. Frances was still at the table, a puddle beneath her.

'My waters have broken.'

Ruby put down the spoons, suddenly panicked. 'What do I do?' She pulled out a chair. 'Sit down. No, don't sit down.' Oh, Lord, where was the mop, the bucket? She stared at Frances.

Frances reached out for the sink and leaned against it while Ruby pulled open the pantry door, looking for the mop. 'Leave it, Ruby. It doesn't matter.'

'But—'

'But nothing.' Frances tried to stifle a groan and failed, pressed her hand to her pelvis. 'Get the midwife.'

'How?'

'The phone. The surgery.'

Ruby dashed into the hallway and picked up the receiver. The doctor's wife said she would pass on the message. Ruby hung up, wishing she'd asked what to do, hoping the midwife wouldn't be long.

Back in the kitchen, Frances was pacing around and panting, avoiding the puddle on the floor. Mr Brown got up from his basket and went to investigate it and Ruby dashed forward, opened the back door, shooshing him out into the garden. Frances groaned again, reaching out her hand behind her. Ruby hesitated, then stepped forward and took hold of it. Frances gripped it. Panted. Ruby panted with her, her breath coming in short bursts. It made Frances laugh. Ruby wanted to cry. 'I don't know what to do.'

Frances tried to smile, gritting her teeth. 'There's a rubber sheet and a pile of towels in my room. Strip back the sheets and put the rubber one on top, and plenty of towels. I'll show you.'

'No, you won't. I can do it.'

'I'll come with you. I need to be up there anyway.'

Frances grabbed the newel post and hauled herself up the stairs, Ruby following close behind and when they got to Frances's room she rushed forward and began pulling the sheets and blankets from the bed. She spread the rubber sheet out as Frances instructed and covered it with towels, all the time Frances panting and groaning between contractions.

'Get some hot water, Ruby. In a bowl. Bring it in here.'

Ruby ran downstairs, got the water and brought it up and placed it on the dressing table. Frances was bent forward, her hands gripping the window frame, her knuckles white. 'Now what?'

Frances groaned, turned from the window. 'Wash your hands in the water, up to your elbows. I don't think this baby's going to wait for the midwife.' She groaned again. 'After all this time, it's not going to wait.'

Ruby felt the blood drain from her body. Frances moved away from the window, one hand at the small of her back and held out the other for Ruby to take hold of. 'Help me onto the bed.'

Ruby did as she asked, and Frances made herself as comfortable as she could. Ruby tried to suppress the panic that was rising in her. She went to the window and looked along the street. There was no sign of the midwife or her bicycle.

Frances hauled herself up, drew up her knees. Ruby tried to calm herself, taking a few deep breaths, closing her eyes as she did so. The midwife would be here soon; all she had to do was stay with Frances and hold her hand. She could do that. Frances released her hand and Ruby shook it to bring back the circulation.

'What do I do now?'

'Be there to make sure the cord isn't around its neck.' Frances groaned, and panted.

Ruby wanted to pass out, but she willed herself to concentrate. She looked between Frances's legs and gasped. 'I can see the top of its head.'

Frances put her hand between her legs and felt below. 'I've got to push, Ruby. Stay where you are.'

Ruby wasn't sure she could bear to look but couldn't tear her eyes away. Frances strained, pushed, grunted, her face beetroot, her dark hair damp with sweat.

'Its head came out.'

'Which way is it facing?'

'Down towards the bed.'

'That's good.'

Ruby strained to hear the doorbell, hoping Mrs Frame would soon return.

Frances panted. 'Ruby, brace yourself, the baby is... coming... any... minute...' She strained for one almighty push and the baby slipped out of Frances's body and into Ruby's hands. Downstairs the doorbell was ringing and ringing, then someone called 'Hello,' and started ascending the stairs.

Ruby called back, 'We're in here.' The baby began to cry.

The midwife came in, put her bag on the dressing table and

calmly removed her hat and coat, washed her hands in the hot water that Ruby had put on the side. Ruby was holding the baby, still connected to Frances by the umbilical cord.

The midwife stood in front of her. 'I'll take over now.'

Ruby stood back while the midwife cut the cord and deftly wrapped the baby into a towel and handed it to Frances. 'Well done, mummy. You have a beautiful son.'

Frances gazed down at her child, her hair clamped about her head, her face puce with the effort of bringing new life into the world and Ruby thought that she'd never looked so beautiful or so tired in all her life. She turned away and looked out of the window and said a quiet prayer of thanks. Johnny would see his child before he left. After that, who knew how long it would be before he saw his family again.

41

Jessie went back to the empty flat, wanting to make a fresh start. She'd got into bad habits, partying when she should have been resting, giving too much away and not holding anything back. Last night had been a wake-up call. Sharing a dressing room with Adele was one thing but sharing a flat was different and Jessie resolved to focus on her career from now on.

In the pigeonhole at the bottom of the stairs, she'd found two letters. One from her mother, and one from Ginny, letting Jessie know that she'd be arriving on 18 April and was there room for her in the flat? It would be a bit cramped in the single bed, but it would be wonderful to have her stay. Adele might swap, just for a couple of days?

She was washing her smalls in the sink when someone knocked on the door. 'Coming,' she called out, drying her hands on a towel as she hurried to answer it. She opened it, expecting to find Adele had forgotten her key but it was the old woman who lived in the flat on the first floor.

'Rent's due,' she said without any preamble. Jessie smiled. The woman did not.

'Let me find the book.' She wasn't sure where it was. Adele didn't leave it lying about. 'One minute. It must be in her room.' She looked on the bedside cabinet, found it in a drawer, gasped when she saw what was written in it. She squinted, thinking her eyes had deceived her, then began to tremble. Adele wouldn't do that to her. They were friends. But it was there, written in dark black ink. Jessie was paying two thirds of the rent.

'I haven't got all day,' the landlady called to her. Jessie shoved the book back in Adele's drawer in temper. She wasn't paying out a penny more than she needed to. She went back to the woman who waited at the door.

'Adele must have the rent book with her,' she said, barely able to hide her anger. 'I don't want to hand anything over without a receipt. Could you come back later? I'm sure she won't be too long.'

The woman folded her arms, huffed. 'I don't like late payers. I can let this room ten times over. Make note,' she said and started lumbering her way back down the stairs.

Jessie closed the door and leaned against it, her fists balled, teeth gritted. Adele had taken her for a fool – and a fool she was. Such a silly little fool. She sank onto a chair. The ashtray was full of cigarette ends, Adele's red lipstick on the paper, and it made Jessie feel sick. What if she'd never found out? Billy had warned her that Adele was trouble, and she'd taken no notice. Not just him, Tabby too. She'd not paid any regard to them, wanting to think the best of her. And because of it, Adele had taken her for a ride.

She was getting herself ready to go out when Adele rolled in. She threw her handbag on the sofa and pulled off her shoes, tossed them in front of her and took off her coat. 'Where did you and Harry get to? You never said you were leaving.'

'I didn't realise we had to.' Jessie was curt and Adele stopped what she was doing and looked at her.

'Lovers' tiff?'

'Something like that.'

Adele stared at her. 'Plenty more fish in the sea. Or the air?' She grinned at her own joke.

Jessie didn't crack a smile. She had the measure of Adele now and she wasn't going to be treated like a child. Her mother had not liked Adele and neither had Harry, but they had let Jessie find out for herself. Oh, how that hurt, how stupid she felt, believing Adele was looking out for her when all the time she was looking out for herself. She thought of the times she'd held herself back, not wanting to make Adele feel uncomfortable, when all the time Adele was laughing at her.

'The landlady called for the rent.'

'Oh, yeah.' Adele ran some water into the kettle and put it on the gas ring.

'I said to call back later.'

'Yeah, I'll take it down to her. Have you got your share?'

Jessie laughed. Adele twisted to look at her.

'Share? Your maths is terrible, Adele. You said you'd adjust the rent. I've been paying two thirds of the rent for the smallest room.'

'Ah.' She gave Jessie a big smile. 'Listen. I can explain.' She held up her hands. 'I'll pay you back. We'll call it half from today.'

Jessie was furious. 'You can call it what you like but I'm not paying more than a third for that tiny room.'

'Take it or leave it.'

'Then I'll leave it. I'll find something else.'

* * *

It was frosty in the dressing room that evening but neither of them spoke of what had gone on to Tabby. Jessie was grateful to have her there and when an extravagant bouquet arrived from Dexter Parker's office, Jessie paid little regard for how Adele might feel.

'Aren't they beautiful, Tabby?'

'They are indeed. Lovely to have flowers this time of the year.'

Adele didn't comment and Jessie would have paid little attention if she did. She read the card that accompanied it.

'He's invited me to lunch at The Savoy.' She was not as excited as she should have been. Only a few hours ago she would have been desperate to tell Harry, to let him know that she was on the brink of something wonderful. Now, she stopped to think, wishing she could talk it over with him, knowing that the first thing he'd ask would be: was it what she wanted? Would it make her happy? She tucked the card into the frame of her mirror.

Adele put down her magazine. 'I know you've every reason to ignore me, but be careful. Dexter Parker can't be trusted.'

Adele's audacity astounded her. 'I've trusted too many people, lately. That was a big mistake. One I won't make again.'

Adele got up and slipped off her dressing gown, stepped into her costume. 'I mean it, Jessie. He's got a reputation. With young girls. Don't be alone with him.'

Jessie reached for the make-up bag to touch up her brows. 'Well, forewarned is forearmed, so they say.' It was a lesson learned too late.

There was another raid, but they carried on as they always did and when the all-clear sounded, Jessie went straight home. There would be no more partying for her, not for a long time. Tomorrow she would go to Albany Street to see Belle and start distancing herself from Adele.

42

Dexter had arranged lunch for 1 p.m. on Friday 18 at the Savoy Grill. Jessie had asked for Bernie to join them, and he'd readily agreed, telling her to come to his office on Regent Street at 11 a.m. Jessie had written to Ginny to tell her to go to the theatre first and not the flat. It would be a bit cramped in the small bed but it was only for a couple of nights. She'd been to see Belle at Albany Street but was disappointed that she couldn't move back until the twentieth. It was a Sunday, a day of new beginnings.

On the day of the meeting, Jessie was up early, took her sixpences for the hot water and went to bathe and wash her hair, wanting to make a good impression when she walked into Dexter's office at eleven.

* * *

Bernie Blackwood had been good to Billy. That he hadn't made the best of his opportunities had not been down to his agent. Bernie had been great at mopping up the fallout from his unfortunate liaison with Maisie Foster. Billy hadn't known until it was too late that she was having an affair with Dexter Parker. Parker had warned him off and Billy had thumped him – a good right hook that had hurt Billy's fist and blackened Parker's eye. The satisfaction hadn't lasted as long as the bruises. Parker had told Billy he'd never work again, and he'd kept his word. Whoever his agent offered him to, he was met with a resounding no.

Bernie had told him to give things a few months to calm down before trying again. In the end he'd got him on the bill at the Windmill. The revue had carried on when other theatres had shut up shop and gone off to the provinces, giving him steady work when others had not been so fortunate – and the scenery was the best in London. There wasn't much he could complain about.

The two of them stood at Bernie's office window, looking out over Piccadilly.

'Things are moving again. They can't keep up this nightly bombing much longer.' He patted Billy's shoulder. 'They think they can break us, but we're made of tough stuff, my boy.'

'Any movement on offers for me? I know a lot of chaps will think I've got the best job in town but I'm itching to move on.'

'Early days, Billy. Early days.'

Billy sighed. 'I thought something would have broken by now. Couldn't you get me on *ITMA*? I don't mind buggering off to Bristol for it.' Tommy Handley and his cast had been a huge success on the wireless in *It's That Man Again*, a comedy set in the fictional Ministry of Aggravation and Mysteries. What he wouldn't give to have even the smallest part in it.

'I can try. But don't get your hopes up.'

Billy turned his back to the window and looked into the room. 'Well, I haven't got a face for films any more. Unless they want the damaged hero type.'

'Better the hero than the coward, son.'

Billy looked at the photos Bernie had about his office and displayed on the walls. 'Things are looking good for Jessie. I'm pleased for her.'

'Still keeping watch?'

'I do my best.' Bernie had told him she was in town, that her mother was worried for her. It had not been difficult to keep an eye on her, reporting back to Bernie if he thought she was in trouble. Jessie didn't have a clue how vulnerable she was. He'd been perturbed when she'd taken the flat with Adele when the show reopened at the Adelphi. The girl was whip smart, knew her way around, but she was not a good person for someone like Jessie to get hooked up with. He'd tried to be a friend to Jessie, to protect her, but it wasn't easy – and for that he only had himself to blame. He'd been an idiot in the past. Everything had seemed such a lark before the war. He'd thought only of himself, what *he* wanted, but being on the beaches at Dunkirk had changed everything. He and his pals had looked out for each other. In the theatre he'd wanted to be top dog; in the army he'd been one of the lads. It was important to belong, to watch someone's back, knowing they were watching yours.

'I'll be seeing her later this afternoon. We've got a lunch meeting with Dexter Parker.'

'This morning, surely?' He sprang away from the window, checked the clock on Bernie's wall that showed 11.15.

'No. Definitely one o'clock at The Savoy. Dexter's office phoned to confirm.'

'I called in at the café before I came here. Adele told me Jessie was meeting Dexter at his office at eleven.' He picked up his jacket that he'd hung on the back of the chair, not waiting to put it on.

'Billy,' Bernie cautioned. 'Be careful.'

Billy nodded and sprinted for the door. Dexter Parker wouldn't be happy to see him at all.

Dexter Parker's office was on Regent Street. Jessie went in the lift to the first floor and stepped out into a dark corridor. She was early but it was better than being late. She wanted to make the right impression, let him know that she was professional and reliable. She knocked on the door marked *Reception* and opened it. A secretary was typing at a smart desk and she eyed Jessie over her spectacles. Jessie wondered whether she should have waited outside for Bernie.

'Miss Delaney?' She nodded to a chair. 'Take a seat. I'll let Mr Parker know you're here.'

Jessie looked at the framed film posters on the walls. Nerves were getting the better of her and she knew she was on the threshold of something exciting. If this meeting went well, she could be doing screen tests, making films, like Deanna Durbin in *One Hundred Men and A Girl*. She was still deep in her dreams when the secretary returned and told her to go through to Mr Parker's office. She got up as elegantly as she could and went into his room.

'Miss Delaney. Jessie. Dear Jessie.' He got up from his desk and came over to her, pressed her hand in his. 'Do take a seat.' He moved the chair a little away from the desk and she brushed her hand over the back of her skirt and sat down. The windows overlooked Regent Street and the office was filled with light. She could hear the traffic below them. It all felt higher up than it was. She stared at the framed photographs and awards on the walls, aware he was watching her.

'Pretty impressive, isn't it?' He pointed some of them out to her. It wasn't at all like Bernie's office. This was very grand and imposing and made her feel small and out of her depth. A large mirror almost filled one wall, a sofa beneath it. 'How are you finding London? Not *too* overwhelming?'

'It was a little, to begin with,' she said honestly. 'But I soon found my way around. And I have friends.' Or she did have. She didn't need Adele, never had, but to lose a friend hurt, and to be used by one even more so. She was suddenly aware of how lonely she'd felt.

'Worst possible time to be here, of course,' Dexter continued, 'but then, there's opportunity for people who want to get on. Who are prepared to go the extra mile to get what they want.'

Jessie drew her handbag closer. 'Oh, yes, I totally agree.'

He came to stand in front of her, his crotch almost in her face, and she pulled herself more upright, looked up. He touched her chin, moved her head from side to side. 'I think your right profile is your best side. Do you agree?'

She'd spent hours in front of the mirror, turning her head this way and that, imagining the very same thing. It was hard to believe he was already considering her future as a done deal. Her heart was racing with excitement, but she fought to remain calm, wanting to find the balance between enthusiasm and expectation.

'I do.'

He smiled and went back to his desk. 'That's good. Always best if we can find something to agree on to begin with. Makes things much easier. For both of us.' He asked her about the show, what she'd done over the Christmas period, what her plans were. He listened, interested, watching her face, her mouth as she talked, and to begin with she was flattered, then became self-conscious, over-aware of how her lips moved when she spoke. He got up and walked towards a cabinet, opened it. 'I believe we have something to celebrate.' He took out a bottle of champagne. 'A toast to the star of tomorrow.'

'Shouldn't we wait for Bernie?'

He ignored her question, watching her, smiling, removing the foil around the cork, twisting the wire, easing the cork out slowly so it released with a pop.

'Have you ever had champagne before, Jessie?'

She nodded, remembering the glass Vernon Leroy had given her on the first opening night in August. How deliriously happy she'd been, with her mother there, and Eddie. She looked at her wristwatch. It wasn't like Bernie to be late. Dexter filled two glasses then handed one to her. She took it, watching the bubbles rise.

'One little glass won't hurt.' She didn't want to offend him by saying no. 'To your bright future, Miss Delaney.' He held out his glass and she touched hers to it, took a small sip. It was dry on her tongue. He beckoned her to the window and she got up and went to stand beside him. 'Wonderful view. Have you seen it?' He placed his hand on the small of her back and she stood there, feeling uncomfortable but not able to move. 'Come and sit down on the sofa with me.'

She looked at the streets below, at the people walking about as if nothing untoward was happening, that everything was normal, but it wasn't. They were just pretending, and he was pretending too. She handed him her glass.

'I have to go. I made a mistake, Mr Parker.'

'Call me Dexter,' he insisted. She managed to smile but her mouth was stiff, and her heart was beating hard against her ribs.

'I should have waited for Bernie.' She smiled and repeated Bernie's words to him. 'That's what I pay him for.'

He put his hand on her shoulder. 'I'll deal with Bernie. This is just you and me working things out. The two of us. We can tell

Bernie later.' He ran his fingers down her arm, and she shuddered. She put out her hands, ready to push him away.

'You're getting too close.' All she had to do was make a noise. The secretary was the other side of the door. She'd scream if she had to. Nothing was worth spoiling herself for. She hadn't given herself to Harry and she certainly wasn't going to give anything to this man. No career was worth that.

He gripped her arm and leered at her. 'You've got the wrong idea.'

'Have I?' She pulled herself free, rage rising up through her stomach.

He caught her again. 'Don't be difficult, Jessie,' he said calmly, ignoring her distress. 'You wouldn't want *me* to be difficult, would you?'

His veiled threat infuriated her. She was ready to bring up her knee between his legs when the door burst open and Billy came striding towards her.

'Lane. What the hell.'

'Billy?'

'You know each other?' Dexter glared at them.

Billy ignored him. 'Jessie. It's your mother.'

No other words were needed. She looked to Billy, her cheeks burning with shame and, with all the dignity she could muster, said, 'My apologies, Mr Parker. I must go.' Billy took her arm, and coolly and calmly led her out of the office. The reception was deserted, the secretary nowhere to be seen, and the sight of her empty chair made Jessie want to faint. Billy ignored the lift, steering her down the stairs and out onto the street. She tried to stop, to catch her breath, but he wouldn't let her go. Tears of panic pricked at her eyes. 'Billy. Billy. What's wrong with Mum?'

He wouldn't answer her until they were well away from the

building and further down the street. Then he stopped, stood to one side, allowing pedestrians to walk past.

'She's fine. She's perfectly fine.' He was breathing heavily.

'What! What do you mean?' She couldn't think properly. 'Why did you burst in like that?'

He leaned forward, his hands pressed to his thighs. 'It was the only way I knew to get you out of his office.'

'What?' Her voice was high, almost a shriek; he took her hand and pulled her into an alleyway.

'You should never have gone in there alone. It was asking for trouble. Men like Dexter don't take no for answer.'

She started to tremble, the shock taking over, feeling her legs would give way. She felt his hands hovering by her then he took hold of her and held her to him, and she sobbed into his chest.

43

When she stopped crying, she pulled away from him, fumbled in her coat for her handkerchief, remembered it was in her handbag.

'I've got to go back.' The thought filled her with dread. 'I left my handbag in his office. It's got my ration books, my savings book. I've got to have it.'

'I'll get it. Don't upset yourself.'

He led her into a café, made her sit down, ordered her a tea and a paste sandwich.

'I couldn't eat anything.'

'You must. You've got a show to do.'

'So have you.' She checked the large clock hanging over the counter. 'Aren't you supposed to be onstage?'

'I won't be missed. They'll think I've been caught in an overnight raid. One of the other chaps will double up for me and I'll repay the favour.'

The waitress put the plates on the table and Billy handed her a sandwich. He waited while she took a bite before starting to eat himself.

'I was meant to be eating at the Savoy Grill.'

'An expensive meal.'

She looked at him. 'Too expensive.'

'Don't beat yourself up about it. He's already on his third wife, and a couple of mistresses on the side, and even that's not enough for him.'

Jessie was scandalised. 'He knew you?'

Billy nodded. 'I had a thing going with a woman.' He grinned. 'You know me. She was single; so was I.' He looked across the café. 'I had no idea she was his mistress. She was using me to get at him. I got caught in the middle.' He screwed his mouth. 'You can guess the rest.'

She nodded, suddenly remembering that Ginny was arriving in a few hours. What would she think if she saw them together, after all she'd gone through because of Billy? But it wasn't just down to him, was it? Ginny had wanted to be with him that summer, she just hadn't expected the consequences. Just as Jessie had walked blithely into Dexter's office, thinking only of the good things, giving no consideration to the danger. Billy was talking but she wasn't really listening, too many thoughts in her head of what had... almost happened. What if Billy hadn't burst in like that – and where was Dexter's secretary? Had she known what her boss was up to? She thought of how close she had been to being another of Dexter Parker's conquests and bile rose in her mouth. She sipped her tea to take away the bitterness. 'He said he could make things difficult for me.' His words echoed in her brain. 'I thought I could take care of myself.'

Billy sympathised. 'It's hard. There are a lot of great people like Bernie. And a lot of sharks. Like Dexter.'

She looked down at her plate. 'I can't tell the difference. I thought Adele was my friend.' She told him about the rent.

'I might have done the same thing myself a few years ago,' he told her. 'Anything to make a bob or two.'

'But not from your friends?'

'It's a fine line. Hard to tell who your friends are sometimes.'

He waited outside the call box while she called Bernie to let him know she wouldn't be there for lunch, but didn't give a reason why, too embarrassed to tell him over the telephone. Billy offered to walk her back to the theatre, but she didn't want him to, just in case Ginny was already there. She needed time to tell her about Billy and what he had done, the kindness he had shown her. Far better to prepare her in case they should meet. 'Don't worry about your bag. I'll go back for it. I'll call in at Bernie's and let him know you're all right.'

She leaned forward and kissed his cheek. 'Thanks, Billy. For being there.'

He put his fingers to his forehead, tipped his hand to her in a salute and disappeared into the crowds.

* * *

Adele came into the dressing room and hung her tin hat on the hook behind the rail of costumes. 'How did it go?' She sounded genuinely concerned, as if she had known exactly how it went, but Jessie didn't trust her.

'He wanted something I wasn't prepared to give. I walked out.' There was no need to mention Billy.

'Good for you.' She held on to the back of her chair and looked at Jessie through the mirror. 'I'm sorry.'

'Hardly your fault,' Jessie replied. 'Dexter Parker is just another man trying to get what he wants.'

'I meant about the rent. I'll pay it all until we're square.'

Jessie shrugged. What was done was done. As long as she

learned from it – and she was learning fast. Staying at the flat was out of the question.

Jessie sleepwalked through the show and was grateful when the curtain came down on the first house. She couldn't concentrate on anything and the sandwich she'd eaten had made her feel nauseous. Tabby brought her a glass of milk. 'You're looking a little pasty. You must rest or you'll not get through the next house.'

She felt empty. Unsure what to do next. Her mother would be appalled. Or would she? Suddenly, it seemed glaringly obvious why she'd been so worried about Jessie being here alone. She observed Adele as she read the newspaper. Perhaps Adele had been innocent once and had had to change to survive. If Jessie had to do that to follow her dream, she wasn't sure she wanted it any more.

There was a knock on the door and one of the stage crew opened it and stood back to allow a young woman to come forward. 'Ginny.' Jessie was suddenly uplifted. Ginny looked tired, but no more than anyone who had had a long train journey. Her hair was glossy and her skin was clear. 'You look so much better.'

'That's down to Olive and George's mollycoddling. They've been so generous.'

Jessie felt a sudden longing for home, for her mother and Eddie.

'Sit down.' She sprang out of the chair and pressed Ginny into her place. 'Where are your bags? When did you get here?'

Ginny laughed. 'My case is at the stage door. I got here just now. Came straight to the theatre from the station.' She grinned. 'You never change, Jessie.'

Jessie felt a sharp pang of regret. Harry hadn't thought so. What would he think of her latest mistake? Should she tell him the truth, or keep it to herself? She hadn't told him about bumping into Billy and he hadn't done anything wrong – and neither had she – and look at the trouble it had caused. She wasn't sure what to do any more, where to go, what she wanted. She felt lost and rudderless but Ginny was here, and she was reminded of how wonderful friends could be. It was best to put the last few days down to lessons learned and move forward, a little bruised, hopefully a little wiser.

When the show went up, Ginny went out front to watch, sliding into an empty seat at the back of the stalls. She was pleased for Jessie, glad that she had come to see the show and to spend a little time with her. It felt like the perfect ending to that part of her life. She'd said goodbye to Dolly and her parents, to Grace and Eddie, called in to see Frances and her new baby. Imogen was besotted and Frances and Ruby seemed to have healed whatever rifts had kept them apart. It was good to be surrounded by so many kind people, but she needed to find her own way in the world again. When she signed up with ENSA this time, she was going to ask to be sent overseas, sensing the distance would make it easier to put the last few years behind her. She was free now, no ties. What had happened couldn't be erased but she didn't want to dwell on what was, only what could be. She'd already told Joe of her decision and he'd been supportive, telling her they could be together when this dreadful war had come to an end. Each and every one of them had to do what they thought was best. It was *all* they could do.

She watched Jessie perform then went backstage. Adele was alone in the dressing room. 'Okay if I wait in here?'

'Take a pew. Any friend of Jessie's is a friend of mine.'

Ginny sat in the armchair, watching Adele through the mirror, wondering how Jessie had fared these past few months in her company. Ginny had got the measure of her as soon as they shook hands, the woman assessing her from head to toe, that sly smile that was meant to hide a cold heart. Ginny had met her type before.

'So, you're one of the girls Jessie's always talking of.'

'Am I? Jessie chatters so much.'

'The one she's been working with recently. You were in a concert party.'

'That's right.' She would never forget Jessie's generosity. Ginny knew full well that Jessie had shared the work she could have taken for herself alone.

'Good on you. That's not for me. I like being in one place. I've had enough of trudging about on buses and trains.'

'It has its advantages.' She didn't have to get attached; she didn't have to stay long enough to think, always on the move. It suited her. She didn't have roots and she no longer wanted them.

Adele put her elbow on the dressing table and cupped her chin. 'Are you the one who got tangled with Billy Lane?'

Ginny tried not to react. What on earth had Jessie been saying about her? She smiled at Adele. 'We walked out together for a while.'

Adele turned. 'More than walking out, though, wasn't it? Jessie told me how much he hurt you. She's still furious with him. Won't let him forget it.' She picked up her lipstick and refreshed her colour, put a paper between her lips and pressed them together, tossed the lip paper carelessly to one side. 'Loyal girl, isn't she?'

'Billy's in London?' She tried not to show her surprise.

Adele paused. 'She didn't tell you?'

Jessie breezed into the room. 'I thought you might need

something to eat; I got one of the boys to get you a sausage roll.'
She held it out. Ginny took it and put it to one side, her appetite
gone.

Tabby bustled in and Ginny made herself small in the chair
to keep out of the way while Jessie changed her costume. The call
boy knocked on the door and gave Adele her cue and she
checked her reflection and got up, smiling. 'I'll leave you ladies
to it.'

Tabby followed her soon after. Ginny could barely hide her
anger.

'You didn't tell me Billy was in town.' She saw the colour
drain from Jessie's face.

'I didn't want to upset you.'

'Upset me! What else have you been saying about me? Telling
all and sundry my business.'

Jessie shook her head, bewildered. 'I never said anything.'

'Your friend Adele gave me chapter and verse on what you've
been saying.'

'She's not my friend, Ginny. I thought she was. I swear I never
told her anything.'

'Really? That's not the impression she gave me.'

The siren began to wail, cutting into her brain, and Ginny
got up.

'Don't leave, Ginny. Please. She's just putting two and two
together and making five. I said Billy had upset my friend. I didn't
say anything more than that, I'm sure of it.' She reached out for
Ginny's hand. 'Ask her when she comes back.'

Ginny pulled away. 'That will make it worse. Oh, Jessie, didn't
you think? Are you really so naïve?' She had to get out of the
small room, to get outside, find a shelter. The bombers would
come as they had in Sheffield. This was London, not Cleethorpes;
there would be no safety here. Jessie tugged at her sleeve, and she

pulled away, wanting to get down to the lower levels. She ran from the room, Jessie following, heading for the stairs and escape, only to meet Billy coming up, carrying a handbag. She stopped, hardly able to believe it was him, the misery of what happened between them filling her head. She didn't want any reminders of the past – it was too painful; she was going forward, to something new, something better. She had Joe. She was waiting for Joe.

Billy smiled. 'Ginny. Jessie didn't say...'

The thought of what else Jessie might have said galvanised her. 'Jessie seems to have said quite enough already.' She pushed past him, stumbling down to the stage door, hearing the drone of engines above.

Jessie caught up with her. 'Please, Ginny. Don't leave. I can explain.'

Ginny picked up her case. 'We were together for weeks and you never said a thing. All that time on the bus, between shows...'

'I didn't want to hurt you.' Jessie's face crumpled and Ginny could see she was trying not to cry.

'But you have, Jessie. And that can't be changed.'

A boy tapped Jessie's shoulder. 'You're wanted onstage, Miss Delaney.'

Jessie hesitated then followed him, hurrying towards the wings. Something exploded close by, and Ginny startled, winced at the blast of ack-ack fire in response. She couldn't face Jessie tonight, nor spend any more time with Adele. As for Billy... if only Jessie had said something, but it was too late for that. Too late for everything. She'd go back to the Underground station to sit it out. There were plenty of other people who wouldn't have a bed for the night; she'd just be one more person hiding from the enemy.

* * *

The light box was on, warning the audience of the raid, and the manager was centre stage asking those who wished to leave to do so as quickly as possible. Jessie waited in the wings until the manager exited stage right and her intro music began to play. She stepped out into the spotlight, giving the audience the best smile she could muster. To her horror she forgot the words, filling in with anything that came into her head, as long as it went with the melody. The conductor looked askance at her, and she carried on as best she could, trying so hard to focus on what she was there to do. To entertain. She concentrated on the music, trying to block out the images of Ginny's stricken face. When she finished her spot, the applause was warm, but she knew she had failed. It only added to the emptiness inside of her. She dashed back up to the dressing room to find Adele gathering her things to take down into the corridor where they would sit while the raid was on. 'What did you say?' She pulled Adele at the shoulder.

'Me? I didn't say much at all. Just like you, Jessie, for all your talking and endless questions. I mentioned Billy to your friend. I didn't know I wasn't meant to.'

'Where is he?'

Adele shrugged. 'I think he went after her.' She pushed past her. 'This is your doing, Jessie. Don't take it out on me. You owe your friend an apology – and Billy. He told me what he walked in on.' Adele picked up her bag, and moved to the door. 'Dexter could have easily overpowered you. I know. It happened to me.' Her face was set hard.

'Why didn't you say anything?'

'Would you have believed me?' She snatched at her tin hat. 'You're so ruddy blinkered. Your eyes are so full of stars you can't see what's under your nose.' There was a huge blast as something hit the building, making the walls shake. Adele looked up to the ceiling as plaster dust fell about them. 'We need to get out of here.'

'Where's Tabby?'

'Probably already downstairs. You need to move. Fast.' She seized Jessie's hand and dragged her out of the door and down to the stage area. The safety curtain was up, and the audience were spilling through the exits, the usherettes standing calmly, checking them all out. Was that what Ginny had done in Sheffield? The last to leave? Billy came running towards them.

'You need to get out.'

Jessie stopped. 'My make-up bag.'

'You can come back for it,' Adele snapped. 'When it's safe.'

'There might be nothing to come back to.' She was looking about her, checking the people who had passed her. The safety curtain was up, and the cast and crew were exiting over the stage and into the auditorium. 'I can't see Tabby. She must still be upstairs.'

'I'll go back. Stay here.' Billy ran up the steps at the front of the stage and into the wings. Jessie followed him, shouting Tabby's name. Adele came after her. The dressing room door was open and she grabbed her father's bag, then out again into the corridor, calling for Tabby. Billy was already dashing up the next flight of stairs. She heard the old woman's bewildered voice, calling to them. Smoke was billowing down towards her.

'It's all right, Tabby, we're here. We're coming to get you.' Billy was at the top of the stairs, urging Tabby to go down before him. Tabby stumbled on the steps and Jessie reached up to catch her hand, letting her father's bag fall to the floor. Greasepaint sticks fell out, rolled about her feet and she lost her footing, fell on one knee. There was a loud rumbling and the walls began to move.

Billy screamed at her, 'Get back, Jessie. The whole ruddy lot's going to go in a minute. Run!'

She scrambled to her feet, stumbling, trying to right herself, the floor shifting beneath her feet. Thick black smoke sank around her and plaster began falling from the walls, the ceiling. She could hear Adele coughing but couldn't see her. She turned back to see where Billy and Tabby were and heard a huge creaking and whining sound. She looked up. Part of the roof had come away and was falling towards them. She saw a huge wall of plaster fall on Billy, knocking him sideways, then thunder as brick and joists fell around them. She put up her arms to protect her face and everything went black.

She lay in the darkness for what seemed like hours but might have been minutes – or days – she had no sense of time, listening to the sounds of fire bells ringing out in the distance. She tried to move but couldn't. Her arms hurt, and it was hard to breathe. Something was wet on her head and dripping into her eye. For a time it was quiet, so very quiet, then there was movement, voices, the sound of rubble falling. Above her something was peeled away and she blinked as a torch beam swept over her. A man's blackened face appeared in the hole. 'Don't be frightened, love,' he reassured her. 'We're going to get you out.'

44

Jessie felt the light on her face, the warmth of the spotlight but didn't hear music, only voices, strange voices. She tried to open her eyes, but she was too tired to sing, and her chest hurt so much that every breath required enormous effort. Someone was holding her hand, warm and soft, and she forced herself to wake up, blinked, realised that it wasn't a spotlight at all. Sunlight was streaming in from a huge window opposite her bed. Someone was pushing a trolley and it smelled of disinfectant. She tried to look to the side, but her neck was stiff.

'There you are, darling girl. Welcome back.' It was Ginny's voice and she tried to move, to look and check that it was. Was she dreaming? Ginny got up and stood over her, touched her forehead then kissed it. Jessie moved her left hand, touched her temple, felt stitches.

'Ginny.' She wanted to cry with happiness, but her throat was thick with misery.

'Shh, shh, now. Don't try to talk. Rest.'

A tear escaped and ran down her cheek. Ginny brought out

her handkerchief and wiped it away. Jessie opened her mouth, croaked, coughed.

Ginny held a glass of water to her lips. 'Sip.'

Jessie did as she was told. 'Where am I?'

'In hospital. Can you remember anything?'

Jessie could, but she didn't want to. She saw the wall falling, Tabby falling too and Billy, like they had dropped out of the sky, like angels. More tears came and Ginny dabbed at them, all the time smiling kindly at her. Was she forgiven? She wanted to tell her that she hadn't betrayed her confidence, that she would never have done that, but when she opened her mouth to speak it came out as a croak. Her throat felt like it had been scratched with a comb. Ginny gave her more water, dabbed at her lips with a wet flannel, wiped her hair away from her face.

'You've broken some ribs. It will make talking difficult. But it will heal, as will you.'

She tried to nod her head, closed her eyes, hoping it was all a dream, saw the wall falling down again, Billy and Tabby falling.

'Billy? Tabby?' Her voice was raspy, her throat raw.

Ginny pressed her hand to her cheek. 'Rest. Don't talk.'

'I... need... to know.' The pain hurt her chest. She closed her eyes, saw the wall collapse again, Billy putting out his arm to protect Tabby. She wanted to cry but nothing happened, no tears, nothing but a hollowness inside of her.

Ginny shook her head. 'When the rescuers got to them it was too late.'

'Adele?'

'She was alive when they pulled her from the rubble but...'

Ginny didn't need to say any more; her face said it all. Jessie couldn't bear it. Why had she survived when they had not?

'I've made a mess of everything.'

Ginny shook her head. 'War makes a mess of everything. We're all of us learning as we go along. Doing our best. That's all we can do. That, and be kind to each other.'

Jessie pressed her lips together, closed her eyes, felt herself drifting. She should have spoken up, she should have said so many things and now it was almost impossible to say anything.

Sleep came. She was disturbed by the sound of planes overhead, the anti-aircraft fire in retaliation, the wail of the all-clear, then peace, the sound of shoes, soft on the lino. When she opened her eyes again it was dark, the blackout blinds down, small lamps at each bedside table. Ginny had gone.

She heard quiet voices, turned to the light that spilled from the corridor. A man in uniform was talking to a nurse. She saw the woman nod, shake his hand. They were coming towards her and as they neared, she gasped, felt the pain sear through her chest. Tears welled up, for all she had lost, for how stupid she had been. Harry took off his cap, smiled. She tried to smile back but she couldn't. The pain in her heart was worse than anything she felt elsewhere in her body. He leaned forward and kissed her lips, so gently that it didn't feel real. 'Jessie Delaney, I can't leave you for a minute and you're getting into scrapes.' He clasped her hand, and she squeezed it as hard as she could, to try and let him know that she was grateful, that she loved him. He came closer still and whispered into her ear, and his breath felt like the warmest of breezes on a summer day. 'I love you, Jessie. I've come to take you home, and when you're well, we'll work something out, you and I, because I'm never going to let you go again.'

The tears came then, and he put his hand to her face and wiped them away. 'I've been such a fool,' she whispered.

'But a kind-hearted fool.'

Was she? She didn't think so.

'I thought I was dreaming.'

He shook his head. 'Not this time. This is real. You and I are real. Dreams. Well, that's for another day.' He sat down on the chair beside the bed and kept her hand in his. 'And we have all the time in the world to make them come true.'

45

By the end of May, Hitler had turned his attention elsewhere and the relentless bombing of London and other cities around Great Britain known as the Blitz had come to an end. Thousands of civilians had died or been injured and many thousands more left homeless. The British people had not been crushed, but they had suffered greatly – some more than others.

Jessie had been given her mother's bed in the room at Barkhouse Lane, where she had come to recover. The stitches from her head wound had been removed and though her ribs had not healed it had become easier to breathe. Each day was a small step forward from the one before and Jessie was learning to take each day as it came. Twelve months ago, Harry had suggested that Jessie take a year to follow her dream of appearing in the West End. It had had the desired effect, and she'd accomplished what she set out to achieve – even though it had ended in a nightmare. She still woke in the night, terrified, and sweating with panic, and her mother soothed her as she had done Jessie's father, many years after he returned from France in 1918. She recalled Belle's words, that the damage of war goes on and on and was suddenly afraid. She reached for Harry's hand, and he clasped hers tightly.

'All right?'

She nodded, glad he was at her side. He had stayed with her in London until her mother had arrived, making sure she was never left alone. Belle had taken care of her mother, as had Bernie, making sure they had everything they needed, until Jessie was allowed home. Now she wasn't sure why she'd ever left. She'd always thought it was her father watching over her but realised that it had been her mother all along. They'd talked on the long journey home, and in the nights when Jessie couldn't sleep.

'I thought I'd left you behind, Mum, but you were with me all the time, weren't you?'

'In the only way I knew how,' her mother had admitted. 'Getting you the place at Albany Street was the start of things, and Bernie of course. He was the one who had Billy keep check on you.'

'He kept turning up like a bad penny. If I'd known...' Would she have been any kinder? The thought that she was betraying Ginny had coloured her judgement of him, but he'd saved her life. 'No one is all bad, are they, Mum?'

'No. No, they're not. Although I think we can make an exception for Hitler. And maybe Dexter Parker.'

Jessie had told her mother and Harry what had happened, the whole unvarnished truth of it, not wanting to be afraid of secrets coming out. She'd written to Ginny to explain about Billy, and Ginny had told her to let it go. It was in the past and they should both be looking to the future.

Her mother got up from the chair beside her and straightened the satin eiderdown on her bed that doubled as a sofa, smoothing her hand over it and turning to Jessie. She smiled.

'Frances thought you might like to go to the Empire this evening, for the singalong. Just to watch.'

Jessie felt panic flutter inside her.

'Harry's here,' her mother said gently. 'He has his car. We can help you up the stairs to the dress circle where it's quiet.'

'I can carry you, if it gets too much,' Harry reassured her. 'Just for half an hour. I think you'll enjoy it.'

Jessie pressed her lips together. She knew what they were trying to do, to get her back to the theatre, to face her fears, but she wasn't sure she could, not yet.

Her mother kneeled in front of her, placing her hands on Jessie's knees. 'Don't keep putting it off, darling. You have to go back into the world sometime.' She glanced to the window. 'We're all here for you.'

Someone knocked on the door and her mother got up as Harry went to open it. A few seconds later, Frances came in carrying two-month-old Thomas, Imogen and Ruby close behind her. Eddie and Harry went to get dining chairs from the other room and brought them in for the ladies. Eddie took Imogen outside to play.

'Somehow I don't think this is a surprise visit?' Jessie said, looking at her mother, then to Frances and Ruby.

'Not entirely.' Frances smiled. 'Your mum thought you were ready for a small outing, and it seemed perfect timing with Harry being here.'

Jessie's chest felt tight with a mixture of fear, and of love. She tried to hold back the tears but failed. Frances gave the baby to Ruby and came to Jessie's side.

'I'm not sure I'm ready. I'm not sure I'm brave enough.'

'Of course you are. Jessie Delaney, you followed your dream. Not everyone's brave enough to even try to do that.'

'But look what happened.'

'That's hardly your fault, sweetheart. But you can't give in, and me and your mum, Harry, Ruby, Eddie, we won't let you. You're not alone. You have a whole army walking beside you. Please come. It would make us all so happy if you did.'

Harry helped her to her feet and her mother helped her on with her coat and slowly they walked with her, down the hall and out onto the street. It was a beautiful evening, the sun full of warmth, and her mother held her hand while Harry opened the door and carefully settled her in the front seat of his Austin Seven. Her mother got in the back and Harry got in the driver's seat. On the pavement, Frances and her children, Ruby, Eddie and Geraldine waved her off then began to walk the short distance to the Empire theatre. Harry waited for them to arrive then dashed around to the passenger door to help Jessie to her feet. She managed to get up the stairs on her own, her mother holding her hand, Harry close behind, the two of them giving her words of encouragement with every shaky step she took. Jack Holland was waiting for them in the dress circle and he gave Jessie a gentle kiss on her cheek.

'Good to see you, Jessie, back where you belong.'

She was ready to cry there and then but managed to hold back her tears. She turned and looked down towards the stage and saw Ruby and Frances talking to the pianist, going over the music, and a small part of her wished she could join them. It was the briefest of sensations, but she knew one day she would. Like Jack had said, it was where she belonged.

She took as big a breath as she could manage, and carefully made her way to the front row. Her mother sat one side of her, Harry the other, both of them holding her hands. In a world that was battling so much hatred, she was surrounded with love and kindness, and she knew how lucky she was. Geraldine shuffled in the seat next to Imogen and Dolly came up with Thomas in her arms. Below them young men in uniform laughed and talked, fell quiet when the pianist began to play an introduction. Jack went on to kick things off and Ruby and Frances opened with the 'Beer Barrel Polka'. It was a sure-fire favourite and the lads were happy to sing along with them. It was wonderful to see Frances and Ruby together. She thought back to how Ruby had been before she left for London, how afraid and unsure. If Ruby could overcome her fears, there was no reason Jessie couldn't too.

After half an hour, her mother asked her if she wanted to go home.

'I don't want you to overdo it and tire yourself out.'

'I won't, Mum. It's good to listen to them singing together.'

'It won't be long before you're up there with them,' Harry said, lifting her hand to his and kissing it.

'There's something else I need to do before that happens, something I've put aside for too long.'

He frowned, not understanding, and she smiled.

'We should set a date for our wedding. Harry.'

He reached forward to hug her, then remembered her fragility and dropped his arms, leaned forward and kissed her cheek. Only she wasn't fragile at all; she was strong, and she had an army walking with her. And she was back where she belonged.

It was Sunday. A day of new beginnings.

ACKNOWLEDGEMENTS

The more I read about what people endured during the Second World War, the more I am in awe of their bravery, whether fighting in the forces or on the home front.

The Adelphi didn't have a variety show in 1940/41, and the bomb didn't explode there, killing members of the cast and crew – but the other theatres mentioned are real, and the Windmill famously never closed throughout the long months of the Blitz.

As always, any mistakes are my own.

Thanks to my utterly fabulous editor, Caroline Ridding, who has been such a wonderful support to me while writing this book. Nia, Claire, and Marcela, who work so hard to let readers know of my books, likewise to Jenna, and Ben and all the fabulous people at Boldwood. Copy editor, Becca Allen, who catches my inconsistencies so brilliantly and keeps track of the cast of characters as I move from one book to another. To Shirley, who picks up those final errors before the Seaside Girls face the audience. And last but not at all least, Amanda Ridout.

Thanks to Gaia, Margaret, Vivien and Helen, who metaphorically hold my hand. Knowing they're there for me makes the difficult days less so.

To local historians and enthusiasts who have kept me supplied with plenty of press cuttings and photographs: Trevor Ekins, Paul Fenwick, Dave Smith, Tracey and Adrian at Grimsby Archives. Thanks to Tracy Pidd Smith for Sheffield details, and Jez and Debi Harper for help with the motorbike.

Wonderful bloggers and Facebook friends who've been amazingly supportive.

Most of all, to you the reader. Thanks for picking up the books and continuing to enjoy them. It makes writing them very special as I've got to know so many of you.

And as always, to my family.

ABOUT THE AUTHOR

Tracy Baines is the bestselling saga writer of The Seaside Girls series. She was born and brought up in Cleethorpes and spent her early years in the theatre world which inspired her writing.

Sign up to Tracy Baines's mailing list here for news, competitions and updates on future books.

Follow Tracy on social media:

 x.com/tracyfbaines

facebook.com/tracybainesauthor

instagram.com/tracyfbaines

ALSO BY TRACY BAINES

Dockyard Girls

The Dockyard Girls

Trouble for The Dockyard Girls

The Seaside Girls

The Seaside Girls

Hopes and Dreams for The Seaside Girls

A New Year for the Seaside Girls

The Seaside Girls Under Fire

Sixpence Stories

Introducing Sixpence Stories!

Discover page-turning historical novels from your favourite authors, meet new friends and be transported back in time.

Join our book club
Facebook group

https://bit.ly/SixpenceGroup

Sign up to our
newsletter

https://bit.ly/SixpenceNews

Boldwood

Boldwood Books is an award-winning fiction publishing company seeking out the best stories from around the world.

Find out more at www.boldwoodbooks.com

Join our reader community for brilliant books, competitions and offers!

Follow us
@BoldwoodBooks
@TheBoldBookClub

Sign up to our weekly deals newsletter

https://bit.ly/BoldwoodBNewsletter

Printed in Great Britain
by Amazon